Love Song
&
Love Shine

Donna Minnix Proctor

Love Song & Love Shine
All Rights reserved
Copyright © 2019 Donna Minnix Proctor
All rights reserved
SDC Publishing, LLC
All rights reserved.
ISBN: 978-1-0878-4901-0

Published and printed in the United States of America

DEDICATION

This book is dedicated to all the strong, independent women who still believe in true love.

ACKNOWLEDGMENTS

Many, many thanks to my readers, who will, hopefully, enjoy reading these stories as much as I enjoyed writing them; to Becky Sink for waiting impatiently to read the next chapter as soon as it was finished; to Mary Minnix and Lisa Mackenhimer for their editing and proofreading skills; and to my patient husband, Cary, for indulging me in this dream of one day becoming a real writer.

LOVE SONG
PART I

When Bill left, she was certain her life was over. For a quarter of a century, she had defined herself in terms of her relationship to him. For the last twenty years she'd been William Austin's wife, and the five years before that, she'd been his girl. Who was she without him? She'd asked herself that question for months after he packed up his things and pulled his shiny BMW out of the driveway. The only answer she'd been able to come up with was an empty, "Nobody."

On the afternoon he'd walked out, Carolee had examined her reflection in the bathroom mirror and realized that Bill's accusations, his clearly outlined reasons for leaving her, were right on the mark. She hadn't aged gracefully. Truth be told, she was downright flabby. Her untouched, graying hair gave her a decidedly worn and aging look. Compared to Bill, who had maintained his youthful appearance and trim, athletic build, she was old, frumpy, and soft.

There was an excellent reason for that difference of course. While she'd been occupied with the drudgery of housekeeping, carpools, soccer games, and homework, he'd been enjoying a stimulating career and regular workouts. Carolee had rarely taken the time to pamper herself, and spent the better part of every day in comfortable old jeans and a soft sweatshirt. Bill, who always prided himself on his meticulously grooming, wore nothing less impressive than hand-tailored suits or pristine khakis and crisp oxford cloth shirts.

Bill had artfully accused her of failing to grow as a person. Instead of living up to her full potential, as he'd told her he'd fully expected her to do, she'd gotten old, worn out, and boring, focused entirely on the mundane tasks of homemaking and childcare. She'd become an embarrassment to him, he'd complained, and had given him no choice but to leave her. Seeing her reflection, graying hair drawn back in a messy tail, grease spots on the front of her baggy shirt, spare tire inflating around her middle, she'd swallowed his well-thought-out line of baloney, and blamed herself.

It was months before the guilt, and the deep ache in her heart, eased up enough for her even begin to think through the flaws in his seemingly logical reasoning. All of the rebuttal arguments, that she should have made when he'd stood there so convincingly placing the full responsibility for the breakup squarely on her shoulders, flooded in. Why hadn't he told her about his complaints sooner? Why hadn't he given her a chance to make things better? She'd always been responsive to his needs, to his desires, so what had made him think the situation was irreparable?

Carolee had given up her career when their first son was born, at Bill's insistence, so she could be the full-time mother he wanted for his boy. And then, standing at the open door with his suitcases in hand, he'd claimed that his dissatisfaction with her was the direct result of her willingness to do just as he had asked her to do – to stay home and take care of their family. When had he changed the rules? Why hadn't she been informed?

The answer to those questions came soon after the final divorce settlement papers were signed. Bill was engaged – to a young associate in his law firm. When Carolee had overheard two of the firm's associates "Oohing" and "Aahing" over the bride-to-be's "enormous" diamond ring, in the checkout line of the small, local natural foods store, the truth hit Carolee like a dagger in the heart.

"It was all so sudden and soooo romantic," one of the sharply dressed women crooned, "Bill got down on one knee in front of the whole office." Carolee hadn't waited around to hear the response, but grabbed up her small package of gourmet coffee and slipped away.

It was an unimaginable shock, that the man she'd loved for more than half of her life, the man she'd believed loved her with his whole heart, and with whom she'd shared wedding vows and two sons was, in truth, a deceitful, selfish liar – a man who was capable of being completely and utterly ruthlessness. But she'd finally seen him for what he was, and despised him for what he'd done to her, and to their family. Bill Austin was a loathsome, calculating, heartless rogue. He'd successfully hidden his true motivation for leaving. He'd deliberately misdirected her, and laid a carload of guilt at her feet.

The secrecy surrounding Bill's relationship with the up-and-coming associate had been most profound. Few suspected that the skillful attorney had been seeing Ms. Clarice Gordon since her first interview with Mattox, Franklin, and Austin PC, believing instead that the whirlwind courtship had only begun following Bill's separation from Carolee. The clever attorney had gone to great lengths to ensure that there was no malicious gossip. Mr. William Austin was determined to keep his naive wife totally ignorant of the true reason for his betrayal.

His plan would have succeeded, had Carolee not known her ex-husband's habits so well. Such spontaneity was simply beyond Bill. He wasn't a man to be swept off his feet by emotion, nor was he prone to romantic gestures. He never allowed his heart to rule his head. To Bill, impulsiveness was a character flaw. The man wouldn't purchase a new lawn mower without weeks of research, comparison, and careful thought, so there was no way he'd enter into another marriage contract, even with the most beautiful and desirable of women, so suddenly.

Carolee was certain that the affair had been going on for much longer than it had been made to appear. She felt sure it has started well before their separation, and she wondered how she could not have known. Most of all, she wondered how she could prove that she was right.

Righteous anger boiled up and filled the void inside her, pushing out all the guilt she'd been carrying. In a moment of complete clarity, she freed herself completely of that burden. Focused now, she dialed the number of the one person who might be able to confirm her suspicions, her ex-husband's personal assistant.

Like most shortsighted, egotistical men, Bill had always felt that it was beneath him to build a friendly comradeship with his assistant, or with any of the many paraprofessionals in his firm. He kept things between them on a strictly boss-subordinate basis, and made sure that his secretary knew her lowly place in the organization. But, as any good wife of an ambitious, and oft-times preoccupied, professional knows, it's essential to make the husband's assistant your ally, so Carolee had done just that.

She'd met Sally Murphy soon after Bill was named a full partner in his firm, earning himself a posh corner office and a private secretary. The two women had hit it off immediately. Together they'd made a great team, promoting and encouraging William Austin, ensuring that he was an unqualified success in everything he attempted.

Sally, a diminutive matron, had an energy and passion that belied her age and years of experience. Despite the tremendous demands Bill put on her, she always completed her work accurately and efficiently, and could be counted on to go the extra mile for the firm. Of course, Bill failed to notice. He was just as stingy with his compliments around the office as he was at home. To her credit, the self-assured legal assistant tired of the man's self-centered insensitivity before his less assertive wife.

On a beautiful spring morning, a few days after overhearing the news of Bill's engagement, Carolee arranged a lunch meeting with Sally. Over huge bowls of fresh fruit salad and a basket of hot muffins, the women discussed information the competent assistant had gleaned, regarding the details of Bill's relationship with the firm's newest associate. Spurred on by her strong sense of justice and fair play, the knowledgeable woman had been able to secure evidence that went way beyond the circumstantial.

"It's just terrible what he's done to you," the petite lady told Carolee. "And to think he had me fooled, too, for a very long time. – too long. Why, it just makes me furious! I can't believe I didn't catch on sooner. We could have hung him out to dry. He might not believe it, but I've learned a few things about the law over the years, and I could've seen to it that he paid for his deceit, and paid dearly. That Bill Austin's a sneaky snake."

"You don't have to tell me," her companion agreed, lowering her sad, tired eyes to her plate. "What made you suspect something had been going on between Bill and that woman for longer than he claimed?

"When he came in the afternoon your divorce was final, flying high, announcing to the entire office that he was finally a free man, the little hairs on the back of my neck stood up. He made a big show of going into Clarice's office and asking her out, acting like he'd been waiting for the settlement decree, pretending to be a decent human being. The very next day, she started demanding that I do work for her, rather than taking it to the steno pool, claiming that Bill had given her permission to do so. It really steamed me; you know." Pausing to take a bite of her salad, she chewed with a ferocity which demonstrated her ire.

"Despite the fact that he's unbelievably self-centered, Bill doesn't usually violate firm protocol. Alarms went off in my head. I agreed to take on her project, so I could keep an eye on her. And I'm glad I did. It was immediately clear that Clarice had something on Bill, something incriminating. She had him wound around her finger a little too tightly. He was doing her favors, giving her perks no one else got. Bill's generally not a generous colleague, as you know.

"Then I hit pay dirt. I was bringing in a contract for her to look over, when I overheard her talking to an engraver on the phone. She was ordering wedding invitations. It seemed improbable that they would take such a huge step after only one date, so I slipped out of her office before she knew I was there. What I heard had convinced me that they'd been seeing one another for quite some time, so I immediately went to work, searching for anything I could find to prove that my theory was correct."

"Were you able to dig up anything?" Carolee asked, her stomach sinking.

"That I did." Sally grinned as widely as her small mouth would allow. "Expense records never lie, if you know what you're looking for. The two of them always made a point to leave the office at different times, so it never appeared that they were off somewhere together. Since I was responsible for submitting his accounts, and Clarice's went through the associates' bookkeeper, no one person ever compared their ledgers, until I decided to take a look. On over a dozen occasions since last fall, Bill and Clarice claimed suspiciously similar travel expenses – lunch at the same restaurant, registration fees for the same conferences, tickets on the same flight, even rooms at the same hotel for the same dates."
"But it could be a coincidence, couldn't it?" the ex-wife asked, frustrated that this information had not come to light sooner, when it could have been used to improve the pitiful settlement she had received from her husband. "Attorneys do attend the same meetings sometimes. Maybe their relationship had been strictly professional, until after our divorce was final."

"Huh, if you believe that you're not as smart as I think you are." Sally wagged a tiny finger at her. "But wait, there's more. The travel expense information was good, but I wanted something really definitive. Then Miss High and Mighty began completely overstepping her authority. She started treating me like I was her maid as well as her secretary, demanding that I bring her coffee and straighten up her office, and Bill's. I saw red, but figured it would be a good way to snoop around in her desk, and his, without raising eyebrows. That's when I found the receipts and gift boxes."

"Receipts? Gift boxes?" came the puzzled query.

"The receipts were in the top drawer of Bill's desk, with the last four digits of his credit card number on them, receipts for things for her, jewelry mostly, and lingerie. I found the empty boxes and bags in her credenza, plus I remember seeing her wearing new earrings and a matching bracelet, just about the same time as the date on one of the credit slips. That's not all. One day I caught a glimpse of her in the restroom, when she was supposed to be changing for the gym. She was putting on a slinky, black teddy under her yoga pants. I remembered that one of the receipts in Bill's desk was from Victoria's Secret, and the gift bag was in her office, with the tags still in it."

When Carolee groaned, Sally added, "Listen, it gets better, depending on your point of view, of course. Some of the things were purchased way back in November and December, before you two had even separated, and months before the divorce was final. I guess Bill wasn't as clever as he thought, leaving those receipts around for me to find. Probably didn't imagine that I would be smart enough to put two and two together. Maybe he even forgot that he'd given me his credit card number last Christmas, so I could order presents for you and the boys. Just to be sure though, I used the account number, called the stores, and pretended to be a credit card rep verifying purchases. Sure enough, the sales people confirmed my suspicions. Your ex bought a bracelet, earrings, and a black teddy, and gave them to Miss Clarice Gordon."

Carolee pushed her fruit around on her plate, but the knots in her stomach made eating impossible. "I should have known you did the shopping for him. Bill's too selfish and too self-absorbed to spend his precious time buying gifts for his family. Thanks, Sally." She reached across the table and squeezed the woman's small hand. "Brett and Bryce were thrilled with the computer games you picked out for them, and I loved the perfume and candles.

"For a little while I thought Bill might be trying, finally, to put some romance back into our marriage. Of course, I found out just I wrong I was when he packed up his things and left me." Raising her gaze and sighing hopelessly, she added, "At least it's nice to hear that he cares enough about someone, besides himself, to buy her something special. He did pick out the gifts for her, didn't he?"

Sally shrugged. "He couldn't take a chance on having anyone else in the loop. But just give him time. It won't be long before that man quits making the effort, especially when his red-haired princess gets more and more demanding, which she will. I predict a very short marriage for Mr. and Mrs. William Austin-to-be. Then he'll really be in a pickle with two ex-wives to support." White curls bounced when she punctuated her point with a sharp nod.

"Only if she makes out better than I did." Shaking her head, Carolee explained. "Bill's a great lawyer. You have to give him that. The judge awarded us joint custody, despite the fact that he rarely sees the boys, so the check we get from him is very small. Bill claimed that keeping up two houses, both set up with bedrooms for the boys, was a financial hardship. So, we barely have enough to get by. I put our house on the market immediately, and thankfully, found a prospective buyer right away. Once the sale closes, we'll get something smaller and more affordable." "Oh, how awful, having to sell your beautiful house," Sally offered sincerely.

"No, it's okay, really. I don't mind. Bill was the one who had to have the biggest house in the fanciest subdivision, not me. I'll be much happier in a small condo, where I won't have to worry with yard work, and where I'll have good neighbors close by. I'm just glad I went against his wishes and kept on taking continuing education classes, to keep my teaching certificate up to date. I've been offered a long-term substitute position at the local high school, which was also my alma mater, so I already know my way around. The extra money will get us through. If we're frugal, we'll be solvent until the end of the term, at least."

"That's wonderful," the legal assistant chirped. "What will you be teaching?"

"English and drama," Carolee answered, her face brightening a bit. "And I'll be directing the spring production for the theatre company.

"Sounds like fun."

"Yes, it should be. It'll help get my mind off this stinking divorce business. Living through betrayal is no picnic." Wiping her lips with the napkin, she added, "I really appreciate everything you've done for me, for us, Sally. I really do. You don't know how much it means to me to have proof that the break-up wasn't entirely my fault."

"Your fault? How could it possibly be your fault?" The tiny lady's white eyebrows went up sharply.

"Bill's very convincing and very manipulative. He blamed me, and I swallowed his well-constructed arguments hook, line, and sinker. Looking back, and knowing what I know now, I can't imagine how I could have accepted his twisted logic so easily, but I did. It has taken me a long time to see things clearly, and the information you've given me helps tremendously.

"For the first three months after Bill left, I was in a deep, cloying fog, fighting my way out of it just long enough to care for the boys, and then letting it envelope me again. In the past couple of days, though, I've been questioning the things Bill said about me, imagining that his accusations might not be true, hoping the blame might not be entirely mine.

"Even though it hurts deeply, to find out that he'd been cheating on me for months, it's a good sort of hurt, you know, like the annoying sting that makes you let go of a live wire. I think I can finally break free of him now." Her soft blue eyes filled with tears. "My husband left me because he wanted someone else, someone who didn't support him through law school, someone who didn't bear his children, someone who doesn't remind him of the silly, irresponsible boy he used to be. The break-up of our marriage was not my fault."

"Good for you," Sally praised her. "Now tell me about the boys. How are they taking all this?"

"Quite well actually," Carolee sniffed. "Bill was always so tied up with work that he rarely saw them anyway. They were usually in bed before he got home in the evenings, and he was away on business every other weekend, so they tell me they don't miss him at all. In fact, the other day Bryce commented that he's seeing more of his dad, since the separation, than he ever did before. I don't know what impact the news of his eminent wedding will have on their weekends with their father, though. Maybe

Clarice won't want teenagers hanging around. I guess we'll just have to wait and see what happens."

"I suppose you will," the kind secretary agreed. "You've got two wonderful young men there, my dear. Good heads on their shoulders. But it's hard for me to believe they aren't angry with their dad for abandoning them, at least a little bit."

"Oh, sure, they're angry with Bill, but not for themselves, for me. Bill has always been way too hard on the boys. They have never been able do anything to please him. He's supremely critical of everything they try, everything they say, their friends, their music, you name it. In a way it's been a relief for them to get him off their backs."

Carolee pushed back a long strand of gray hair. "They're furious with him because of my response to the separation and divorce, because I've been so devastated, so immobilized. It was after I realized what I was doing to my boys, by wallowing in my pain, that I decided I had to put it all behind me and move on."

"They must understand how hard this has been for you," Sally offered sympathetically.

"They do and that's the problem." Sighing deeply, Carolee explained, "At first I was so wrapped up in my own sorrow that I barely noticed them. I made sure they had good meals, and clean clothes, and got to school on time, but except for basic caretaking, I just sat for hours listening to music – love songs, Dylan St. Claire ballads, that sort of thing – longing for the true love I believed I'd lost. I must have played his latest song, 'I Will Cherish You,' a thousand times. I know my guys got tired of hearing it, but it helped me to cry, and I needed to cry. Even before you told me the truth about Bill and his new girl, I was coming to realize that I hadn't really lost my one true love, because I'd never had it to begin with. For years I had been romanticizing Bill and my relationship with him. Thanks to you, I can see him clearly now, for the first time in my life."

"He's a self-centered, egotistical jerk!" the tiny woman declared firmly.

"Yes, he is," her friend agreed with a smile. "And I'm not going to waste any more energy on him. From now on, I'm investing my love where it will pay dividends, in my children. They're going to be surprised to see the change in their old mom."

"Good for you, girl." Pushing her chair back, the efficient legal secretary sighed. "Well, as much as I hate the thought of doing anything for your slimy ex-husband or that haughty witch he's about to marry, I've got to get back to the office before he comes looking for me. We have a big deposition this afternoon." Picking up the check, she offered, "Lunch is on me, but you can leave the tip. Give my love to Brett and Bryce, will you?"

"I will, Sally, and thanks again, for everything." Carolee hugged her tightly.

"It was my pleasure. Just wish I'd figured out his deceitful game sooner," Sally said sadly, "when it would have done you some good."

"Don't worry yourself about that. It might be too late to affect my divorce settlement, but it still helps me, emotionally, to know for sure. Take care and call me soon." She waved goodbye to the rapidly retreating form.

Arriving at home a few minutes before her sons were scheduled to come in from school, the newly emancipated woman took a second, more realistic look at herself in the mirror. The extra pounds she'd carried for the past few years had been melted away by the recent suffering and worry. Yes, her hair was gray, but today she looked at it in a fresh light. Those silver strands were no longer merely telltale signs of advancing age. Now each one shone brightly, a medal of courage, earned in the lifelong battle of nurturing and protecting her family. Examining her face, she noted that the corners of her mouth were softer and more relaxed than they had been for months, and the thin frown lines and dark circles under her eyes had almost disappeared. She smiled.

Who was she without Bill Austin? She asked the question again and memories of the first day of the fifth grade came flooding back to her. Her homeroom teacher had encouraged each child to stand up in front of the class, introduce him or herself, list their favorite things, and describe what career they hoped to pursue. Carolee could still remember her words exactly. "Hello, I'm Carolee Stone. I love horses, grape Popsicles, and Bon Jovi. When I grow up, I'm going to be a famous actress." She smiled again. Who was she? That little girl with the big dreams was still there, deep inside her, but now she was more, much more.

After several long moments of reflection, she took a deep breath and attempted to redefine herself. "I'm not a wife any longer, but I'm still a pretty darned good mother. I'm an accomplished teacher and a thoughtful friend. I could be a talented actress and even a passionate lover." She thought of her parents and her sister and added, "I'm a faithful daughter and a caring sister."

Rephrasing her fifth-grade introduction, she said, "Hello, I'm Carolee Austin. I love horses and grape Popsicles. I still like Bon Jovi, but the music of Dylan St. Claire moves me more now. I'm not famous, but I have been a great actress, for I've spent over twenty years intrenched in the role of the dutiful wife. From this day on, I'll be satisfied and happy with the other parts I play each day – roles of mother, teacher, daughter, sister, and friend. Most of all, I am a woman who is worthy of devotion and capable of love."

That declaration made, she gave herself a wink and moved to the kitchen to prepare the snack she knew her sons would be wanting as soon as they hit the door. Moments later, they bounded into the house, dropping heavy backpacks and athletic bags in their rush to greet her. For the first time in weeks, her response to their question, "How're you doing, Mom?" was sincere.

"Fine, just fine," she told them, and meant it.

Grabbing up the glasses of cold milk she'd poured for them, along with a small plate of homemade oatmeal-raisin cookies, the teens plodded downstairs to the family room. Thirteen-year-old, Bryce, ensconced himself in front of the TV, while his older brother settled in with his smart phone. At sixteen and a half, Brett thought he was far too grown up to pay any attention to his brother's juvenile choice of programs, and preferred texting with his friends.

Bored by the choices provided by the local cable company, the younger teen surfed the channels, stopping briefly on the newest talk show to hit the airwaves. Fresh, sophisticated, and polished, *The Olivia Wells Show* had taken off like a rocket, leaving its competitors in a dense cloud of low ratings dust. Even though the show originated in Atlanta, rather than New York or LA, it had made huge inroad into the afternoon lineup nationwide.

The show's namesake, bright, smart, witty, and outspoken, Olivia Wells, was primarily responsible for its unqualified success, even with the under twenty-five crowd. Her flaming auburn curls and magnetic smile had become immediately recognizable to the majority of the afternoon TV viewing audience. Bryce liked her.

He laid the remote aside to dunk a cookie. "Hey, Brett, you've got to see this," he mumbled to his brother, his mouth full.

"Not now, I'm busy," the elder complained, not looking up.

"Come on. It's important," the youngster begged. "It's just what Mom needs."

Intrigued by the idea of helping his mother, the teenager laid his phone aside and listened intently as Miss Wells explained the rules of the latest of her very popular viewer contests. This one, entitled *Make Dreams Come True*, would recognize several worthy individuals, who had encountered setbacks or disappointment in their lives. The show's producers would select the most deserving winners, and attempt to make their fondest wishes a reality. The announcer encouraged viewers to make their entry right away, and gave the link to the nomination form and instructions.

"We've got to do this," Brett decided firmly, ordering his younger sibling. "Go check and see where Mom is. We don't want her to overhear. I'll start working on it."

When Bryce returned, his brother was furiously rattling keys. "She's lying down in her room. I shut her door."

"Good. Now help me with this, will you? The deadline's tomorrow, so we need to finish it up right now. What else should we say?" He slid his chair back to give the smaller boy a view of the screen. They worked furiously, explaining how alone and sad their mom had been since their dad left them, pouring out their hearts, expressing how helpless they'd felt as they'd watched their mother being crushed, so unjustly, by the unexpected separation and divorce, and suggesting how *The Olivia Wells Show* might help make her dreams come true.

By the time Carolee startled them from their efforts with a call of, "Dinner's ready!" they were convinced they'd composed a great nomination letter.

"Send it now, Brett," Bryce urged. "So Mom won't see it."

"Aw…she rarely uses the computer," his big brother reassured him. "Let's wait until after we eat. Then if we can't think of anything we want to add, I'll submit it before I start my homework, okay?"

"Okay," he agreed with a huge, self-satisfied smile.

PART II

Weeks passed before the boys received a response to their contest submission. Carolee began her new teaching job, and spent every afternoon rehearsing for the spring musical, "West Side Story." She convinced both of her sons to take small roles in the production. They liked the idea of playing opposing gang members. Brett, with his dark, swarthy good looks, so like his father's, was a stereotypical *Shark*, while the fair-haired, Bryce, fit in well as a *Jet*. Every evening they spent an hour or more, joyfully choreographing their mock combat for the rumble scene opening in Act One.

The afterschool rehearsal was usually the topic of the boys' animated discussion on the trip home. This afternoon, Carolee let Brett drive, while she sat quietly in the back seat, caught up in her own thoughts, anxious for the weekend to arrive. She had finally closed on the house she and Bill had purchased together, and had found an affordable condo in a neighborhood near the high school and the small church she and the boys attended. A successful yard sale had produced a much-needed quantity of ready cash, and had reduced their household belongings to a more manageable level. They planned to move on Saturday, with the help of friends and neighbors.

When Brett wheeled the family van into the driveway and rolled to a stop, Bryce slid out and sprinted to the mailbox. What he found inside delighted him. It was a letter from *The Olivia Wells Show*, addressed to his mother. He brought it to her proudly, urging her to open it immediately. She put him off long enough to get inside and drop her briefcase on the kitchen counter. Then the boys surrounded her, one on either side, each peering over a shoulder.

"What in the world could this be?" she asked, turning the envelope over and examining it carefully, prolonging their agony unbearably.

"Come on, Mom," Brett pleaded. "Just rip into it!"

A strange suspicion occurred to her and she asked, "Do you guys know anything about this?"

"Open it and find out," was the only response she received.

Shrugging in acceptance, she slid her fingernail under the flap. Inside she found an announcement that read, "Congratulations! You have won our *Make Dreams Come True* contest," and gave instructions to call the show's producer for further instructions.

"Yippee!" the youngest Austin cried, grabbing Carolee and spinning her around. "You won! You won!" Both teens were dancing in delight.

"What do you mean, I won? What did I win? And how did I win? I didn't enter any contest," she complained, obviously confused.

"We entered for you," the older explained. "Bryce was watching the show the day of the deadline to submit nominations. The contest sounded perfect for you, so we sent in a letter and application form that night. This is so great! You're gonna love it."

"I'm gonna love what? I don't understand." She shook her head in confusion.

"Just call 'em and find out. We're not going to tell you any more. It's supposed to be a surprise," Brett urged her firmly.

Sighing in defeat, the baffled woman grabbed her cell phone and punched in the number listed in the letter. A cheerful voice on the other end of the line answered, "Hello. Thanks for calling *The Olivia Wells Show*. How may I help you?"

Fumbling with the paper, Carolee searched for the name of the contact person. "Uh…may I speak with Jennifer Thompson? This is Carolee Austin."

"Certainly, Ms. Austin. One moment, please."

After several clicks on the line, she heard, "Hi, this is Jenny Thompson, associate producer. It's good to hear from you, Mrs. Austin. You've got a couple of really special sons there. I know you're very proud of them."

"Why yes, they are and I am, thank you," Carolee replied, hesitantly.

"Well, I guess you're wondering what this is all about, huh?" Her youthful voice was full of excitement and energy. "How much have your boys told you?"

"Nothing, except that they entered me in some sort of a contest, sponsored by your show, and I have this announcement from you saying that I've won. Just what have I won?" She didn't mean to sound so demanding and skeptical, but the newly divorced woman was too recently burned by misfortune to believe that anything good could come to her so easily.

"Oh, this is great. I'm glad they haven't let the cat out of the bag. It will be so much more fun that way. You'll be receiving the prize they suggested for you, plus several surprises they don't know about. I believe our plans for you will please them. So, I'd better not tell you anymore until we get you on the show. Wouldn't want to ruin the surprise, would we?"

"And why not?" the caller snapped, irritated by the young woman's evasiveness. "I've had my fill of surprises lately. I refuse to go on national television and allow your show to make a fool of me. If you aren't willing to tell me exactly what's going on here, I'm not willing to cooperate with it."

"Mom, don't be like that," Bryce whispered. Seeing the wistful look in his eyes, she softened a bit.

"I understand how you feel, Mrs. Austin, honestly I do. Have you ever seen *The Olivia Wells Show*?" Jenny asked her, accustomed to dealing with reluctant guests.

"Well, yes, I have," Carolee admitted reluctantly.

"Then you know how we operate. We're an above-board, respectable show. We never belittle or make a spectacle of people. Our contests are straightforward and fair. If we say we're going to make your dreams come true, then that's exactly what we intend to do."

Jenny could obviously sense that her quiet, calm manner was having the desired effect on the unsure woman, as she continued. "In this contest, we asked our viewers to nominate a worthy individual, someone they feel deserves to have their dreams come true. They outlined why their nominee should be chosen, and what we could do to make his or her dreams a reality.

"I guess you've figured out by now that Brett and Bryce sent us a letter about you. It was wonderful. It's obvious that they love you very much."

Tears welled and the lump that had suddenly formed in her throat made it hard to speak. "Yes, and I love them very much, too."

"I know you do. And it's our goal to encourage and support the connection you have with them, not break it down. Though I'd rather not tell you any more about your specific prize at this time, I will do so, if you still don't feel you can trust me," the associate producer offered.

"No, no, it's all right, I guess," Carolee relented. "Since my sons have gone to such trouble to win this prize for me, the least I can do is to accept it graciously. What do I need to do now?" Beginning to allow herself to feel hopeful, she smiled.

"I'm so glad," Jenny exclaimed before giving her detailed instructions. "We've booked you on a flight to Atlanta on June eighteen, returning home on the evening of the twenty-first. I hope those dates will work for you."

Mentally checking her calendar, Carolee said, "Yes, school's out by then and Mom should be able to look after the boys. That'll be fine. It definitely won't interfere with any vacation plans."

"Good. You'll be staying at the new Southern Hospitality Hotel in downtown Atlanta. A car and driver will be provided for you, so you won't have to worry about getting around the city on your own. All of your expenses will be covered by the show, and I will send you a complete itinerary with your schedule, important contacts, and anything else you might need. Oh, and Mrs. Austin, there's one more thing." Jennifer hesitated.

"What's that? And call me Carolee, please. I've grown quite uncomfortable with the Mrs. Austin label."

"Sure, Carolee. You'll need to bring one outfit to wear on the set during the initial taping. Solid colors work best. Stay away from extremely large patterns, vivid multi-colors, or white, and no big, shiny jewelry. If you choose a skirt or dress, pick a length that's comfortable when you sit down, and a safe, stable shoe. Being on TV for the first time can make your knees a little wobbly. Be sure to wear a jacket or something with a collar, to clip the microphone on, and with pockets or a waistband, where we can attach the transmitter."

"That's no problem. You're describing my entire wardrobe, dull and conservative." Carolee laughed, catching the producer's enthusiasm.

"Don't worry about remembering all this stuff. I'll put the instructions in the confirmation email I send. My contact info is on the bottom of the award letter. If you'll drop me a short note, then I'll have your email address."

"Of course," Carolee agreed. "Do you need my cell phone number?"

"I've got it already. It's on the nomination form your sons sent. You're going to have a wonderful trip, Carolee, and an even more wonderful surprise. I promise. I'll meet you at the airport when you arrive, but if you think of any other questions before then, please call or text. I'll send you my cell number so you don't have to go through the switchboard." The young woman's voice rang with sincerity.

"Thank you, Jenny. I'm sorry I was so suspicious. You've been very kind and helpful. I'm looking forward to meeting you."

"Oh, it's no problem. I've handled tougher customers than you, believe me," Jenny teased.

"I'll just bet you have. Thanks again. Goodbye." Carolee waited for her to sign off before hanging up.

Immediately, the boys bombarded her with questions. "What did they tell you? Are you going to Atlanta? When do you leave? Are you gonna be on the show?"

"Hold on guys and let me catch my breath," she begged them. Giving in to the weakness that had suddenly attacked her knees, she pulled a chair out from under the kitchen table and dropped into it. After a couple of deep, relaxing breaths, she was able to relate Jenny Thompson's instructions to her impatiently waiting sons.

"So, she didn't tell you what you'd won?" Bryce asked, wanting to be sure he didn't ruin the surprise by saying too much.

"No, she said the show has something special planned, in addition to whatever it is you asked them for – a surprise you two don't know about either. It all sounds pretty mysterious." Getting into a celebrating mood, she prodded him. "It's confession time. What in the world did you write in that nomination letter you guys submitted? What do you believe would make my dreams come true?"

"Oh, no, I'm not falling for your tricks," the younger boy said, shaking his head firmly. "You won't talk me into telling you anything."

"Then I'll just have to guess. Let's see, you asked Olivia Wells to find me a knight in shining armor to come to my rescue on a white charger. No, that can't be it, we don't have the space for a white charger in our condo. Wait, I've got it! You asked her to get me a recurring role in a soap opera. Oh, I forgot, my life's pretty much a soap opera already, so I guess that's not it. I know, you asked for a truckload of Dylan St. Claire CD's to replace the ones I've worn out over the last months."

The teens eyed one another suspiciously, but said nothing.

"Not ready to spill the beans, huh? Well, just give me time, I'll get it out of you," she threatened. Forcing herself back to her weary feet, she sighed. "I sure hope you wished for a younger body for me. This one feels pretty tired and used up right now."

Moving to the refrigerator, she began pulling out plastic containers of leftovers. "I'll have something ready for you guys to eat in just a few minutes. I know you're hungry. Then after dinner we'll call Grandma and tell her about this mysterious surprise you've cooked up. I've got to make sure she'll be around to help out while I'm in Atlanta. Unfortunately, we can't depend on your father."

By lunchtime the next day, the news had spread all over Thomas Jefferson High. Students she barely knew stopped Carolee in the hallway to offer her their congratulations. Her colleagues, curiosity eating at them, formed countless conjectures, regarding the prizes she might be receiving once she reached Atlanta. While she graded papers in the staff lounge during her free period, various possibilities were flung around the room.

"I'll bet it's a vacation of some sort," the math teacher suggested, trying repeatedly but unsuccessfully, to tuck his shirt into his pants over his protruding belly. "You know kids, they usually ask for a trip to Disneyworld, or something frivolous like that."

"No, no, it must be a makeover," the pretty, young volleyball coach countered. "*The Olivia Wells Show* is always doing makeovers."

"The good Lord knows I could use either one of those, for sure" Carolee admitted with a sigh. "Though right now I'm not sure which one would do me the most good."

"Wait, wait," the librarian stuttered, fluttering her plump hands with excitement. "I know what it is – it's an audition for a part in a movie. Your boys are sharp. They know you've had acting aspirations since you were a little girl. Or maybe it's a cameo appearance on a TV show."

Cindy Lawrence, a short, cuddly bookworm, who always looked like she was just a little lost, had been Carolee's best friend since the second grade, when they had met in a summer reading program at the local library. Cindy clearly took pride in the fact that she knew more about her old pal than the rest of the faculty. Her newly acquired reading glasses slipped down to the end of her upturned nose when she added, "Wouldn't that be a dream come true?"

"It would, I guess," Carolee agreed, somewhat reluctantly. "But I don't think I'd be up to such a demanding, nerve-wracking surprise. Wouldn't want the pressure at this point in my life. Honestly, I hope it's something more, well…more fun, and less stressful."

"Whatever it turns out to be, I know one thing for sure," Cindy declared.

"What's that?" her friend asked.

"You deserve it more than anyone I know, and I'm very happy for you." The tiny librarian wrapped her arms around Carolee in a sincere embrace.

"Here, here!" the portly mathematician chimed in. "With all the bad stuff going on in this world, it's a pleasure to see something good happen for a change, and to such a nice person, too. We're all excited for you, Carolee. Wild horses won't be able to drag us away from the boob tube when you're on."

"Thanks, to all of you." Carolee's gaze swept around the room, touching lightly on each one. "I really appreciate everything you've done to help me get settled in here. You've all been wonderful. I'm going to miss you so much when this job is over."

"Don't fret about that just yet," the trim, athletic coach told her, unfolding her long, muscular legs and stretching. "I have it on the best authority that Ms. Parks, the full-timer you're filling in for, may not be wanted back. She's been out because she's going to have a baby, you know; but unfortunately, there's no husband in the picture. In fact, there's a wife." The word seemed to twist in her mouth as she spat it out.

"The administration looked the other way at first, until she started flaunting her sexual preferences in everyone's faces. Don't know what she was thinking, getting married to another woman **and** having a baby. That sort of thing is not looked upon favorably by our provincial school board. It doesn't set a good example for our kids. So, her bad luck may be your good fortune, Carolee. There's a better than average chance they'll keep you on. Talk to your ex. I hear he has some pull with the superintendent, since he got him out of that DUI charge a while back. The board's already in a huff over this, so I don't think it would take much to push them to can Parks."

"As much as I'd love to keep this job, I wouldn't want it at such a cost to anyone else." Carolee declared, heading for the door, deciding it was time to leave before she said something she'd regret later. "Thanks again, folks, and I hope to see you all tomorrow, at opening night." A chorus of affirmative responses echoed behind her.

Cindy Lawrence followed her friend into the hallway. Grabbing her by the elbow, she said, "You can't let the narrow-minded types get to you, Carolee."

"I know, I know. Figured it was best to retreat rather than sit there biting my tongue till it bled."

Changing the subject abruptly, Cindy asked, "Have you gotten your invitation for the class reunion yet?"

"Yeah," Blue eyes darkening sadly, the taller woman nodded.

"Well?" the librarian probed.

"Well, what?" Carolee snapped, unable to hide her irritation.

"Are you planning to go? Twenty-five years, I can hardly believe it's been so long. I know it's going to be a lot of fun."

"You've got to be kidding." The taller woman stubbornly folded her arms across her chest. "Bill wouldn't miss the opportunity to show off his new, trophy wife, and I couldn't stand the humiliation."

Looking more lost than usual, Cindy urged, "Oh, come on, you can go with Danny and me, just like old times. Remember all those sock hops we used to go to? Danny would drive us, and then you and I would dance together, because he was too self-conscious, too afraid he'd look silly, to get out there and give it a try."

"How could I forget? We've had a lot of great times. After I started dating Bill, we became a foursome instead of a threesome, but still did everything together, at least until the kids came along. Remember the trip to the beach when we tent camped and practically melted in the heat, and the motorcycle ride in the mountains when we practically froze to death?"

"Yeah, those were the good old days!" Cindy laughed.

"How can I go to the reunion and face all those people again, without Bill?" Carolee looked stricken. "I can just imagine the snide comments and nasty jokes that will be repeated behind my back. I couldn't bear it, Cindy.

"I can hear them gossiping now. 'It's no wonder he left her, look how she's let herself go,' or 'I always wondered what he saw in her anyway.' And you know Marlo Grimes will be there, gloating because she always wanted Bill for herself. She'll have something especially ugly to say. You know she will. She won't be able to resist rubbing it in. I just can't do it. I just can't."

"You don't know it will be like that. You're just imaging the worst. Think of it this way - It'll be a great opportunity to show Bill that he hasn't gotten the best of you." Carolee gave her friend a determined look that said this decision was non-negotiable, so Cindy relented, and her shoulders slumped in defeat. "It just won't be the same without you there. That's for sure."

The librarian let the subject drop for the time being, but Carolee knew her friend too well to believe that she'd let go of the idea entirely. "See you at church on Sunday," Cindy called behind her as she scooted off down the hallway.

PART III

Thomas Jefferson High School's production of "West Side Story" was an unqualified hit. The auditorium was packed to capacity for the dress rehearsal and all three performances. A local theatre critic gave the cast, crew, and director rave reviews in the town newspaper. With the hustle and bustle surrounding the play, combined with exams and end-of-the-semester activities, the spring term flew by for Carolee and her sons. Almost before she had time to think about the contest, her prize, or the trip to Atlanta, June had arrived.

As promised, Jennifer Thompson was waiting for Carolee when her plane touched down in the huge airport. The energetic associate producer deftly steered the nervous traveler through the concourse, helped her locate her luggage, and loaded it into the waiting car. She introduced her to the driver of the big, black Lincoln, which waited for them on the curb outside the terminal.

"'Lo, Ms. Austin, name's Doss, Arnold Doss, but most folks call me Arnie," the big man offered, holding the open door for her. "I'll be chauffeurin' you roun' town for the next couple o' days."

"Thanks, Arnie. It's a pleasure to meet you, and I'm Carolee," the excited woman responded before sliding into the luxurious interior. Jenny slipped in beside her and provided a running commentary on Atlanta, as they rolled past interesting landmarks. With traffic unusually light, they arrived at the city's newest luxury hotel in less than half an hour.

Arnie lifted her suitcase out of the car's generous trunk and onto a cart provided by the valet. Accustomed to waiting on herself, Carolee shouldered her overnight bag. "Here, ma'am, let me git that for you," the beefy chauffeur said, reaching for the case she carried. "You go on, now. We'll bring all your things to yer room directly."

"Thanks." She smiled warmly at him before following the producer through the revolving door and into the ornate lobby of the Southern Hospitality Hotel.

"You're already checked in," Jenny informed her. "So, we can go right to your suite. I know you're going to love it. This place is really something." They rode the glass elevator up through the middle of a huge atrium, designed to resemble the exterior of a white-columned antebellum mansion. Carolee felt like she'd stepped into a scene from <u>Gone with the Wind.</u>

The sumptuous appointments in her rooms served only to enhance that illusion. Standing in the sitting area, she could truly imagine herself in the parlor of *Tara*. The furniture was predominantly nineteenth-century reproductions, crafted in warm, dark woods and upholstered in pleasing, cool shades of green and rose. A delicate china tea service, bearing an understated floral pattern, had been placed in the middle of the small dining table. Fresh magnolias stood in crystal vases around the room. An obvious effort had been made to keep all evidence of the modern world out of sight, by hiding the television inside a mahogany hutch, and tucking the tiny kitchenette and wet bar behind a collapsible screen.

The young producer was pleased with Carolee's reaction to the suite. "If you think this is great, wait until you see the bedroom. Come with me," she urged. Throwing the double doors open wide, Jenny revealed a huge poster-bed, topped with a beautiful, white lace canopy, and piled high with fluffy pillows. In one corner, two overstuffed chairs, in coordinating pastel fabrics faced each other, with a wide ottoman between them. An antique armoire, concealing yet another TV and sound system, numerous storage compartments, and stocked mini-bar, covered the better part of one wall. The one opposite was not really a wall at all, but a floor-to-ceiling window, overlooking the city.

"Wow!" Carolee breathed.

"Yeah, wow," Jenny echoed. "It's really great, isn't it?"

A rap on the exterior door interrupted their admiration of the spacious accommodations. Arnie and the valet entered, pushing a loaded cart. They quickly stowed her bags in the bedroom closet. "Thanks so much," Carolee told them, reaching into her pocket for the bills she had folded and ready for use as a tip.

Before she could hand the money over, Jenny touched her arm and whispered, "It's all taken care of, remember, on us." She handed an envelope to each man.

The bellman nodded his appreciation and departed, but the driver hesitated, doffing his hat. "Just ring the front desk whenever you need me, hear? I'll be on duty ever' day, and 'til eleven or so in the evenin'. You want to go somewhere, or want me to pick somethin' up fer you – whatever, I'm yer man."

"Thank you, Arnie. I really appreciate your thoughtfulness." Carolee's blue eyes twinkled brightly.

"We'll be down in about half an hour," the efficient producer informed him. "I'll get our guest settled in, freshened up, and ready for this afternoon's broadcast. She's not expected at the studio until 1p.m., so we should have time to stop for a bite to eat on the way."

"Okey, dokey. I know jest the place for lunch. I'll call ahead and get everthin' set up so's ya'll won't have to wait." He flopped his cap back over his close-cropped, thinning hair and grinned widely. "See ya in a bit, then."

Right on schedule, the driver pulled the long, dark auto up to the rear door of the television studio. "I'll be waitin' right here to take ya back to the hotel when you're done," he informed Carolee politely.

Miss Thompson whisked her guest inside and down the hallway to the dressing room, introducing her to several members of the show's staff along the way. Leaving her in the make-up artist's capable hands, Jenny rushed off to finalize last minute details.

"Hi, I'm Denise." With a well-manicured hand, the tall, statuesque woman patted the back of a swivel chair placed in front of a large, brightly-lit mirror. "Sit over here." Once Carolee had complied, she draped a silver plastic cape around her shoulders and over her suit.

"You don't usually wear much make-up, do you?" Denise asked her.

"Not for years. There just doesn't seem to be any use in it," the anxious guest answered, shrugging.

Laying out the tools of her trade, the efficient cosmetologist worked quickly, chatting all the while. "This foundation will probably feel pretty heavy to you, then, but we've got to make sure your nose doesn't shine under those hot lights." She applied powder with a large, soft brush. "You've got beautiful skin, you know, and great eyes. Some folks get contact lenses to make their eyes look that color." A few touches of shadow, mascara, blush, and lip color, and she was done. "That's it, I guess. Jenny told me to keep it minimal for today's show. She wants you to look really natural."

The assistant producer returned to guide Carolee to her next stop, the green room, where she waited, along with three other contest winners who would be featured in their own segments of the show. A technician came in and helped her attach a microphone to the lapel of her navy jacket. He complimented her on her clothing selection and understated jewelry, saying she looked perfect for TV. Just minutes before airtime, the show's star popped through the door.

"Hello everyone, I'm Olivia Wells. It's a great pleasure to meet y'all. We're going to have a terrific time today." Shaking hands all around, and tossing her bright curls carelessly, the popular host's friendly, casual manner made all of her guests feel welcome, comfortable, and relaxed.

"Now before you go on air, I want you to know a bit more about our production schedule. One thing that makes *The Olivia Wells Show* unique is that we're live, every weekday. We always broadcast a show on Friday that will hook our viewers in and get them back on Monday. So, that's the theme for today's show – cliffhanger – and all of you will participate. The hook we give them will make folks tune in next week to see how everything turns out for each of you."

Nodding in Carolee's direction she added, "Ms. Austin, you will complete your post-prize show on Monday." Gesturing toward a pretty brunette, she said, "Theresa, your *Dream Come True* follow-up will be produced Tuesday." Her gaze moved to a boy whose small size seemed incongruent with his apparent age. "Ricky, we'll feature you on Wednesday." Finally, she focused on an elderly couple seated on the sofa, holding hands. "And you folks will go last, on Thursday's broadcast. Is that clear with everyone?"

All heads nodded in the affirmative. "Good. Your special surprises will take place between the end of the broadcast today, and your next scheduled appearance. Each of you has been assigned an associate producer, whom you've already met, along with a camera technician. They'll accompany you and shoot the action as we make your dreams come true. Do any of you have questions?"

"Uh, yes, Miss Wells, will there be a lot of people watching us?" Ricky asked, his voice surprisingly deep.

"Just the usual studio audience. Nothing to be worried about," she answered with a reassuring smile. "You'll be joining them in just a couple of minutes, then I'll bring you up to the stage, individually, to announce what you've won. We'll go in reverse order of show production. Mr. and Mrs. Johnson will go first, then you, Ricky, next Theresa, and finally Carolee."

Clapping her palms together in encouragement, she moved to the door. "Okay, is everyone ready? Let's go. Follow me."

Carolee did as she was directed, claiming the seat on the end of the front row. Almost before she could take a calming breath, the lights came up and Olivia's peppy, jazz-inspired theme song blared. A neon "*Applause*" sign flashed, prompting the audience to rise, cheering, as the vibrant host made her way through them and up onto the stage.

"Hello and welcome," Olivia announced, flashing her brilliant smile. "You'll be very happy you tuned in today, because we're going to announce the winners of our *Make Dreams Come True* contest!" Cheers resounded throughout the studio. "Here they are folks. See them for yourselves." The cameras left her and panned the row on which Carolee was seated. "We'll introduce you to our first winners, right after this."

During the commercial break, the Johnsons were moved to chairs on the raised platform, next to Olivia. When broadcasting resumed, she welcomed them and read excerpts from the nomination letter their granddaughter had sent in to the show. The child's words were deeply touching. She explained how her granny and grandpa had given up their dream trip to Hawaii, to celebrate their fiftieth wedding anniversary, when she'd become seriously ill.

Her family was financially strapped, and had no health insurance. Mr. and Mrs. Johnson had happily contributed their second honeymoon savings to pay off their granddaughter's medical bills. The child's final words were, "My grandparents shouldn't have to sacrifice so much for me. Can you please make their dream come true and send them to Hawaii?"

There was hardly a dry eye in the house when Olivia outlined the travel plans the show's staff had arranged for the elderly couple. It truly would be the trip of a lifetime, and one they would always remember.

After another short break, it was Ricky's turn to take the stage. This time the nomination was a video recording sent in by a group of the boy's closest friends. They described how he had struggled through long years of surgery and therapy, to correct a congenital abnormality in his heart. The boys spoke of Ricky's untiring good humor and never-complaining attitude, despite the constant pain he endured, and of his complete lack of self-pity.

"He never feels sorry for himself," one tow-headed youngster said, "even though he can't run and play sports like the rest of us. And he's so little, too. Some of the kids in our fifth-grade class make fun of him because he's only the size of a kindergartener, but he never seems to mind."

The last snippet of the video asked *The Olivia Wells Show* to send Ricky to Disneyworld, since, they claimed, he'd always wanted to go there, but his family couldn't afford to take him. "We want to see pictures of him on the tallest roller coaster," one of his friends had said. "He'll be just as big as everyone else way up there."

The audience went wild when Ricky's prize was detailed – four days in Orlando for the boy, his family, and his friends from the video, complete travel arrangements, hotel accommodations, food, and admission to all of the theme parks in that area.

Following the next break, Theresa was escorted to the platform. A woman's voice was piped into the studio, reading portions of the nomination she'd sent the show, asking for assistance in locating her daughter's siblings.

"I adopted Theresa when she was four years old," the voice said. "She's been the finest daughter any mother could want, and I'm very proud of her, but I know there's always been something missing in her life. Theresa was the youngest of five siblings. They were separated and sent to different foster or adoptive homes after their parents died. I can't tell you how many nights she cried herself to sleep asking for her brothers and sisters. I've tried to track them down for her, but have only run into roadblocks. Please help me."

When Olivia announced that Theresa's family had been found, and a reunion arranged, the attractive young woman burst into tears and threw her arms around the delighted host. She would be spending the next few days in Atlanta with her siblings, getting reacquainted.

One more commercial break and it was Carolee's turn. Just before the cameras started rolling again, Olivia squeezed her hand and whispered reassuringly, "You're going to be fine." The director cued her and she began, "Here with us now is our last *Make Dreams Come True* prize winner, Carolee Austin. Hello, Carolee. It's good to have you with us."

"I'm very happy to be here," the nervous guest replied, forcing her face to relax, and trying her best not to look scared silly.

"Carolee's sons nominated her for this prize. I'd like for you to see their letter now." A huge screen behind the stage lit up, displaying the message Brett and Bryce had written. Everyone in

the studio and viewers at home could follow along as Olivia read
their words:

*"Our mom is the greatest. She's always here for us, cooking,
cleaning, doing laundry, taking us places, helping us with
homework, watching our soccer games, telling us stories, and
listening to our problems. Other guys complain about their
mothers sometimes, but not us. We know how good we've got it!*

*The problem is, our dad left us a while back, and it's been
really, really hard on mom. We don't have money now, like we
used to, and she worries about that all the time. She tries to hide it
from us, but we know she's very sad. Sometimes she sits and listens
to the music she likes, and we can tell she's been crying, even
though she smiles and says she's okay. We have each other and
our friends, and Dad has his new girlfriend, but Mom doesn't have
anyone now, so she's pretty lonely. We think she deserves to have
her dreams come true.*

*"Mom's favorite singer is Dylan St. Claire. She listens to his
CD's all the time. We tease her that she's going to wear her old
CD player out! Mr. St. Claire's tour is coming to Greensboro,
North Carolina in July. That's only about two hours from our
town, Dogwood Valley, Virginia. We know mom would love to go
to that concert, but she won't spend the money for a ticket, because
we need new soccer shoes. She's always doing stuff like that,
giving up things she wants for us.*

*Today we heard that the concert's sold out. But, since you're
such a famous person, we thought you'd probably be able to get
her a ticket to that Dylan St. Claire concert. We don't think this
would be too much to ask, since it won't be very expensive,
compared to some of the stuff other people ask you for, but it
would definitely make our mom's dreams come true. Thank you
very much."*

The letter was signed, *Your fans, Brett and Bryce Austin.*
When the camera returned to Carolee, her eyes were brimming
with tears.

"My goodness," Ms. Wells said with a sigh. "Aren't they something? You must be extremely proud; it's obvious that they love you very much."

"I'm very lucky." the guest said, sniffing. "My boys are so sweet and selfless. The divorce has been hard on them, too, but they're always worried about me. I can hardly believe they've done this. It's so thoughtful, such a wonderful surprise."

"So, you're a Dylan St. Claire, fan huh?" the host prompted with a grin. "I love his music, too. And, he's a good friend."

"Well, you won't see me screaming after him like a silly teenager." Carolee clarified, smiling brightly, "if that's what you mean by being a fan. I got that silly nonsense out of my system when I was thirteen and head over heels for Jon Bon Jovi, but I do appreciate Mr. St. Claire's songs. They speak to my heart.

"It's easy to imagine that his music is a reflection of the man; and if it is, then he just seems to know how to get under a woman's skin – to make her believe that true love is still possible, even when the real world is proving otherwise."

"I think you're right. Dylan's work is something very special. Not to mention that he's a real hunk! Wouldn't you agree, folks?" At her prompting, the audience broke into enthusiastic applause.

"A single ticket to a Dylan St. Claire concert seems a very simple and inexpensive request. We should have no trouble making this dream come true." Reaching into her pocket she pulled out a strip of heavy off-white paper, imprinted with dark green ink. "I just happen to have one on me."

Demonstrating her dramatic flair, which consistently drove up her ratings, Olivia extended the ticket toward Carolee, but just as the guest's fingers touched it, the host drew it back. "No, wait," she pretended to examine the print carefully. "Your boys asked us for a ticket to Dylan's concert in Greensboro, next month. This one is for his Atlanta concert, tomorrow, front row center." Turning to her guest, she asked, "Would that be all right with you? Could you hang around town for a couple of days? We'd make it worth your while by throwing in a back stage pass."

"Yes, of course," Carolee stuttered eagerly. "Can't think of anything else I have to do this weekend."

"Oh, good," the host handed over the ticket with a flourish.

"Since you didn't come to the show prepared with concert-worthy attire, I think it's only fair that we treat you to a complete make-over. What do you think about that, folks? Doesn't Carolee deserve to look her best for her evening out at the Dylan St. Claire concert?"

The audience offered their whole-hearted support once more.

"Thank you so much. This is incredibly exciting," Carolee gave the dynamic redhead a warm hug.

"You're very welcome, my dear, but hold on. That's not all."

A chorus of curious whispers filled the studio. Olivia waited for them to fall silent before she continued. "I mentioned that Dylan and I are friends. When we received this nomination from your sons, I had it forwarded to him. After he read it, he called to see if there was anything he could do to add a few special surprises to your dream come true. We talked for a while, and decided that you might enjoy a quiet dinner alone with him, before the concert. How does that sound?"

Squeals of delight could be heard over the din, as the entire audience exploded in wild cheers and applause. Carolee could hardly believe her ears. She didn't know what to say. Her mouth moved, but no words came out, so she nodded her head furiously. "I'll take that as a yes," Miss Wells teased.

"Yes, yes," the dumbfounded guest croaked, her throat as dry as paper.

"And we'll expect you back here on our next show to tell us all about your special evening with Dylan St. Claire. Is that a deal?"

"Of course!" Carolee agreed, finally finding her voice. Turning to face the camera directly, Olivia offered her concluding words. "As soon as our award winners leave the studio today, they'll begin their individual *Dreams Come True* adventures. We'll be sending a camera along with them to catch every second of the excitement. All next week we'll run that footage for you, as we bring each of our winners back into the studio to describe their experiences, in detail. You won't miss a minute of the fun, adventure, and romance." She shot a quick wink in Carolee's direction.

"On Monday's show, you'll go along on Carolee's dream date with Dylan St. Claire. I know you won't want to miss that one. Tuesday, you'll witness Theresa's reunion with her long-lost brothers and sisters. Be sure to have plenty of tissues on hand. Ricky will be back with us on Wednesday, to tell you about his once-in-a-lifetime trip to Disneyworld; and finally, on Thursday, the Johnson's will return from five glorious days in Hawaii, to share their second honeymoon with you. Please join us."

"That's a wrap!" the director yelled.

PART IV

Carolee was anxious to get back to the privacy of her room at the hotel to call Brett and Bryce. As she expected, they were waiting by the phone, anxious to hear all about her trip, the show, and the prize they'd won for her. The boys talked for over half an hour, remarking on how great she looked on TV, and reassuring her that they'd recorded every second. After thanking them profusely, she reminded them to record Monday's show, so she could see it when she returned home.

Signing off with, "I love you guys," she ended the call, plugged her cellphone up to charge, and headed for the huge spa tub and a long, hot soak. Afterward, she ordered a light supper from room service and fell into bed.

Despite the fact that she was physically exhausted, the excited woman found herself unable to relax. Her mind was awhirl with jumbled thoughts. Whenever she closed her eyes, she began reliving the events of the thrilling day, the early morning flight and arrival in a new, bustling city, the fabulous hotel, and the studio with its bright lights and expectant tension, all jumbled up with the anticipation of the promise of tomorrow.

"I've got to stop this and get some rest," she scolded herself. "Jenny said they'd be here first thing in the morning."

In desperation, she got out of bed and crossed to the armoire where she'd noticed a compact disc player and an assortment of CD's, thoughtfully provided by the *Olivia Wells Show*. "Am I old-school or what?" she asked herself. "Maybe I'll figure out how to stream music one of these days."

She quickly located a Dylan St. Claire album and popped it in the slot. Before returning to the big four-poster, she pulled open the draperies, exposing the enormous window, and letting the lights of the city pour in. Crawling back under the soft eyelet comforter, she snuggled down to listen to her favorite song, "I Will Cherish You," while she watched the brilliant skyline. By the time the first notes of last cut on the disk began, she was sound asleep.

The associate producer and cameraman arrived just as Carolee was finishing breakfast. "Good morning," Jenny said cheerfully. "This is Dale Marks. He's going to be filming your day."

"Hi there," he said, sticking out his hand. "It's nice to meet you, Carolee."

"You, too, Dale." She slipped her long fingers into his square palm and squeezed firmly. His friendly, outgoing approach impressed her. "I hope you don't get too bored following me around today."

"Never," he declared with conviction. "This is going to be fun."

Turning to the producer, the prizewinner plucked at her attire, a faded T-shirt and jeans. "I didn't know what to wear. Is this all right?"

"It's perfect. You're getting a skin-out makeover, so right now, it's just important that you're comfortable." Jenny put her long arm around the older woman's shoulders and aimed her toward the door. "Ready?"

"Ready as I'll ever be, I guess." Carolee took a deep breath.

Their first stop was the Talbott Salon, situated a few blocks from the hotel. George Talbott had made a name for himself, and his successful business, because of his close affiliation with *The Olivia Wells Show*. Producers, technicians, and even Miss Wells herself frequented the salon, and Talbott's staff had proven astonishingly adept at turning out the most remarkable makeovers. Carolee was placed into George's very talented hands.

"My, oh my," he exclaimed, examining her skin and bone structure with a practiced eye. "You're going to be so beautiful you won't recognize yourself." As he worked, he related, in complete detail, how he was transforming the ex. Mrs. William Austin, nondescript housewife, into the reborn Carolee Austin, sexy school teacher. Dale diligently recorded every minute of the process, occasionally peeking around the digital camera to give his subject an encouraging wink.

First, George set out to lighten and highlight Carolee's mousy, gray-streaked tresses. "Your coloring is so fair, Cherie. You should have been born blonde."

"Actually, I was," she told him. "My hair didn't turn darker until I was in my teens; and then, I started to go gray while I was in college. I tried frosting it at first, but my hair grows so fast, and I just didn't have the time to maintain it after the boys were born. Too much trouble when there's so many, more important things to be done.

"Once you see how this glorious color lights up your beautiful face, you'll never go back to the way you were, I assure you, my dear." His competent fingers flew. When that step was completed, he directed her to his best cosmetician. "When your face is complete, you'll return to me for the final styling of your fabulous hair, mais oui?" he added, with a flourish.

Carolee followed George's instructions and moved into the next room. She was surprised when Denise greeted her. "Come with me," she urged, seating the prize winner in a comfortable chair, complete with a relaxing back massage feature. "I'm going to do a deep facial cleansing and apply your makeup."

Noticing the puzzled look on her client's face she added, "I actually work for Talbott. George contracts me out to the studio to do faces for the show. That's why I was there yesterday. I'll be back to do your TV makeup when you tape next week."

The exfoliating massage and refreshing scrub felt wonderful. Carolee let herself enjoy the unaccustomed pampering. Like her boss, Denise also explained each step as she performed it. As a bonus, she gave her customer tips on how the look she was creating could be reproduced at home, without too much time or effort.

"Like I said, you have great skin. All you need most of the time, besides moisturizer, is a light foundation, plus a little cheek color. You'll want to keep your brows well shaped, and use natural tints and a soft pencil liner on your lids. See, there. That really makes your eyes pop." She turned the woman's chair toward the huge mirror so she could see her reflection. "I'll give you some samples of the products I've used. You can take them with you and practice applying them."

Carolee said, "Thanks," automatically, but with little comprehension, as she was totally spellbound by the woman gazing back at her. Even with her straight locks still damp and unshaped, the change was remarkable. She was a new woman, literally. The bright, revitalizing hair color, and expertly applied makeup, had taken at least ten years off her face.

Noting the Carolee's shocked reaction to the change, Denise smiled a pleased smile and asked, "You like?"

"Um…yes, I can hardly believe that's me." Clear blue eyes misted. "You did a wonderful job."

"I just put on a little paint and highlighted your natural beauty, that's all, but I appreciate the praise." Denise gathered up the cosmetics she'd promised her client, and packed them neatly in a gift bag.

Turning back to Carolee, whose eyes were still glistening, she teased, "Now, you aren't going to go all mushy on me, are you? Wouldn't want your mascara to run." Sensing the prize winner's hesitant gratitude, she patted her hand and reassured her. "Don't worry, with a little practice, you'll be able to do this at home every day."

Sniffing back the threatening tears, Carolee told her, "I doubt that, but you make me want to give it a try." With a hug and a final, "Thank you, Denise," the schoolteacher graciously accepted the gift and waved goodbye.

Moments later, she was back in George Talbott's chair with his scissors flying around her ears. "Didn't I tell you? You look fab-u-lous already. Once I'm finished, you will be perfection itself." His outspoken self-confidence, combined with his practiced affectations and the unexpectedly feminine voice, which emanated from his rather oversized body, made Carolee giggle. "My words were intended to inspire, Cherie, not to amuse," he quipped, somewhat miffed. "Do you doubt me?"

"Not at all," she quickly denied. "You've already proven that you're a genius." Her praise brought a bloom of bright color to his pudgy cheeks. "I never imagined I could look this good. You've made me as giddy as a schoolgirl." She hoped her words would assuage his wounded pride.

With the videographer turning circles around them, George worked, continuing to offer a running narrative. "I'm giving you a cut that will take full advantage of your hair's exquisite texture. When I'm finished you will have a style that is loose, carefree, and most important of all, very, very sexy."

"Are you taking off much of the length?" Carolee was somewhat concerned. She'd never worn her hair short. "I like to keep it long enough to pull back into a pony tail or roll into a bun, to get it out of my face."

"Ponytail!... Bun!... Mais non! Oh, my goodness, no. Say it isn't so; I beg you, Cherie," he exclaimed, incensed. "I'm trimming the ends to stop just below your chin. Then I'm adding layers for fullness and movement. The style will accentuate your exquisite cheekbones, and make your eyes smolder. And I assure you, the cut will be easy for you to keep up with nothing more than a blow dryer and brush. I'll write down exact instructions on how the cut and color were accomplished, so your own hairdresser can reproduce the look.

"There now. C'est fini!" Taking her chair by the arm, he spun her around to face the mirror. "Well?"

Once again, Carolee was struck speechless. She couldn't believe the woman staring back, the woman with shining, ash-blonde tresses framing her face, the woman with prominent, classic cheekbones and dramatic, sapphire eyes, couldn't possibly be her – the aging, frumpy, invisible housewife and mother. This woman was fabulous – a vibrant head-turner.

"I...I just don't know what to say," she stammered. Giving up on the inadequacies of verbal expression, she flew out of her seat, threw her arms around the stylist's neck, and kissed him lightly on the cheek. "Thank you so much," she whispered against his ear.

Overcome by her display, the big man returned her hug, and cleared his throat. "It was my pleasure," he breathed softly. When she drew back from the embrace, he played to the camera. "Well, there she is, folks, our dear Carolee. And can you believe the miraculous transformation we've accomplished? She's gorgeous, n'est pas?"

After a light, lunch, the next stop was Neiman-Marcus, where Jennifer led the way to the designer clothing department. Dale shouldered his heavy equipment and followed closely behind. A knowledgeable fashion consultant was waiting to assist them with finding the perfect outfit to set off Carolee's height, figure, and chic new look.

She tried on dress after dress, suit after suit, finally deciding on a soft, clingy knit in a luscious shade of cornflower blue. Jenny remarked that the color matched Carolee's eyes almost perfectly. The dress's deeply scooped neckline, long tapered sleeves, knee-length hem, and flowing princess lines, made the most of its wearer's assets. It narrowed her waist, drew attention to her long, slender legs, and accentuated her full, well-curved bosom. The consultant also encouraged her to accept a double-breasted, charcoal pantsuit, which Carolee especially liked, to wear for the post-prize taping.

Visits to the jewelry, lingerie, and shoe departments followed. A strappy, pewter high heel and gray, beaded purse were chosen to accessorize the dress, along with a smart ankle-boot and big, leather handbag, to go with the suit. Carolee picked out an exquisite pair of heart-shaped, white-gold, filigree earrings, with a necklace to match, which would go equally well with both outfits.

Jenny tried to convince the prizewinner to choose a few more pieces, but the frugal woman refused, feeling it would be too extravagant. Finally, the necessary undergarments and personal items were purchased, and the threesome headed back to the hotel. Jenny and Dale said goodbye to Carolee when Arnie pulled the long black car up to the curb. They promised to return at 6:00 p.m. sharp, to get set up for the evening's festivities. Their departure gave the anxious prizewinner a couple of precious hours to relax.

Once she was safely inside her luxurious suite, Carolee treated herself to another long soak in the whirlpool tub. Just as she stepped out of the cooling water, and drew on the heavy, complimentary robe, she heard a tap on the door.

"Ms. Austin, your delivery has arrived from Neiman-Marcus," called a young male voice from the hallway.

Carolee opened the portal and swung it wide. "Please, come in. You can put everything in the bedroom." She followed him, taking charge of the smaller accessory bags, while he hung the larger garments inside the huge closet. "Thanks," she told him.

"No, problem," he responded, his long legs striding for the door. "Oh, I almost forgot, the catering supervisor asked me to tell you that he'll be here shortly, to set up everything for your dinner with Mr. St. Claire. It's scheduled to be served, here in your suite, promptly at 6:45."

"Here?" she asked, a bit puzzled. "Nobody said for sure, but I just assumed we'd have our meal in the dining room."

"Oh, no, that would never work," he informed her confidently.

"The crazy fans would swamp you. Things have been wild around here since Mr. St. Claire and his people got in this afternoon. Doesn't seem to matter how hard we try to keep our famous guests' arrival a secret, someone always finds out. Sometimes I think they stake out all the hotels, and the first one to spot the star gets on the horn to all the others."

"He's staying here?" Unexpected nervousness suddenly drew Carolee's stomach into a tight knot.

"Of course." The tall, thin valet shrugged. "Where else? We're the newest, the fanciest, and the best." Noting the look of sheer panic in her clear blue eyes, and the nervous way she was twisting the belt of her robe, he added, "Don't worry. You're gonna have a swell time."

"Mr. St. Claire's a real down-to-earth guy. I helped carry his stuff up to the penthouse. Most of the celebs I've met so far are pretty uppity and arrogant. They think a whole lot of themselves, you know? But Dylan's not like that. He pitched right in with the bags and things, shook my hand, and introduced himself to me, like I didn't already know who he was. Most stars, as big as him, act like they don't even see us peons."

Glancing at his watch, he bolted for the exit. "Gotta book. Promised Dylan I'd get a newspaper for him."

"Well, thanks for the encouragement, uh..." she paused, hoping he would take the hint and fill in the blank.

"Jason, ma'am," he obliged.

"Thanks, Jason. I'm Carolee."

"You're very welcome, Carolee. Have fun tonight." He bounded out, letting the door slam shut behind him.

Returning to the bedroom, she removed the plastic bags from her dress and suit, set the shoeboxes on the closet shelf, and folded her undergarments into the top drawer of the chest. The small, burgundy velvet jewelry box drew her attention. Opening it slowly, she admired the sparkling baubles nestled inside, before placing it on top of the dresser.

It didn't take her long to touch up her makeup and run a brush through her hair, despite the time she spent studying her unfamiliar reflection. Then she retrieved the new lingerie, tossed aside the robe, and shivered with delight as the silky fabric caressed her skin sensuously. So much better, she decided, than the practical, inexpensive cotton she usually wore.

Next, she took the dress off its hanger, stepped in, and pulled it up into place. Once she had her arms inside the clingy sleeves, she found it extremely difficult to manage the long, back zipper.

She was still struggling with the closure when she heard Jenny's voice, "Carolee! We're back. Are you here? We knocked, but you didn't answer, so we let ourselves in. Hope you don't mind."

Popping her head around the doorframe with a relieved sigh, she waved for the producer to come to her aid. "Thank goodness. You're just in time. I can't reach this blasted zipper. Help!"

The insightful young woman could see anxiety, bordering on panic, reflected in Carolee's eyes. Jenny fastened the dress with skilled fingers and addressed her guest with calming words. "Hey, it's all right. I've got it. There." She laid a reassuring hand on the older woman's shoulder.

"I'm sorry," Carolee offered, embarrassed by her distressed state. "It's just that silly little things, like not being able to zip up my stupid dress, remind me how hard it is to be alone. When you're married, there's always someone there to do up the buttons you can't reach, or to brush the stray lint off your back.

"Most of the time I can put Bill and what he did to me, to our marriage, out of my mind, but then some insignificant thing brings it all back up again and, wham, I'm just as angry and hurt as ever. I bet that sounds ridiculous."

"Not at all." The producer shook her head. "I think any woman would feel the same way. He broke his solemn promise to love and to cherish you. You have every right to be hurt and angry. I'd be furious, and I'd have a hard time getting over it, too." She grinned when she saw a tentative smile return to Carolee's generous lips.

Taking a step back, so she could get the full effect of the new clothes and the makeover, she declared, "Wow, you look great!"

"Do I, really?" the nervous woman asked.

"Yes, you're a knockout. Trust me." Jenny beamed at her. "Now get your shoes. I can't wait to see Dale's reaction to the new you."

Carolee transferred her wallet, cell phone, key card, hairbrush, and lipstick to the evening bag, slipped on the shiny sandals, and clipped on the necklace and earrings. When she was finally all put together, Jenny called out to the cameraman, "Here we come," then she pushed her guest toward the door ahead of her.

When Carolee stepped out of the bedroom and into the sitting area, Dale was facing her, his camera shouldered, lens focused, his finger on record. He didn't press that button as usual; however, because his eyes were filled with the vision in blue before him. His mouth hung open in surprise, his record finger was momentarily frozen. He whistled appreciatively before he began recording.

"Dale thinks you look pretty terrific, too," Jenny said, laughing.

PART V

Dylan St. Claire arrived early. Carolee rushed to the door, anxious to greet him, only to have Dale instruct her to wait, while he situated his equipment, just right, and adjusted the lighting. She fidgeted nervously, as she waited. When the cameraman was satisfied that he'd chosen the perfect angle to capture Carolee's reaction as she greeted Dylan, he nodded.

Sighing deeply, she swung the door wide, forced her trembling mouth into a hesitant smile, and slowly raised her eyes to the popular singer's familiar face. Her first glimpse of the real man, in the flesh, struck her like a blast of frigid air, stealing her breath away. She'd seen him often enough, on TV and CD jackets, to know he was ruggedly handsome, but she was completely knocked off balance by the masculine appeal of him.

Sharp gray eyes, framed by long, dark lashes, and topped by expressively arched brows, studied her thoughtfully. His longish hair, a tawny golden-brown, was shot through with sun-bleached highlights.

At first, his solemn expression lent an unapproachable, catalogue-model look to his classic features, but when he grinned his wide, confident, signature grin, his face was transformed. Suddenly, he was the easy-going charmer, the man who had successfully convinced every female fan that his fabulous, full-of-promise smile was intended for her and her alone. The effect was not lost on Carolee.

Before she could find her voice, he spoke, his deep, fluid tones echoing in her ears. "You must be Carolee. I'm Dylan. It's great to meet you." His quicksilver gaze slid over her again, leaving sensitized nerves everywhere his eyes touched. "My, my, my," he breathed, obviously pleased by her appearance. "You're stunning."

"I…uh…thank you," she croaked out, her face flaming. Finally realizing that she was keeping him standing out in the hallway, while she stared, she added, "Please come in.

"The hotel people have everything set up over there," she gestured toward the alcove where a table was laid with sparkling china and crystal. Nervously, she added, "The show's producer said you'd be on a tight schedule tonight, so I hope you're hungry, it smells wonderful."

"I can eat," he quipped, grinning again. He gestured for her to precede him, followed her to table, pulled out a chair, and held it for her. As she skirted around him to take the proffered seat, her head filled with the clean, fresh scent of his soap and light aftershave. The close-up look also revealed that he wasn't as young as his media photos made him appear. There were tiny laugh creases around his eyes and mouth, and the blond streaks of his hair, as well as the light scruff sprouting on his strong chin, were liberally sprinkled with silver strands. She thanked him for his gallant gesture with another, more convincing smile.

After he took his place across the small table from her, they sat in silence for a few long moments, each seemingly unable, or unwilling, to begin the expected conversation beneath the watchful lens of the ever-present camera. When Carolee could bear the searching look he was giving her no longer, she asked, "Do you do this often?"

"What's that?" he responded, hesitantly, "have dinner with a beautiful woman?" He flashed her a flirtatious, heart-pounding grin. "Not as often as I'd like."

Carolee blushed again and laughed softly. "I'm not…no, I mean, I'm sure beautiful women stand in line, waiting to have dinner with you. I'm wondering how often you agree to meet, one-on-one, with someone like me, someone who enjoys your music…uh…a fan.

'I'm sure this kind of personal attention would be extremely time consuming, since there are thousands of adoring fans, who would do almost anything, to get this close to you."

"Well, I…" he began, then paused while the waiter filled their bowls with steaming clam chowder, and poured a dry, white wine into their goblets. "I love my fans. I wouldn't be anything without them. I know that, and I appreciate them more than I can say; but no, I don't make it a habit to meet with them, individually or privately." Pointing to the camera, he added, "If you can call this private.

"To tell you the truth, the really determined ones, the obsessed idol-worshiping types, scare me to death. I do whatever I can to avoid them. After a concert, I usually hang around to sign a few autographs, as long as the crowd is pretty calm and well-behaved, but once the screamers, clingers, and clothes-grabbers arrive, I beat a hasty retreat."

He treated himself to several spoonsful of the thick, delicious soup before continuing. "Honestly, I was nervous about this dinner-date thing, even though I suggested it to Olivia. It was my first impulse, when I read the nomination letter from your sons, but after thinking it through a bit more carefully, I almost backed out. Now though, I'm glad I didn't cancel."

"Why?"

"Why was I nervous, or why am I glad I didn't back out?" he asked with a mischievous grin.

"Either… uh…both," she prodded, wanting to keep him talking, so she could drown in the echoing fullness of his incomparable voice.

"First question – Why I'm nervous. Well…I've had a couple of close calls, when I let some of my more passionate admirers get a little too close. So, personal contact with fans tends to put me on edge. It can start out all sweet and innocent, and then go south in a split second. Before you know it, things can get completely out of control.

"I'm a regular guy, believe it or not, a regular guy who's just lucky enough to be born with a little talent, and the determination to make something of it. I've been very fortunate, and I'm grateful that lots of people, especially women, like my work. Without them, I'd be a nobody, a hack picking guitar in some backwater bar for tips.

"I'll never be able to understand why my music turns otherwise sensible females into mindless banshees. It's great to be appreciated, but I don't want to be adored." He gestured for the waiter to remove the soup bowls and serve the next course, a spicy, succulent shrimp Alfredo over angel hair pasta.

"I think I understand. You were afraid I'd be just another groupie, ripping at your clothes and begging for a lock of your hair." Carolee chuckled at the ridiculousness of that image. "Let me put your mind at ease. I'm not the screaming, grabbing, or clinging type."

Laughing, too, he assured her, "I can see that. You seem to be pretty levelheaded, as well as exceedingly easy on the eyes. And that's the answer to your second question – Why I'm glad I decided not to cancel this dinner. It's been a long time since I've had a blind date with a smart, beautiful woman."

Insides quivering, her mind reeling at the suggestion that this might be a real date and not simply an opportunity for free publicity for Dylan's concert tour, Carolee forced herself to swallow a bite of the succulent seafood. Then she told him. "I find that extremely hard to believe."

"What?"

"That you don't have a date every night of the week, considering the thousands of gorgeous female fans who are anxiously waiting for you to choose one of them," she explained.

"I could, I guess, if I wanted to hang out with that sort. But I hope I'll always be able to recognize, and avoid, those gold-digging hangers-on, the women who only want me because I've had a couple of platinum records."

After a breath, he elaborated. "I've gone out a few times, since my divorce three years ago, but I haven't had a serious relationship." The lines of his face hardened and a muscle in his jaw twitched. "It was pretty messy and left me downright skeptical about the 'happily ever after' thing."

"I'm sorry. I didn't know you'd been married…or divorced," Carolee apologized.

"Then you really aren't a hardcore fan, otherwise you'd have read all about it. My marital problems were splashed across the tabloids." He reached for the bottle of wine, topped off both their glasses, and took a sip from his. Turning to Jenny, he asked,

"Could we shut off the tape for a bit? Olivia promised you would oblige me if things became uncomfortable. This is getting just a little too personal for TV."

"Sure," the assistant producer agreed politely. "We have plenty of dinner footage anyway. Dale and I will go grab a couple of sandwiches and be back in an hour."

"Thanks, that'd be perfect" Dylan said, flashing her is million-dollar grin. He waited for the show people to leave before continuing. "I was in the process of recording my first top-ten single when I found out that Sandra was having an affair with my business manager. 'I Will Cherish You' hit the charts the day she had me served with separation papers."

He raised his long fingers, gesturing as if emblazoning the headline in the air. "'Rising Star Dumped by Neglected, Furious Wife.' It made great copy. I was devastated. She'd stood by me through the hard times, the years of trying to make good, only to leave me just as I was on the brink of success."

"By why?" his concerned companion asked.

"You and your 'whys," he quipped lightly. "Is that the only question you know how to ask?" Not waiting for a response, or expecting one, he went on, "It's hard to say, really, but I think it was because Sandra was tired of the uncertainly of living with a struggling musician. She was desperate for a sure thing.

"While she was packing up her things, she told me she was convinced that I'd never make it, despite the fact that I had a song shooting up the charts at the time. It was a fluke, she claimed, a one-hit-wonder.

"

With Steve, my agent and business manager, she thought she'd have a future she could count on, and the luxuries she deserved, after the deprivations she'd endured, scratching out a meager living with an unsuccessful songwriter-husband. She said Steve had time for her. He could afford to meet her needs. I couldn't."

Carolee was deeply touched by his story, and surprised by his willingness to share his private heartbreak with her. His words also pricked a sensitive spot inside her, and she had to struggle hard to keep the tight knot of sorrow from welling up and overwhelming her. "That must have been unbelievably difficult for you. What did you say to her?"

"I told her I understood, and I said I was sorry. She made me feel so guilty, Carolee. It's hard to explain, but I was certain the break-up was entirely my fault. If I'd been better at my craft, if I'd been the success I should have been, sooner. If I hadn't been so preoccupied with my work, she wouldn't have been forced to reach out to another man. I knew I'd let her down. My incompetence, my failure, had destroyed our marriage. It took me a long time to realize that I wasn't completely to blame."

Her name, breathed through his lips, echoed in her head. She trembled. Taking a tiny sip of the wine, she prayed it would steady her voice. "Uh…I get it. I've been there. You read the nomination my boys sent to the show, so you know my husband left me. It took me a very long time to get past the guilt and self-blame. Divorce is a terrible thing."

"Yeah, it is, especially for the kids." Dylan hung his handsome head and studied his hands. "I'm not sure my girls will ever get over their mother walking out on us."

"You have daughters?"

"Yes, teenaged daughters, a father's nightmare," he sighed. "Kristen is eighteen. She graduated in May and is busy getting ready to attend college this fall. Leah's a rising sophomore, and a very mature fifteen and a half. Just ask her." Pride shone clearly in his sparking gray eyes.

"They're not much older than my kids, then, respectively. Brett turned sixteen a few months ago. I had to teach him to drive." She shuddered at the memory. "Bryce will be fourteen soon, and is very excited about moving up to the high school.

"Adolescent boys really need their father, you know. I wish Bill would spend more time with them. Mothers have a very special relationship with their sons, but there are some things moms are just not suited for, like teaching their sons self-defense or automobile maintenance."

"Imagine what it's like for a father when his girls come to him with questions about make-up and fashion, or heaven forbid…boys. It's awful! Sandra should be around for them."

"Why isn't she?"

"Oh, no, not another 'why!'" He feigned exasperation. "Will they never stop?"

"I…I just want to understand why any mother would abandon her daughters." Carolee's sincere blue eyes regarded him steadily. "No matter how bad things get between a husband and wife, I can't comprehend what could possibly force a woman to leave her children."

"It depends on the woman, I guess," Dylan noted, running his talented fingers through his hair. "Sandra claimed that our girls were old enough to get along without her. She always accused me of I babying them too much. But I think she was jealous, because I had a better relationship with them than she did. It wasn't all her fault, to be fair.

"We had a sort of turn-about family. My career kept me out at night, in clubs, recording studios, and such, so I was there for the girls during the day, when they needed me. Sandra always worked days.

"I have to admit, I wasn't much of a housekeeper or disciplinarian. I would sleep the morning away and get up just before the school bus arrived in the afternoon. Then Kristen, Leah, and I would spend a couple of hours talking about their day at school, playing games, maybe going out to the park, you know, having fun." He grinned sheepishly.

"When Sandra got home, she'd find the place in a mess, homework undone, no meal prepared, and kids who didn't want supper, anyway, because they'd been eating junk since they came in the door. She'd start ranting. At the time, I thought she was being rigid and harsh, but since I've finally grown up myself, I don't blame her for that anymore.

"I forced her to be the big bad adult, the strict disciplinarian, and she got tired of it. If I've learned anything from our divorce, it's that both parents should behave like grown-ups most of the time, and both parents need permission to act like children occasionally."

"Oh, you are very wise, sir." Carolee smiled at him, liking this sensitive, self-aware man more and more by the second. Chuckling softly, he reached across the table and laid his hand over hers. "Thank you, sweet lady. That's high praise indeed." A short, expectant pause followed as he studied her face.

Clearing his throat, and pulling back to wipe his full lips with the linen napkin, Dylan finished his story. "Of course, it's possible that I've overanalyzed the whole situation. It could be that Sandra is just too self-centered and selfish to be bothered with having her daughters in her new, affluent life. Plus, there's no love lost between Steve and the girls. He resents me enormously, and them, because they're an extension of me."

"Brett and Bryce hate their father's fiancée, too. From what I hear through the rumor mill, Clarice is planning a huge wedding. I don't think she's very happy that Bill asked the boys to be his groomsmen. It should be very, very interesting, that wedding. Wish I could be a fly on the wall."

"This Clarice is the reason your husband left you, I assume," he suggested astutely, taking another small sip of wine.

"Yes, but most people don't know it. Bill did a great job of hiding the affair and covering his tracks. The majority opinion is that they started dating **after** he divorced his frumpy, boring wife, the albatross who was holding him back, keeping him from achieving his full potential." Her obvious sarcasm wasn't wasted on her quick-witted companion.

"Humph," he sniffed. "I'd bet the only thing holding him back was his lack of imagination, and willingness to indulge his mid-life cravings." The line of his finely chiseled jaw grew firmer. "I hope you didn't buy the line of garbage he was spewing."

"I did, for quite a while longer than I should have, but not anymore. Thankfully, I have a good friend, with inside information, that helped me find out the truth. So, I'm not his victim anymore. The boys and I are getting along mighty well without him, thank you very much." She nodded assertively.

"I can see that," he told her, his voice low and silky smooth.

"Do your sons know why their dad really left?"

Unsure of how to answer, she stalled a few seconds, considering, then said, "I didn't tell the boys, if that's what you're asking. I couldn't do it, despite how much I wanted to get revenge on Bill, by turning his sons against him. Even in my fury, I realized that I had to protect their feelings. Bill is their father, and they need to love and respect him. Criticizing him to them will only hurt them in the long run."

Dylan didn't comment, but simply waited for her to finish. "But yes, they know, or at least I think they know. I'm not sure how they found out, or figured it out, but they seem to despise and distrust Clarice. And I believe the feelings are mutual."

"Kids are pretty darn smart, and plenty tuned-in to what goes on between adults, even if the adults believe they're being discrete. If your guys have spent any time with their dad and his new woman, I'm sure they've overheard things that clued them in to the truth. Your ex and his fiancée have probably made plenty of little slip-ups. Your boys likely picked up the clues."

Laying aside his fork, Dylan leaned back in his chair, while the waiter removed his half-empty dinner plate and replaced it with a dessert dish, heaping with a huge slice of luscious, peanut butter pie.

"You're probably right," Carolee agreed, nodding for the server to take her plate as well, even though it was still piled high with uneaten food. When the creamy confection was place before her, she sighed, her eyes wide. "I don't think I could eat another bite."

"If I eat any more, I won't be able to sing a note. But we have to taste this, at least." Taking up a clean utensil, he dug in.

"One bite," she agreed, following his example. Several deliciously rich mouthfuls later, they pushed themselves away from the table.

Rising and taking Carolee by the hand, Dylan led her across the room and out onto the tiny balcony, which overlooked the city. For a few moments they stood silently, holding hands, watching the traffic and descending sun. Then he turned to her and whispered, "What is it about you, and your endless questions, that have me opening up and telling you my life story?"

When she shrugged one shoulder and sent him a quizzical look, he returned it with a wink. "It's really not like me at all," he admitted. "I'm usually pretty darned reserved, but with you I'm an open book. Who woulda thought it?

"It's great that we have so much in common, but I'm tired of talking about kids and failed marriages. Tell me more about you, Carolee Austin. Why do you like my music?"

She studied him carefully before answering, subconsciously comparing the tall, graceful singer to her ex. Dylan had a significant height advantage. Even in her high heels, he towered above her. Bill always made her wear flats, since he was barely an inch taller than she. It felt great to look up to a man, instead of looking him straight in the eye. In spite of the hours Bill spent in the gym, he'd never achieved the lean, well-toned musculature, that fit so naturally on Dylan's lanky frame.

Bill was dark, compact, and squarely built, a powerful man in a three-piece suit. The musician was fair, imposing, and deeply sensuous, an elegant man in faded blue denim. Carolee liked the latter much better than the former.

"So now it's your turn to pose the whys?" she suggested, delaying.

"You bet," he countered and repeated, "Why do you like my music, Carolee?"

Sighing deeply, she tried to explain, "I'm sure you've been told this many times, but that doesn't make it any less true. Your songs speak to the heart, especially 'I Will Cherish You.' The words you write create the illusion that it is possible for a man to love a woman with all of his being. You make me believe in the kind of love I thought I had once, the kind of love I think every woman longs for, but will likely never find."

"An illusion, huh?" His eyes darkened and the solemn, thoughtful expression returned to his face.

"Isn't it? You said yourself that you'd grown skeptical about, how did you put it, the 'happily ever after?' After what you've experienced, do you think that the sort of love you sing about really exists?" Her voice took on a note of desperation.

Before he could respond, the associate producer and cameraman announced their return. "Better get a move on, Dylan" Jenny prompted. "You're due at the concert venue in 30, and your car's waiting."

"Guess our time's up. My public calls," Dylan grimaced. After a beat, he added, "Hey, why don't you ride to the auditorium with me, in my limo? Then we can discuss your question at length. Looks like I have my work cut out for me, trying to convince you that my songs are more than smoke and mirrors.

"Come on, I'll tell Jenny and Dale we've changed their plans. I want a little more time alone with you, Carolee Austin, and since I'm such a big star, I usually get what I want." He threw her a teasing wink.

PART VI

Camera rolling, they fled the hotel, hand-in-hand, through a hovering line of roadies and security guards, and dove headlong into St. Claire's waiting limousine. Once inside, the cheers and screams of the noisy throng of fans, each one hoping to get a close-up look at the star, faded. The *Olivia Show* staff dropped back, following in Arnie's car, as Dylan had insisted, telling them that he had to center himself for the concert. The maneuver gave him a few more moments alone with Carolee, and away from the prying eye of the camera. Though the trip to the civic arena was a short one, the sincere musician made the most of it.

"All men aren't like that bastard husband of yours, you know," he told Carolee, his silver-gray eyes boring straight into her own. "Some of us keep our promises." Settling into the seat, he elaborated, "I learned a lot from my failed marriage, and I grew as a man – as a human. I may have some doubts about the institution of marriage, after what I've been through, but I'm still optimistic. I think I'd be better at it next time around, if there is a next time.

"As for love, I am sure about that. Maybe my songs do create an illusion, to some extent," he admitted, "but you'll never convince me that love, in its purest form, doesn't happen – at least once in a while. I couldn't believe in myself, or my music, if I didn't trust in the reality of true love."

The huge lump that had lodged tightly in her throat made speech impossible, so she simply stared back at him, her eyes filling with glistening tears. One welled up and slid down her cheek. He caught it on the tip of his finger. "Don't cry, my lovely Carolee," he whispered, encircling her with his long arms and holding her tightly. When her body relaxed against his, he asked her, "Will you do me a favor?"

She nodded, still not trusting her voice.

"Keep your mind open to the possibility that pure, selfless love might exist. Give me a chance to show you that it can be real. Will you try?"

She whispered, smiling tentatively, "I…I think I can do that."

"Good." He grinned at her, his unexpected openness and intimacy shaking her well-guarded composure.

Then quite suddenly, he changed the subject. "I want to get back to something you said, earlier. I have to make sure I heard you right. Did you say that your stupid ex accused you of being…uh…What were your words, 'frumpy and boring'?"

Her smile widening, she jabbed him with her elbow, "That's what I said, but you didn't have to remind me. I hate to admit it, but when you come down to it, Bill was right. That's exactly what I was."

"I don't believe it! You could never be frumpy or boring. I mean, look at you. You positively sparkle." His sincerity was evident. Dylan wasn't trying to flatter her. He meant every word. "Has he seen you lately?"

"Not in the last forty-eight hours," she replied, with a broad smile. "Whether you believe it or not, I'm not the same person I was when I arrived in Atlanta yesterday morning, Dylan. My trip to the Talbott Salon and Neiman-Marcus literally transformed me."

"Oh, I bet you haven't changed all that much. All the paint, polish, and fancy window dressing in the world can't create beauty where none exists. Nope," he said with conviction. "It was there all along; he just didn't have the brains to notice. Wait until the stupid man sees you again, face-to-face, his eyes are gonna pop out of his head. He's going to be darned sorry he let you get away."

"I doubt that," Carolee denied. "It would a nice, though – a little bit of payback. I don't have any use for Bill Austin, or any desire to have him in my life. I no longer care what he thinks about me, but it would be pretty sweet to know that he regretted his decision to leave me for his new trophy wife."

Carolee blew out a breath, and stared at her hands. "Clarice is young, sophisticated, and strikingly attractive. Even with my new look, I can't compete. No matter what Bill thinks about my appearance, after this make-over, one quick glance at his fiancée will remind him that he's moved up in the world."

She paused to draw a mournful sigh. "Which is why I'm refusing to go to our class reunion this fall."

"I'm sorry. I'm not usually dense, but I don't follow." His arched brows were drawn together in concern.

She laughed softly. "I guess I did take a bit of a detour there, didn't I?" Tossing him an apologetic grin, she explained. "Bill and I were high school sweethearts, you know, the perfect couple everyone adored. I can't go to the reunion knowing he'll be there with Clarice. Snide comments will be flying around all over the place – mean-spirited gossip about Bill's lovely new wife, and poor old Carolee. It would be too humiliating to endure." Her cheeks flushed hotly and tears threatened.

"I see." Dylan scrubbed his strong chin with his knuckles. "I guess it could be embarrassing, but there is another possible scenario." She felt her expression go from hurtful to hopeful as he continued, "Your old classmates might look at you, blossoming, beautiful, a mature, independent woman, and wonder why in the world Bill would desert you for such a superficial Barbie doll."

"You've met Clarice?" she asked with a teasing chuckle.

"I've met her type," he declared. "And you've got to stop selling yourself short. I bet there'll be plenty of guys at that reunion who'll be thrilled that you've been cut loose. Just wait and see."

She eyed him skeptically. "You should go. Give the other fellows a chance to fill your dance card. Promise me you'll think about it."

Before she could answer, the driver pulled up to the stage entrance of the huge civic auditorium. Dylan waited while his security team filed out of their vehicles, and formed a protective line from his car to the building. Pulling Carolee behind him, he made a dash for the door, waving to the crowd with his free hand, and flashing a grin in Dale's general direction as he followed, hot on their heels, digital recorder light glowing.

Once inside, the entire entourage made for the VIP suite. The gracious performer invited Carolee to stay with him, while he made the final preparations for the concert. He even allowed the show people to record the private, tense moments just before the show.

While Dylan disappeared into the dressing room to change into his stage costume, Jenny asked Carolee questions, and Dale videoed her response. "Are you having a good time?

The camera caught the answer, in the bright twinkle of her blue eyes, even before she spoke. "I'm having a wonderful time."

"What is Dylan St. Claire really like?"

Without hesitation, she said, "He's very kind and surprisingly real, almost untouched by his success. He's definitely not what I expected."

"What did you expect?" came a deep, familiar voice from behind her. Turning slowly, Carolee found herself staring straight into Dylan's piercing silver eyes.

"I... uh..." she stuttered.

"Get this," Jenny urged Dale in a whisper. "It'll be good." He pulled in for a tight shot on the couple.

"I'm waiting," Dylan teased her. "What did you expect?"

Straightening her shoulders, she rose to meet his challenge. "You told me that you were afraid I'd be a shallow, idol-worshiping groupie. Well, I was afraid that you'd be an egotistical, self-promoting jerk."

"I'm not?"

Smiling at him warmly, she breathed, "Far from it."

"Glad to hear it. Your good opinion means a lot to me, Carolee." He kept his cool gaze on her for another long moment before turning away.

"Okay, out you go," he shooed the show staff off, along with his own people. "Everyone but Carolee, get out. And send my make-up lady in. It's time for her work her magic and make this mug of mine presentable." They all hurried off at his command. Seconds later an efficient-looking woman entered, carrying a large, orange case.

Dylan took the swivel chair that sat in front of the lighted mirror, and let the cosmetician take over. Carolee curled up in the corner of the soft sofa, where she could quietly observe the process. His stage make-up was quickly applied, since Dylan's classic good looks needed little enhancement.

Offering the make-up artist a sincere, "Thank you," when she removed the protective napkin from under his chin, he rose and faced Carolee. "What do you think? Will they like me?" With his thumbs hooked in his belt, and his head cocked at a jaunty angle, he looked like a cross between a mischievous Tom Sawyer and a cocksure Brett Maverick.

Struck once more by the powerful magnetism of the man, Carolee whistled softly, trying to appear coolly unaffected. He wore a silver shirt, tucked neatly into tight, black leather jeans, and topped by a form-fitting suede vest. Ebony snakeskin boots, polished to a high gloss, and a silver-buckled belt, completed the effect. Her casual, "Not bad," brought out his boyish grin, which left her tingling.

"Come on," he urged, taking her arm. "It's time."

"I guess I'd better head out front and find my seat," she said.

"No way," he corrected, squeezing her elbow. "I'm not letting you out of my sight. I'll get the boys to find a place for you to watch the performance from the wings. I want to know where to find you after the final encore."

Carolee was sure she had the best seat in the house. Perched on a high stool, just out of sight, stage left, she felt like she was part of the action. She was close enough to see the beads of sweat breaking out on Dylan's upper lip, as he belted out tune after tune under the blazing lights, but with a clear view of the enormous video screen covering the entire wall behind the musicians. Several times, the singer moved across the wide stage toward the wing where she sat, standing less than yard from her, and making it seem as if he was serenading her alone.

Dale Marks glided around the platform, expertly interweaving shots of the performer with close-ups of the prizewinner. He caught the suggestive, raised-eyebrow wink Dylan shot Carolee, and the tears sparkling in her clear blue eyes, when he sang a verse which particularly touched her.

About forty-five minutes into the show, Dylan took a short break, while his band played on. Backstage, he grabbed a bottle of water and shucked out of the vest and long-sleeve shirt, replacing them with a soft, black tee. After flashing his special guest a heart-stopping grin, he reclaimed the stage, sparking a redoubling of the cheers and applause. The noise was almost deafening.

Raising his arms, he called for quiet, and the boisterous throng obeyed, falling reverently silent. Nodding to the drummer, who tapped out the signal to begin, the talented singer launched into the second part of his show, beginning with a soft, soulful ballad. For the next half hour, he played his audience like the consummate professional he was, taking them from the depths of heartache and despair, to the dizzying pinnacles of joyful exuberance, using only his incomparable voice and innate sense of timing.

As he brought his final number to a close and made his first attempt to exit the stage, the auditorium went wild, demanding an encore. Dylan stepped into the wing briefly and whispered something to Carolee, but his words were drowned out by numerous chants for "I Will Cherish You!"

Realizing she couldn't hear him, he repeated, almost shouting, "Do you trust me?" When she nodded in the affirmative, he squeezed her hand and stepped back out into the spotlight. At the sight of him, silently waving for them to settle, the noise abated, expectantly.

"Thank you, thank you," he told them, bowing graciously. "You're too kind." Returning the microphone to the stand and readjusting its height, he added, "I promise we'll do 'I Will Cherish You' in just a moment." Once more, the cheers rose in a deafening crescendo, forcing him to plead for quiet. "But first," he continued, as soon as he could be heard, "I want to thank the City of Atlanta for its gracious hospitality." More applause ensued.

"In case you've been wondering why the cameraman has been flitting around the stage, it's because this concert is being recorded for Monday's *Olivia Wells Show* as a part of their *Make Dreams*

Come True contest. It's been my sincere pleasure to spend the evening with one of the winners of that contest, and I would like to introduce her to you now." Turning toward the wings, he held out a beckoning hand. "Carolee, come out here."

When she hesitated, obviously surprised and unsure, he urged, "Come on. Let these nice folks see your pretty face."

Woodenly, focusing her attention entirely on Dylan, who was encouraging her with its trademark grin, she stepped out into the glaring lights. The handsome singer crossed the distance between them quickly, and took her by the hand, pulling her to center stage, before she could turn tail and run. He whirled her around to face the waiting audience.

"This is Carolee Austin, y'all," The crowd was hushed. "Carolee's boys wrote a beautiful nomination letter to Olivia Wells, asking her to send their mom to one of my concerts. I tried to make the evening a little more exciting for her, by throwing in dinner and a backstage pass." A few 'Ooohs, Aaahs,' and envious sighs, broke the silence. "I thought I would be the one granting gifts to this deserving contestant, but I have to tell you, there has been more than one winner here tonight."

As his words penetrated her terror-numbed brain, Carolee forced her gaze away from the blinding glare of the footlights, and looked straight into his sparkling eyes.

Taking both of her hands in his, he drew her closer, speaking only to her, his voice almost a whisper. "I can't explain it, but from the very first moment I laid eyes on you, Carolee, everything changed for me. We've only had a few hours together, but I feel like I've known you all my life."

Raising his gaze to look out over the crowd, he addressed the audience, "I'm going to dedicate this last number to Carolee, since I understand it's her favorite. I want her to stay right here, with me, as I sing it for her, and for you." Whistles and shouts of approval went up as the musicians struck up the first chords of "I Will Cherish You."

Carolee's wobbly knees threatened to give out from under her. She clung to Dylan's hand in desperation, tears welling and overflowing as the words of the song touched her heart, more deeply than ever before. Despite the thousands of people in the auditorium, he sang just for her. Time was suspended. She felt like she was drowning in a sea of rolling emotion, kept afloat by the compelling attraction of his sparking silver-gray gaze.

When his electrifying voice echoed the last note, Dylan surprised them both by pulling her into his chest and lowering his lips to hers. The tender, impulsive kiss was displayed on the huge screen behind them, for the entire audience to see, inciting yet another round of joyful applause, this one bigger and longer than the last.

PART VII

Ignoring the ear-splitting pleas for one more song, Dylan fled the stage, his arm still wrapped tightly around Carolee, stopping just long enough to wave a final farewell to the raucous crowd. Once they were back inside the VIP suite, he pulled the door closed behind them, shutting out the roar. Cradling her trembling hands, he waited for her to raise her eyes to his. Her heart was trying to pound its way out of her chest, and her body shook in time to every ragged beat. His cheeks were flushed, his pupils dilated, his palms clammy. His breath came in ragged gulps. Neither spoke.

Then Jenny popped through the door, with Dale close behind, breaking the spell. Dylan released his grip on Carolee and let his arms fall to his sides. The look of unexpected longing slid from his handsome features, leaving only the telltale evidence of his recent exertion. "Wow!" the associate producer exclaimed. "That was unbelievable! The audience is still on its feet."

Self-consciously moving away from the intrusive lens the cameraman had pointed in his direction, Dylan grabbed a clean towel from one of his bags, and draped it around his neck. "I guess we'd better not tarry too long, then. Maybe we can get out of here unscathed, while the crowd is still waiting for another encore. If y'all are ready, we'll go. Carolee will ride back to the hotel with me." The hint of annoyance in his clipped tone prompted immediate compliance with his orders.

As before, safe passage to the waiting limo was provided by a dozen or so burly men. The overwhelmed woman sank back into the luxurious interior of the huge automobile, and sighed deeply.

Slipping in beside her, the superstar singer signaled the driver to proceed. They rode in uncertain silence, each wrestling with the tumultuous emotions brought on by the spontaneous kiss.

The man spoke first, studying the fists he had clenched together in his lap. "I don't know what came over me, Carolee. I never meant to put you on display like that. It seemed like a great idea at the time, hauling you out on stage for the last song. And when it was over, I just couldn't help myself. You looked so lovely, so desirable, so kissable. Some irresistible impulsive grabbed me…I couldn't control it…I didn't want to control it."

"It's okay, Dylan" she told him softly, laying her fingers over his hands. "I was caught up in the moment, too."

"You're not angry? Not too embarrassed?" He regarded her with the open, hopeful face of a repentant lad.

"I can honestly say that embarrassment was one emotion I didn't feel," she admitted, smiling at his apologetic demeanor, her voice low and sultry.

Raising one perfect eyebrow, he asked her, his grin cocky and blatantly suggestive. "Were you experiencing other feelings that you'd like to share with me?"

Playing along with his teasing, she hedged, "Quite a few, actually, but I'm not sure I remember any of them very clearly now."
"Perhaps this will refresh your memory." Not waiting for her to respond, he enfolded her in his arms and sought out her mouth with his, gently, tenderly. When she eagerly returned the kiss, he deepened it, tasting, exploring, and setting every nerve on fire.

Long moments passed before he withdrew, asking her shamelessly, "Does that bring any particular emotions to mind?"

Smiling sweetly, she refused to answer, but pulled him to her once more, anxious to have his lean body pressed tightly against hers, hear his ragged breath in her ear, feel the irresistible touch of his lips on hers. They remained thus, drinking their fill of one another, completely unaware that the limousine had rolled to a stop, until the driver stuttered, "Uh... Mr. St. Claire, we have arrived. Should I give you and the lady a few minutes alone, sir?"

Shifting self-consciously away from Carolee, who giggled at the befuddled look on the chauffeur's all-business face, Dylan told him, "No, thanks. We'd better move out before those *Olivia* people get here with their blasted camera. I don't want them recording any more private moments than absolutely necessary, though I'm sure the celebrity gossipmongers would love it."

As expected, Dale and Jenny were waiting when they stepped out of the car. The camera followed them closely, all the way up to the door of the prizewinner's suite, determined to capture every last second of the evening's excitement. Since it was obvious that they weren't going to steal any more time alone, the deliberately subdued superstar made his good-bye short and light. "This has been an utterly delightful experience, my dear Carolee. I have enjoyed every moment of my time with you."

Still holding tightly to his arm, she responded, her blue eyes regarding him sincerely, "Thank you so much for everything, Dylan. It was a wonderful evening. I'll never forget you."

"My pleasure," he assured her with a soft peck on the cheek. Squeezing her hand tightly, just outside the view of the ever-watchful camera, Dylan backed away slowly, his gaze locked on hers. Halfway to the waiting elevator, he shot her one last, gut-wrenching grin, and turned away. Carolee watched him step through the retracted door and into the car. Then she retreated into her room.

Jenny called a wrap to the recording session, and sent the exhausted cameraman home, before following Carolee into the suite to review the schedule for Monday. It didn't take long to go over the details. The exhausted prizewinner promised the efficient production associate that she would be at the studio, packed and ready for her trip home, by noon on Monday. Immediately after the broadcast, the car would take her to the airport to catch her return flight.

"It's really late," the ever-cheerful Miss Thompson noted, checking her watch. "I'm sure you'll need tomorrow, just to rest up, but if you should feel like doing any sight-seeing, ring the front desk and have them page Arnie. He'll be at your disposal all day, and I understand he's an excellent tour guide."

"Thanks again, Jenny, for everything. It was absolutely wonderful, truly a dream come true," she told the young woman softly, smiling to hide the pall of disappointment the singer's departure had dropped over her.

"Hey, it's my job," the perky producer replied. "We got some great footage. Dylan's a terrific sport. Your show's going to be spectacular. Every woman in the audience will be green with envy. Now, get some sleep; you look tired. Enjoy your free day tomorrow and I'll see you on Monday. You have my number if you need anything."

Reassuring Jenny that she understood the instructions, and that she would call if she had any problems or questions, Carolee closed the door tightly, sighed deeply, and slid the bolt. She briefly considered calling the boys, to tell them all about her thrilling evening, but decided not to wake them.

Unzipping and removing the new dress proved easier than fastening it up, so within moments, she was lowering herself into the jetted tub, filled to the brim with steaming, lavender-scented water. She forced herself to relax and let the warm bubbles soothe away the tension.

The unexpected events of the past few hours had sparked feelings in her that were still too fresh and too tender to explore, so she made a conscious effort to put them aside. "I'll think about that tomorrow," she said to herself and laughed. "Look at me – a little too old to play Scarlet O'Hara." Giggling now, she chirped, "Fiddle-de-de!"

A rap on her door brought her out of her reverie. Stepping from the bath, she pulled on the heavy terrycloth hotel robe and went to investigate. She peered through the peephole and blinked, afraid to believe her eyes. Standing outside her suite, barefoot toes peeking out from under the hem of his faded jeans, longish locks damp, was Dylan St. Claire. As soon as she unfastened the lock and opened the portal, he stepped inside, sweeping the hallway with a quick glance. "Are they all gone?"

"Yes," she answered, surprised by his unexpected reappearance. "The story was over once you left, so Dale took off immediately. Jenny stayed a little while to go over plans for Monday, then she headed home too."

"Good." He grinned widely, sending a shiver of delight through her, and prompting her foolish heart to skip a beat. "Now we can say our farewells properly, without that damned camera stuck in our faces."

Noting Carolee's attire, he backpedaled, "Oh, shoot, I'm sorry. You must be dead on your feet. I shouldn't have barged in on you without calling. I'm always so wired after a concert that I have trouble unwinding. It didn't occur to me that you might be ready to call it a night."

Reaching for the knob, he offered, "Ask the desk to ring my room when you get up in the morning. I'll leave word that I'm expecting your call. Maybe we can get together for a few minutes, before I leave for Chicago tomorrow afternoon."

"Wait," she insisted, removing his hand from the latch, and leading him into the sitting area. "I was just trying to unwind a bit myself, enjoying the spa. It's a luxury I don't have at home. Please stay. Promise you'll wait right here while I get dressed?"

"Okay, if you hurry," he teased. "I'll raid the fridge while you're gone. I could use a snack. Performances always leave me hulled out."

She pulled on her most comfortable denims and cotton shirt, ran her fingers through her hair, brushed her teeth, and returned to find him relaxing on the sofa, draining the contents of a huge glass. In front of him on the coffee table was another tall tumbler, a pitcher full of ice water, two enormous sandwiches, and a variety of pickles, chips, and cookies. "I fixed you something, too. You didn't eat much dinner," he noted.

"Thanks," she said, grinning, grabbing a plate, and curling up beside him. "I guess I was too nervous, or too excited, or something. You found all this in there?" She gestured toward the kitchenette.

"Yeah, the chef left you pretty well stocked. Guess those *Olivia* folks thought of everything. There're some soft drinks, if you'd prefer them to the water. I don't need to put any caffeine in my system, since I'm already wound up just a bit too tight." He paused briefly to take a bite of his sandwich. His mouth still half full, he mumbled, "We could call downstairs and have room service bring up some cold beer and a bottle of wine, or we could break into the mini-bar, if you want."

"No thanks, water's fine. A glass of wine with dinner's my limit. Bill always complained that I was a bore at his company cocktail parties, because I didn't drink much. He thought I was being antisocial when I refused to indulge. He repeatedly told me I needed to loosen up." She shook her head sadly before diving into the tasty snack.

"You look pretty loose to me," Dylan teased. "Any looser and you'd fall limb from limb." He jabbed a long index finger into her ribs just to watch her squirm.

"Ha," she said, pushing his hand away. "You think you're pretty funny, don't you, St. Claire?" Attacking the sandwich, she remarked, "Hey, this is really good."

"Don't sound so surprised. I'm a pro at throwing together a midnight snack. I have two teenagers to feed, remember?"

They ate quietly for a while before he added, "Your ex is a complete idiot. You do know that, don't you?" When she made no comment, he went on, "He's a fool for not seeing what a gem you are, for trying to force you to be someone you're not, and for not loving you the way you deserve to be loved. You've got to stop beating yourself up, Carolee. He let you down and not the other way around. Got it?"

"Yessir, got it!" she said, snapping a mock salute. After a second, her smile faded. "I know you're right, in my head. But my heart is having a little trouble catching up. It still hurts too much."

"Yeah, tell me about it. I've been there, remember? There's no way to describe how awful it is to be deserted by the one person you expected to stand by you forever."

Taking her empty plate, he stacked it on his. Then he turned toward her, took both of her hands in his, and stared straight into her eyes. "I want to be here for you, to help you get through this, to prove to you that all men aren't like your stupid ex-husband."

He lowered his face and paused, collecting his thoughts. "Look, Carolee, this seems really weird – since we only met a few hours ago – but strange as it is, I feel a real connection between us, a connection I'm not willing to break, at least until we've had time to find out if it's something real or just wishful thinking. This concert tour is going to require most of my time for the next few months. I'm not sure when we'll be able to get together, or for how long, but I'm willing to do whatever it takes. I want see you again. I want to get to know you better. Give us a chance to find out if there could be more. Are you in?"

Sniffing back tears, she nodded joyfully. "I'd like that, very much."

He kissed her quickly and softly before turning his attention to a huge chocolate chip cookie. When he was finished, he wiped crumbs off his mouth with a large linen napkin. "Here," he said, leaning forward and pulling his wallet from his back pocket. "Take my card. It has my agent's number on it. He can reach me anytime, anywhere. Call him and leave your cell number. I'd give you mine, but I've lost my phone – again, I'm always leaving the darned thing somewhere."

"This couldn't be the agent who stole your wife, could it?" she asked, running her fingers over the embossed print.

"Uh…yeah, it is," he admitted a bit shamefaced. "Losing Sandra to Steve was awful. I was furious with him, but I couldn't stand losing him as my business manager too. He stepped way over the line personally, but he never let me down professionally. Steve had a lot of time and effort invested in me. He believed in me when others didn't, so I stuck it out with him, and tried to put my wounded pride aside."

"To tell you the truth, I'm glad your ex-wife wasn't faithful," Carolee admitted.

"What do you mean?" he snapped, clearly offended. "You think I'm not worthy of a wife's devotion?"

Realizing she had touched a sore spot, she soothed. "Wait, that's not what I meant, Dylan. You're completely worthy – worthy of faithfulness, loyalty, love, and devotion. And I'm still glad she dumped you."

"Really?" His full lips were drawn into a tight line, making it clear that he wanted to argue the point.

"Yes. I'm thankful Sandra is out of your life – so I can be in it," she quipped with a sly smile. "My motives are purely selfish." Moving in close, she pressed a soft kiss to his still pouting mouth, and felt it warm and respond to the interaction. It was a long time before she drew away, breathless and shaking.

"Oh, my," she sighed. "You overwhelm me, Mr. St. Claire." Flushing hotly, she ran her fingers through her newly cropped hair. "Your ex must be one of the most idiotic women on this planet, to walk away from you, but I'm sure glad she did." When she regained the composure to face him again, he was grinning too, his eyes sparkling with silver lights, and her heart did another flip.

He reached out to pull her back to him, but she scampered away. "That's quite enough of that," she teased. "We've got to stop before we both get carried away."

"What's wrong with getting carried away?" he asked, still leering. "I haven't let myself get carried away for a very long time, and it feels great."

"That's the problem," Carolee explained. "It feels too good, and I'm completely unprepared for this…this…whatever this is. I'm unbelievably attracted to you, Dylan, and I feel that connection you mentioned, too. I feel it so strongly that it scares me, but the reality is – I don't know you. You've had time to get your balance after your divorce. I'm sure you're had many women in your life since Sandra, but I haven't even begun to think about that. Bill was my first and only lover. Being here, like this, with you, is so tempting, so thrilling, but also terrifying. I'm sorry, Dylan, no matter how much I want to be with you, I'm not ready."

His deeply sensuous laughter surprised her. "Oh, I haven't been around as much as you might think. I've had offers, but not many that interest me. I'm sure you've heard stories about the women who chase after guys like me. Lots of musicians get caught up in that scene. But the groupies don't appeal to me. Those women only want a notch on their headboard with my name on it. They're only interested in Dylan St. Claire, the guy with a platinum record or two on his wall. Without the fame, they wouldn't take a second glance at Dylan St. Claire, the man with as many failures to his credit as successes."

"But you've dated, haven't you?" Incredulity shone from her twinkling blue eyes. "I'm sure there are dozens of women, not groupies, but other celebrities, like you, who've jumped at the chance to have their names linked with yours."

"I've gone out some, but most of the women, in the glitzy circle of music and showbiz hype, are more interested in how a match with me will further their careers, than in how we click as a couple. It's difficult to feel any fireworks for someone who measures you by how they're reflected in your eyes."

"I don't pay much attention to entertainment news shows, but I remember hearing something about you dating some beautiful, young starlet, not too long ago," she accused. "Or was that just gossip?"

"If you mean Marsha Walters, the rumors are somewhat true. We've dated, but it's nothing serious." He guiltily studied his hands.

"Is that how she would see it," Carolee prodded, "as nothing serious?"

"Yeah, I'm sure she'd agree," he confirmed, raising his face to look squarely into her questioning eyes.

"But you have made love to her, haven't you?" She swallowed hard, trying to force down the tight knot of dread rising in her throat. She knew she was on shaky ground, because she had no right to ask, but she had to know. Not that she was jealous…well, maybe a little bit jealous…but mostly she needed to identify the competition she was up against, vying for the affections of Dylan St. Claire.

"I wouldn't call it making love exactly," he hedged, clearly searching for the right words to make Carolee understand, because he seemed to need her to understand. "Marsha is unbelievably self-absorbed. Sex, for her, is nothing more than personal gratification, never an expression of caring and commitment. She uses a man, sexually, to feel his adoration of her, and to enjoy her power over him. And as much as it embarrasses me to admit it, she's used me a time or two." Dylan took Carolee's hand, turned it over and kissed the palm.

"When Sandra left me, I was devastated, my self-confidence was in the toilet. I became laser-focused on getting my girls through the divorce. I avoided women. Don't get me wrong, I'm a normal, healthy male, but I wanted to set an example for my daughters. How can I tell them that casual sex is unwise, unhealthy, and just plain wrong, if I don't practice what I preach? After a while though, my bruised ego demanded proof that I was still desirable, and my libido won out over my convictions and my better judgment."

"How could you doubt yourself with millions of screaming females throwing themselves at you?" Skepticism was clear in the jaunty tilt of Carolee's head.

"My thousands of adoring fans didn't help, because they're only attracted to the image my publicist creates. They scream for the celluloid version of me. They don't even know the real me."

Dylan rubbed his jaw with a fist and took a deep, steadying breath. "I met Marsha just after my second album went gold. She did a cameo in the music video of the first track. She's very sexy and came on strong. She made me think she wanted Dylan, the totally screwed-up man whose wife dumped him, and not Dylan St. Claire, the pop-music icon who's desired by women all over. I didn't catch on until too late.

"I bought her act, and let myself get pulled along by the waves of public adoration. It was good for a while – having a gorgeous woman on my arm, being followed by the paparazzi, seeing our faces on every gossip rag in the supermarket – but after a few months, things went sour. Marsha demanded more time and devoted attention than I had to give. I finally realized that I was just a trophy to her, a conquest to be flaunted and to incite envy in other women. Once I stopped pursuing her, she lost interest, and the relationship sort of dried up."

"So, you didn't have to deal with a difficult break-up."

His hangdog expression confirmed her suspicion. "No, because I didn't really end it – officially."

"Then how is she going to feel about that hugely public kiss? You know it will be broadcast everywhere next week. The *Olivia Wells* folks are drooling over that clip. You'll be lucky if it isn't shown on every network's entertainment news show tomorrow morning. If she stills thinks you're involved with her, she'll be furious,"

"I didn't end it with her, Carolee, because there was nothing to end." Anxious frustration burned in his clear, gray eyes. "I don't mean to be insensitive, but I don't care how Marsha Walters reacts. She's selfish and shallow, and more in love with herself than with anyone else. Whatever I had with her is over and done. From the start, it was a pale imitation of what a serious relationship should be, and I wish I'd never wasted my time on her.

"It's hard to believe, but you and I know more about one another, after a few hours together, than Marsha and I learned in months."

Carefully considering his words, she regarded him longingly before she responded, "I think I understand, Dylan, really, I do, and I'm sympathetic, but it's just one more reason to take things slowly. You're not the man I imagined you'd be. I never dreamed you'd have any interest in me, but I've seen the real you, and I'm blown away. I'm completely overwhelmed, trying to wrap my brain around the wonderful things you've said to me.

"I don't trust my feelings. And your kisses, those are even more heady and confusing than your words. If I'm not careful, you'll sweep me off my feet and into something I'm not remotely prepared to handle." Dropping her eyes and studying the hands she had tightly clenched in her lap, she added, her voice almost a whisper, "The only thing I know for sure is that I can't begin to compete with a woman like Marsha Walters."

Seeming to understanding her hesitation and fear, Dylan smiled, encircling her shoulders with his arm, pulling her close, and pressing her head into the hollow just beneath his collarbone.

"It's okay, Carolee. There's something special and magical between us; we both know it. But you're not ready to risk your heart. I get it. So just relax. We'll take it easy, like you say, move slowly, really get to know each other, and build trust.

"One day soon, I'll convince you that no superficial sexpot can hold a candle to you in my eyes. I can wait." He kissed the top of her head and fell silent.

Reassured by his heartfelt declaration, Carolee obeyed his urging and relaxed, tucked under his arm, safe and warm against the hard wall of his chest. She could hear his heartbeat thudding in her ear, and his clean, freshly scrubbed, manly scent filled her head. Tears of joy and promise squeezed out between her lowered lids and fell onto his T-shirt.

When his breathing slowed, and his arm sagged heavily across her, she gently slipped out of his embrace. She found a throw pillow to cushion his head, and retrieved a blanket from the bedroom to cover his long, lean form. She watched him sleep for long moment, his face unguarded and boyish, before realizing she may already be falling in love with this tender, exciting, frustratingly handsome man. Clearing those dangerous thoughts from her mind, she tiptoed away.

PART VIII

The enticing aroma of freshly brewed coffee pulled Carolee out of a blissfully dreamless slumber, and into a reluctant consciousness. Blinking her eyelids to rid them of the cloyingly sticky remnants of sleep, her vision slowly cleared. When her eyes finally focused, she was startled to find herself staring straight into the mischievous grin of Dylan St. Claire. The man was perched on the edge of her bed, holding an open carafe in one hand. The other he waved back and forth through the billows of steam emanating from the top of the pot, trying to coax her awake with the delicious smell.

"Finally," he sighed impatiently, his smile growing even wider and a bit one-sided. "I thought you were going to waste the day away. Get up girl. There're croissants and muffins to go with the coffee. Come on. Let's move. We've got lots of sight-seeing to do." At her half-hearted attempt to slink back beneath the duvet, he yanked the cover down. "No, you don't. You're getting up. I'll pour you a cup while you get ready. What do you take in it?"

"Milk and sweetener, thanks," she croaked, deciding there was no use to protest. Crawling out of the tall bed, she headed for the bathroom.

From the sitting area, he called to her, "I'm going up to my suite to change. Arnie is bringing the car around in twenty minutes. I'll be back to pick you up in fifteen." Before she could respond, she heard the door close behind him.

As instructed, she was brushed and polished, dressed in comfortable jeans, chambray shirt, and tennis shoes, and feeling a little more alert, following a half-cup of coffee, when she heard him approach her suite, whistling. Opening the door before he could knock, she waved him inside. "I know Arnie's waiting, but I've got to call my boys before we go. I know they're dying to hear all about last night. It won't take a minute."

"No problem," he agreed, reaching for a pastry. "I could go for another muffin, anyway."

Clearing a number of texts from her sons, to which she hadn't responded, she asked him, "Would you say 'Hi' to them? They'd really get a kick out of that."

"Sure, I'd be happy to. Should I tell them I think their mother is pretty special? Maybe I should ask their permission to court you." he teased.

"Court me?" she laughed. "Now that's an old-fashioned notion. You're showing your age, St. Claire."

"That's me, just an old-fashioned guy," he quipped, his mouth full.

Brett picked up on the first ring and put his cell phone on speaker so Bryce could participate in the conversation. Talking at the same time, they quizzed her about the dinner and concert. The older teen was particularly interested in hearing all of the details of the huge production, from her backstage perspective. Both boys were pleased by her enthusiastic description of her dream-come-true evening.

As she'd expected, Bryce was the one who asked her how she liked Dylan St. Claire, and how he liked her.

"Well, I think he's great, but you'll have to ask Mr. St. Claire his opinion of me yourself. Here he is." She handed the phone over to the singer, who hastily cleared his throat.

After a long, comical silence, Dylan begin to answer their anxious, yet skeptical, questions. "Yes, it's really me," he assured them. "Your mom and I are going out sight-seeing." Another pause, then he added, "Don't worry, I'll look after her. You're right. I think she's great, too... No, no, I wouldn't hurt her for the world. Please don't worry... Sure, I hope I get to meet you sometime soon." He ended with, "I'm counting on you guys to take care of your mom for me while I finish this tour. She's really terrific and means a lot to me. Here she is," and handed the phone back to her.

Laughing over their exuberant response to the brief conversation, Carolee promised to check in, via text, first thing in the morning. "I'll see you at the airport tomorrow night. I'll have plenty of time to fill you in on the rest of the details when I get home. Right now, I've got to go, Mr. St. Claire's on a tight schedule. I love you guys!"

"Schedule's not as tight as you think," he informed her. "I was planning a one-day rest break in Chicago, before the Tuesday evening concert, so I had some wiggle-room to rearrange things. My people are taking the bus on ahead to get set up, and I'm catching a flight later on. I'm happy to say that we have all day to spend together."

Placing a palm in the small of her back, he propelled her toward the door. "I thought your car would be less conspicuous than mine. Your driver's arranging a picnic lunch for us, and driving us to a private spot where we can enjoy the scenery, and each other, without the prying eyes of my ever-present fans."

Pulling a tattered red cap out of his back pocket, Dylan crammed it down over his hair. Then he added a pair of aviator-style dark glasses to complete his makeshift disguise. He wore his ever-present, faded blue jeans, topped off with another black T-shirt, and beat-up cowboy boots. Together they made a very attractive, if nondescript, couple.

The hotel lobby was surprisingly deserted, so they made it to the waiting car with no trouble. Carolee slid inside and bid the driver a cheerful, "Hello, Arnie," before asking her companion, "How in the world did you manage to arrange such a clean get-away? There wasn't one groupie in sight."

He motioned for the driver to proceed, "I've learned the hard way that it's essential to have a contingency plan to outwit the more determined followers. We usually travel from city to city by bus. It takes two full-sized motor coaches, and a semi, to haul all the people and equipment needed to put the show together. Since our tour busses all have *Dylan St. Claire* emblazoned on their sides, like huge rolling billboards, they're too obvious to use around town. We leave them on the parking lot of the arena or auditorium, where we're performing, and arrange for rented vehicles to move us to and from our hotel.

"I don't understand how, but at least one group of my most persistent fans inevitably spot my car, follow me to the hotel, and set up a twenty-four-hour stakeout. They make it impossible for me to come and go without being mobbed. You won't believe the lengths these women go to. Heck, somehow, they get through the tightest security. After I got trapped, several times, with no way out, except to run the gauntlet and go through them, I decided to hire a stand-in."

"A stand-in?" Carolee was puzzled.

"I found a guy who looks a lot like me, same build, same height, etc. We had him grow his hair out a bit, and dyed it to match mine. We dress him up in an attention-getting, concert outfit, and send him out to battle the crowd, you know, create a diversion."

His pride in the success of the sly strategy was evident in the flash of his trademark smile. "Then I slip out, usually unnoticed, in my old jeans and ball cap, and go about my business with none the wiser."

"Those women really fall for your bait and switch?" she asked, giggling at the thought of his delighted followers chasing after a fake Dylan St. Claire.

"Sure," he confirmed, taking her hand and entwining his fingers in hers. "One afternoon in St. Louis, a parade of more than ten cars followed my twin for two solid hours, while I was out all alone, having a great time looking over the sights. I took a city bus, believe it or not, and even went up inside that arch thing. Nobody recognized me. It was terrific."

"So, what does this look-alike do when he's not impersonating you?"

"Oh, this and that, just like any of the roadies – stage set up, lighting, toting stuff – like that. We do tend to keep him behind the scenes, and out of sight, most of the time. Wouldn't want anyone to see him, and catch on to what we're pulling. He's a hard worker, but he'd be worth his salary, even if he didn't do anything else but pretend to be me. No one could call me an introvert, but even an extravert like me needs private time occasionally. I like being able to go places where I'm not recognized. Having my twin around makes that possible."

When Dylan paused to squeeze her hand and brush her lips with a light kiss, Arnie interrupted apologetically, to call their attention to some of the more important architectural wonders of the city. Conversation lagged, as they peered out through the tinted windows to follow the interesting descriptions the chauffeur provided. As promised, the driver was a good tour guide. He showed them many of Atlanta's interesting sights, before stopping at his favorite deli to pick up the picnic basket he'd ordered. Then, he steered the big, black car onto the interstate and out into the open countryside.

A half-hour passed before Arnie powered down an exit ramp and turned off on a quiet, two-lane road. Ten minutes later, he slowed the big car to take a narrow side road. The lane was beautifully picturesque. Blooming shrubs, in pastel colors, dotted the shoulders, while the branches of ancient trees created a verdant, green canopy above. Sunlight dapples filtered through the heavy overhang, like a sprinkling of gold dust. In less than a mile, the driver pulled off the gravel track, through an almost imperceptible break in the trees, and into a sylvan clearing overlooking a small, crystal clear lake.

Dylan helped Arnie unload the cooler and enormous basket, while Carolee grabbed a blanket from the trunk. The driver led them to a grassy knoll, in the shade of a looming oak, where he and the singer put down their burdens and unfolded the thick spread.

"No one's gonna bother you here," the rotund man assured them. "It's private property, been in my family for three generations. Our place is just up the road a piece." He shook a beefy arm in the direction opposite the way they'd come in. "I'll head on over to the house, to rest for a spell."

"Oh, no, Arnie, you should stay and have something to eat with us. There's enough here to feed an army!" Carolee exclaimed, as she opened the wicker container and examined the contents.

"Wouldn't think of it," he refused. "You young folks need your time alone, without an old coot like me hangin' 'round.

'Sides, the old lady's expectin' me for dinner. She always makes fried chicken on Sunday." He licked his ample lips in anticipation.

"I'll be back for you in a couple o' three hours."

As he waddled toward the Lincoln, he called back to them, his tone teasing, "Hey, just so's ya'll know. I allow skinny-dippin' in my lake. In fact, I encourage it!" Contagious laughter followed him, until his crewcut disappeared inside the car.

"Well, we certainly won't go hungry," Carolee noted, quickly changing the subject, and hoping Dylan wouldn't see the bloom of color on her cheeks. "Look at all this food." There were thin slices of rare roast beef and smoked ham, cold grilled chicken, and tangy deviled eggs, large containers of coleslaw, potato salad, and fresh fruit chunks, an assortment of cheeses, relishes, breads, and rolls. A sparkling wine, several bottles of imported beer, and a variety of soft drinks had also been provided, to wash down the impressive repast.

"Looks like old Arnie planned for a few leftovers," Dylan commented, chuckling. "There's no way we'll finish off all this in an afternoon. Especially since I'm not even hungry right now, at least not for food." He reached out for Carolee, pulling her into his long arms and caressing her lips with his. Long, delicious moments passed.

Her head spinning, she bracing her hands against the firm wall of his chest and pushed away, dizzy and shaken. He offered no resistance, but released her to study her face thoughtfully. "I promise you, Carolee, I won't push you into anything you don't want to do."

"But I do want it, Dylan. I want it...I want **you** so much it scares me." She knew her expression was one of sheer panic.

"Correction...I won't push you into anything you aren't ready for. You can trust me." The reassuring words finally sunk in, and she let herself relax against him.

"Let's go for a walk, then maybe we'll consider that dip in the lake Arnie suggested, followed by a few more friendly kisses, a little lunch, and to top it off, some dessert. How does that sound?"

"Great. Except for the skinny-dipping part! This middle-aged body is definitely not up to stripping bare in front of a superstar recording artist, even for a bit of carefree fun." She offered him a tiny kiss to take the bite out of her refusal.

Grabbing her hand, they strolled leisurely around the lake, while he threw out all of his most convincing arguments, in support of the naked swimming option. "I'll turn my back. I won't look. I promise," he cajoled.

"Come on Carolee, it's time you had some guilty fun. Wouldn't it be thrilling to go back home and tell your friends that you went swimming in the altogether, with Dylan St. Claire? What would they think about that?"

"I don't care what they think," she declared firmly. "It's what **you** think that matters to me. I'm over forty, Dylan. I've had two children. Keeping my body fit and trim has not been the first priority in my life. You date skinny models, and young starlets with silicone implants and abs of steel, not mature homemakers with stretch marks and cellulite. I won't stack up very well in comparison, and I'm not anxious to see the disappointment in your eyes."

"Wait just a minute," he complained. "I'd hoped you'd realized by now that I'm not your average, superficial male. I'm not interested in the plastic, Barbie-doll types, Carolee. I want a woman my own age, a real woman who has lived a real life, had real problems, has grown in real ways, and who has a real woman's body. I want you, my dear woman – stretch marks, cellulite, and all."

To punctuate his declaration, he looked her over from top to toes. "What I see before me is a very warm, very loving, and very beautiful lady. Any figure flaws you might have aren't obvious to me."

"Heavy denim and a good bra can cover a multitude of sins." She half-joked, shooting him a wry smile. Blushing again at the thought of being naked in front of him, she added, "Without the benefit of surgery, gravity takes its toll on all of us gals, Dylan. Besides, that's not my only concern."

"No?" he asked.

Tossing him a teasing grin, she added. "I'm not sure my old heart could take seeing you in the buff, out here like this, in broad daylight."

Laughing too now, he countered. "Okay, okay, have it your way. No skinny-dipping! But since it's such a warm day, our clothes should dry pretty quickly. You can swim in your shirt, and I'll keep my underwear on."

Not giving her a chance to refuse, he tugged off his boots and socks, and wriggled out of his jeans. The hat and glasses were thrown on top of the pile, as he bounded for the water, wearing nothing but a pair of tight-fitting, dark gray, cotton boxer shorts.

"Hurry, hurry, it feels wonderful," he urged her, diving under and kicking up a plume.

Shrugging in defeat, she slipped off her shoes. Turning her back to the lake, she unbuttoned her pants and peeled out of them. The tail of her over-sized chambray shirt came halfway to her knees, affording her some measure of modesty. The water was spring-fed and chilling.

Carolee waded in slowly, trying to get adjusted to the cold temperature, but Dylan, bristling with impatience, took matters into his own hands. Submerging and circling behind her, he grabbed her legs and pulled her out into a deeper pool, hastening the adjustment process.

"It's freezing!" she squealed breathlessly.

"Give it a second. You'll get used to it," he assured, grinning smugly, his long limbs gracefully treading water. Thankfully, he was right. It didn't take long for the numbing cold to dissipate, as Carolee's body acclimated. The gentle current felt like a sweet caress, smooth and silky, against her skin. They played teasing games in the cool water, splashing and chasing one another, like a couple of love-struck teenagers. When Dylan decided he'd had enough of the horseplay, he scooped her up and held her tightly against him, letting the water buoy them up.

"Now comes the kissing part," he warned her. Several minutes later, following a deeply stirring entangling of lips and tongues, he withdrew without prompting, whistling between his teeth.

"Heavens, woman, you make it damned hard for a man to keep his promises." Then changing gears abruptly, he added, "I'm getting hungry. Let's go raid that picnic basket. What do you say?"

They climbed out of the lake, shook off the clinging water drops, struggled to drag their jeans back on over wet skin, and stretched out on the welcoming blanket, warmed by the sun.

Carolee piled two plates high, with the delectable goodies, while Dylan scooped ice into plastic glasses and poured soft drinks. It pleased her to see him pass up the wine and beer in favor of her preferred beverage. They ate in comfortable silence.

Setting his empty plate aside, he rummaged through the basket, "I'm sure Arnie didn't forget the dessert. There must be something sweet in here…Eureka!" he exclaimed, holding up a box of flaky, bite-sized pastries. There were cookies, too, and brownies. "I think I hit the jackpot," he added, cramming a cherry tart into his mouth.

"How do you eat so much and stay so slim?" she asked him, giggling at his antics.

"I don't eat this much, ordinarily, but when I'm in love, I have a huge appetite," he explained, his sparkling gray eyes shooting her a sideways glance, as he chased the tart with a small brownie.

"Oh, so you're in love?" she taunted, taking the bait.

"Could be," the singer noted. "I have been eating a lot the last couple of days. Could be a sign that I'm falling in love with you."

"Could be, huh? Well, please let me know when you decide for sure," she quipped, her tone light, despite the rapid beating of her heart and the anxious knot in her stomach.
"You'll be the first one notified," he promised, sliding close and planting a quick kiss on the tip of her pert nose.

PART IX

Arnie returned to find them both sleeping soundly. Dylan was propped up against the rough bark of the huge oak, with Carolee's head cradled in his lap. Using his thigh for a pillow, the exhausted teacher lay curled on the blanket beside him. The singer's head lolled back against the tree trunk, and he snored softly.

The snap of a camera lens startled them to wakefulness.

"Couldn't resist that there shot," Arnie crowed, obviously pleased. "It could bring me a small fortune from one o' them tabloids."

The sour, almost threatening glare Dylan directed his way prompted the portly man to add, "Only kiddin, Mr. St. Claire.' I like to take pictures of the famous people I drive around, just for my own album. I never share them with anyone. Would y'all mind?"

Graciously obliging the old man, Dylan posed in front of the enormous tree, first alone, then with Carolee, and finally with Arnie himself, while the accommodating woman clicked the shutter. "Thanks," Arnie said, tucking the small digital camera into his coat pocket. "My wife'll git a kick out o' those. She's a big fan o' yers."

"And you're not?" Dylan goaded.

Unruffled, the driver responded matter-of-factly. "I got nothin' agin your style, mind you. I just like country music better, is all. You got to admit, your stuff's more for the ladies than the gents."

Slapping him good-naturedly, on his broad back, the singer laughed heartily. "You're okay, Arnie, and you're absolutely right. If I depended on men to buy my records, I'd still be a starving nightclub singer."

As they gathered up the leftovers, and carried everything back to the waiting car, Dylan asked, "Speaking of good country music, do you know a roadhouse around here, where we could kick up our heels a bit without causing a stir?"

"Sure." Arnie winked at them. "I know jest the place. Leave it to me."

As they bumped back along the rough gravel and made for the highway, Carolee voiced her apprehension. "Dylan, I just don't know about this. I must look a mess." To demonstrate her point, she ran damp palms down the set-in wrinkles in her shirt. "And I don't know anything about country-style dancing."

"You look just perfect, and I'll teach you the steps," he reassured her.

"But what if someone recognizes you?" The shrill edge of concern sharpened her tone.

"Not likely. My music's not particularly popular with the bluegrass set, like Arnie said. But if someone does ID me, we'll handle it. Arnie'll back me up. Won't you, Arnie?"

"Anythin' you say, Mr. St. Claire," the big man echoed, flashing her a wink in the rearview mirror.

Turning toward Carolee, Dylan whispered, "This is our last night together, for who knows how long. I'm not ready for it to end just yet. Are you?" She shook her head, the whirl of emotion stirred up by his declaration making it impossible for her to answer.

"If we go back to the hotel and spend the evening together, in private, it's going to be next to impossible for me to keep my hands off you. I don't want to break my promise to you, Carolee, so the alternative is to find a public place, where I'll be forced to behave."

Put that way, the roadhouse idea seemed a reasonable one. "Okay," she breathed, smiling into his shining eyes. "Let's party!"

"All right! That's my girl." His wide-eyed, victorious grin nearly broke her heart.

A few minutes later, Arnie steered the shiny black car into the parking lot of a low, dilapidated-looking wooden structure, with a blue neon sign over the door which read, *The Silver Spur*. "I'll park around on the side, where folks'll be less likely to notice this big buggy, and catch a cat nap, while you young-uns have yerselves a grand old time.”

“Thanks, Arnie,” Dylan told him, opening his door and offering Carolee his hand.

“Jest holler if you need any hep!” the driver urged, waving his cell phone.

“Will do,” the younger man assured him.

As soon as they stepped out onto the gravel lot, Carolee could feel the boom, boom of a heavy electric bass reverberating in her chest, raising her apprehensions. Inside, however, the volume seemed less intimidating, and the patrons appeared friendly. The place wasn’t crowded, so they had their pick of tables. Dylan chose one that was off to one side and out of the way, but still near the dance floor. Instead of a live band, one lone cowboy-type stood on a raised platform, spinning records and taking requests.

“Hey there, name’s Lacy,” a perky, young woman in short denim shorts, and bright red boots, greeted them, pad and tray in hand, dipping a hip and directing a seductive smile in Dylan’s direction. “Haven’t seen you folks round here before. What’ll you have?” she asked him between chomps on a wad of pink bubble gum.

“Yeah, we’re just passin’ through,” the tall man informed her, dropping into a very convincing drawl. “Jest bring us a couple of Dr. Peppers. Will ya?”

“Sure thing, sweetie,” she chirped, batting her mascara-caked eyelashes at him. Popping her gum and swinging her hips, she sashayed toward the bar.

“I think she likes you,” Carolee teased, leaning across the small table.

“Aw, she’s just a kid, probably not much older than my Kristen,” he responded, dismissing the idea entirely. “She’s just working every angle, hoping for a big tip.”

“I’m afraid you don’t look like a big spender, in your rumpled jeans, and you ordered soft drinks, remember? She can’t be expecting much of a tip. Nope, she’s pretty impressed with you all right.” He eyed her sideways and shook his head.

"My goodness, St. Claire, you honestly have no clue about the effect you have on the female of the species, do you?"

"Yeah, yeah, yeah," he denied dismissively. I hear all those silly women screaming for me, but they've got stars in their eyes. They can't get past the phony, Dylan St. Claire media image. If they ever really looked at me, all they'd see would be an ordinary man who's a little worn around the edges."

"That's baloney!" she huffed. "Even if you're blind, the women in this bar aren't. Every single one of them has checked you out. There's nothing ordinary about you, Dylan." Fighting the tears that threatened, she added, hoping her flirtation skills weren't too rusty, "You're a drop-dead, gorgeous hunk of man." Heart twisting painfully, she winked at him, forcing down the knot of inadequacy twisting her belly.

"Well, if I'm so irresistible, why aren't you dancing with me?" he asked playfully, taking her hand, and hauling her out onto the floor.

Despite her inexperience, Carolee proved to be a quick study. Dylan taught her a few moves, and soon they were two- stepping their way around the dance floor like a couple of old pros. To her surprise, the hesitant schoolteacher enjoyed herself immensely, especially with Dylan's strong hands holding her tightly, and every eye in the place on them.

When they returned to their beat-up table, breathless and sweating from the exertion, they were pleased to discover that Lacy had delivered their drinks. Condensation dripped off the tall, icy glasses onto round paper coasters. Dylan drained his in one long pull, and waved for the waitress to bring him another. A movement from the far side of the room caught his eye. He nuzzled his companion's ear and whispered, "Don't look now, but here comes trouble."

Carolee turned to follow his gaze and noted three, big-haired women sashaying across the room in their direction, faces alight with unexpected discovery. "Just be cool. Don't worry. I can handle them." Keeping his face close to Carolee's cheek, her hand tucked in his, he pretended he hadn't seen the bevy approaching, until they stood right next to the table.

The boldest of the trio cleared her throat to get his attention, though her pungent floral cologne had already announced her arrival. "Uh, 'scuse me…but has anyone ever told you that you look just like Dylan St. Claire, that singer?" The other two nodded their heads furiously, encouraging their leader.

Adopting an almost unbelievable, aw-shucks-ma'am attitude, Dylan grinned crookedly, and answered in his most convincing drawl, "Cain't say they have. Fact is, I never heered o' no, wha'd you say his name wuz, St. Cloud? Have you, honey bunch?" Carolee couldn't answer. She was too busy choking back the shudders of laughter which threatening to break out.

"No…St. Claire, Dylan St. Claire. You look just like him. Don't he girls?" The big redhead fidgeted nervously, and looked back and forth from one of her friends to the other. Their heads bobbed in agreement, like papier mâché dogs in the back window of a car.

Dylan rubbed his chin where late-day stubble generously sprouted. "Don't know 'im. What kind o' songs does he sing, anyhow?"

"Rock ballads, love songs, you know, like that." The woman's expansive, crimson-lipped smile disappeared, as doubt clouded her mind.

Playing the redneck cowboy role to the hilt, Dylan slapped the table. "Well, that splains it then. I don't like me no rock n' roll racket. I only listen to real Amurcan music. Now if'n you was to say I look like Randy Travis or Lyle Lovett, then I'd a known 'xactly who you wuz talkin' about, but I never heared o' that there St. Cloud fella. Sorry ladies. Sure do wish I had me some o' his money, though. Bet he's got a pile of it."

Dismissing them with a shrug, he slid his chair closer to Carolee's and nuzzled her ear again. The determined spokeswoman opened her mouth to try again, but closed it with a pop, when one of her girlfriends pulled her sleeve.

"It's not him, Flo. It couldn't be. What would a big star like Dylan St. Claire be doing in a dump like this, anyway?"

Slowly, dejectedly, the buxom threesome turned away, the redhead still waving her hands in frustration. "Well, that fella sure looks like St. Claire, and he was in Atlanta for a concert last night, you know."

Her friend argued, "That was last night. He's probably long gone, and we made fools of ourselves for nothing." They argued their way across the floor, picked up their gaudy, beaded handbags, and beat an embarrassed retreat. Once they were out the door, Carolee let a giggle escape her tight control.

"Shhh," he warned her. "We're not out of the woods, yet. People are still gaping." She let her eyes sweep the room, and discovered he was right. "Just sit quietly for a couple of minutes, and they'll forget about us." Again, he was right. In a matter of moments, the bar's patrons went back to minding their own business. Only nosy Lacy seemed curious about the goings-on.

Refilling his glass from a large pitcher, she asked him, deliberately ignoring Carolee, "What was that all about?"

Deciding that honesty was the best approach, he told her, "Oh, those gals seemed to think I look a little bit like some rock and roll hotshot, that's all. But I set 'em straight. Didn't I, sweet cheeks?" The ridiculous endearment caught Carolee off guard, and she had to choke off another giggle.

Unfortunately, his explanation set Lacy to thinking. "Yeah! That's it. I knew you reminded me of somebody. It's that singer who had a concert downtown last night…Dylan St. Claire."

Dylan shot Carolee a smug, I-told-you-so look, and nodded toward the door. Just as he slipped his wallet out of his back pocket, and slapped a twenty-dollar bill down on the table, the waitress called out, "Hey, everybody, you see this guy here? Don't he look just like that Dylan St. Claire fella?" She pointed at the singer, encouraging him. "Stand up, honey, so's everyone can get a good look at you."

Taking Carolee by the arm, he complied with the waitress's request, but didn't pause for the crowd's reaction, as he bolted for the exit, pulling his companion along behind.

"Well, of all the rude things!" Lacy yelled after him, more than a bit miffed.

Shrugging off the puzzled looks of the other patrons, she bent to clear the glasses, her lip stuck out in an obvious pout. The large bill she found there lightened her mood considerably. "Hey, he left a twenty! Maybe it really was that St. Claire guy."

When the chauffeur saw his passengers shoot out of the roadhouse, he fired up the engine, and pulled the big Lincoln around to meet them. They tumbled into the back seat, laughing hysterically. "What's up?" he asked, curiosity getting the best of him.

"Oh, just a minor close call," Dylan explained. Turning to Carolee he teased, "Now you have to admit that was fun."

"Yes, it was. I had no idea you were such a good actor. I almost fell for your good ol' boy routine." She ran her fingers through her hair, smoothing out the tangles, and stared into his bright, shining eyes.

They rode in silence for a while, enjoying the quiet and each other's company. As they approached the lights of the city, Dylan re-visited the conversation they had begun in the bar. "Carolee, I know my popularity worries you, but I hope you'll try to overlook it, or at least learn to live with it. You're the first woman, in a very long time, who really sees me for me.

"That thing back there, with the waitress, just proves my point. Most women react to me, even if it's on a sub-conscious level, because of my public persona. I can't escape it. But you're different, and that's why you already mean so much to me. You like his music, but you don't worship Dylan St. Claire, the famous recording star, you care about Dylan St. Claire, the regular guy."

Kissing him tenderly, she agreed, "I do care, Dylan. I don't know how I've grown to care so much in 24 hours, but there it is. But I can't pretend that your public image doesn't scare me silly. There's been a special connection between us, from the first, but

I'm still afraid that I won't be enough for you. You're a bright, shining star, and I'm a mousy, boring schoolteacher.

"I'll never forget this weekend, these dreamy days set apart from reality. I'll hold the memories we've made together close to my heart, and pray that we will see each other again sometime, but I won't count on it. Tomorrow you'll go back to being adored by the world, and thoughts of me will fade into the background. And that's okay. I'll always be grateful for the time we've had together, and for the kindness you've shown me."

"Now hold on a minute," he protested. "I hate it when you diminish yourself like that, Carolee. You're beautiful and accomplished, and I'm already a little bit in love. You don't believe it yet, but you will. No matter what you think you know, you haven't heard the last of me, not by a long shot. If you can put up with the petty annoyances of my crazy life, we'll be seeing a lot more of each another, and I mean that in more ways than one." He wiggled his eyebrows suggestively, and punctuated the assurance with a series of intensifying kisses.

As they rolled up to the curb in front of the Southern Hospitality Hotel, Dylan pulled aback and offered, "Come up to my suite with me. I'll order a light supper from room service. It'll give us a few more hours together. You have a big day ahead of you tomorrow, so I promise not to keep you up too late."

"That sounds nice," she agreed. Before sliding out of the back seat, they expressed their gratitude to Arnie, for making their day together special, and wished him well. Carolee followed Dylan through the revolving door and into the lobby.

He cautioned her to hurry along, just in case a hanger-on or two remained on lookout. Thankfully, it seemed that even the most determined groupies had given up, or had been fooled into leaving when the tour busses pulled out, for the large, marble and glass foyer was almost deserted. The happy couple reached the elevator without being accosted. When the door slid open, they stepped inside. Dylan pushed the button for the penthouse.

As the state-of-the-art car glided effortlessly upward, the singer took the teacher's hand, squeezed it tightly, and kissed her soundly. The car deposited them just outside his suite. Pulling the key-card out of his pocket, he held it against the lock until the light blinked, opened the door, and held it for her, placing his hand in the middle of her back to guide her inside.

An involuntary sigh escaped her as she took in the expansive elegance of the suite. It was utterly magnificent. "I thought my room was grand, but this one…." She paused. "Wow!"

"Yeah, it's nice, but a little too ostentatious and impersonal to suit me," he remarked. "Make yourself at home."

Her exploration of the rooms was cut short, when she heard a squeal from the adjoining chamber. Two pretty teenagers burst out of one of the bedrooms. "Dad! You're back…finally. Where have you been? We've been waiting for you since noon."

"Kristen! Leah!" he exclaimed, clearly surprised. He hugged them both tightly before asking, "What are you doing here?"

"Well," the oldest began. "When Marsha saw that picture of you in the entertainment news, the one of you kissing the woman at your concert, she called us and said we'd better catch up with you, and find out what in the world is going on."

In her typical, distracted way, she added, "The review of your performance was excellent, by the way." Dylan shook his head in confusion and waited for her to continue. "We tried your cell, but you didn't answer…as usual," her tone held just a touch of patient annoyance. "So, we called Steve and found out you weren't planning to go on to Chicago with the rest of the crew, and then we decided to come here and surprise you."

"Our plane got in at noon. We've been waiting for you ever since," Leah snapped, not hiding her irritation. "Where have you been? What have you been doing? And who is this with you?"

Gradually digesting her words, Dylan responded hesitantly, "Carolee, these are my daughters, Kristen and Leah. Girls, I'd like you to meet the lady from the picture you mentioned, Ms. Carolee Austin. Ms. Austin and I have been out sight-seeing."

Before the schoolteacher could voice a proper hello, the door to the other bedroom flew open, and out swept Marsha Walters, perfectly made up, and resplendent in a billowy gown and peignoir of creamy peach chiffon. She flowed across the floor toward them, practically swimming in a cloud of expensive perfume.

"I thought I heard the girls talking with someone. Dylan darling, it's about time you got back. We've been waiting impatiently all day." She gathered his bristly face in her long-nailed fingers, and planted a warm kiss on his lips.

"You need a shave, precious," she commented softly, and patted his cheek, before turning to the other women. "Ah, and who do we have here? The lucky prizewinner, I assume. Dylan dear, aren't you taking your responsibilities a little too seriously? This silly date thing was supposed to end last night, at your concert, wasn't it?"

Dylan looked back and forth between the two women, clearly unsure. Ignoring the impertinent actress, he turned to Carolee and took her by the shoulders, trying to make her look at him, and trying to drive the pain and disappointment from her brimming blue eyes. His attempt was unsuccessful. She twisted away from his grasp saying, "Miss Walters is right. I have intruded upon your time for much too long. Thank you again for everything, Mr. St. Claire. I'll always remember you and cherish our time together."

Gathering the last ounce of her strength, Carolee sprinted for the door, refusing to look back. The elevator car was still open, waiting and empty, so she ducked inside. She raised her eyes in time to see Dylan's handsome, anguished face framed by the doors as they slowly slid together.

PART X

The room phone was ringing when she reached her suite, but she ignored it, determined to put Dylan St. Claire, and the impossible hopes he had sparked within her, out of her mind. When it finally stopped, she laid the receiver off the cradle, pulled out her cell phone and dialed her home number.

Once she had assured herself that her sons were well and getting along fine without her, she cut the conversation short. They wished her luck on tomorrow's show. She told them she loved them and signed off.

After a quick shower, she pulled on clean underwear and a big cotton T-shirt, and set her mind to getting ready for the next day. Laying out the things she'd need for the broadcast, and flight home, she packed everything else, streamlining her morning regimen. Then she set her phone alarm to wake her at the appropriate hour, and climbed between the covers.

The night crawled by. Her troubled heart tormented her, despite her vain attempts to relax. The neck of the soft, oversized shirt seemed to choke her. She tugged at it with no relief, seeing visions of the gorgeous actress, so utterly delectable, in yards of peach chiffon, standing beside her, dowdy and dull in her favorite blue tee. That scene melted into another, even more disturbing, in which the handsome singer ignored her, and drew the young, glamorous bombshell into his welcoming arms.

Knowing it would be utterly stupid to hold onto any false hope, that Dylan would choose her over the seductive Miss Walters, she finally stopped struggling and allowed the tears to flow unabated. As she wept, one thing became exceedingly clear. She'd had a wonderful, magical weekend with the man of her dreams, but the fairytale was over. And though her head told her that her *Dream Come True* date had come to its inevitable end; her rebellious heart grieved the loss.

The tender songwriter's words echoed in her ears, and the memory of his kisses burned her lips. She would cherish those words, and those memories forever, but she would not allow herself to hope for more.

Hours later, having cried herself out, she drifted into a fitful slumber, finally rationalizing that Marsha Walters's sudden appearance had been a blessing after all. A quick break was best, she declared, before Dylan's magnetic appeal ensnared her completely. Though the pain was intense at the moment, she was certain she'd been saved from an even greater hurt later on. Better to face stark reality, than to hold out vain hope for something more with the popular star. Better to bear the sharp, unexpected twist of the knife now, than to be completely hacked apart, bit by bit, over the coming months.

The alarm woke her much too soon. A quick glance in the bathroom mirror confirmed her worst fears. Her eyes were impossibly swollen and red-rimmed. Retrieving a few remaining shards of ice from the bucket, she folded them inside a soft face cloth and held them over her lids, hoping the cold would work magic. It did help a little. Thankfully, the cosmetics Denise had given her provided excellent camouflage.

After doing what she could with her face, and dressing quickly, Carolee forced down a few bites of the delicious brunch that had been sent up to her suite, and gulped several cups of hot, black coffee. By the time Jason arrived, to carry her bags down to her car, she felt almost normal again. Taking one last look at herself in the full-length mirror, she smiled. The dark gray suit was most becoming. It made her look tall, statuesque, professional, and much more confident than she felt.

Both the bellman and the chauffeur offered her warm complements on her appearance, along with kind words of encouragement. Calling her 'Thanks," to the young man, she ducked through the door Arnie held open for her. He rounded the car and took his place in front, accelerating into traffic.

"Just want you to know it's been a real pleasure to meet you, young lady," the sweet old man told her. "I wish you and that St. Claire fella the very best o' luck."

"Thanks, Arnie, but I don't think I'll be seeing him again. His girlfriend arrived yesterday, so I'm sure he's already forgotten about me. They're probably on their way to Chicago by now."

Though she was surprised that she could discuss Dylan so unemotionally, she praised herself for thinking practically and realistically. It was better for everyone, she knew, that her budding romance with the pop music superstar had ended before it had really begun.

"Well, it's a shame, I say," the driver sighed, glancing at her in the mirror. "You two looked real good together, if you ask me."

"We were good together," she admitted. "But the fantasy couldn't last. A famous recording star and a simple schoolteacher? It would never work out."

"Still say it's a real shame," he grumbled. "Here we are." Stopping the car at the curb in front of the studio, he added, "I'll pick you up in this very spot, and take you to the airport, after you're done."

She nodded and slid out. Jennifer Thompson was waiting for her just inside the building. "Hey there. You're right on time. That suit is smashing." Carolee followed the assistant producer, letting her chatter on, without really listening.

"Denise is here to put the finishing touches on your make-up, but it looks like you've done a pretty good job all by yourself. When she's finished, I'll meet you in the green room." Not waiting for Carolee's acknowledgement, the young woman bounced off down a long hallway.

The cosmetician spotted the telltale signs of her client's restless night almost immediately. "You've been crying," she remarked, sympathetically patting Carolee's arm. "Don't worry. I'll fix it so no one will notice." While she worked, she couldn't resist the temptation to quiz her client about the talented, and decidedly yummy, Dylan St. Claire.

Carolee assured her that the man was just as good-looking, in the flesh, as he was in his videos, and that he was a down-to-earth, wonderful guy. Her feelings were still exquisitely tender, so she balked at revealing too many details about the time she'd spent with him. Instead, she spoke in vague generalities.

Denise took the hint, and bit off the other questions she obviously wanted to ask. It seemed to take all of her will power to keep further inquiry to herself.

Soon the reluctant prizewinner was ready to face the cameras once more. From the green room, Jenny led her onto the stage area, where she was mic-ed and seated in a comfortable chair next to Olivia's customary one. Carolee was alarmed that the broadcast would begin immediately, without any further preparation, but the producer assured her that a run-through would only ruin the genuine, spontaneous nature of her responses.

"Just be yourself and go with it. You're going to be fine."

The director yelled, "In 5… 4… 3… 2… 1." The lights blazed, and the audience rose to their feet, as Miss Olivia Wells made her entrance. When the applause lulled, the host introduced her guest.

"Hello and welcome, to the first follow-up show of our *Make Dreams Come True* contest. With us today is Carolee Austin, the winner of an evening with superstar singer, Dylan St. Claire. When we come back, you'll see all the best parts of Carolee's makeover, dinner with the man himself, and her trip to his concert this past Saturday night, here in Atlanta. Don't go away."

As promised, the next segment was a replay of the digital video footage Dale had recorded, at the salon and department store. Carolee was asked to narrate and comment throughout. A before-and-after makeover shot was shown, bringing "Ooohs" and "Aaahs" and a few "Wows!" from the viewers.

"You really do look wonderful," Olivia told her. "Was Dylan impressed?"

Flushing hotly, Carolee smiled and answered softly, "He was very kind, very complimentary."

"Oh, I think you're being too modest," the hostess prompted. "And we have the video footage to prove it. That and more when we return."

After a short break, clips from their dinner date were broadcast onto the huge screen behind the stage. The shot of the popular performer, as he appeared at the door of Carolee's suite, brought a roar of approval from the audience. "Looks like you had a nice long talk over your meal," Olivia observed. "Did you find out a lot about one another? Do you have anything in common?"

"Actually yes, we both have teenaged children, among other things." Carolee hedged.

"Well, well," Olivia sighed. "Bet there's more to this story, but in the interest of time, we'll move on to the concert. Roll that piece. Will you?" she directed the crew. A short snippet of Dylan's dressing room was displayed, followed by a couple of minutes from the performance itself, interspersed with close ups of Carolee's face, as she reacted to the songs he was singing.

"Did you enjoy the concert?" Olivia asked her.

"Very much. It was absolutely perfect. I had the time of my life," the embarrassed guest admitted.

"I'm so glad you did." The bubbly hostess squeezed Carolee's fingers affectionately. "And this, I believe, is one of the highlights of your evening with Dylan St. Claire." She gestured widely, drawing all eyes toward the enormous view-screen behind her.

Lights flashed, and the viewers went wild. The clip was the last few bars of "I Will Cherish You." Carolee stood at Dylan's side, her hands in his, while he sang his heart out, just for her. When the final refrain ended, he swept her into his arms and kissed her. Screams of delight, and sighs of longing, burst out of the women in the audience. For enhanced effect, a frozen image of Carolee, enfolded in Dylan's embrace, flashed across the screen, repeating and repeating, over and over.

"Wow, that must have been something!" Olivia exclaimed. "How did it feel to kiss Dylan St. Claire, on stage, in front of thousands of adoring fans?"

Her face was so hot she was afraid t it would ignite. She took a deep, soothing breath, trying to calm the knot in her stomach. Panic, bitter and sharp, clawed its way up the back of her throat. She swallowed hard. Silently ordering herself to suck it up, she forced a smile and answered, "It took me by surprise, and…was very nice."

Knowing what was expected of her and warming to the role, she added. "I'm sure all the ladies out there are dying to know. Yes, Dylan St. Claire is a great kisser. It was probably the best kiss I've ever enjoyed."

Obviously delighted with her guest's response, Olivia beamed at her encouragingly. "All of us here at the *Olivia Wells Show* are thrilled that you had such a wonderful evening. Would you say we made your dreams come true?"

"Yes. Definitely," Carolee confirmed.

"Good, then we did what we set out to do. But that's not all, folks. After a short break, we're coming back with one more surprise for our guest. So, stay with us." The dynamic hostess smiled into the camera until the red light went out.

"Surprise? What surprise?" the schoolteacher asked shrilly, unsure of her capacity to handle any more surprises.

"Don't worry," Olivia assured her, patting her hand. "You're going to love it."

A few terrifying moments later, the lights came back up and the cameraman signaled to the star. "I promised you a surprise, and here he is, in the flesh, my very dear friend, Dylan St. Claire!"

The audience was on its feet, screaming. Olivia rose, too, greeting the handsome singer with an affectionate hug. He smiled and kissed her cheek, before turning to Carolee. Taking the empty chair on the other side of the amazed guest, he slipped his fingers into her palm, and brushed his lips against her ear. "I told you that you hadn't seen the last of me."

Carolee was too stunned to respond. Her heart was pounding so hard against her ribcage, that she was sure the microphone would pick up its staccato beat.

Laughing brightly, the hostess teased, "I think our prize winner is shocked, speechless. So, tell us, Dylan, why did you rearrange your travel plans to be with us today?"

"Well, Olivia, it's like this," he began, his trademark grin prompting whistles and cheers. "This date with Carolee was a dream come true for me, too. She's a very special woman. Have you ever met someone and known immediately, that your lives were meant to be interconnected?"

The hostess signaled her agreement and understanding with a nod.

"That's what it was like for us. We just clicked. Carolee and I had a terrific weekend, so I wanted to come to your show today, to declare, publicly, that I think our relationship has real potential. She's skeptical, of course, and I don't blame her for that, so I wanted to be here, to make sure she knows that I intend to follow this through and see where it goes." When he shifted his gaze from the host to the teacher, she looked away to hide the tears filling her eyes.

"What do you mean, 'weekend?' We only arranged one evening for the two of you. Are you saying that you spent some time together that we didn't capture on video, time that wasn't officially part of the dream date?" the curious host probed.

Dylan nodded. "I talked Carolee into doing a little sightseeing with me yesterday. Atlanta's a beautiful city."

"Yes, it is, but you're not getting off the hook that easily, my dear. Carolee, what's the story here? Did you and Dylan St. Claire make a love connection?" She laughed at her clever phrasing, and directed another question at the prize winner. "We want the truth, now. What really happened between you and our gorgeous Mr. St. Claire?"

Taking a deep, fortifying breath, she answered, "We had a great time together. Dylan is a caring, thoughtful man, and I will never forget him. As he said, we made a connection. I felt it too, but I'm not sure what to make of it. I know your viewers would like a happily-ever-after ending to a fairytale love story, but that's not how it is. In Cinderella stories, the peasant girl may capture the heart of the prince, but in real life, the prince always chooses the princess."

"Are you saying there's no hope for the two of you?" Olivia asked, noticing the dark look of disappointment settling across Dylan's handsomely expressive face.

Carolee shrugged. "There's always hope. If Dylan can find time in his busy schedule, I'd be happy to stay in touch, to continue our friendship. But it would be foolish, and naïve, of me to expect anything more."

A small, pleased grin tugged at the corners of the man's wide mouth. "Just give me a chance. It's all I'm asking, Carolee." He lifted her hand and placed a tender kiss on her fingers.

"How about that, folks?" she prompted, and the crowd cheered once more. "I wish we had more time to spend with Dylan St. Claire and our first prizewinner, Carolee Austin, but the hour has flown, and we must say farewell until tomorrow.

"Join us then as we show you how we made our second prizewinner's dream, of reuniting with her long-lost family, come true. And be sure to bring your tissues. It's going to be a tear jerker!"

The music swelled as the credits rolled. The camera continued to record Dylan and Carolee, as he leaned toward her, trying to be heard over the deafening roar of applause. "You have to let me explain about Marsha. I called your room last night, but you didn't answer. I left you a message at the front desk, but you didn't pick it up. Please, Carolee, you're not being fair."

His eyes snapped with frustration when she failed to respond. "Man, I could throttle that ex-husband of yours, for what he did to you, for what he's doing to us!"

The director finally cried, "And we're out!" Dylan jumped up and waved an enthusiastic goodbye to Olivia and the audience. He ignored the pleading cries of protest from the jubilant crowd, and bolted for the soundstage door, pulling Carolee along behind.

Olivia caught up with them in the greenroom, and thanked Dylan profusely, for his unplanned appearance. "This was really a wonderful show. Better than I'd ever hoped." Noting the look that passed between her guests, she cleared her throat. "Well, I can see when I'm not wanted. Take care you two, and best wishes!"

As soon as they were alone, Carolee said bluntly, "Arnie is waiting for me. I have to get to the airport." The determined look in her clear blue eyes, and stubborn set of her chin, was intended to discourage.

During her sleepless night, she'd built a wall around her vulnerable heart, a wall she wasn't about to allow him to breach with a beguiling smile and a kiss on the hand. "There nothing to explain, Dylan. It's very clear to me that I am not the woman you need."

"Yeah, I heard that line about the prince and the peasant girl, and it's rubbish," he growled. "But I'll forgive you for being so short-sighted, because you're exhausted, and stressed-out, and wounded. So, I'll just say, I'm sorry I am for hurting you, and I'll let you go, for now, if you'll tell me how to reach you." He took a pen and a card out of his pocket, and waited for her to recite her cell phone number and email address. That accomplished, he kissed her soundly, leaving her more than a little weak in the knees.

"You think on that for a while, my lovely Carolee, and when I call, be ready to do some serious talking." His gray eyes shot fiery darts straight through her. Then he turned and left her without another word.

Moment later, Jenny appeared to escort her to the waiting car. Helping her guest inside, she chirped cheerfully, "Carolee, I'm really glad you had a good time. It was a fabulous show. You're the envy of women everywhere!"

"Thank you, Jenny, for everything," the forlorn teacher responded.

Seeing his passenger's pensive mood, Arnie turned the radio to an oldies station and drove in silence. When they arrived at the airport, he unloaded her bags and handed them to a porter. "Thank you, Arnie," she said, offering him her hand.

"My pleasure," he replied and kissed her softly on the cheek.

Carolee made her way through the enormous, bustling terminal in a fog of hazy emotions and confusing thoughts. Moving in a vague, exhausted stupor, she reached the proper gate, somehow, then managed to get onboard and seated comfortably, in the first-class compartment. Before the airplane took off, she was sound asleep.

PART XI

Brett and Bryce greeted her at the airport, all smiles, hugs, and jittery excitement. The short ride home was filled with rapid-fire questions, which she answered circumspectly. They insistently quizzed her about when they would get to meet Dylan St. Claire, in person. She warned them, repeatedly, not to get their hopes up, explaining that Dylan's schedule was very demanding, and that it might be some time before she heard from him again. They seemed to understand and accept her reasoning.

Bryce insisted she watch the videos of the shows, as soon as they walked in the house, but before he could get the DVR fired up, her phone rang. The caller was Cindy Lawrence, bubbling with excitement and another barrage of questions. Carolee cut the exchange short by promising to meet her friend later in the week, for a long lunch and a longer talk.

Almost immediately, her phone jingled again. This time, it was her mother, with her sister, Deborah, listening in on speaker. Mrs. Stone had been apprehensive about allowing Brett to drive to the airport, to meet Carolee's flight, and was much relieved to hear that he'd managed the confusing traffic patterns quite well.

Deborah wanted all the juicy details of her sister's dream weekend. It was a good twenty minutes before the tired traveler could break off the conversation.

The boys, restless with waiting, started playing a video game. "It's okay," Carolee told them, when the pesky cell jangled for the third time. "You guys enjoy yourselves. We'll watch the shows later. Looks like I'm going to have my ear stuck to this blasted phone all evening."

She answered with a forced, but cheerful, "Hello."

"Well, well, well, don't you sound pleased with yourself?" The caller's tone dripped disdain. "Who's been taking care of my boys while you were off making a complete fool of yourself, playing kissy face with some piece of Hollywood trash?"

"Hello, Bill," she responded meekly, heading for the kitchen, where she could talk without being overheard.

"Don't 'Hello Bill' me," her ex snapped, fury giving a cold, sharp edge to his voice. "What in God's name is wrong with you, Carolee? Explain it to me, if you can. How could you submit yourself to such public humiliation?!"

Not pausing for a response, he cranked up his attacked. "You are truly unbelievable! I know you're still upset about our divorce, but I can't believe you would deliberately set out to embarrass me, the father of your children. How could you do it? How could you go on national television, and make me out to be such a selfish monster? How could you cozy-up, so publicly, to that long-haired, self-promoting fake!"

Seeming to sense, by her silence, that Carolee might not be overly concerned about the wounds her television appearance had inflicted upon him, the calculating attorney shifted his attack to a more vulnerable spot. "How could you abandon our children, leave them to fend for themselves, while you fly off to indulge some foolish, adolescent fantasy?

Never mind what your self-indulgent, injudicious action has done to me, or to my reputation, I can't begin to imagine the distress your participation in this ridiculous farce has caused my boys. You're a mature woman, Carolee, with adult responsibilities, which you seem to have forgotten. My sons' well-being is one of those responsibilities. I'm sure Brett and Bryce are utterly humiliated by your indecent behavior."

Unable to hold her tongue one second longer, she snapped back. "I'm not the one who runs away from my responsibilities, Bill. And you know perfectly well that I would never leave Brett and Bryce alone. Mother stayed here while I was away."

Determined not to let him know that he was getting under her skin, she straightened her spine, and kept her voice low and calmly controlled. "The trip to Atlanta was their idea. Your sons entered the contest, Bill, for me. Let's just assume that you already know that, and you're feigning ignorance, to manipulate me into feeling guilty. Well, that tactic isn't going to work this time. Our sons aren't embarrassed by my TV appearances, not in the least. The question is, why are you?"

When his usually compliant ex refused to cave in as easily as he'd expected, he pulled out the most effective weapon in his arsenal. As he'd done, quite successfully, many times before, he attacked her self-esteem. "Dammit Carolee, stop being completely obtuse. I know you're not very sophisticated, or particularly intelligent, but you're not usually completely dense.

"You aired our dirty laundry in public, damaged my reputation, and potentially sabotaged my ability to support our children; nevertheless, my primary concern is for you. I can't believe you don't realize that you made an utter fool of yourself.

This whole contest thing was a stroke of marketing genius, and you fell for it hook, line, and sinker. Olivia Wells gets a huge ratings bonanza for her show, while that St. Claire prick gets sold-out concerts and platinum records. They used you, Carolee. How could you be so damned stupid? You played right into their hands, sitting there like an air-headed dope, all goo-goo eyed, over that slick, sickeningly artificial bastard, while he feigned sincerity and pretended to have fallen for you."

Her knees suddenly weak from his vicious attack, Carolee sunk helplessly into a chair, her stomach feeling like he'd punched her with a well-aimed fist. Numb and shaking, she listened silently, her gut a mass of knots, as his tirade continued.

"Did you think this contest was about some honest desire to make your infantile dreams come true? That's plain crap, and you know it. It wasn't about **you** at all. You and your dreams are not important to anyone. It was about money, and making more of it.

"Your wide-eyed, gullible display will foster the utterly ridiculous notion, in the heads of all of the other plain, average females, like you, that Dylan St. Claire is just a regular guy who wants a regular girl, and who just might notice them the same way he noticed you. They will flock to his performances, and he'll sell millions of his damn records.

"Gotta give the conceited bastard credit. He's a marketing genius. You're going to make the self-promoting jerk another frigging fortune."

"No, no, it's not… I mean, he's not like that," she stuttered, confused and unsure. She wanted to defend herself, and Dylan, but she didn't know how to begin, when Bill's accusations had put her worst fears into words.

"Don't tell me you've fallen for the slick bastard?" Bill snarled. "For God's sake, Carolee, you can't possibly be that pathetic. Take a good look at yourself. All the makeovers in the world won't put you in the same class with a superstar like St. Claire. Stop kidding yourself. You're never going to hear from the sonofabitch again."

He paused, waiting for her reaction. When none was forthcoming, he apparently assumed that his words were having the desired effect, so he softened his voice. "Look honey, you were duped and played for a fool, but you don't have to let him get the best of you, going forward. Honestly, I think the whole thing's over, but if the guy should try to milk it a little while longer, you know…call you and try to drag this charade on, to garner a little more free promotion…you just shut him down."

Carolee felt sick and disgusted. Bill's slimy, manipulative tone made her slightly nauseous. Intuition and experience telling her where Bill was headed with this phony pep talk, her voice was edged with skepticism when she asked, "How do you propose I do that? Dylan is so much more sophisticated and clever than poor old, backward me."

"Cut the flippant crap!" the insistent man, snarled, his calculated niceness disappearing without a trace. "Dammit, you know exactly what I expect, Carolee! If St. Claire phones, reject the call. If he texts or emails, tell him you're onto his deceitful, self-serving game and want no part of it.

"He won't be very persistent, I assure you. Look, you know I'm right. You don't really believe he has any interest in you. He's using you to keep other twits, like you, on the hook, making their farfetched fantasies seem possible, while they continue to buy his music. He'll move on quick enough, once you lay down the law.

"Now, you do what I say!" he demanded. "You hear? You're a grown woman, Carolee, and the mother of **my** children. What you do reflects on me, and on my sons. You will not go gallivanting off, like some star-struck groupie, panting after that conceited no-talent, who is only using you for self-promotion. I'll not stand for you embarrassing me like that again. Do you understand?"

"Yes, Bill, I understand completely." Righteous indignation bubbled up and overflowed, giving her a reserve of strength that she hadn't known she possessed. "I'm not nearly as stupid as you think. I know exactly what you want me to do. You needn't worry.

"When," she stressed the word. "When Dylan St. Claire calls, I will handle him appropriately."

"See that you do," he added, just for emphasis. "Now, let me talk to my sons."

"Sure," she agreed sweetly. "But, first there are just a couple of things…

Sighing with irritation, he broke in before she could finish, "What is it now?"

"Do not call me honey, sweetie, sugar, sweetheart or any other form of endearment, ever again. Do you hear me? You don't mean them, and they won't work on me anymore, so save your breath.

"And stop using profanity. It offends me. From now on, watch your mouth around me, and around the kids. Is that clear?" She couldn't believe she was speaking to him this way; but suddenly, she felt strong and empowered.

"No problem," he complied without rebuttal, hopefully surprised by the intensity of her demands.

"Then, I'll get the boys." She carried the phone into the den and handed it to Brett. "Your dad wants to talk to you." When Bryce screwed up his face in distaste, she shook her head at him. Carolee refused to encourage his negative attitude toward Bill, no matter how well deserved.

Leaving them to talk, she plodded, on wooden legs, into her bedroom, and flopped down on top of her comforter, completely drained. She could hear the boys' muted voices carrying in from the next room, as they chatted with their father. When the electronic beeping of the video game started once more, she hauled herself up and began unpacking.

Raised voices, emanating from the living room, distracted her from her task. She found them bickering, deliberately sniping at one another, faces drawn up in tight frowns and belligerent pouts. "What's going on?" she quizzed.

"Brett's being a bully," Bryce complained, sticking out his tongue at his brother.

"He started it, the big baby," Brett countered, throwing a Nerf ball in his younger sibling's direction.

"Did not!"

"Did so!" Seconds later they were rolling on the floor, fists flying.

"Hold it!" Carolee insisted. "That's quite enough. Get up."

Dragging Brett by the collar, she shoved him down in an easy chair, and pointed to another one on the other side of the room, throwing Bryce an I-mean-it stare. He meekly shuffled over and took a seat in the indicated place. Looking from one boy to the other she repeated, "One more time now, what's going on?" When no response came, a thought dawned, "What did your dad say to you?"

Brett glared at his brother, as if daring him to speak, but Carolee was determined to wait them out. It didn't take long for the softhearted Bryce to break down. "He jumped on us for entering you in that contest. He said we were silly, thoughtless children, and that you'd made a fool of yourself because of us." Tears welled in his pale blues. "Gosh, Mom, I'm really sorry. I didn't know. I guess I am just a silly kid, 'cause I thought it was cool."

Kneeling on the floor in front of his chair, she hugged him tightly. "It was cool. Your father's completely wrong. What you boys did for me was kind, selfless, and thoughtful. It was a thoroughly wonderful experience, and I had the time of my life. Your Dad's just angry right now.

"Think about it," she encouraged them, smiling. "I know it wasn't your intention to show your father in a bad light, but that's how it came across to him. He's too proud and stubborn to admit it, but deep down he feels badly about how his leaving has affected you guys, and having it talked about on national television was hard for him to take.

"To top it off, the old boring wife he threw away, is grabbed up by a famous, handsome man. He's probably been getting a lot of ribbing from his colleagues."

"He sure is mad," Brett added, deciding cooperation was best.

"I know he is," his mother confirmed. "Did either of you tell him you were entering the contest? Did you prepare him for it in any way?" Two downcast faces told her the answer. "Then, I imagine he was totally blindsided. His reaction is understandable, isn't it? From your dad's point of view, he believes he has a right to be angry."

"Did he say that?" Bryce asked, his face contorting with pain.

"Did he say he thought we tried to make him look bad, to embarrass him?"

"Oh, no, sweetheart, he knows better than that." She tried to soothe their worried frowns. "Your father won't challenge you, about what you said in the letter, because he knows you were just being honest. The thing is, he doesn't think he was wrong to leave. He believes he was fully justified, and will take on anyone who dares to disagree. He just hates being accused, publicly, without having the opportunity to defend himself.

"His complaints about Dylan and the show folks taking advantage of me, for ratings, is just a smoke screen. He's scolding you to make himself feel better. Your father knows your intentions were completely pure, and he would never dare to suggest otherwise. You told the simple truth, and you can't help it if that truth stings him a bit. Don't worry about it, guys. He's man enough to take it."

The older teen sat up and leaned forward, his dark eyes brightening. "That's right. All we did was tell it the way it happened. If Dad doesn't like it, that's tough. He shouldn't have left us if he wasn't ready to handle the consequences."

"Your father didn't leave you, Brett. He left me. No matter how he acts sometimes, your dad still loves you very much. Don't forget it," she told them, repeating the litany she'd used so many times before.

Trying to lighten the mood, she suggested, "If he's still this furious, can you imagine how he reacted when he saw the shows? I bet he was seething. Miss Clarice must have thought she had a raving lunatic on her hands."

Giggling, Bryce embellished, "He was probably screaming at the top of his lungs, stomping around, with his face as red as a beet."

Not moved by the comical image, Brett asked his mother, his brows drawn together in concern, "What did he say to you, Mom?" Taking a deep breath, she thought carefully before answering, not wanting to further prejudice her sons against their father.

"Much the same as he said to you. He told me the contest was nothing more than an elaborate publicity stunt. He said I'd made a fool of myself, and embarrassed him. He assured me that Dylan has no interest in me, and that it was all a big put-on. He told me to grow up and stop living in a fantasy world. If I do hear from Dylan, he ordered me to make it the last time."

"Yeah, he told us that, too," Brett added. "He said if Dylan calls, and either of us answers your phone, we're supposed to tell him to never call back." He stuck out his bottom lip in defiance.

"But I'm not gonna do it!"

"Me neither!" his brother chimed in.

"It's none of Dad's business if Mr. St. Claire contacts you. I can't believe he's so selfish. He's got a new life and a new love. Why doesn't he want you to have somebody?" Brett's brown eyes snapped with the injustice of it all.

"He probably wouldn't care, if that someone wasn't Dylan St. Claire. If I'd found a man who was less successful than your father, it wouldn't be an issue. But now, he's feeling threatened. He doesn't want me anymore, but it chafes him to know that a man like Dylan St. Claire might. So, to save face, your dad insists that the idea of Dylan having any interest in me, is a fabricated sham."

"Dad's not right, is he?" Bryce wondered. "It wasn't all a big put-on, was it? Mr. St. Claire sounded real nice on the phone. He didn't seem like he was fakin' it to me."

"No, he's not right." She tousled his fair hair playfully. "Dylan's a good guy, totally authentic. His intentions are completely honorable; but still, his work is extremely demanding. When he says he'll call, and promises he'll see me again, and meet you guys, he means it. I'm sure we'll hear from him, but I'm not expecting this to turn into a true relationship. I just don't think it's in the cards."

"Why not?" The younger son looked crestfallen. "I think Dylan really likes you."

Shrugging hopelessly, Carolee found it very difficult to express her apprehension, without exposing the excruciatingly painful conflict raging within her. "And I like him, but our lives are just too different. He needs a woman who's his equal in every way, talented, beautiful, and famous – not plain, unsophisticated, and ordinary."

Brett objected, "But, Mom, you're not..."

Carolee dismissed his attempt to dissuade her with a wave of her hand. "I have to be realistic about this, sweetheart. I can't give myself false hopes; my heart won't take another rejection."

Though the angry frowns and creased foreheads had disappeared, their handsome, young faces still showed strain and sadness.

"Hey, that's enough of this brooding over things we can't control. How does an ice-cold milkshake sound right about now? You guys could make a run to the Dairy Queen. Wha'da ya say?"

Grabbing the opportunity to exercise his driving muscles, Brett sprinted to retrieve the car keys, Bryce following closely on his heels. Carolee knew that, on long, hot summer evenings like this one, the popular restaurant would be crowded with Dogwood

Valley teenagers, out cruising and looking for something to do. She was sure the boys would run into some of their friends, and the quick trip would turn into something more prolonged. Thankful for some quiet time, she turned on the CD player, flopped into the recliner, rested her head against the back of the chair, and tried to clear her mind.

When she heard the first strains of "I Will Cherish You" emitting from the speakers across the room, she smiled. Relaxing and letting her thoughts wander, she had almost drifted off to sleep when her cell rang again, bringing her back to reality with a start.

Reluctant and apprehensive, she answered with a sharp, "Hello," her tone thick with the irritation.

"Wow, guess I caught you at a bad time," came a deeply melodic baritone from the other end. "Should I call back later?" The disappointment in Dylan's voice cut her like a knife.

"Oh, no, sorry. Actually, your timing couldn't be better," she assured him, feeling her heart melt, and unable to do a thing to stop it. This time when she spoke, her words flowed like silk. "It's wonderful to hear from you, Dylan, but I didn't expect you to call so soon."

"Who did you expect?"

"Seems like everyone I know has checked in since I got back, including Bill. I was afraid he might be calling back to berate me some more. He's pretty angry at me." She hadn't intended to involve Dylan in the conflict with her ex-husband, but the words had popped out before she could stop them.

"Why's he upset with you? You haven't done anything wrong that I know of, unless you've broken bad in the past few hours."

Despite his teasing tone, she could tell he was annoyed by her ex's unreasonable treatment of her.

"Can't say I have." She laughed, then hedged, "It's difficult to explain." Not wanting him to know that Bill had accused him of leading her on, and playing her false, she deflected, "I'm never quite sure why William Austin reacts to anything the way that he does, and I've stopped trying to figure him out."

"Good girl. Forget the guy. He's not worth one hair on your pretty head. He's probably just jealous, feeling sorry that he let you get away."

"He didn't let me get away, Dylan. He threw me away. And I don't think he regrets it a bit. He's just, well… He's just Bill. That's all I can say." Wanting desperately to talk about anything, else, she changed the subject. "Where are you, anyway?"

"Chicago, finally. I had to get my girls on a plane for California before I could catch my flight, so I just got in a couple of minutes ago." He sounded tired. "I need to get some sleep, but I couldn't turn in until I straightened things out with you, Carolee."

"Dylan, it's okay. Really it is. I understand," she offered, hoping to come across as upbeat and accommodating.

"No, Carolee, you don't understand," he insisted. "Listen to me, please. I need to explain about last night." Taking her lack of response for agreement, he went on, "My relationship with Marsha Walters never amounted to much. I told you that. I hadn't seen or heard from her in weeks. As a matter of fact, I never expected to hear from her again. Out of courtesy, I was planning to call her, one last time, just to make certain that she knew, that I knew, it was over.

"When she showed up at the hotel, I couldn't believe it. I was looking forward to an evening alone with you, and – bam! There she was. The shock knocked me for a loop."

"Why did she come?" Carolee whispered the question, afraid to hear the answer.

"I don't know for sure. She claimed that seeing a tabloid picture of us kissing, made her realize how much she cared for me, and how badly she felt for treating our relationship so casually. Personally, I think she just needed to prove that she could get me back on the string, whenever she wanted."

"And did she succeed?"

"Heavens, no, Carolee! How could you even imagine it?" His desperation seeped through the line. "I let her know, for good and all, that it's over, definitely and completely over. I told her she couldn't treat me like a child's plaything – tossing me away when she was bored with me, only to grab me up again, and fight over me, when someone else wanted me."

He paused to let the truth of his words sink in. "After that, I helped her pack, had Arnie put her on the red eye for LA, and spent a great evening catching up with my daughters."

Unable to suppress the smile tearing at the corners of her mouth, Carolee decided that she could spend the rest of her life listening to his precious voice.

PART XII

The week went by in a blur. Dylan called every day. Whenever Carolee or the boys were available, they chatted for a while. Other times, he left them a brief voice mail.

After the Chicago concert, the Dylan St. Claire entourage traveled east. Following performances in Boston, New York, Philadelphia, and DC, a whirlwind trip south to Greensboro and Charlotte was scheduled, before the performance company could head home, to Los Angeles, for a short rest. But despite his hectic schedule, Dylan seemed determined to stay connected. Carolee was impressed by his persistence.

As promised, she met Cindy Lawrence at their favorite neighborhood café, on Friday afternoon. Her dear friend was anxious to get a complete rundown of Carolee's trip to Atlanta, and weekend with the handsome singer. Putting the anxious librarian off until after the waitress had taken their orders, she finally offered, grinning foolishly, "Okay, shoot. What do you want to know?"

"Why everything, of course! Details, girl, details! Is Dylan St. Claire as dreamy in person as he is on TV? Is he as nice as he seems? What was it like being on *The Olivia Wells Show*? Is she cool or what? Was it fun shopping for all those clothes? What was it like, getting the make-over?" Cindy's words bubbled up and flowed out in a seamless stream of excitement.

"Hold on! Take a breath. Which question do I answer first? What are you just dying to know?" Her friend's enthusiasm tickled Carolee, and she couldn't help teasing her a little.

Pausing to think, as if the decision was critical, given the myriad of important options, Cindy waived a finger in the air and responded with an aah-haa look, "Is Dylan really a good a kisser, like you said on the show?"

Unable to suppress her amusement, Carolee burst into laughter, feeling like a giddy teen, sharing guilty secrets with her BFF. When the fit of giggles finally subsided, she nodded her head, tears dripping down her very pink cheeks. "Oh Cindy, he was better than good. I could hardly walk off the stage the first time he kissed me; my knees were so weak."

"The first time? You mean he kissed you more than once?" Her bright brown eyes flew open wide, and an incredulous smirk settled across her bow-shaped mouth.

Knowing she was rubbing it in, and not caring in the slightest, Carolee grinned smugly. "Yep, we kissed many, many times – in the car, in the elevator, and in my suite, among other places."

"In your suite? Dylan St. Claire was alone with you in your suite?" Cindy shook her curls in unbelief, happy for her friend's good fortune.

"Sure, silly, you saw the video of our dinner, didn't you? That was in my suite," she teased again, deliberately dragging out the explanation.

"Well, I know that, but I didn't see him kissing you there, not with the camera stuck in your faces. How many times was he in your suite? What happened on that sightseeing tour he mentioned on the second show? This is your old pal, Cindy, remember? Why are you keeping secrets from me?"

The pleading expression, on the librarian's pixie face, spurred Carolee to show mercy. She stopped stalling, and related the events of the entire weekend to her dear friend, in detail. When she was finished, Cindy sat in a stunned silence, staring blankly, in amazement. Opportunely, the waitress arrived with their sandwiches, giving her a chance to pull her thoughts together before responding.

They each took a small bite of the tasty fare, and chewed thoughtfully. The teacher waited expectantly for her best buddy's reaction. "You want me to believe that Dylan St. Claire spent the night alone with you, in your room, took you on a romantic picnic, in a secluded little spot in the woods, stripped to his skivvies to go swimming, made it very clear that he wanted to make love to you, and all you did was kiss?"

"Yep, that's what happened," Carolee said firmly.

"Good grief! What's wrong with you, girl? I would have jumped his gorgeous bones so fast he wouldn't have known what hit him." Cindy's tiny chin jutted out in fierce determination, setting Carolee off in another series of uncontrollable giggles.

"Cindy, you're terrible! You know that's not true. You wouldn't have had the courage to go through with it any more than I did, but don't think for a second I didn't want to. Dylan was…well, let's just say that I've never before felt the way he makes me feel," she admitted.

"Not with Bill?"

"No, not even at first." Carolee studied her hands for a few seconds before continuing. "Months before he walked out, Bill called me a cold fish. It really hurt. I'll admit that I rarely initiated love making, but I never turned him down, even when I was exhausted. I actually thought we had it pretty good, you know, in the bedroom. Clearly, he didn't agree. I guess I was just too naïve and inexperienced to know better."
She lowered her voice conspiratorially, and leaned closer to her friend. "It always took me a long time to get into it, you know, but if Bill was in the mood to be patient, I usually enjoyed myself."

Carolee flushed hotly and admitted, "He never turned me on with just a glance, a touch, or a word. I never felt about Bill the way I feel about Dylan. Oh my gosh, Cindy, when the man smiles at me, I melt. His kisses take my breath away. His voice sends shivers up and down my spine."

"I've said it before, and I'll say it again. William Austin is a complete jerk. Serves him right that you found a man who appreciates you, and gives you the love and respect you deserve. I'll bet your slimy ex is green with jealousy." The pert librarian's eyes twinkled gleefully. "I hope the thought of you and Dylan St. Claire, making a love match, is eating him alive. Serves him right."

"Don't count on anything much coming of this…whatever this is…with Dylan. It's a long, long way from being a love match," the wary divorcee warned her caring friend. "I have to be cautious, keep him at arm's length – for my own good. I don't think I could endure another heartbreak. Plus, I have my boys to think about. I don't want them to get their hopes up. You know I have to protect them, and set the right example for them. I can't let my heart rule my head, as much as I'd like to do just that."

"I understand, believe me. But I think there's something you're not admitting to yourself. You're running scared, afraid to love. You're expecting to be rejected and abandoned again. I don't blame you, Carolee, really, I don't. But Dylan isn't Bill. Give him a chance." She looked straight into her companion's soft blue eyes, and patted her arm. "Has he called yet?"

"Yes, every day," Carolee said, smiling tentatively.

"Every day! See there. He's a man of his word, a man you can depend on," Cindy tried to assure her.

"Maybe," Carolee agree hesitantly, fiddling with her fork.

"Bill says this whole thing is just a sham, a slick marketing promotion to get foolish women like me to buy concert tickets and stream his music. And when I look at myself in the mirror, I think he might be right. What could a man like Dylan St. Claire possibly see in me?"

"For goodness sakes! Why do you pay any attention to one word that conceited boor says? He proved his stupidity when he walked out on you. That's Bill's voice you're hearing in your head, chipping away at your self-confidence. Stop listening."

Cindy leaned in and added softly, "Carolee, sweetie, what does your heart tell you? In my experience, the heart is always right. You should trust your heart. It's a very reliable organ." The librarian's eyes, two shiny pools of warm chocolate, studied her friend with sympathy.

"It says…'Grab that wonderful man with both hands and hang on tight!'" Carolee croaked, choking back tears.

"Then do it," Cindy urged, taking the last bite of her sandwich, and following it with a gulp of iced tea.

"Dylan wants me to bring the boys down to the Greensboro concert next month. Do you think I should?"

"Ab-so-lute-ly! Stop playing it safe. What have you got to lose? Be courageous for once in your life. Go for it!" Her brown eyes twinkling, Cindy waved the waitress down and ordered dessert for both of them.

An hour later, her stomach uncomfortably full, Carolee hugged her old friend tightly, and ushered her into her beat-up SUV. Circling back to her own van, she headed for home. When she rolled into her driveway, the boys were sitting on the front stoop, waiting anxiously, soccer shoes in hand and sports bags thrown over their shoulders.

"Where're you off to?" she asked them, handing her car keys over to the eldest.

"We're gonna meet some of the guys at the high school field and kick the ball around a while," Brett informed her. "If it's okay."

"Sure. Just be home in time for an early supper. Your dad is picking you up at 6:30 sharp," she reminded them. "Do have your weekend bags packed?"

"Yeah…but I don't want to go to Dad's." Brett folded his long arms over his chest in defiance.

"I don't want to go, either," Bryce whined. "If I have to go, so does he."

"Come on, guys, you know you have to go. This isn't negotiable. Your father expects you. I'm sure he and Clarice have a lot of fun things planned for you to do." She hoped she sounded more optimistic than she felt.

"Yeah, right," Brett complained sarcastically. "All **she** wants to do is talk about their dumb wedding. If I have to look at another bridal magazine, I'm gonna puke. I wish they'd just elope and get it over with. It seems pretty stupid to me anyway. They've been living together for a long time, so why get married now?"

Surprised at his conclusion, Carolee asked, "What makes you think they've been living together, Brett?" Doesn't Clarice have her own apartment?"

"She does, and she never stays over at Dad's when we're there, but it's not hard to figure out that she's there the rest of the time. Her stuff's all over the house –you know, stuff like girly shampoo, pink razors, and makeup. His closet is full of her clothes, and she's always slipping up, and saying things that make it pretty plain they're living together. Dad gives her a dirty look when she does it, but that doesn't stop her.

"The last time we were there, he tried to change the subject, when she started complaining about his mattress being too hard to sleep on, and wanting to buy a softer one. But Clarice flipped out. She told him to stop being such a hypocrite, and to start being honest with us, because we're old enough to understand how it is."

"Sounds like there's some trouble in paradise." The possibility made Carolee smile, despite her annoyance at Bill for setting such a poor example for his sons.

Sticking to her promise, not to engage in any overt criticism of him, she encouraged her sons instead. "All the wedding hubbub will be over in a few of weeks. I'm sure you can stand it until then. And honestly, I know you guys are going to look smashing in your tuxedos. I wish I could be there to see you."

They grimaced simultaneously. "Hey, I just remembered something," she interjected, hoping to lift their spirits. "The last time Dylan called, he invited us to come down to his concert in Greensboro next month. Would you like to go? He'll be on a tight timetable, arriving the morning of the performance and leaving immediately afterward, but he said we could spend a couple of hours on the bus with him, before the show. And we can see the concert from backstage. What do you say?"

"Wow!" Bryce exclaimed, his eyes wide. "That would be awesome!"

"Yeah, I could go for that," Brett agreed with more composure. "But what about Dad? He'll have a fit when he finds out we're planning a trip to meet Dylan."

"To borrow an old cliché, what your father doesn't know won't hurt him. The timing is perfect, because he and Clarice will be in Paris, on their honeymoon. So, if you guys can keep it a secret, he'll never know."

She placed a quick kiss on each forehead and shooed them off. "Go on now, you're going to use up all your playing time. Be home by 5:30. Be careful, and have fun." An eager light shining in their young faces, they hurried off to meet their friends.

As ordered, the boys were home right on time, rushing to shower while Carolee put the final touches on dinner. They were shoveling in the last few bites of barbecued chicken, macaroni and cheese, and steamed broccoli, when their father strode into the kitchen, his manner as presumptuous and demanding as usual. His fiancée followed closely behind him, looking smart and professional in a bright, form-fitting, lime-green suit, and spiky, patent leather pumps.

Ignoring the accusatory look Carolee shot him, for barging in without knocking, Bill greeted his sons, a superficial smile plastered on his thin lips. "You guys ready? Clarice and I have a big weekend planned. So, hop to it. Chop! Chop!" He clapped his palms together for emphasis.

When Brett and Bryce looked at her for permission to leave the table, Carolee saw irritation flicker across the serious attorney's darkly attractive visage. The forced smile evaporated, and a stern scowl replaced it. Automatically appeasing him, Carolee urged them, "Go get your things. Don't keep your father waiting."

Picking up their dirty plates, silverware, and glasses as they rose, they deposited them in the sink, and bolted for the stairs, the younger hot on the heels of the elder. "Hold it just a minute!" Bill bellowed, when they blew past their stepmother-to-be without a word of acknowledgement. "March right back here and say 'Hello' to Clarice."

Dragging their feet, they turned back. "Hello, Clarice," they mumbled simultaneously.

"Hi, boys," she returned smugly.

"Now, go do as your mother told you," Bill ordered gruffly. Once they were out of earshot, he rounded on his ex-wife. "I can see we have our work cut out for us this weekend, trying to get those two in line. What in God's name is wrong with you, Carolee?

"Don't you know anything about discipline? You're spoiling them rotten, dammit, and I won't stand for it! The next time

Clarice and I arrive here, we **will** be treated with proper respect. You don't seem to have the backbone necessary to instill proper manners in my sons, so I'll have to take them in hand."

Surprisingly calm and unaffected by his bluster, Carolee told him, "It's funny, Bill, but I rarely have any trouble with Brett or Bryce. They're always polite, considerate, and respectful to me, just as I am to them. Perhaps the way they behave around you, is a reflection your treatment of them. Did you ever consider that possibility?" Not waiting for his response, she added, "No, of course you didn't."

His face darkened threateningly. "This is all your doing, you conniving, vengeful bitch. You're trying your best to turn my boys against me, and I won't have it. Whatever you're telling them to undermine me, it had better stop immediately! Do you hear me?"

"How could I help it? The entire neighborhood heard you." She smiled sweetly and replied in a hoarse whisper. "I have never deliberately demeaned you in front of our boys. As a matter of fact, I've gone out of my way to make excuses for you, even to apologize for you, when you stomped all over their feelings, or selfishly ignored them.

"No matter what has gone on between us, Bill, you're still their father, and they're bound to take any criticism of you to heart. I would never hurt them by attacking you. Despite what you think, I want them to love you, and to be proud to be your sons."

"Bullshit!" he spat.

"Bill, stop," she pleaded. "You're an educated man with a vast vocabulary. I warned you about the profanity."

"Why have you become such a prude all of a sudden?" he accused, more enraged than ever. "My choice of words never bothered you before."

"No, it always bothered me. I just didn't have the courage to speak up about it before," she informed him softly.

"Is that right? So, what has given you such guts now, your little tete à tete with that St. Claire bast...uh, Dylan St. Claire?" He took an aggressive step toward her, trying to intimidate. "I was right about him, wasn't I?"

Deciding that avoiding this battle was the best tack to take, Carolee lowered her eyes, unconsciously biting her lower lip, and allowed him to draw his own conclusions.

Taking her submissive posture as the affirmation he expected, his calculated grin slid back into place. "Good. Maybe one of these days you'll learn to listen to me. But I doubt it." He turned away, the dismissive gesture clearly indicating that he was finished with her.

He might be done, but she wasn't. "I listen to every word you say, Bill." Her eyes shot blue fire. "Unfortunately, you refuse to give me the same courtesy." Caught off guard by her biting tone, he whirled back to face the challenge.

"Why should I listen to you? You never say anything important," he accused, arms folded aggressively across his chest.

His unmitigated arrogance inflamed Carolee's temper. "Well, hear this and make your own judgment about its importance." She stood facing him, toe-to-toe, and fired back. "This is our house, Bill, the boys' and mine. Do not come waltzing in here like you own the place. If you want to teach your sons to respect you, you can start by respecting them, and respecting me."

Taken aback by the ferocity of her tone, he stepped back. "My, my, if you haven't turned into a little hellcat. Got your back up and claws out, all ready for a fight, haven't you? Be careful, Carolee. You don't want to make an enemy out of me," he warned, dark eyes snapping.

He aimed his most intimidating glare at her, and for several long seconds, the atmosphere cracked between them, with megawatts of negative energy. Clarice cleared her throat to bring Bill's attention back to her. After a quick glance in the younger woman's direction, the man's demeanor changed abruptly.

"But then again, I don't take on weaker opponents, who have absolutely no chance of winning. It isn't very sportsmanlike. So, have it your way, this time, Carolee. I'll honor the sanctity of your dreary little cottage. It is yours, as you say, though I've no idea why you're so possessive of it. It's certainly not much to be proud of."

The reappearance of Brett and Bryce cut his rebuttal opportunely short. Clapping both boys on the back, he beamed at them. "Great! You're ready, finally. Let's go."

"You go on ahead, Bill," Clarice ordered her fiancé as he helped gather up his son's bags. "I'll be right there. I just need to talk with Carolee a minute, in private."

As soon as the boys, and their father, disappeared out the front door, the hard-charging lawyer cornered Carolee in her tiny kitchen, where the younger woman used her aggressive green suit, and impossibly high heels, to their fullest advantage. Clad as usual in a faded T-shirt and denim cut-offs, the former Mrs. Austin felt like a defenseless gray mouse being stalked by a brightly feathered, heavily clawed bird of prey.

"Bill might be hesitant to take you on, since you're the mother of his children, and you make him work hard to protect them from your devious machinations, but I have no such compunctions. I'm on to your little game," her green eyes shot darts of pure vitriol straight at Carolee.

"What game, Clarice? I have no idea what you are talking about," the older woman replied, shocked and amazed by the unexpected attack.

"Don't play stupid, Carolee. Your, not-little-old-naïve-me act might fool Bill, but it doesn't work on me. You've played this whole thing with Dylan St. Claire and the *Olivia Wells Show* for everything it's worth. I have to give you credit, though, you've been very clever. But I see it all for what it really is – a ruse, a well-thought-out ploy to get your revenge against Bill, by publicly humiliating him.

"When you heard about the contest, you convinced the boys to play along with your scheme, and got lucky. But your lucky streak has come to an end."

Carolee opened her mouth to protest, but before she could utter a single syllable, Clarice redoubled her siege. "As an attorney with a well-respected firm, I have more than a few well-placed contacts. I called in a favor from one of my friends in Atlanta."

Patting her slim leather briefcase, she continued, "I have right here, in my possession, an eye witness account placing you and Dylan St. Claire together, in your suite, this past Saturday night…all night.

"The sworn statement says that you and he left together on the following morning, and confirms that you went with him, to his rooms, when you returned to the hotel. Should I allow this information to fall into Bill's hands, you know that he would immediately file for full custody of his sons, since it proves, in no uncertain terms, that you are an immoral, unprincipled, and totally unfit mother. You, my dear, with all your high and mighty airs, are nothing more than a groupie slut."

Heart pounding in her ears, Carolee's thoughts whirled frantically. Did Clarice really have what she claimed? Who had seen them, kept track of their comings and goings? Stomach clenching, she realized that any of a dozen or more staff members – maids, waiters, valets, and even front desk personnel, could provide information regarding her whereabouts, and Dylan's, while they were in the hotel. Room service had been in and out of her suite, and likely his as well, on numerous occasions.

It was more than possible that her comings and goings had been noted, and well documented. She hadn't slept with Dylan, or stayed the night in his suite, but eye-witness evidence to the contrary would be damning. The light went out of her eyes. She chewed her lip in anxious frustration.

Sensing an imminent victory, the wily attorney went in for the kill, "Not that I blame you. Any woman in her right mind would jump at the chance to get naked and sweaty with a hunk like Dylan St. Claire. Actually, I'm pretty impressed that you could pull it off. Can't imagine the guy being that hard up, but maybe he likes banging skanks. Too bad for you, though. Judges won't see it the way I do. Most of the ones I know expect the mothers of teenaged sons to set a good example for their impressionable adolescent offspring, not to go bed-hopping with rock stars."

"Clarice, don't do this, please," Carolee begged, fear welling up inside her. "My boys are everything to me." She wanted to deny the charges the daring young lawyer was making against her, to explain what had really happened, but one glance at the gleeful look of victory in Clarice's sea-green eyes, told her that any attempted explanation would be a waste of breath.

"Well, then, you'd best remember that, hadn't you? If you want to keep the boys, that is. Now, here's what you're going to do." Clarice moved in closer, waving an orange-tipped nail in Carolee's face. "You will follow Bill's orders, to the letter, particularly where this St. Claire business is concerned.

"Bill thinks it's over, but I'm not convinced. Keeping the gullible public thinking St. Claire is interested in you, a plain little homemaker, will definitely sell his songs, and I think he'll milk the sham a while longer. So, I'm not taking chances. I don't want any rumors flying."

She lowered her voice to a hiss. "If I get the slightest hint that you're in contact with the man, if I see any photographs, or hear any gossip, whatsoever, I will place these affidavits into your ex-husband's expert hands. I will not be made a fool of – by you or anybody."

Wrenching up her courage, Carolee swallowed hard and said, "Before I agree to your demands, there are a couple of things I need to understand."

"Of course, by all means, let's make sure everything is completely clear."

Ignoring Clarice's condescending tone, she asked, "Why are you doing this? I know Bill's angry, and rightfully so, but how does any of it reflect badly on you?"

"How could it not?!" Clarice ranted, enraged. "You go on national television, making my fiancé out to be a selfish, heartless man who abandoned his poor, sweet, deserving wifey, leaving her heart-broken and helpless. Then you get all lovey-dovey with a famous recording star, who pretends to be interested in you.

"I can't believe you're so naive. Your calculated, selfish actions were a direct attack on Bill, and by association, on me. You've made my fiancé the laughing stock of the partnership, and you know it."

"If that's true, I'm sorry." Carolee felt her self-confidence returning slowly. She calmed her teeming emotions, and took control of the conversation, determined to get in at least one shot.

"If the public disclosure, of truthful details surrounding the breakup of our marriage, makes you, or Bill, feel guilty, then perhaps there's just cause. But whether you believe me or not, I didn't set out to point fingers."

"Don't give me your self-righteous crap! You knew exactly what you were doing when you put your boys up to entering that contest. I'm onto your vindictive game, and I'm putting a stop to it." Clarice's fair complexion flamed red, which clashed with her suit.

"Okay, all right." Carolee held up her hands in mock surrender. "I'm not to have any contact with Dylan St. Claire, or you will make sure Bill gets a copy of the lies and embellishments you've collected against me."

"That's right," Clarice declared. "Finally, you've got it!"

"Since I don't have your experience in the courtroom, I'll have to take your word about the likely outcome of a custody suit. Though I do wonder if a fair, open-minded judge would really be more likely to chastise a mother than a father, for similar offenses.

"What do you mean?" the younger woman asked, obviously curious to see where her adversary was heading with this line of thinking.

"If you and Bill go before the court, with this so-called 'proof' of my unfit behavior, then you'll have to explain why you're living together, without the benefit of marriage." she paused, watching Clarice's face closely. "What will the judge say when I present evidence that you were having an adulterous affair, prior to our separation, an affair which precipitated that split?"

"You can't prove anything," Clarice challenged.

"Are you sure?" Carolee asked, her blue eyes sparkling.

Going back on the offensive, Clarice struck again. "By the time a petition could get on the docket, Bill and I will be legally married, so your petty allegations would be inadmissible. The causes of the divorce would be irrelevant. The suit we bring would be about your parental fitness – or lack thereof.

"Besides, you've totally missed the point, as usual. It doesn't matter if the accusations I hold are true. What matters is that, if you defy Bill's demands, you will be forced to fight it out in court, in front of your sons. I will make it as painful as possible for you. I enjoy fighting dirty." The thought of that terrifying possibility turned Carolee's blood to ice water.

Realizing she had struck her opponent's weakest spot, Clarice smiled slyly and twisted the knife. "With a case like this, involving a man like St. Claire, it would be all over the internet, exposed in the tabloids, broadcast from coast-to-coast. Bill and I would love the fight, and the exposure, our firm would profit immensely from the publicity, but would you? How would your boys feel about having their mom labeled a self-serving whore, a gold-digging groupie, in front of the entire world?"

Recognizing that she was completely outmatched by the unscrupulous attorney, in the sneaky and underhanded department, Carolee acquiesced, her shoulders sagging, "You've made your point. You win, Clarice."

PART XIII

In mid-July, the days turned swelteringly hot, making the thought spending an entire day dressed in stiff, scratchy tuxedos almost unbearable for Brett and Bryce. The closer it came to their father's wedding day, the more they whined. It was only the anticipation, of the planned excursion to Greensboro, that kept them pacified and cooperative. Carolee didn't have the heart to disappoint them, so she kept putting off telling them the trip wasn't going to happen.

Dylan continued to call her almost every day, pressing her to commit to the concert. She kept the conversations short and superficial, knowing she had to end all contact with him, but dreading the inevitable, unbearable emptiness that would follow their final goodbye.

On the evening of the wedding rehearsal, it was still a blazing ninety-two degrees, when Carolee shuffled her sons off to the church, amid a hail of protests and complaints. Home alone, the house blessedly quiet, she made a glass of iced tea, and curled up in front of a fan, with the new suspense novel she was anxious to read. She jumped, heart pounding, when her phone chimed, startling her out of a deeply intriguing passage.

"Hello," she answered, taking a deep breath to settle her frayed nerves.

"Hello, beautiful," Dylan's warm, honeyed tones sounded from the other end, raising goosebumps, and quickening her pulse. "Whatcha doin'?"

"Just sitting here reading, and feeling sorry for myself," she admitted before thinking.

"I wish I could be there with you, to kiss away your blues," he breathed, his sensuous voice sending shivers down her spine. "What's got you down?"

"The kids just left for the rehearsal. The big wedding's tomorrow, and I well, I..."

"Oh, the ex's wedding, yep, I understand," he said, and she knew he did. "You're feeling left out and rejected, but you know what? You should be feeling relieved."

"Why's that?" she asked, warming to the exchange.

"Another woman has finally taken your hateful ex off your hands, spoiled, pain-in-the-fanny that he is. Now he can boss **her** around and leave you alone," he finished.

"If only that were true," she sighed, her heart heavy. "Clarice is a lot smarter than I am, when it comes to dealing with Bill. She's already grabbed the upper hand in their relationship."

"Good for her," Dylan crowed. "The man needs someone to take him down a peg or two, and show him his place."

"Maybe, but that doesn't help me or my situation." Carolee's stomach twisted into a tight knot, as she tried to get up the courage to tell him their budding relationship was over. Her long silence spoke volumes.

"Something else is bothering you, Carolee. What is it? Tell me. Whatever it is, I can handle it. I might even be able to help," he encouraged and assured her.

"Dylan." She whispered his name, softly, lovingly. It felt so wonderful, tripping off the end of her tongue. "We aren't going to be able to come down to see you in Greensboro." Before he could object, she added, "And…this is the last time we can talk. As much as I hate it, I have to break things off. Our friendship can't go on any longer."

Shocked and disappointed, he demanded, "Why? What's happened, Carolee?"

"I... I can't explain," she stuttered, tormented by the pain and longing in his voice.

"You have to!" he cried. "You owe me that much. If you don't tell me what's going on, right now, I'll cancel this tour, park my bus up in front of your house, and wait until you do. Is that what you want?"

"No, Dylan, no, please. You deserve to know everything, but it's just too hard to talk about." Tears of agony tore at her throat.

She knew he could hear the hoarse sound of her breathing, ragged and strained, and hoped he could feel the torment this decision was causing her.

"Calm down, sweetheart," he urged her softly. "It's all right. Take your time. Start at the beginning and tell me everything."

Allowing his soothing baritone to seep into her, straightening out her jumbled thoughts, she began with a deep sigh, "The day I returned from Atlanta, Bill called me, positively livid. I told you about it, remember? He accused me of making a fool of myself, and of humiliating him. He demanded that I break things off with you, immediately."

"You obviously didn't take him seriously," Dylan noted.

"Not at first. I couldn't bear to let you go," she admitted. "I thought he was just angry, because he'd gotten a little ribbing from his colleagues, but apparently it goes much deeper than that."

"I'm sure he was mortified to see the woman he threw away, looking like a million bucks, and being swept off her feet by another man. It proved to the whole world that he didn't know a good thing when he had it." The caring singer's words had a ring of truth that she couldn't deny.

"It pricked him fiercely, that the man who did the sweeping, was famous, talented, and gorgeous," she added playfully.

"You think I'm gorgeous?" he prompted in the same teasing tone. "Then why, my dear Carolee, do you still shun my attentions?"

"Hang on, there's more to the story," she parried, feeling more relaxed and comfortable with the disclosure. "Initially, I dealt with Bill as I had in the past, by telling him what he wanted to hear and then doing as I pleased, until the clever Miss Clarice intervened."

"Clarice?" he asked, puzzled.

"Yeah," she verified. "She threatened me, Dylan. If she finds out that we're still in touch with one another, she'll push Bill to file for custody of Brett and Bryce, by accusing me of being an unfit mother. I should have broken it off immediately, after she confronted me with her demands, but I couldn't bear the thought of losing you. I've been taking a terrible chance, letting things go on this long."

"You, unfit? Impossible! She can't have any grounds for such an accusation. You're a wonderful mother. I can't imagine that Bill could build any case against you." Dylan's surprise was plain, as was his confusion.

"Clarice claims to have a sworn statement, from someone at the Southern Hospitality Hotel, who says that you spent the night in my suite, the Saturday I was in Atlanta. And also claims that I went with you to your rooms, on the following evening.

"She's sharp and ruthless, Dylan. A weapon like that could be very destructive in her skilled and vindictive hands," Carolee told him, choking back tears. "She'll paint a horrible picture of me. I'll come out looking like a gold-digging groupie who slept with a man she barely knew, just because he's famous."

"Who in the world did she talk to?" he asked, fury building.

"It could be any of the hotel staff," she answered, "maids, valets, and servers were in and out of our suites all weekend. And I'm sure there were surveillance cameras everywhere. The only time I didn't pass a hotel employee was when I left your suite, Sunday night. So, there are many people, and likely video footage, that could provide eye-witness testimony against me. In the right hands, with the right editing, and with the right twist, it could be very incriminating."

"But we know nothing happened, Carolee." He sounded desperate. "Let him sue. We'll tell the truth, and that will be the end of it."

"It's not that simple, Dylan. I can't take a chance on going to court, period. I can't put my boys through such an ordeal. If this comes before a judge, Bill will be vicious and merciless. He'll say unbelievably damaging things about me – and about you. Can you imagine the fodder that would be for the gossipmongers, the tabloids?

"No, Dylan, I won't risk it. I won't have my good name and reputation destroyed in front of my sons, and I won't damage your career with the bad press. No, this…this…whatever this is between us, is over. There's no choice."

"Carolee, you know what this is between us, even though you're still trying to deny it. Your heart feels a connection to me that is deep, and real. I can't believe you're giving up so easily." Amazement, tinged with anger, came through in his hoarse whisper.

"I'm being realistic, Dylan," she coaxed. "Yes, I have very strong feelings for you, but no matter how I hard I try, I can't see a future for us. We're too different; our worlds are light-years apart. Saying good-bye now will not only save us heartache, it will protect your career, and my sons."

"I reject your conclusion, Carolee. We could make it work. I know it. But you're giving up without a fight, and that infuriates me." She could imagine his face, arched brows wrinkled in determination, full lips drawn tight, strong jaw jutted forward stubbornly, and it wrenched her heart.

"I won't endanger your family, but if you think I'd sacrifice you for the sake of my career, then you don't understand me at all. I'm ready and willing to go the distance here. Let's face them down, together. I think that sneaky, controlling witch your ex is marrying is bluffing, big time. Maybe he's getting what he deserves after all." Dylan was clearly ready for a fight.

Doubt seeped in, making her question the decision she'd made. "What makes you think Clarice is bluffing?"

"She's trying to bully you," he said, "but she's played her trump card too soon."

"What do you mean?"

"Does she know you're defying Bill's gag order?"

"I doubt it. Brett or Bryce would never tell, and I certainly haven't."

"Then why is she pulling out all the stops, to guarantee that you break off our relationship, when she's not certain one still exists?" Not giving her the chance to respond, he answered for her,

"I'll tell you why. She's scared stiff.

"I've known a few women like her, the sort who not only like to win, but delight in leaving their opponent ravaged. Once she gets someone down, she wants them to stay that way. Taking Bill away from you was a victory she relished, as long as you were the defeated, helpless victim.

"But, your growing independence and confidence, and the potential for a budding romance with me, moves her out of the winner's circle and you into it. She's left with the consolation prize, and she can't stand it."

Carolee was still uncertain. "You could be right. But if she is who you think she is, won't she do exactly what she threatens – force Bill to file for custody, wage a bloody court battle, and do whatever she can to take my boys from me?

"Not at all." Dylan seemed smugly sure of himself. "A prolonged court battle, involving me, would bring entertainment reporters, and rumor hounds, out in droves. Clarice would be crazy to take a chance on having her unethical behavior exposed. You did say she and Bill were carrying-on long before he left you, didn't you?"

Sensing where he was headed and gaining confidence, she confirmed, "Yes, and I can get sworn testimony to prove it. I can also prove that she used her affair with Bill to get special privileges within his firm."

"Good girl," he praised. "Now you're getting the idea. If you show her that you're willing to play her game, show your hold cards so to speak, then my bet is you won't have to call her bluff. She'll fold, because you have the better hand."

"I like that analogy," she admitted, somewhat relieved.

"Then grab your boys, hop in the car, and drive down to Greensboro to see me," pleaded. "I'll take measures to ensure that we're not disturbed, and you're not recognized. No sense borrowing trouble, if it can be avoided. My twin will be happy to act as a decoy, to keep your ex and his new wife off your trail."

"Sounds like a lot cloak and dagger stuff," she hesitated.

"Come on. It'll be fun," he encouraged.

"The truth is, I'm aching to see you, and the boys are over the moon about the trip. I've been putting off telling them that it was off, because I couldn't bear seeing the disappointment on their faces," she admitted.

"See, now you won't have to. Aren't you happy I called?"

She imagined him grinning from widely, and she shivered at the image. "I'm always happy when I'm talking to you. It's the time in between calls when I feel empty."

"Yeah, me too," he responded, his voice low and heavy with emotion. "I didn't realize I was so lonely until I met you, Carolee. Now I feel like you ripped my heart out of my chest and took it with you.

"Maybe I could arrange an unscheduled stopover. It wouldn't be too much of a detour to swing west, as we roll through Virginia on our way south. Imagine what your neighbors would think if my big old bus pulled up in front of your door."

"This little town would never be the same," she giggled, deeply moved by his declaration. "It would add four hours to your travel time, just to drive by and wave. And blow our cover in the process. A motor coach with *Dylan St. Claire* emblazoned all over the side might be a dead give-away. It'll be better if we meet you at the coliseum in Greensboro."

"If you insist," he joked, then added, "I'll make the arrangements, but don't you back out on me, Carolee. I can't wait to hold you again." Before she could respond to him, voices and noise in the background distracted him.

When he came back a moment later, he excused himself, saying, "Sorry, but I've gotta go. The crew needs me to do a sound check before the doors open for early seating. I'll call you soon to firm up details for next week."

"Dylan, break a leg, huh? Bye." She hung up smiling, her heart lighter than it had been for a week.

On Saturday afternoon, in spite of the blazing sun and smothering humidity, the society-showcase wedding, of Clarice Gordon and William Austin, went off without a hitch. As predicted, the young Austin groomsmen looked very dashing in their charcoal gray cutaways. Carolee anxiously awaited their return, from the reception at the local country club, so she could get the scoop on the much-anticipated event. She wanted details on everything, from the bride's dress, to the church decorations, and the menu for the lavish celebration that followed.

It was well past midnight when she heard her old van pull into the driveway. Brett and Bryce were hot and tired, but still excited and full of information. They told her that their dad had looked good, in his expensive, well-tailored tux, but honest Bryce admitted that he thought Clarice's pristine, white dress, and billowy veil, had made her look a bit green.

Recalling the bride's brassy, orangey-blond hair, green eyes, and golden complexion, Carolee was surprised that she hadn't chosen a more flattering, ivory or cream gown. They all had a hearty laugh when Brett announced that he thought the redheaded bride had looked like a huge, flaming meringue.

As they shucked out of their uncomfortable formal wear, her sons expounded on everything they could remember about the extravagant production. All the partners and important clients of Franklin, Mattox, and Austin had been in attendance, of course, along with numerous members of Clarice's extended family.

Bill's brother and his wife had made an appearance, along with his mother, though the regal Austin matriarch hadn't appeared pleased. Brett and Bryce had been seated with their grandmother at dinner, and said she'd been uncharacteristically quiet. Though she was always a woman of few words, her reticence at the reception had gone beyond her normal reserve. The boys guessed that she was angry with her son, for abandoning his family and for marrying Clarice, pointing out that there didn't seem to be any love lost between the bride and her new mother-in-law.

The very last thing Brett said, before sauntering off to bed, was that he would be relieved when Bill and his new wife left for their month-long honeymoon in Europe. His weary, frustrated tone told Carolee that he needed a break from the pressure his dad regularly put on him. His younger brother echoed his sentiments, declaring that he was sick of Clarice's incessant interrogation. Smiling encouragement, Carolee thanked them for their loyalty, and promised to make the last month of their summer vacation as much fun as possible.

A week later, they piled into Cindy Lawrence's beat-up SUV, laughing hysterically at the outrageous disguises they'd devised, and cruised south. Getting into the spirit of the clandestine adventure, Carolee had dug up the long, brown wig, Bill had insisted she wear after she'd started to go gray, and tucked her platinum-streaked locks beneath it. A pair of holey, cut-off bib overalls, frayed cotton shirt, and battered cowboy boots completed her Daisy Mae outfit.

Brett had chosen a preppy approach - Izod shirt, khaki trousers, and deck shoes, topped with a cool pair of sunglasses, while Bryce had gone for the skateboarder look - long, baggy shorts, a voluminous 'Dragon Force' T-shirt, run-down Vans, and a worn baseball cap turned around backwards. Cindy rounded out the foursome, looking like an out-of-place biker chick in her tight jeans, Harley Davidson crop-top, shiny black ankle boots, and bandana.

The tiny librarian had been thrilled when her friend asked her to tag along, on the trip to meet the St. Claire tour. She'd quickly offered up her aging, but reliable, transportation, in hopes of throwing the more diligent paparazzi off the track.

Just before they reached the Greensboro Coliseum, Dylan sent his twin off in a hired limousine, accompanied by a beautiful, young woman from his backup chorus, and then notified security to deliver Carolee and her entourage discretely to his bus, as soon as they arrived.

As expected, the ruse worked. The largest group of paparazzi followed the long black car, as it sped out of the parking lot. The few who stayed around were serious photographers, who busied themselves taking shots of the staff and crew, as they set up for the performance.

Dylan laughed so hard he doubled over, when he saw the ridiculous disguises his guests had chosen. Then he took his time openly admiring the long length of leg Carolee's shorts displayed.

The singer's down-to-earth sincerity, and irresistible warmth, won the boys over with little effort, and charmed Cindy into a bashful silence. Dylan arranged for his chief technician to show Brett and Bryce around the control booth, and they enthusiastically jumped at the chance to see the magic behind the scenes.

They were given V.I.P. passes, and treated to great back-stage seats in the wings, during the concert. Afterward, the handsome singer hugged Carolee tightly, and kissed her soundly. Then he shook the boy's hands, and told them to take care of their mother. The little librarian flushed hotly when Dylan gave her a goodbye peck on the cheek, and thanked her for playing chauffer.

Once they reached the car, Cindy found her voice again. She babbled continuously, all the way home, while the boys played the new video game apps the singer had given them, allowing Carolee time to daydream. Ignoring the chatter, beeps, and whoops, she thought about the way Dylan had looked at her, the way he'd kissed her, and the way her body had responded. She let herself hope that she'd see him again, soon.

Reviews of the Greensboro concert hit the media early Sunday morning. <u>USA Today</u> ran an online piece, by an ambitious freelance writer, featuring photos he shot of Dylan's twin leaving the parking lot of the coliseum, in the company of the sexy back-up singer. The pictures were picked up by entertainment news outlets and blasted all over the country.

Legitimate music critics' columns claimed, "The Dylan St. Claire concert tour just keeps getting better and better," while tabloids screamed, "Fickle Heartthrob Dumps Talk-Show Teacher for Curvaceous Cutie." Monday editions of *Entertainment Tonight* and *E! News* picked up the story and embellished upon it. Carolee was delighted.

PART XIV

Summer drew to a close in a whirlwind of pre-school preparations. In early August, the school administration offered Carolee a full-time contract for the fall term, in the position she'd previously filled at Thomas Jefferson High. After a couple of phone calls, she found out that Ms. Parks, the teacher she'd been subbing for, had voluntarily resigned from her job, to stay home with their baby girl. Satisfied with the offer, she happily signed the one-year agreement, returned it immediately, and made a lunch date with Cindy and her sister, Deborah, to celebrate her good fortune.

Brett and Bryce spent their days hanging out with friends, at the neighborhood pool or soccer field, and their evenings watching streamed movies, playing cards, or battling it out on video games. Carolee knew it was killing them to keep their visit with the Dylan St. Claire tour a secret. It would be an impressive story to tell, sure to earn them more than a few brownie points with their peers, but they fought the temptation to brag, and kept mum. Their mother was grateful for their sacrifice.

Dylan completed his concerts, and returned to Los Angeles and the recording studio. He called and video-chatted frequently, offering to send airline tickets, so Carolee and her sons could fly out to visit him and his family. But since Bill had returned from his honeymoon, the concerned mother was afraid to take the risk.

No matter how desperately she yearned to talk to Dylan, their conversations became more and more painful for Carolee. Each time she heard his voice, her heart leapt for joy, and each time she said goodbye, that same, delicate organ ached to bursting.

Talking to Dylan filled her with great joy, but in the spaces between calls, she was left feeling abandoned, lonely, and hopeless. Sometimes she could hear the longing in his voice, too, making her acutely aware that his feelings mirrored hers. Never had she gone from such exhilarating highs, to such excruciating lows, in a matter of minutes. Never had she felt such love mixed with such pain. Through it all, though, she kept faith, faith in herself and her newfound independence, faith in Dylan and his assurance that one day soon he would hold her in his arms.

Once the fall term began, Carolee's family fell into a comfortable routine, as the boys' resistance to the alternate weekends with their father eased. The fortuitous publicity, hinting at a budding romance between Dylan and his young back-up singer, pleased the new Mrs. William Austin immensely.

When the newlyweds dropped by to pick up Brett and Bryce, they treated Carolee with benign condescension. Though she was grateful to have them off her back, their I-told-you-so smirks irked her. She wished she could set them straight.

As fate would have it, Dylan's twin was quite taken with the up-and-coming performer, and had dated her several times after their return to L.A. The ever-present paparazzi follow them, cameras snapping, giving the gossips more fat to chew. The look-alike had perfected his photographer-dodging skill so well, that any shot taken of him was easily mistaken for a photo of his employer.

Dylan was also impressed by the woman's talent, and was helping her cut a solo demo record, which guaranteed her continued cooperation with the deception. It didn't hurt that she was developing a strong affection for Dylan's double, and enjoyed spending time with him, tricking the publicity-seekers, especially since the St. Claire tour was paying the tab.

As Carolee reluctantly dressed for her dreaded class reunion, two wishes occupied her thoughts. The first was to give up the charade, go public with her relationship with Dylan, and accept the consequences. The second was to blow off the upcoming ordeal, and stay home with her kids. But knowing she could do neither, she tugged up her pantyhose, grimacing. She was obligated; Cindy had made her promise to make an appearance tonight, and she hadn't, as yet, gotten up the courage to take on Bill and Clarice.

Slipping on the soft, cornflower blue dress the *Olivia Wells Show* had purchased for her, she breathed a relieved sigh. The elegant frock was perfect for this occasion. With back-to-school expenses, she was strapped for cash, and couldn't afford to purchase a new outfit. She struggled with the difficult zipper for several minutes, before finally achieving success.

She found her sons watching a baseball game. Brett looked up when she walked into the room, and whistled. Bryce's mouth flew open. "Wow, Mom, you look great!"

"You think so?" she asked, encouraged by their praise, but still not feeling up to the challenge facing her.

"Yeah," they chimed-in together.

"You're gonna turn every head in the room," Brett added, trying to reassure her.

"Oh, heavens," she sighed, "that's the last thing I want to do. I'll be thrilled if nobody notices me, but that's not very likely. My plan is to put in a short appearance, stand quietly in a corner somewhere, and slip away as soon as possible."

"That won't be any fun," her younger son told her, his eyes alight. "You should have a good time. Think about it. Your old classmates will want to know all about your trip to Atlanta. That'll be great, right?"

"Maybe, if I could tell them the truth," she answered, shaking her head sadly. "But I'll look pretty silly, talking about the wonderful time I had on my date with Dylan, when they all think he's moved on to a much younger, more beautiful woman. Just like your father did. It's going to be so embarrassing."

"Aw, Mom," Bryce whined. "Don't say that. You'll be as pretty as anyone there, prettier even, and I know Dylan will think so too."

Brett coughed and elbowed his brother. "You mean Dylan **would** think so, **if** he was going to be there."

"Yeah, that's what I mean," he amended.

Ruffling his fair hair with affection, she smiled. "Thanks, sweetie. You're so thoughtful. If Dylan were here, I'm sure he'd be just as complimentary as you guys, because he really knows how to make me feel special."

"Well, you are special," her eldest son affirmed, bringing tears to her eyes. Retrieving the van keys from the hook by the front door, he called, "You ready?"

"I guess," she signed deeply. "You don't have to drive me. I'll take the van so I can come home when I want."

"Absolutely not," Brett insisted. "It could be late, and we won't have you driving home alone. Danny Lawrence said he'd drop you off afterwards; and besides, Bryce and I might need some wheels later on."

Chuckling at his take-charge attitude, she acquiesced, "Okay, okay, but if you do go out, text me so I'll know where you're headed… and don't be too late."

"Sure, no problem," he agreed, grinning sheepishly.

The short jaunt to the high school took only a few minutes. Brett deposited Carolee at the cafeteria door, waving as he wheeled away. Taking several deep, calming breaths of the cool autumn air, she steeled herself and went inside.

Her friend, Cindy Lawrence, was the first to greet her. As chairman of the committee, the librarian had been responsible for all of the arrangements for the reunion, and was anxious to show off the attractive decorations.

The two walked arm-in-arm around the huge room, which was usually set up to seat and serve hundreds of hungry teens. The transformation of the facility, from functional lunchroom to elegant ballroom, was miraculous.

The center of the tiled floor had been cleared to make room for dancing. A dozen or so, tastefully appointed tables remained, spaced around three walls. The overflowing buffet enticed early birds to fill their plates from a wide variety of delectable choices. On the fourth wall, a raised, skirted platform had been erected, so the band could be seen above the crowd. The musicians had already taken their places upon the risers, and were busily warming up, their sequined jackets sparkling. Aside from the spotlights highlighting the buffet tables, stage, and dance area, long, white tapers, set in glittering silver candelabra, provided the only illumination.

"You've done a fantastic job, Cindy," Carolee praised her buddy. "Everything looks gorgeous."

"Thanks," Cindy said, grinning from ear to ear. "As do you, my dear. You're a knockout! Clarice is going to be sooo jealous."

"I doubt it very much, but thanks anyway." The taller woman shook her fair head. "At least I hope I won't get too many pitying looks."

"Don't worry. This is gonna be great. Wait and see." Hands planted firmly on her hips, Cindy looked like a determined pixie.

"Fix yourself a plate and something to drink. Danny saved us a place over there." She indicated a table between the buffet and the stage.

"Okay," Carolee agreed, anxious to move to an inconspicuous location. "But let me know if I can help you. I'm sure you have your hands full."

"Hey, you know me. I wouldn't be happy without a dozen irons in the fire. Thanks, I'll holler if I need you," her friend called back to her, as she scurried away to answer a summoning wave from the caterer.

Rich, sweet food was the last thing the nervous woman wanted in her roiling stomach, but a cold drink sounded good, so she headed for the beverage service. Everything on the buffet looked scrumptious, but nothing tempted her. On the very end of the long stretch of linen-covered table, behind a crystal punch bowl filled to its sparkling brim, a hired bartender waited. At her request, he filled a tall glass with ice, and poured it full of ginger ale.

Drink in hand, she retraced her steps. She'd almost reached the safety of the seat Danny Lawrence had staked out for her, when a familiar, yet decidedly unwelcome, voice stopped her.

"Yoo-hoo… Carolee, over here!" A taffeta and lace bedecked form trotted across the dance floor in her direction, beckoning. It's Marlo, Marlo Grimes, remember? Well, it's Marlo Cravens now." Tossing her sable-brown mane, still cut in the eighties, mall-bang style she'd worn years ago, the determined woman maneuvered herself between Carolee and the safe haven she was seeking.

"Hello, Marlo, of course I remember you. How've you been?" Squirming like a mouse cornered by a big Persian cat, Carolee pasted on a polite smile.

"I wasn't sure it was you when I saw you over here. You've changed so much." Marlo's dark eyes twinkled with mischief, and her lips drew up into a wide smile. The two rows of tiny, sharp teeth, revealed by that smile, reinforced the prowling-feline image.

"No offense, but the last time I bumped into you at the grocery store, you were positively dumpy, but now look at you. Those *Olivia Wells* people did a great job on you."

Carolee offered her a non-committal, "Thanks," silently noting her former classmate's failed attempts to maintain her youthful appearance. The dark hair dye, thick make-up, and gaudy jewelry Marlo had chosen, made her appear old and outdated. Tactfully, the taller woman added, "You haven't changed much."

Not put off by her target's lack of enthusiasm, Marlo went on, patting an imaginary stray lock back into place, "We all do our best with what we have, don't we?" It was clear that Marlo Grimes Cravens thought what she had was better than most.

"I'm so sorry to hear about you and Bill, though I must say, I wasn't shocked. It's the thing successful men do these days – trade in the first wife for the trophy wife, especially when the old wife let's herself go to pot. I'm sure it must have been terrible for you."

"Yes," Carolee admitted, wishing she could be somewhere, anywhere, else. "It was pretty rough."

"Well, you sure are looking great now. That little fling you had with the singer, what's his name, St. Claire? That must have helped you get over Bill. I bet the old boy was green. Bill was always insanely jealous, couldn't stand for any other guy to glance in your direction. Pity the thing with the singer didn't work out. It would have served Bill right for dumping you."

Marlo had always been shameless in her pursuit of interesting tidbits or tempting hearsay, particularly when it was at the expense of anyone who was more popular than she. In high school, Carolee had often been pricked by the sharp barbs that flew off her glib tongue with practiced ease. It was clear the scheming woman's character hadn't changed. If anything, she'd become more callous and jaded than she'd been at eighteen.

Carolee edged away, but the determined cat sensed her attempt to flee, and cut off her escape. "Your recent escapades are the topic of the hottest gossip in town. You must tell me, Carolee, what was it like, hooking up with that gorgeous hunk of a man? Is he really as sexy as he looks?"

Her thirst for scandal spurred her on. "On the second show, he said you two spent the weekend together. You did you sleep with him, huh? You're a fool if you didn't. Of course, knowing your prudish ways, I bet you didn't have the guts.

"What did Bill say? He was livid, wasn't he? But maybe, since he's gotten himself such a beautiful, young wife, he's given up on running your life. Come on, Carolee, out with it. I just have to know all the juicy details."

"There's really not much to tell, Marlo," the cornered woman explained, fighting to control her rolling stomach. "My trip to Atlanta, and time with Dylan, was great, but it's over now, and I'm going on with my life. If you want to know Bill's thoughts on the subject, you'll have to ask him."

"Oh, I see," Marlo smirked, going in for the kill. "Dumped by two men in a matter of months. Poor thing, I can't even imagine the pain and humiliation. How did you get up the nerve to come here tonight? I'd be hiding at home, afraid to show my face. You are sooo brave."

A flurry of activity at the entrance distracted her. "Oh, look. Speak of the devil. There's Bill now, with his new bride. I must go greet them. I'm dying to get his take on this. Bye, Carolee. Take care, huh?"

Sighing with relief, Carolee's bright blue gaze followed the retreating busybody. Her noisy taffeta gown rustling loudly as she crossed the dance floor, Marlo's trek claimed the attention of everyone in the room. All eyes were on the conniving woman by the time she reached the newlyweds.

Unable to force herself to look away, Carolee was caught staring, self-consciously, at her ex-husband and his new wife, when Marlo gestured in her direction and the threesome turned to regard her. Flushing hotly, the embarrassed woman's imagination ran away with her. What was that trouble-making female saying about her? From the looks of smug satisfaction on the faces of Mr. and Mrs. Austin, it was clearly something denigrating. Carolee turned away, wishing she could fall through the floor.

To her relief, Danny Lawrence noticed her distress and came to her rescue. Taking her elbow, he led her on shaky legs, to the seat he'd saved for her. Dropping into the chair he held, she whispered, "Thanks," and offered him a sad smile.

Sensing Carolee's need to calm her ragged emotions, Danny sat quietly, giving her time to settle. After a couple of minutes, he told her, "Don't let them get to you, gal. They're just jealous. You're the first celebrity this town has ever had."

"Oh, so now I'm a celebrity?" she quipped, thankful for his thoughtful attempt to lighten her mood.

"Sure. You're famous," he replied, nodding in affirmation.

"Infamous is more like it," she corrected.

Chuckling at her wry sense of humor, he observed, "You have to admit, old Bill looks pretty sharp tonight, and Clarice isn't half bad either – a bit on the obvious, slutty side for my taste, but not bad."

Taking note of her ex-husband's dark, well-tailored suit, spotless white shirt, and classic red, striped tie, she was forced to agree, "This marriage seems to suit him. There's no doubt he and Clarice were made for one another." His new wife was resplendent in a slinky gold cocktail dress and her usual high, spiked heels. They're a striking couple.

"You're not bothered by that." Danny's comment was a statement, not a question.

"No. I'm glad that part of my life is over. A few months ago, I wouldn't have imagined it, but I'm much happier now, without Bill, than I ever was with him." She smiled thoughtfully, beginning to feel better. "I was afraid to come here tonight, afraid of seeing Bill and Clarice together, of being humiliated in front of all of our old classmates. But, you know, I just realized that it doesn't matter to me anymore."

"For real?" he asked.

"Yeah, I can't keep defining myself by what others think or say about me. The contest, the TV show, the concert, my time with Dylan, has drawn a lot of attention to me – unwanted attention, but attention still. People know my name now, and some, like Marlo, are dying to see me belittled, put back in my place, and made to pay for my fifteen minutes of fame. But I don't have to give them that pleasure, do I?"

"No, you don't," he encouraged. "Keep your chin up girl, and this evening may be more fun than you think." He patted her hand in a friendly gesture of reassurance. "Oh, look, there's Cindy," he added, pointing toward the stage.

"Attention everyone!" the tiny librarian announced. "On behalf of the Class of 1991 of Thomas Jefferson High School, and the twenty-fifth reunion committee, I want to welcome you all to a great night of fun and fellowship. Please help yourselves to the food and refreshments. The music will begin shortly, but first, we have a very exciting surprise. As most of you know, one of our classmates, Carolee Stone Austin, recently had the pleasure of being a guest on *The Olivia Wells Show,* where she was introduced to the brilliant singer-songwriter, Dylan St. Claire."

Despite her efforts to remain cool and unaffected, Carolee felt heat rising up her neck, and her heart pounding furiously in her chest. It took a tremendous effort to concentrate on her friend's words, and ignore the eyes boring holes into the back of her head.

She could hardly believe her ears when Cindy said, "Though you may have read tabloid stories to the contrary, Carolee and Dylan have maintained a close relationship. In fact, I had the pleasure of spending some time with him myself, a few weeks ago, at his Greensboro concert. That's when he told me he wanted to surprise Carolee with an appearance here, tonight.
Let's show him that good old TJHS school spirit. What do you say? Here he is folks, direct from Los Angeles California, live and in person, Dylan St. Claire!"

PART XV

Murmurs of stunned disbelief greeted the popular singer, when he moved out of the inconspicuous spot behind the drummer, where he'd been waiting. Flashing his dazzling, heart-wrenching grin, he winked at Carolee, who stared at him, open-mouthed. A wave of cheers and applause built gradually, as the audience reacted to his magnetic appeal. The clamor grew louder and louder, until the tall, charismatic man raised his arms to call for quiet.

"Thank-you, thank-you," he said, taking the mic from its stand, and stepping up to the very front of the platform. Dressed in a black, form-fitting suit, pearl gray shirt, and coordinating tie, he looked more handsome than ever. When his shining eyes, alight with anticipation, touched on her again, Carolee shivered, every nerve aflame, anxiety knotting her stomach.

She was desperate to see Bill's reaction, but she couldn't take her eyes off Dylan, as he put his million-dollar voice to work. His velvety tones brought involuntary sighs from many of the women in the group. "It is truly a pleasure to be here with you this evening. I'm very grateful to Cindy Lawrence for inviting me." He motioned for the band to strike up the first chords of his latest single.

When the song was finished, he had to beg for silence once more. "You're too kind," he told them. "I promise I'll do another number for you a little later, but right now I want to spend some time with my dear friend, Carolee." Bowing gallantly, he jumped down from the stage, and crossed quickly to the vacant seat beside the surprised teacher.

"May I join you?" he asked her, his warm gaze shooting straight into her heart.

Unable to speak, she smiled and nodded her welcome. He pulled out the chair and dropped into it, leaning over to take her fingers in his, and brush his lips across her cheek. "You look gorgeous tonight, my love," he whispered against her ear. Then he asked, his face buried in her hair, "Is everyone still looking at us?"

Once again, Carolee nodded, dumbfounded. "Come on then. Let's give them something for their trouble." As if on cue, the band launched into a soulful version of "When a Man Loves a Woman." Smiling a challenge, Dylan rose and offered her his hand. "Honor me, please, Carolee."

Unable to refuse him, she placed her palm in his. Seconds later, they were gliding gracefully around the dance floor, his lean, hard body pressed tightly against hers, his warm gray eyes devouring her adoring, upturned face. For several long minutes, they continued to be the center of attention; but before long, a few of the other couples gave up their ogling to join them, swaying to the beat.

When the music stopped, several classmates approached and introduced themselves, anxious to meet the well-known star. Carolee noticed Bill and Clarice, standing within earshot, and the knot in her gut twisted again. They listened without comment, though their faces were drawn into closed, angry masks.

For the most part, Carolee's inquisitive classmates were courteous and polite, but a few hinted that they'd heard the rumors linking Dylan to his back-up singer. When Marlo Cravens openly confronted him on the issue, he simply laughed, saying, "You shouldn't believe everything you read in the gossip rags."

Clearly anxious to talk privately with Carolee, he insisted, "Please excuse us. I promised my lovely partner another dance. The music swelled as he whirled her onto the floor. About half-way through the number, Dylan grabbed her hand and led her outside. The night air was cool and refreshing. It caressed her face like a lover's breath.

"Why, Dylan? Why did you come here?" she asked him, her tone frightened and bordering on frantic. "Bill and Clarice are furious. Don't you realize the trouble they'll make for me?"

"Shh, shh," he soothed her, enfolding her in his strong arms, kissing her hair. She knew he could feel her body shaking in anguish. "I wouldn't put you or your family in any danger. Trust me, Carolee. I have things under control, and I couldn't stand being away from you one more day." Pulling back, he stared into her glowing face for a long second, then lowered his mouth to hers, trying to drive the tortured look from her tear-filled eyes.

"Ah, hem!" A harsh bark broke them apart. "Sorry to interrupt this touching little reunion, but we have a couple of things to clear up here, Carolee." Recognizing Bill's voice immediately, Carolee stumbled backward in dread.

He swaggered toward her, belligerently, his stocky body aggressively poised for action. Though his face was partially shadowed, it was easy to see the fury in his dark, snapping eyes. Clarice followed closely on his heels, ready to back-up her man. Dylan, anticipating trouble, placed his taller, rangier form between Carolee and the advancing threat.

"It's no use trying to hide behind your fickle lover." Bill spat.

His arrogance infuriated her, pushing back the fear and allowing her suppressed anger to bubble to the surface. "It's okay, Dylan," she said, touching his shoulder. "What do you want, Bill?"

When Carolee stepped forward to face him, the furious attorney snarled at her, "You're going to listen to me, and do what I tell you. Do you hear? I warned you to stop this ridiculous farce, but you refuse to show any common sense.

"Now you've forced my hand. Clarice told me how you two carried on in Atlanta. I am shocked and appalled, Carolee. Despite all your shortcomings, I never imagined that you were also a whore, but then you continuously surprise me lately."

"It's nice to hear I've put a little excitement in your life," she needled, her serene smile giving no hint to the fury burning inside her.

"You bitch!" he shrieked. "I'll wipe that silly grin off your face with a petition for sole custody of my boys. You won't be nearly so smug when the judge demands that you defend your immoral behavior."

Determined not to be cowed by his attack, Carolee responded, "I'm sure you can recognize immoral behavior when you see it, Bill, since you have first-hand experience with adultery."

"Wha... What do you mean? I never...," he stuttered, obviously taken off guard.

"Don't bother to deny it. I have more than enough proof. Just ask your assistant about it, if you dare." Carolee's blue eyes flashed dangerously. "Go ahead, Bill, take me to court. Let's see whose character proves to be the most lacking."

When her new husband stood sputtering, searching for words, Clarice jumped in, her pointy chin stuck out belligerently, and her voice shrill, "If you want a fight, bitch, you've got one. But I warn you; we'll wage a battle that will make your life a living hell. Even if you win, and keep your sons, in the end your relationship with them will be ruined. I will personally make it my goal to destroy you!"

"Hold on just a minute," Dylan interjected. "Let's not let our tempers get the best of us."

"Shut-up, St. Claire!" Bill shouted, his face scarlet. "Stay out of this. You've caused enough trouble, by indulging Carolee in this stupid fantasy. It's time she stopped this foolishness and started behaving rationally, or else make ready to suffer the consequences of her injudicious actions."

"I guess 'behaving rationally' means being your doormat, quietly putting up with all the crap you and your pretty mistress dish out. Right, Austin?" Dylan's gray eyes snapped indignantly. "And those consequences are your unfair, malicious attempts to separate her from her sons? Well, this stops right here. You will not be filing suit against Carolee, now or anytime in the foreseeable future."

"How dare you?" the lawyer ranted. "You can't tell me what I will, or will not, do!"

"I wouldn't be so sure about that." Flashing his signature grin, Dylan expounded, "At ten a.m. this morning, I signed a contract with your firm's controlling partner, Robert Mattox, authorizing Mattox, Franklin, and Austin to serve as my advocate and agent, in all future professional negotiations. I implied that it was Carolee who had prompted me to seek out this partnership, and I insisted that **you** handle my portfolio, personally and exclusively. In case you're not following me, Austin, this means you work for me now."

"B... b... but you can't! I won't!" he choked. "I won't work for you."

"Oh, you will, unless you and your ambitious young wife want to go looking for new jobs." Dylan draped a long arm around the shorter man's shoulders. "Cheer up man. We're going to make loads of money together."

Leaning in conspiratorially, he added, "You'll be able to buy sexy, little Clarice here all the nice things she demands."

Carolee was delighted by the look of utter disbelief clouding her ex's darkly handsome visage. Dylan clapped him on the chest, playfully, and asked, "So that's the end of the petty threats. From now on, you're going to be caring and supportive, for the sake of your sons and your ex-wife."

When Bill's shoulders sagged, and he sighed his acceptance, Dylan beamed. "Wise choice. Now come on. We're missing the party."

Leaving the newlyweds outside, angrily sniping at each other, Dylan tucked Carolee's hand into the crook of his elbow and led her back inside.

"You're unbelievable!" she told him. "My knight in shining armor." Hugging him tightly, she offered up her lips to be kissed.

He graciously accepted. A long moment later, he responded, "Why thank you, my lady. I'm always happy to come to the aid of a damsel in distress."

"But won't this cause problems with your business manager?" Carolee was pleased with his clever solution to her situation, but concerned that Dylan had created additional problems for himself.

"The contract I had with Steve expired over a year ago. I hadn't done anything about changing it, because I thought I was proving something by staying with him, showing Sandra that I'm a better person than she is, or something ridiculous like that."

Dylan's handsome face twisted with distress. "When I started thinking of ways to help you out, it occurred to me that, by hanging onto the past, I was hurting myself, dredging up old pain, every time I spoke to the man. I finally realized it was time to move on."

"But do you think you can trust Bill? He can be very vindictive. Aren't you afraid he'll sabotage your career? He might not do something deliberately, but he has no experience representing show business talent."

"I've thought this through completely, Carolee," he assured her. "I did my homework, and from what I can gather, despite his numerous personality flaws, the guy is a top-notch attorney. He does his homework, and he's a quick study on whatever project he takes on. He's earned the respect of his peers many times over.

Obtaining this contract for his firm is a coup of sorts, so he'll be expected to make it highly profitable for his partners. He won't be allowed to fail. Besides, my future is pretty well established, and I have PR and promotion people to handle the pieces Bill can't. There's not too much he can do to screw things up, even if he tries."

"I hope not. I'd hate to be responsible for the downfall of a pop music icon," Carolee teased him, her heart fluttering like butterfly wings. "Of course, if such a come-down would mean we could be together more often, then maybe I should re-think things entirely."

Pulling her into a quiet corner, partially hidden from prying eye, he held her close and whispered, "Don't worry, my love. I've taken care of everything. Before you know it, you're going to be tired of having me around."

"Never," she denied.

"I hope you're right," he said, his devilish grin setting her nerves tingling. "Because I'm moving to Dogwood Valley."

"Here? You're moving here?" she uttered in disbelief. "Your job, your family… they're in LA. How can you move here?"

"You're here. So how can I not?" He studied her face intently. "I can work from anywhere, Carolee. Airline connections are easy to make. My girls are excited about the change. Leah's been unhappy with her current school for a while, so she's anxious to give your old alma mater a try. Matter of fact, she came with me.

Brett and Bryce are taking her on a tour of your town as we speak." Carolee shook her head in amazement.

"Kristen started college at William and Mary in August. She's thrilled that I'm going to be living four hours away, instead of clear across the country." A look of smug satisfaction settled over his face.

"But what about Sandra? Won't she make a fuss? You're taking her girls away from her, and a huge wad of money out of her new husband's pockets."

"Sandra's never had much interest in our daughters, but I'll send the girls to visit her in California whenever they wish, which will probably be more often than she'd like. As for my partnership with Steve – that's none of her business, and I'll be happy to tell her so. She never expected me to be a success, so why should she benefit from any of the profits my career generates?"

"But what if your girls don't like me? They didn't seem too happy to meet me at the hotel in Atlanta." Pressing back the surge of hope swelling within her, Carolee angled for reassurance.

"Don't worry about Kristen and Leah. They'll find you every bit as endearing as I do, once they get to know you, away from the negative influence of conceited starlets. Besides, whatever pleases me, pleases them. They just want me to be happy, and being with you makes me happy." His gray eyes sparkled with excitement.

"Trust me, my love. I've thought of everything."

Not yet willing to give into the joy that was rapidly filling her heart, she made one final attempt to assure herself that he had considered every pitfall. "Where will you live? This isn't Hollywood, Dylan. Folks around here aren't used to having famous celebrities in their midst. How will you and Leah have a normal life, with the constant attention?"

"You won't accept a good thing when you hear it, will you?" he teased her, smiling. "I asked your sister, Deborah, to start a search for houses with some acreage, which might suit my, uh… our, needs. We're going to take a look at a couple of properties tomorrow."

Almost laughing at the dumbfounded expression on her lovely face, he addressed the final hurdle. "As to the fame thing, that will fade. Most people have a hard time keeping anyone on a pedestal for very long. Once your neighbors get used to seeing me around town, at the supermarket, the local McDonald's, high school football games, that sort of thing, I'll become just another familiar face. And my girls will be much more likely to have a normal life here, than they ever could in LA. That place is a zoo. Think about it, Carolee. You know I'm right."

Taking note of the people around her, who were no longer following them with curious eyes, she conceded the point. "I can't believe you talked to Deborah without telling me, and that she's in cahoots with you in this little scheme."

"She and Cindy helped me surprise you. It was a bit of a challenge at first. When I called them. out of the blue, they were both skeptical. I had a tough time proving that I was sincere. Carolee, you have many, many people who love you, and I'm happy to be one of them."

To emphasize his point, he swept her into his arms and kissed her deeply. When he released her, he gazed into her brimming eyes.

"So," she whispered hoarsely, a teasing lilt to her voice. "Have you come to a decision about the little issue you mentioned, while we were picnicking at Arnie's lake?"

"What issue is that?" he asked, feigning confusion.

"The one related to your sudden increase in appetite. Remember?" She clarified, hoping against hope.

"Ah, yes, the appetite issue." Taking her cue, he grabbed her tightly once more, and grinned. Her stomach lurched in response. "Since I met you, Carolee Austin, I have been ravenous, ravenous for you. I've definitely decided that I love you."

She answered him by throwing her arms around his neck, and kissing him soundly. When she reluctantly pulled away, she breathed, "I love you, too."

"Then marry me, Carolee," he demanded, sticking his hand into his jacket pocket and withdrawing a purple, velvet box, which he offered to her. "I know this fame thing still worries you, but I'm sure we can manage it. We won't rush into anything, I promise. We'll take our time, so I can prove that I honor my commitments.

"I want us to get to know each other so well, that you'll never have to worry about my constancy, my dedication to you, to us. You are the love I've longed for. Without you I'm incomplete."

The tight wedge of emotion constricted her throat, making speech almost impossible. "I...I..." she choked, then swallowed. "I will marry you, Dylan." Taking a deep breath to calm her shattered nerves, she told him, "I've spent my entire life in fear, fear of displeasing others, fear of being rejected and alone, but I refuse to be afraid any more. I want to live my dreams without fear."

Slipping her free hand into his warm, welcoming grasp, she smiled into his intense silver gaze. "I love you more than I ever imagined possible, and I'm ready to take a chance again. I want to be with you, to be your wife."

Opening the tiny box she still had nestled in her palm, she gasped. Inside was a wide platinum band, intricately carved with a series of stylized hearts, and set with one perfect stone, an opal with such exquisite fire it seemed to glow from within. "Oh, Dylan, it's beautiful. How did you know opals were my favorite gem?"

"I did my homework," he beamed at her, sliding the ring onto the third finger of her left hand. It fit perfectly. "Now come with me. I owe your classmates and friends another song."

Before she could object, he strode off toward the stage, whisking her along behind him. Waiting patiently for the band to finish their number, he boosted his fiancée onto the platform, and hopped up beside her. Once the crowd recognized his honeyed tones, emitting from the microphone, an anticipated hush fell over them.

"Well folks," he began. "Before I give you that song I promised, I have an announcement to make."

Ignoring Carolee's protesting tug on his sleeve, he told them, "In recent weeks you've heard gossip linking my name with a certain movie star, and one of the back-up singers in my band. I want to set those rumors straight. Since my concert in Atlanta, I've been involved with one woman, and one woman only, your friend and classmate, Carolee Austin. And I'm very pleased to announce to you that, just a few moments ago, she agreed to become my wife."

A shocked silence fell over the group. Seconds passed before the speechless surprise was replaced with cheers and shouts of approval and congratulations, the loudest coming from Cindy and Danny Lawrence. Calling for quiet, Dylan said, "To celebrate our engagement, I want to sing the song that brought us together." On cue, the music swelled, and the audience was treated to the first strains of "I Will Cherish You."

The powerfully moving words of the song, which Dylan expressed so brilliantly and with such intensity, such adoration, shot straight into Carolee's heart, filling it to overflowing, and leaving her trembling. She was enthralled by him, his incomparable voice, his larger-than-life presence, his determination to make her his own. All else faded into the background. Nothing existed except the man and the woman at his side. Dylan sang the final note, then cupped her face in his hands and kissed her, deeply, tenderly, and Carolee knew, without question, that everything his love song promised her had been fulfilled.

LOVE SHINE
PART I

A stubborn lock of shaggy, dark hair fell across her face for the hundredth time that day and for the hundredth time, she carelessly swiped at it with a resigned sigh. Pulling her dog-eared pad from the pocket of her dingy apron and slipping the pen from behind her ear, she faced the table of boisterous teenagers with a practiced bland expression, and offered them a softly spoken, "What will it be, boys?"

With her usual efficiency, she took their orders, waiting patiently as they tried, repeatedly, to grab the attention of the girls seated in the adjoining booth. When she turned away from them, they called back to her, snickering, "Thanks, gorgeous!"

Though she'd never understood why the insensitive oafs, like these boys, believed that making her the object of such crude ridicule would impress their female counterparts, she let the ridicule flow over her, refusing to allow the sharp barb to sink into her tender flesh.

She was plain, that was a fact she'd known and accepted since childhood. She'd heard the taunts and teasing all her life and was long past caring what others said about her appearance.

Sliding the order sheet into the clip above the kitchen window, she answered the cook's gruff call, "Order up, Les!" She grabbed up a plate of meatloaf and mashed potatoes, smothered with gravy, and set it down in front of an aging trucker who was seated at the counter. Then she retrieved the carafe from the hotplate and topped off the coffee in the thick porcelain mug he cradled between his meaty fingers.

"Um, looks good," he commented, sniffing the aromatic steam wafting off his food, "Don't let those little snots get to you, gal." She placed the pot back into its warming niche before shrugging her indifference.

"I'm used to them, Sam. They don't bother me." Her blue-gray eyes watched him through smudged horn-rimmed spectacles, as he shoveled forkfuls of the greasy fare into his mouth and chewed with relish.

"Well, you never done nothin' to them and don't deserve to be treated that way," he complained between bites.

"They're just kids who don't know better. Kids just like them have been teasing me all my life. I learned not to pay them any mind a long time ago," she assured him, noting the salesman, another regular, out of the corner of her eye, as he claimed the end stool. "You enjoy, Sam. I'll check back with you in a minute."

A mumbled, "Um, kay," was the only response she received.

She skimmed through the afternoon in a daze, running on autopilot. While she took orders, cleaned tables, made coffee, sliced pie, filled salt shakers, and generally managed the chores required for the efficient running of the small diner, her mind was preoccupied.

The spiteful insult of the heartless teenagers was all but forgotten. But what cut her more deeply than being made the brunt of an insensitive joke, was being ignored entirely. A few, like the teenagers, ridiculed her, but the majority of the folks who came into the diner barely noticed her. Most days she felt invisible.

In the restaurant, when customers wanted coffee refills or a piece of pie, she was, "Les, honey," but when she passed the same customers on the street, few bothered to acknowledge her existence. The good people of Red Valley knew her only as that poor homely girl from the diner, the one with the funny name.

She was so invisible that they rarely noticed, or cared, if she was within earshot when they tossed out unfeeling assessments of her. Over the years, she'd overheard it all. "Poor girl. So homely and with such an unfortunate name," or the clever, "Les certainly isn't more, in her case," and even, "The name Les sure fits her because she's less to look at than any woman has the right to be."

That particularly cruel cut was accompanied by several snickers of agreement. Shutting out these cowardly assaults was impossible because they were so stealthy. The thoughtless attacks always seemed to sneak up on her and take her by surprise. The straightforward ones, like those mounted by the childish boys showing off for the girls, were much easier to defend against. Those she expected.

Shaking off the self-pity, Leslie forced her mind on to more peaceful and productive thoughts. Her tired feet and aching legs were screaming for a long, hot soak. A lazy smile spread across her generous mouth when it dawned on her that she had tomorrow off. After church, she could spend the entire afternoon relaxing in the front porch swing with a good book and her orange tabby, Marmalade, curled up contentedly in her lap.

Henry Simpson, the town's pharmacist, finished up a huge slice of apple pie a la mode, slid his empty plate across the counter, and glanced at Les long enough to witness the mysterious look of pleasure and promise steal over her broad face. For a brief second, her plainness was transformed into a beguiling beauty. But the look quickly vanished, leaving him wondering if he'd seen it at all. He blinked several times to clear the vision, then asked her to bring him a cherry soda to go. When she placed the paper cup in front him, he asked her, his voice a bit tentative, "How's it going, today?"

Surprised by his unexpected attempt at small talk, she answered hesitantly, "Fine. Thanks for asking." His eyes were fixed on her mouth, staring. She turned away self-consciously, hoping she didn't have something in her teeth.

Sipping his drink thoughtfully, as he headed for the door, Henry wondered if he was seeing things. A backward glance in Les's direction confirmed that she was just as homely as always. He made a mental note to get his eyes examined.

Though the day had seemed endless, closing time finally arrived. Les refilled the last of the napkin dispensers and pulled off her apron. "I'm going now, Carl," she called to her boss, the diner's owner. "See you Monday."

Just as he popped his balding head through the window behind the counter to bid her farewell, the front door opened and the bell tinkled. "Oh no, you're not going nowhere, yet. There's another customer." He nodded toward the slim figure entering the diner, then drew his glistening pate back into the kitchen and began banging pots and pans.

Sighing tiredly, Les knotted the apron around her narrow waist once more, and trudged to the booth the tall stranger had chosen. Pad and pen in hand, she approached him, trying not to show her annoyance. "What would you like, sir?" she asked, letting her eyes slide over the man who was keeping her from that relaxing bubble bath she'd been eagerly anticipating.

He raised his gaze from the plastic covered menu and leveled it at her. Piercing hazel eyes, shot through with green-gold lights, met hers. Her stomach clenched like he'd aimed a punch straight to her midsection. "What do you recommend?" he asked her, his voice deep and rich, his smile warm and sincere.

Irritation evaporating, she struggled to swallow the lump in her throat. "I…uh…" she croaked, her mouth as dry as paper. Swallowing again, she made another attempt, which, though audible, was still little more than a whisper. "Anything from the grill is good, but I'd avoid the special. It's been on the warmer for hours."

"Sounds like sensible advice to me," he agreed, winking at her conspiratorial tone. The playful twinkle in his eye, teamed with his slightly crooked smile, hit her like a second salvo. Lowering his voice to match hers, he told her. "Just bring me a hamburger with the works and a Dr. Pepper, please. Oh, yeah, and a piece of pie; your favorite. I trust your judgment."

With shaking hands, she jotted a note on her pad. On wobbly legs, she crossed to the counter to put in the order. Drawing in deep, calming breaths, she filled a large glass with crushed ice and stuck it under the fountain. Silently scolding herself for her foolishness, she set the soft drink on a small serving tray and added a fresh slice of lemon chess pie from the cooler.

By the time she reached the man's table, she'd regained her composure, and then he spoke. "Lemon chess pie! Perfect." he exclaimed, his angular face lighting up with delight. "How'd you know?"

"You said to bring my favorite," she croaked, her eyes downcast, afraid to take another straight-on look at him.

"I knew I could trust you," he beamed at her. The look conveyed a basic gentleness of nature that many men with less self-assurance would have taken pains to disguise.

This stranger was too intensely attractive, and she was standing much too close, she decided, so she assured him, "Your burger'll be up in a minute." Then she backed off to a spot behind the counter where she could watch him from a safer distance.

He wasn't handsome, exactly, she decided, but his face was interesting, all planes and angles, rugged and strong. She studied his profile while he gazed out of the window at passersby, noting his broad forehead, expressive brows above wistful eyes, the color of a sunlit forest glade, straight nose, sensuous lips, and square jaw, all framed by a tawny, windblown mane. Two thoughts crossed her mind. First, that he needed a haircut, and second, that his face had been created for her eyes.

Cook's gruff, "Order up!" startled her. Scooping up the plate, she added a handful of crisp potato chips from the large plastic bag she kept under the counter and hurried to serve him. She shivered when she felt his piercing gaze follow her as she moved across the worn floor tiles toward him.

"Enjoy," she said, falling into her comfortable, well-used vernacular as she placed the still sizzling hamburger before him. "If there's anything else you need, just yell." Her intention was to beat a hasty retreat until he required a soda refill or the check, but he had other ideas.

Grabbing a work-callused hand before she could escape, he pulled her toward the opposite bench. "Sit with me, please. I hate to eat alone, and it doesn't look like you're too busy at the moment."

Though her confused brain urged her to refuse the invitation, her rebellious body immediately moved to accept. Before she could think of some excuse, any excuse, she slid across the cracked red vinyl and propped her elbows on the table. She watched him silently while he savored his dinner, desperately searching her suddenly empty thoughts for something witty to say.

"So," she began hesitantly. "I don't remember seeing you around here before. Are you just passing through?"

"No," he answered, crunching a chip. "I'm a transplant from the city, just moved in. I got tired of the rat race and decided to give country living a try. Do you think I'll fit in?" The way he intently studied her face while he waited for a response, made her drop her gaze to her ragged fingernails self-consciously.

"Sorry," he apologized. "I'm not usually this pushy, or this rude." Offering her his hand, he added, his dazzling smile leaving her breathless, "Name's Gallagher, Ray Gallagher. It is a pleasure to meet you…mmm?" His voice rose questioningly at the end, encouraging her to fill in the blank he left.

Slipping her icy fingers into his warm palm, she supplied, "Les."

"Les," he repeated. "That's an unusual name for a woman, must be short for something."

Surprised, yet pleased, by his straightforward inquisitiveness, she added, "Leslie, uh…, Leslie Grace Willow, but everyone just calls me Les." An embarrassed frown furrowed her brow as she silently kicked herself for her conversational clumsiness.

"Not everyone," he disagreed, chuckling. "I don't think Les does you justice, but Leslie's a beautiful name. So that's what I'll call you – Leslie. Leslie Grace Willow, the girl with eyes the color of a stormy sea. Is that okay? Do you mind if I call you Leslie?" Not seeming to notice the flush of bright color streaking across her prominent cheekbones, he turned his attention to the thick slice of pie.

Uncertainty washed over her and her stomach churned. At first blush, she thought he was making fun of her, but as she watched him innocently savoring the tangy pastry, his wonderful face open and honest, she slowly accepted his sincerity. "I'd like that," she whispered, tears of gratitude stinging her eyes.

He smiled at her again, then drained his glass. "I'll get you a refill," she offered.

"Make it a go-cup, if it's not too much trouble. And bring the check, too, if you don't mind," he mumbled through the last bite of pie. "I've got to get back to the unpacking."

A couple of minutes later, she returned with his bill and the paper cup of soda. "Thanks," he prompted. "Gotta go. I won't have any place to sleep tonight if I don't find the boxes with the linens in it." She was dying to ask him where he was staying but couldn't muster the courage.

He dropped two fives on the table, unfolded his long legs, stretched, and rose. Les, the too-tall girl who towered over many men, found herself looking up at him, not peering over the top of his head, but directly at his mouth. She had difficulty tearing her gaze away from his full, expressive lips, and wondered how it would feel to have those lips pressed against her own. Her body warmed in response.

"Thanks, Leslie, for the wonderful meal and the great company. I'm surprised this diner isn't more crowded, considering the quality of the food and the exceptional service."

"Well…," she reluctantly explained. "We close at seven-thirty or eight most nights, since the folks around here generally like to eat early."

"But you're too gracious to turn away a hungry stranger," Ray concluded, glancing at his wristwatch. "I guess I'm still running on city time. Sorry to keep you working late."

"Oh no, you didn't – that is – we always serve anyone who comes in before Carl locks the door." She tried to reassure him with the flurry of words, but flushed scarlet when she realized that her bumbling efforts to brush off his apology could be misinterpreted. She didn't want Ray Gallagher to think he was just another customer to her, because the tall stranger had already found his way straight into her heart.

Taking a deep breath and smiling apologetically, she corrected, "What I mean is, it was my pleasure to serve you, Mr. Gallagher. I'm happy you enjoyed your meal." She nervously pushed back the straggling lock of hair.

"I did," he said with a grin. "And I also enjoyed the company." She felt his green-gold eyes bore straight into her. He reached for the hand that hung limply at her side and asked, "Would you show me around your town sometime?"

Surprised by the request and unable to find her voice, she nodded agreement.

"Great. I'll see you soon, Leslie." He waved a cheerful farewell promise as he strode out the door. She watched him through the window until his blue-jean clad form disappeared around the corner. Then she quickly cleared his table, untied her apron and hung it on its hook, called good-bye to Carl, and headed home.

Despite the bone-deep weariness of fourteen hours on her feet and a long, relaxing soak in a hot bath, Leslie was still too keyed up to sleep, so she went outside to the wide front porch with its inviting swing. The night air was cool and soft on her face, and the rhythmic movement gently calmed her.

Slowly she felt herself unwinding, her teeming thoughts coasting to a reasonable speed. The pleasant encounter with Ray Gallagher had brought on a flood of memories, sending her thoughts back to a time, years before, when a young man had shown her the same sort of kindness.

Suddenly she was fourteen again, just graduating from junior high. Each year, Red Valley Junior High School honored its eighth-grade class with a social, to celebrate their accomplishments and send them off to high school with a bang. Les's granny had made her a new dress for the occasion. It was bright green taffeta with layers of ruffles and flounces. Leslie had hated it, but not wanting to disappoint the kind woman by refusing her lovingly made gift, she'd put it on with a groan.

Mary Ellen Fisher, Les's best friend, had agreed to help her control her impossible hair. They'd tried everything, rolling it on empty orange juice cans, spraying it, teasing it, and even pressing it; but nothing had worked. When all else had failed, they'd pulled the unruly mass into a tight knot at Leslie's nape and subdued it with a half can of lacquer. Once the bun was wrapped with a ribbon that coordinated with her dress, her abundant, curly locks had seemed almost tame, except for the one stubborn strand that had won its independence from the others, and had fallen over her forehead determinedly. That night her trademark hairdo had been created – the very same style she'd stubbornly recreated every day since.

Catching a glimpse of her reflection in the window, Leslie chuckled, remembering the peculiar picture she and Mary Ellen had made, marching off arm-in-arm to the school gym – a petite, blond pixie and a gangly, dark giant – ridiculously mismatched. No wonder the boys had laughed when they'd come in through the heavy double doors.

As she'd expected, Les had spent the better part of the evening holding up the wall and feeling like a bright green thorn among dozens of pastel roses. Mary Ellen had stayed loyally plastered to her side, until the cutest boy in the class had pried her away. Watching them walk toward the dance floor, hand in hand, Leslie had wished she could melt into the institutional gray of the gymnasium walls.

But then, the unexpected and miraculous had happened. A tall, thin lad with a mop of unruly tan hair had crossed the floor and headed straight for her. Sticking out a palm, that had seemed a bit too big for his lanky frame, he'd asked her to dance. Shocked speechless, she'd nodded her acceptance, trembling as he pulled her into his arms. Her heart had thudded so loudly in her chest that she'd been sure he could hear it. They'd moved to the music silently, his hands on her narrow hips, hers on his broad shoulders.

The sweet interlude had ended abruptly when a gang of rowdy boys, led by the class president and unrelenting bully, Walter Lewis, had approached them jeering insults. Her embarrassed swain had left her to join his compatriots, but not before he'd thanked her for the dance, his sincere hazel eyes boring a hole straight into her heart.

"That's it!" she cried, startling Marmalade, who dug his sharp claws into her bare knees. "It's the eyes, Marme," she told the fluffy feline, stroking him gently. "There was something about the man in the diner tonight, something familiar that I couldn't put my finger on until now. It's his eyes. I haven't been able to get those eyes out of my head, because they remind me of the sweet boy who danced with me at the junior high social, over twenty years ago." That mystery solved, she let her thoughts return to the past and less pleasant memories.

Walter Lewis, the son of the wealthiest family in Red Valley, had tormented Leslie for as long as she could remember. Why he'd chosen to waste his time on a poor, plain farmer's daughter was beyond her comprehension – but he had. In primary school, he'd made daily efforts to belittle her. Insults like "knobby-knees," "skinny-bones," "scared-hair," and the unimaginative, "four eyes," were typical, but the one that had hurt the most had been the particularly mean-spirited, "fish-face." Walter and his cronies had taken perverse pleasure in pointing out just how much her countenance, with its large, wide-set eyes, magnified by thick lenses set in dark, horn-rimmed frames, broad, high cheekbones, and rosy, pouting lips, resembled that of a big fish.

As they grew up, his attacks had become more subtle. He'd taken advantage of every opportunity to humiliate Leslie in front of their classmates with some teasing jest, often using her nickname to ridicule her plainness and her unusual height. His favorite had been,

"Hey, Les. How'd you get that ridiculous name, anyway? I bet it's because everyone wishes they could see a lot less of you!" The laughter his malicious attacks generated still echoed in her ears.

When she recalled the deep, unforgettable pain she'd suffered at his hands, she shuddered. She would always wonder why Walter was so incredibly cruel to her. He had everything she didn't, a wealthy and powerful family, a huge group of devoted followers, and success in whatever he attempted.

Though Walter was neither handsome nor particularly smart, his father's money and influence paved the way for his achievement. He'd risen to the top, in the eyes of his classmates, becoming president of the student government, editor of the school newspaper, and captain of the baseball team. Those accomplishments, plus the thick wad of cash he always carried in his pocket, had made Walter Lewis the catch of the county.

All the popular, status-conscious teenage girls had vied for his attention. Though his grades didn't earn it, Walter's dad had bought him a place at the State University, where he'd eventually received a degree in business. After graduation, he'd stepped into a prestigious position created for him by the local bank and trust. Not surprisingly, he'd inherited the position of Bank President when his good old dad had retired.

Soon after establishing himself in the business community, Walter had married Sharon Vaughn, the town's resident beauty queen. Sharon had numerous crowns in her collection and never hesitated to boast about them. The Lewises had built a huge, pretentious house in the most prestigious part of Red Valley, a section Les liked to call "Snob's Knob," where they had birthed three very average, very spoiled children.

As the first two offspring had been female, Walter had insisted they continue to reproduce until Sharon had pushed out a male child. Then, his ego satisfied, Walter had left his wife to her garden club, historical society, afternoon teas, and other social obligations, while he had invested his time in making more Lewis family money.

Leslie shuddered, as an even more disturbing memory of the high and mighty Walter Lewis flooded her. In a flash, she was back in the President's office of the First United Bank, overcome with grief and loss. She remembered ordering herself to stop wringing her hands, as she listen to Walter's weak attempt at sincerity.

"Now, Les, honey, I know things have been real hard for you, and I'm gonna do the best I can for you," he had assured her, his thin lips drawn into a self- satisfied smirk.

Bile rose in her throat, stinging and bitter, when she recalled his revolting offer. He had thumbed through a manila folder marked *Willow,* as if it contained a crystal ball, cleared his throat, sighed, and looked up at her over the rims of his reading glasses. "Seems ya'll haven't been doin' too well lately. Your loan's over six months in arrears."

She had hesitated, breathing deeply, biting back tears. "Yes, I know. I've tried to keep the farm running smoothly during Granny's illness, because Grandpa just didn't have the heart for it, but her hospital bills and burial expenses put us behind. Then with his death coming so quickly after…Even with my jobs waiting tables and doing the books for Carl's diner and Mary Ellen's beauty shop, I don't bring in enough to make ends meet. Now that Grandpa's gone too, I can't manage the farm alone. I have to sell."

Leslie hadn't expected Walter to express any compassion for her, but his calculated cruelty took her by surprise. His excruciating offer was etched on her heart in indelible ink.

With a feral grin, he'd told her, "You're a hard worker, Les, and smart, too. Even though we've never been friends, I can see that about you. Problem is, you're too proud. If you'd come to me right after you finished up at the community college, I could have given you a job here at the bank. All you had to do was ask. But no, you have that blasted Willow pride. That's what's wrong with your whole dang family. If old John hadn't been so prideful, if he'd a come to me when Emily took sick, we could've worked something out on this mortgage. But now it's so long overdue, the situation is pretty desperate. There's only one thing I can do."

He had waited, deliberately forcing her to ask the question, "And what's that?"

"The Board of Directors won't extend you any more credit without additional collateral. The only way to keep you from default is for me to buy Willow Spring Farm myself," he had said, feigning benevolence. "Since I'm just plumb full of charity today, I'll go you one better.

"I've always felt sorry for you, Les, losing your folks like you did at such a young age, and having to live with your old grandparents on that rundown farm, working like a hired hand from sunup to sundown. So, I'll buy you out of that worthless ball of dirt, and give you a job, too.

"You can live in the house, until I can find someone to develop the property, and you'll come to work for me here at First United. I can always use another bookkeeper, especially one who's single and available. You aren't much to look at, and that's a fact." He slapped his knee and grinned. "But I think we can make you presentable enough for what I have in mind."

Tears had rolled down her cheeks, unbidden, as she absorbed his words. "Which is?" she'd choked out, dreading the answer.

"Occasionally I have clients and business associates who need an escort for an evening or weekend. Pickin's are slim in this little town, and despite your plainness, you have a nice body on you. I'd even bet you're a virgin. Most men I know would be willin' to overlook your homeliness, considering you're such a clean, wholesome girl. That's what they make paper bags for, right?" He chuckled at his own cleverness.

Then, clearly expecting her reluctance, he'd leaned back in his huge leather chair, laced his fingers over his ample belly, and bullied her. "Oh, come on, gal. Don't be such a prude. My offer is better than fair – a nine-to-five job with a few evenings out in the company of some nice gentlemen, and you keep the old home place, for now. It would get you outta that greasy-spoon diner and off your feet." His grin widened into another suggestive sneer. "It's a great opportunity.

"Now I'll have my secretary draw up the necessary papers, leaving out the clause about the overtime duties, of course. We can't put anything like that in writing, so our agreement about the side work will have to be our little secret, an extra perk." He winked.

Anger and disgust bubbling up inside her, Les had seethed, "The only thing for sale here, Walter, is my farm. If you're willing to purchase it at a fair price, I'm willing to sell. If I'd had any other offers, I would never have come to you. Blame it on Willow pride if you want, but I am not part of this deal. I will never work for you, in any capacity, or live on any property you own. If you still want to buy my land on those terms, then by all means, have your secretary draw up the papers."

She had stood there trembling, fully expecting him to throw her out of his office; but instead, he'd calmly given instructions for the transfer of deed and for a check to be cut from his personal account to Les Willow. Though the total amount was woefully below the market value of the farm, barely enough to pay off the mortgage and purchase her tiny, run-down bungalow in town, she'd left his office with her future, and her dignity, intact.

Shaking her head to clear the clinging cobwebs of the unpleasant memory, she scratched the big tabby's chin and told him, "Poor old Walter. He doesn't know what it means to have a real family. My grandparents were the only mother and father I ever knew. They were loving and kind, and growing up on the farm was wonderful.

Except for Walter and his sort bullying me, my childhood was perfect. He's the one who needs pity, Marme. Well, I can tell you one thing for sure, sweet cat, I'd starve before I'd go to work for Walter Lewis.

"If Granny hadn't had the stroke, we'd be living over in Westlake and I'd be working in the finance department at the Community College. They offered me a position, you know, but Grandpa needed me to help out, and I never regretted staying home with him. Waitressing's hard work, but Carl's a great boss. He let me cut back to part-time while I was in college and when Grandma was so sick. Now he gives me a little extra for doing his accounts and that keeps my skills sharp. Mary Ellen's a blessing, too, letting me do the bookkeeping for her beauty salon. So, I have some very special friends, including you, my furry fellow. I wonder if Walter Lewis has any real friends?"

At the mention of her dearest friend an animating thought popped into her head. "I'm going to call Mary Ellen and see if she's still at the shop. Sometimes she works late on Saturday night, getting everything cleaned up and ready for the next week." The large cat's feet made a loud plop when she dropped him onto the wooden floorboards. She scooted inside, grabbed the phone, and punched the number for the Clip N' Curl.

A few minutes later, Leslie was seated in front of the big mirror, pink plastic cape draping her shoulders. Mary Ellen stood behind her, scissors in hand. "Are you sure you want me to do this, Les?" She regarded her dearest friend's reflection with concern.

"Cut away," Leslie confirmed with conviction. "I'm tired of the old me. I'm ready for a change."

"Okay, you're the boss," her friend declared clipping off a long curl. "I've wanted to get my hands on this head of yours for years. The last time you let me touch it was junior high. I've learned a lot about styling hair since then, Les, and I'm glad you finally decided to trust me," Mary Ellen reassured her.

"Yeah, yeah, you can finally stop your nagging! Here's your chance to show me that special style you've been dying to try out on me for so long. I want to see shocked looks on the faces of the gossiping old biddies at church tomorrow."

They both laughed at the idea of heads turning to take a second glance at the usually invisible Leslie Willow. "Your transformation can't be too dramatic. I'd hate to distract Glenwood from his sermon." The tiny blonde grinned broadly, a dreamy look crossing her pixie face. Mary Ellen always managed to insert her husband, Glenwood Cooper, pastor of the Red Valley Fellowship Church, into every conversation.

"Honestly, Mary Ellen, you've been married to the man for over ten years. Isn't the honeymoon over yet?" Les sparred.

"It's never over when you find the right one, dearie," she answered, her fingers flying.

"Well, I wouldn't know about that, would I? I've never had any beau at all, much less the right one," Leslie countered, her tone frank but not bitter.

"Oh, I remember one special fellow who grabbed your attention for one dance," her friend prompted, swinging the chair around to find better light.

"For heaven's sake, that was years ago. We were barely fourteen. He doesn't count. I'm talking about men, Mary Ellen, not adolescent boys." Leslie sighed in frustration.

"Ha, got you!" the tiny woman teased. "Nice to know I still can

push your buttons." Her clear blue eyes twinkling with mischief she added, "Admit it, Les, there were a few guys who asked you out in high school and college, but you always compared them to that handsome lad who stole your heart at the junior high social. And you turned them all down."

"Don't be ridiculous. The only invitations I ever had were from Pete Brown, who smelled like hog slop and thought we belonged together because we both lived on a farm, and followers of Walter Lewis, who were only out to humiliate me on his behalf," Leslie defended.

"What about the guy from Westlake? You know, the one in your accounting class. Didn't he ask you out?" Mary Ellen asked innocently.

Shrugging her broad shoulders, Les said, "Yeah. We went for coffee a couple of times, and a movie once, but things just didn't click between us. Then when Granny got sick, I couldn't make it back to the city very often, and he never came out to the farm, so nothing came of it."

"Did you ever invite him for a visit?" her inquisitive friend asked.

"Well, no," Leslie admitted. "I assumed he would invite himself if he really wanted to see me."

"There you go, proving my point. You compared him to your mysterious admirer and found him lacking, so you deliberately let him slip away. Men have to be encouraged, my friend, otherwise they take your reticence for disinterest. A polite guy would never drop by without an invitation. You brushed him off."

"I did not! Maybe I didn't encourage him, exactly, but I didn't brush him off. Why would I? He was the only real date I ever had. It wasn't my fault it didn't work out." Leslie's eyes flashed on the verge of anger.

"Oh, no? Then why can't you remember his name?" Mary Ellen challenged, swinging her yellow curls.

"Who says I can't remember? His name was…. um, let me see, it was…Joe, no, Jim, no…Josh, I think. I'm sure it started with a J," the dark-haired woman stuttered, laughing at herself. "Okay, okay, you're right, maybe I did brush him off. But I didn't compare him to that boy who danced with me at the social. I'd never seen him before that night, and I haven't seen him since. I never even knew his name or why he was in Red Valley."

"And it's tormented you ever since," her friend concluded. "He was with Walter and his crew. You could have asked about him, like I told you to; but no, you were too stubborn."

"Come on, Mary Ellen," Les complained. "You know I couldn't ask Walter. I heard those monsters laughing it up and giving the poor guy grief. Knowing them, they dared him to dance with me in the first place, and he called their bluff. Maybe he was just putting on a good show, an act for their benefit."

"There you go, selling yourself short again," Mary Ellen scolded. "Is it so hard for you to believe that any person of the male persuasion could find you attractive?"

"Yes, it is," came the frustrated response. "How can I think anything else, Mary Ellen? Look at me!"

"I am looking, Les!" She swung the chair around to face the mirror. "And what I see is a woman with a glorious head of hair. Take a gander at yourself."

Leslie couldn't believe her eyes. Her hair was magnificent. The cut was nothing short of perfection. Thickly curling locks, in colors ranging from deep chestnut to warm honey brown, cascaded around her shoulders in silky waves. Auburn highlights flashed when she shook her head. "What did you do? I can't believe the difference!"

"I shaped it up, added layers so it would move, and applied a henna rinse when I shampooed. The rest is all you, my girl. You have beautiful hair. Like I've been telling you for ages." The tiny hairdresser's smile was very wide and very smug.
Leslie ripped open the Velcro closure on the neck of the cape, tossed it aside, and hugged her friend tightly. "Oh, Mary Ellen, thank you so much. I love my haircut and I love you." Pleased tears slid down her cheeks. Wiping them away with the back of her hand,

Leslie grabbed a broom and began sweeping up. "I've kept you out too late tonight. Glen will be livid. I'm sure the twins have worn him out completely. Tell him I'm sorry for monopolizing you and give him my best."

"He'll never notice. He's completely engrossed in sermon prep on Saturday night, which gives me the time to do clean-up detail. Mom comes over and entertains the girls so Glen can focus on his work, but I'll give him a kiss for you," Mary Ellen promised, emptying the dustpan into the trash and picking up her handbag.

"I'm sure you will," Leslie told her with a wink. "Well, good night and thanks again. See you at church tomorrow morning."

Leslie rose early and spent a few extra minutes touching up the new hairdo. To her delight, the cut stood up well under her amateur touch. Deciding to make the most of the change, she searched through her tiny closet for something more flattering to wear than her usual shapeless denim jumper.

Sighing in frustration at the slim pickings, she finally located the dress she wanted, tucked in the very back behind her winter coat. Slipping the soft, burgundy sheath over her head, she smoothed the straight skirt and checked the mirror. The scooped neckline was perfect. It didn't interfere with the curling tendrils as they lay against her bare throat, and the warm reddish hue of the dress made her auburn highlights gleam.

"Not bad," she breathed.

She cast aside her heavy, dark-framed glasses and pulled a box of seldom-used contact lenses out of the drawer. Inserting a pair, she blinked back tears, remembering how her grandmother, Emily, had insisted on purchasing her first lenses, even when they couldn't afford it. Les had rarely worn them, despite her granny's repeated protests, fearing she would lose one. Now contacts were cheaper and disposable, but she still didn't bother with them, believing they weren't worth the trouble for the minute difference they made in her appearance. But today was special.

Finally, she added a streak of blush to her cheeks, straightened and shaped her brows with a sable pencil, curled and darkened her long lashes with mascara, and brushed a smoky pink shadow into the creases of her eyelids. Not wanting to draw attention to her too-full mouth, she usually avoided lip color, but her look-at-me-now hairstyle had given her courage. So, she carefully applied a shiny lip-gloss in a complementary shade called mulled wine.

"Well, Marme," she told her ever-present feline companion.

"That's the best I can do with what I've got. What do you think?"

Purring his approval, the huge tabby rubbed against her ankles as she tried to put on her shoes. "Oh, you! You love anyone who feeds you. Now let me go. I don't want to be late."

Long legs quickly covering the four blocks between her house and the Red Valley Fellowship Church, Les arrived just as Sunday School was letting out. She watched the Lewis children, decked out in their finest, climb into the big Cadillac Sharon had pulled up to the curb. Walter and wife rarely attended services here in Red Valley. They preferred the prestigious Congregational Church over in Westlake, where they rubbed elbows with the state senator, hospital CEO, a local judge and the county DA, and several highly placed business executives.

Before Leslie could take her usual seat on the back row in the corner, Mary Ellen appeared at her elbow. "Wow, you look great!" she beamed, propelling her friend down the center aisle. "I won't let you hide out where no one will see you and waste my fine handiwork. Come on, girl. You're sitting up front with me."

"But…I," the tall woman protested.

"Huh-uh, no buts today," the petite blonde insisted, pulling her along. "I want to show you off."

Les followed reluctantly, feeling the eyes of the congregation following their progress, the flush of embarrassment adding an unexpected glow to her striking new look. As quickly as she could manage, she slid into Mary Ellen's customary pew.

"I'll be right back," the preacher's wife assured her, patting her hand. "Got to get the girls."

Les kept her head down, self-consciously studying her bulletin, until she felt a tug on her skirt. "'Scuse, Les," little Mary Grace peeped as she bumped past Leslie's knees and into the center of the pew.

"Me, too," Martha Joy echoed, close on her sister's heels.

The twins settled themselves, eagerly spreading out their Sunday School papers and searching for pencils in the little racks on the back of the pew. Les helped get them settled, smiling at their energy and exuberance.

"Please, sit here with us. There's plenty of room," Leslie heard

Mary Ellen's cheery voice offer. She turned to find herself looking squarely into warm, hazel eyes, bright with pleasure.

"Oh, Les, meet Ray Gallagher. He's new in town. Ray, this is my dearest friend, Les Willow."

"Hello, Leslie. It's nice to see you again," he said, taking her hesitantly proffered hand and sliding onto the bench beside her.

"You two already know each other?" Mary Ellen asked, surprised and pleased by the newcomer's reaction.

"We met last night at the diner," he explained. "Leslie served me a great supper and agreed to show me around town sometime. Didn't you?"

Unable to find her voice, Les nodded, thankful the choir chose that moment to make their entrance, raising a hymn of praise. As the music swelled, Reverend Cooper crossed the riser and took his place behind the pulpit.

When the church fell silent, Ray leaned toward her and whispered, his breath tickling her ear, "You look beautiful today, Leslie. I really like your hair."

"Thank you," she croaked, more self-conscious than ever. She kept her eyes on the pulpit, not daring to meet his gaze.

When he raised his arm and placed it along the back of the pew behind her, cradling her shoulders possessively, Leslie tensed involuntarily. She was grateful when the choir director gestured for the congregation to stand for the invocation.

The worship service seemed interminably long with Ray's disturbing presence so intimately close. The twins were their usual, fidgety selves, particularly Mary Grace, affectionately nicknamed "Wiggle Worm" by her dad. Her incessant squirming pushed Les closer and closer to Ray, until her thigh rested against the long, firm length of his.

To add to her discomfort, Glenwood kept giving her curious looks from behind the podium, drawing curious stares from other members of the congregation. For the first time in her life, Leslie wished for invisibility.

When it was finally time to stand for the benediction, she sighed in relief and looked for the most direct route out of the sanctuary. She wanted to get away from Ray as quickly and unobtrusively as possible, but her escape was thwarted when Mary Ellen insisted, "Les will introduce you around, Ray. I promised Carol Simpson I'd help her in the church library for a bit."

Not waiting for Leslie to agree, she urged her daughters, "Come on, girls. Let's leave Mr. Gallagher to Auntie Les. I'm sure the entire parish is anxious to meet him."

Mary Ellen was right about the curiosity of the congregation. As soon as Les and her charge disengaged themselves from the pastor's wife and her twins, and stepped into the aisle, they were swamped by well-wishers and gossip-seekers. For interminably long minutes, the shy woman introduced Ray Gallagher to members of her church family, repeatedly responding with an embarrassed, "Thank you," when each commented on her surprisingly improved appearance.

Inch by inch, they made their way to the back of the sanctuary, where the pastor stood grinning, his bright eyes twinkling. He stuck out his hand eagerly, not an introverted bone in his big body, clasped the newcomer's palm, and shook it enthusiastically. Before Leslie could offer an introduction, he burst out, "I'm Glenwood Cooper, but I guess you've figured that out by now. It's great to have you with us."

"Glad to be here. Enjoyed the service and the company," her companion acknowledged, winking at her. "Leslie's been taking good care of me. She's beginning to make a habit of it. The name's Gallagher, Ray Gallagher."

"Nice to meet you, Ray, "Glenwood beamed, throwing a sly grin at his wife's dearest friend. "Our Les is a real prize. It's good to see you've noticed."

"Hush, Glen," Leslie warned, her voice low. "That's enough nonsense."

"Nonsense, huh? You look particularly fine today, my girl. I saw plenty of heads turning to take a second look at you," he defended, his pudgy cheeks aglow.

Uncomfortable with the compliment, Leslie brushed it off. "They were curious about Ray, that's all. I'm sure they wondered who he was and why he was sitting with me."

"I doubt that, but have it your way. It's much too nice a day for a debate," he agreed, changing the subject. "Ray, we're planning a little picnic at the parsonage this afternoon. We'd love for you to join us." He leaned into the taller, slimmer man and added, "Mary Ellen will be disappointed if you don't come. First-time visitors are always invited to Sunday dinner. And Les will be there."

"Then count me in," Ray announced, clamping his palm on the reverend's arm. "Thanks."

"Good. See you at two p.m. sharp and you, too, my dear, Leslie." He deliberately ignored the dirty look the embarrassed woman shot him.

Leslie tried to make another escape from Ray, telling him she had to go home to change clothes, feed her cat, and finish up the fruit salad she was bringing to the picnic. Ignoring her excuses, he insisted on driving her. Four minutes later, he pulled his battered Land Cruiser up to the curb in front of her tiny bungalow.

"Thanks for the ride, Ray," she said, throwing open the door and sliding out. "Guess I'll see you in a while."

"My pleasure, Leslie. I've got to ride out to the ranch, check on a few things, and get out of this necktie," he replied. "But I'll be back here to pick you up at one forty-five." Before she could open her mouth to point out that the Cooper's home was only four blocks away, or to tell him that she preferred to walk, he sped off, waving goodbye,

Les changed into her nicest jeans and a cotton sweater in a becoming shade of green. Then she fed Marmalade, added a few banana slices and strawberries to the salad, and touched up her hair and make-up. An hour later or so later, she sat on the top step of her porch waiting for Ray, crystal fruit bowl neatly wrapped and at her side.

She spotted his dusty red SUV as it rounded the corner. Unfolding her long legs and grabbing up her dish, she met him at the curb, fingers extended to grab the handle. He reached across from inside and pushed the heavy door open wide for her to slide in. "Thanks," she said, smiling shyly.

"Hey, you didn't give me a chance to show you what a gentleman I am. Most of the women I know wait for me to open the car door for them," he teased, helping her settle in and find a secure spot for the large bowl.

"I haven't had much experience with the proper etiquette of door opening," she parried, flattered by his attentiveness. "I'm not like most women anyway."

"You sure aren't," he breathed, openly admiring her. "I think the good Lord broke the mold when He made you."

Flushing hotly, her heart pounding in her ears, unaccustomed as she was to hearing a sincere compliment, Leslie turned away from him and stared out of the window, suddenly unable to put two words together. The silence didn't seem to bother her companion, who whistled merrily as he drove along, intermittently casting sideways glances in her direction. The questions she had been dying to ask him about his new home, his occupation, and his family, congealed in her throat.

When he deftly steered his Land Cruiser into the driveway of the parsonage, she fought against her innate independence and waited for him to circle the vehicle and open the door on her side. Offering him a timid smile of thanks, she grabbed up the bowl and hopped down from the high seat. "Here, let me take that," he offered, grinning.

Before they could reach the porch of the parsonage, the twins burst out of the front door, surrounding them with gleeful squeals. "Hey, Les," they chimed together, hugging her knees. "Who you got with you? Is he the new man from church?"

"This is Mr. Gallagher," she told them. Turning to Ray she added, "These little sprites are Mary Grace and Martha Joy."

"Hello, ladies," Ray responded. Handing Leslie the salad bowl, he knelt down to greet them eye to eye. "It's a real pleasure to see you again." He took one of their tiny hands in each of his and planted a light, chivalrous kiss on pudgy knuckles, bringing forth yet another squeal of delight from the girls. "Call me, Ray. It's easier," he urged them.

"Okay, Ray," Mary Grace obliged. "You're nice. I like you," she declared, not one to mince words.

"Me, too," Martha Joy mimicked. "Hurry up. We're hungry," she added, still holding Ray's hand and pulling him toward the back yard.

Leslie followed Ray and his cherubic escorts around the brick, two-story house. They could smell the mouth-watering aroma of grilling meat before they turned the corner. As soon as Mary Ellen spotted them, she drew them into the bustle of meal preparations. As directed, the women set out the side dishes and poured tall glasses of iced tea, while the men put the final touches on the burgers sizzling on the grill.

When the food was ready, Glenwood called to the girls, insisting that Ray take the place beside Leslie one of the long wooden benches. He and Mary Ellen seated themselves across the wide picnic table and tried unsuccessfully to tempt Mary Grace away from the tall newcomer's side.

"Let her stay," he urged, his deep baritone sending shivers down Les's spine. "It's been such a long time since I've had a tot around. I really enjoy her company." The more accommodating twin, Martha Joy, quietly climbed up on the bench at her mother's elbow and folded her little hands reverently, waiting for her father to bless the food.

"It's wonderful to have old friends and new ones with us today," Glenwood began, nodding at his guests. "Let's join hands as we pray, to symbolize our unity as members of God's family."

The touch of Ray's warm fingers against hers was electric, and Leslie found it impossible to concentrate on the words Glenwood spoke. She wondered if Ray was having the same difficulty, because he continued to hold her hand for a long moment after the blessing was finished.

Mary Grace's, "Pass me a hamburger, please," prodded him to loosen his grasp self-consciously, and sent a flush of bright color to Leslie's prominent cheekbones.

Grinning broadly at their interaction, the pastor posed the very question Leslie had been burning to ask. "Well, now, Ray, I hear you're a city fellow. So, what brings you to small town life?"

"Guess you heard right. I was born and raised in Greenville. Lived there most of my life, too, except for my college years," he answered between bites of the savory burger. "But I never cared for the city much. Always preferred the country. I like to hear crickets in the evening, you know." Heads all around the table nodded in agreement, politely waiting for him to continue.

"If it had been up to me, I'd have moved here years ago, but Wanda, my wife, insisted that we stay close to her folks. She said we'd have more opportunities in the city, and I guess she was right. Business was good for me, and we were able to send Richard, our son, to the private schools she thought were best for him."

"Oh…I assumed you were single. You don't wear a wedding ring," Mary Ellen interjected, noticeably concerned that she'd been pushing her best friend at a married man. Before Ray could answer the accusation, she probed deeper. "How did you get your wife to agree to leave the city? When will your family be joining you?" Leslie held her breath, eyes brimming, and listened intently for his response.

"No, I'm not… that is, I am… I mean…" Ray sputtered, suddenly at a loss for words. He lay down his sandwich, wiped his mouth and hands on the large paper napkin and cleared his throat.

"I'm a widower. Wanda died early last year, of breast cancer. She was sick for a long time. The doctors tried everything, even stem cells, but it was just too late for a cure. Wanda always hated to go in for check-ups, so she didn't do it very often. Unfortunately, she paid the ultimate price for her fear."

"I'm so sorry," Mary Ellen burst in again, much chagrined. "It must have been terrible for you and your son."

"Yes," Ray acknowledged. "It was tough on us both, and it took me months to convince him that this change is what we both need. Richard reluctantly agreed, as long as I let him stay and help his grandfather this summer, doing inventory in one of the family furniture stores. I'll move him here in time to register for the fall term at the high school."

"How old is your boy?" Glenwood prompted.

"Fifteen." The golden highlights in Ray's eyes flashed in distress. "Going on twenty-five! He needs to get out of Greenville and into a smaller school. Sometimes he's too stubborn for his own good, kind of like me, I guess." His helpless shrug and crooked smile tugged at Leslie's heart.

"Pity he couldn't come with you and help set up the house. That's such a chore. Can't imagine how you've managed, a man alone," Mary Ellen observed, convinced as she was of the basic helplessness of men.

"I did all right, I guess. Besides, that's part of the plan. I want everything to be different for us here, a new start, and I don't want

Richard seeing the place until I have it just right." His hazel eyes darkened seriously, hinting at hidden pain. "He promised Wanda's father he'd help out until after the restocking is finished, and I appreciate his determination to keep his word."

Sensing that this was an uncomfortable topic for the tall stranger, Leslie diverted the conversation to a tangent. "Of all the small towns around, why did you choose ours?"

"Fate," was Ray's curious reply. "I spent a summer in Red Valley years ago, visiting with my cousin, and loved it here."

"A cousin you say?" the preacher asked. "So, I probably know him."

"Oh, I'm sure you do. Everyone knows Walter." A wave of the coldest dread welled in Leslie's throat, threatening to choke her.

Ray grinned wryly and shook his unruly mop of tawny hair. "As much as I hate to admit it, Walter Lewis is my first cousin. His mother and mine are sisters. We spent a couple of months with them, way back, over twenty years ago. Came into town right after my school let out. Even got to go to a school dance. I felt like a real big man, too, being older and a city kid to boot. Thought I was more grown up and sophisticated than the local boys, you know." His eyes twinkled, remembering his childish whims.

"We stayed until just before my classes started in late August. It was a wonderful summer, best of my life, except for having to put up with Walter, of course. That's when I decided Red Valley was the place for me. Always knew I'd come back here someday."

The conversation lulled while everyone savored the delicious food. Mary Ellen chewed thoughtfully for a while and then added, "Well, we're all glad you were drawn back here, Ray. We hope you'll like it as much now as you did when you were a kid."

"So far it's been even better than I remembered," he confirmed, smiling into Leslie's face, setting her cheeks ablaze and her pulse aflutter.

Sensing there was more to this story, Mary Ellen probed, "This morning you mentioned something about getting yourself settled on your ranch. Whereabouts is your place? I haven't heard of any large parcels of land being sold recently."

"I guess I have Walter to thank for finding me a patch big

enough to meet my needs. He sold me this old farm about three miles south of town. He took over the mortgage on it a while back. Gave me a great deal, but knowing Walter, he still made a bundle on the deal." Ray flashed his crooked grin.

"He'd been looking for a developer for a while, but most companies won't come this far out of the city without a rail connection or interstate highway access. I think he'd even tried selling it to a large agricultural production operation, but the farm is too small for anyone to bite on that; so, it worked out for me. Thank goodness.

"The house and barns are still in great shape, and there's more than enough ground for my requirements. It'll be the perfect place to set up my business and raise my son."

"Now that sure sounds like Willow Spring Farm, doesn't it, Les?" Glen observed. "Can't think of anyplace else it could be."

The stiffening posture of the woman at his side alerting him, Ray turned toward Leslie just in time to catch her almost imperceptible nod. Then he watched helplessly as her eyes filled with tears and heard her mumble, "Excuse me." He reached out to stop her retreat, but his attempt came too late. His fingers only brushed the sleeve of her sweater as she bolted for the house.

"Now, Glen," Mary Ellen scolded. "Look what you've gone and done. I'll go see if she's okay." She slipped off the bench and gathered up the girls.

Though Glenwood looked chagrined by his lack of sensitivity, Ray reacted first, jumping up. "What's wrong?" Concern was obvious in his darkening expression.

"It's nothing. She'll be fine. Sit and finish your meal. Glenwood will explain. Won't you, honey?" she prompted tactfully.

Shrugging his wide shoulders in resignation, Ray sat and stared at the remnants of his meal. "What did I say?" he asked.

"Wasn't nothin' you said, Ray," Glenwood assured him, dropping into a comfortable drawl which belied his advanced seminary training. "It was me. Sometimes I speak without thinking. It's one of those bad habits a preacher shouldn't have, but I seem unable to overcome."

He paused, sighed, and went on, "That old farm you bought

used to belong to Les's family. It's her home place. She's still real sensitive about having to sell it like she did. I should've known better than to spout off about it. I'm sure she'd already figured it out. Didn't need me to make it public."

"Of course. *Willow Spring Farm*, you said. I wonder why Walter never told me it had a name."

"Not because he felt bad for the way he practically stole it from Les, that's for sure. Sorry to say it, being as he's your kin and all, but Walter Lewis doesn't have an ounce of conscience in his over-indulged, money-grubbing body. Most likely he didn't want you to go looking into the place's history and find out how he came by it so reasonable."

Glenwood had a minister's gift for finding the good in most people, but the banker was an exception. Glen had been unable to detect even one genuine, worthy characteristic in the man. "What are you planning to do with the land, develop it?"

"Oh, no!" Ray seemed horrified by the thought. "I've had a contractor enlarging and updating the barns, paddocks, and corrals, so they'll be more suitable for my patients."

Glenwood looked puzzled, "Patients?"

"My business is medicine, Glen. I'm a vet. In the city, I saw the spoiled pets of spoiled people, but I've always wanted the challenge of working with large animals. Now I have that chance.

"It'll take several years to get things going; but eventually, I want to make it a working ranch – raise corn, hay, alfalfa, rye, vegetables, and a few head of my own livestock." Ray's excitement and enthusiasm about the opportunity and promise he'd found in Red Valley was clear.

"Les will be glad to hear that," Glen signed, somewhat relieved. "She's worried herself silly over the old farm, afraid that Walter would sell it to someone who would destroy the land she grew up loving, in some ruthless scheme to make a fast buck. She must've thought her worst fear had come true, and you were that someone."

"No wonder she ran away from me," the tall newcomer concluded. "I'll do my best to reassure her that her family farm is safe in my hands. And I'm going to have a talk with my cousin. You say he practically stole the farm from her? How could he do that?"

"Knowing Walter, it was all legal and above board. He wouldn't have it any other way. Les's grandfather was a few months in arrears on his mortgage and Walter claimed the bank wanted to foreclose. He pretended to be doing Les a favor by buying it himself, but Walter doesn't do favors for anyone who can't offer him large return. He never lays out one penny unless he expects to make two.

"That's all Les will say about it, but I think something else went on between them, too, something sleazy. It's just a suspicion of mine that she won't confirm. She refuses to talk about it, even with Mary Ellen," the pastor told him.

"Wouldn't put anything past Walter," Ray confirmed. "He's too much like his father, too conniving and too sly by half. We've never seen eye-to-eye about much. I'm going to get to the bottom of this. I know the garbage my arrogant cousin can dish out, and Leslie's too special to be exposed to his particular brand of torture."

"You like her, don't you?" Glenwood asked, smiling with satisfaction.

"What's not to like?" Ray acknowledged. "She's sensitive, smart, independent, and exceedingly easy on the eyes."

Unable to suppress his delighted laughter, Glen's large frame shook.

"What's so funny?" his companion quizzed.

Between chuckles, the preacher explained, "Our Les is considered quite plain by most folks, and even homely by some. She's been the brunt of teasing and bullying most of her life, much of it started by your cousin Walter."

"That's hard to believe," Ray declared, running his hand through his shaggy hair. "How could anyone look at Leslie and not see beauty? She moves with an unusual grace, her voice is captivating, and her face is striking. When I saw her in the diner last night, I just had to get to know her.

"Those stormy eyes of hers just suck you in. And then this morning in church - WOW! There are no words to describe her, except totally gorgeous!"

"There definitely was a change in her today. I think everyone noticed it," Glen admitted. "When you look at her, you see the real Leslie. That's something most people don't take the time to do. Growing up,

Leslie didn't fit in and that hurt her deeply.

"She was too tall and too thin. Her hair was too curly and her glasses too thick. She wore homemade clothes and second-hand shoes. But her worst sin was being smarter than most, and refusing to follow the crowd. Walter Lewis hated her because he knew she could see through his bravado, to the corruption and insecurity inside. She ignored him like you ignore a pesky bug, and he punished her for making him feel small. Folks allowed their perception of Les to be colored by the pictures he and his friends painted."

"No wonder she seems so shy." His hazel eyes clouded in sympathy. "Lots of kids get teased and even bullied in school, but most don't carry that burden into adulthood. I'm surprised that Leslie hasn't shaken it off and moved on."

"Most get away from their home towns and leave their bullies behind," Glenwood noted. "Les couldn't do that. She had to stay here to take care of her grandparents. And she had to watch her tormenter gain more power and authority over others, power and authority he didn't deserve, of course, but still, his influence has grown, exponentially. With his success, Walter seemed to grow up a bit, moving on to bigger targets.

"For the years before he bought the Willow farm, he'd actually stopped going out of his way to humiliate Les, but since she transferred the deed to him, the skunk has redoubled his attacks on her. For reasons known only to Walter, he goes out of his way to take a jab or two at her whenever the mood strikes him – always in a public place, like the bank or the diner, where he has an audience for his abuse."

"Why would he do such an infantile thing?"

"Beats me. But my intuition tells me that it has something to do with the deal he made with her over the farm – the deal everyone knows was underhanded and unfair. As I said, I'm sorry to say this since he's your kin and all."

"Look, you can't tell me anything bad about Walter that I don't already know. Insulting him doesn't insult me. Tell on."

Glen sighed and continued, "I find it hard to understand the twisted mind of Walter Lewis – but I believe his attacks are an attempt to convince the town that Les deserves what he's done to her, along with what he continues to dish out. Whatever his motive, he has the town making fun of our girl again."

"I came on pretty strong last night," Ray noted thoughtfully. "I'm lucky I didn't scare her away."

"Well, I don't know what you did, or said, but I do know you've touched a place inside her that no one else has been able to reach. She's been so beaten down by all the jokes made at her expense, that Mary Ellen and I have given up trying to convince her that she isn't ugly and unlovable. But you got through. You brought her spark back.

"It's pretty clear that she's taken a shine to you and that's put a shine on her." Glenwood chuckled again, at his clever turn of phrase. "I've never seen a woman undergo such a radical transformation in such a short time, and I can't wait till your cousin gets a glimpse of the new Leslie. His face will turn green!"

The picture Glen had created of an apoplectic Walter Lewis, his fat, fleshy face tinged chartreuse, his bulbous nose glowing, and his loose jowls flapping in anger, caused laugher to erupt. When Mary Ellen, Leslie, and the twins rejoined the picnic, tears were rolling freely. With difficulty, the men quieted their guffaws and welcomed the women back.

"It's nice to see you boys found a way to amuse yourself in our absence," Mary Ellen quipped, still a bit annoyed with her husband.

"What'cha laughin' at, Daddy?" Mary Grace asked.

Taking a deep, calming breath, Glen explained the reason for their hilarity. Mary Ellen immediately joined in the mirth, but the twins look puzzled, unable to figure out what their parents found so funny about mean, old Mr. Lewis.

Ray rose from his seat and held out a hand to help Leslie, pleased to see a hesitant smile on her full lips. "I'm sorry, Leslie," he began. "I... I didn't know..."

"It's all right," she interrupted, refusing to sit down. "You couldn't have. Besides, it had to happen sooner or later." Her voice was tight. The hesitant smile and the hopeful openness had disappeared, closing her off. In a flash, she'd retreated to safer ground, putting her emotional defenses in place.

"Please sit a minute. Let me tell you about my plans for the farm," he offered hopefully.

"I'd rather not hear any more about it, if you don't mind," she stated flatly. "I'm going home, now." Turning to her friends, she said, "Thank you for a very lovely picnic."

"Ain't you gonna stay for dessert, Auntie Les?" Martha Joy asked, disappointedly. "Me and Mary Grace made a nana puddin' just for you and Mr. Ray."

Not wanting to hurt the tiny girl's feelings, Leslie knelt down and kissed her soft cheek. "Some other time, dear heart. Will you save some for me?"

"Sure," she agreed, squeezing Leslie's hand.

"I'll drive you," Ray offered politely.

"That's not necessary," the tall woman refused. "I don't want to take you away from the fun. You stay."

"I said I'll drive you," he insisted, impatiently, offering a handshake of thanks to Glenwood, a quick hug to Mary Ellen, and two hand-kisses to the girls.

With no energy left to continue the resistance, Leslie shrugged her goodbyes and followed Ray to the car, waiting patiently for him to assist her inside. The Cooper family watched them drive away, the twins' lower lips stuck out in identical, disappointed pouts.

They rode in silence. Ray's frustration at her stubborn refusal to give him a chance to explain his plans for her family's farm prevented him from wasting the effort on small talk. Leslie, overcome with loss and despair, ignored him. She couldn't bear to hear anything more about the fate of Willow Spring Farm. That wound was too raw. She would not break down in front of Walter Lewis's cousin. She would not let him see how her spirit had been crushed by his news.

When he pulled up to the curb, she flung open the door and jumped out, throwing back an insincere, "Thanks," and ran for the safety of her small bungalow.

"Leslie, wait," he called after her over the top of the SUV, but if she heard, she ignored him, never slowing. "You promised to show me around town," he murmured at her retreating form, his heart heavy.

PART II

Leslie was determined to put Ray Gallagher out of her thoughts, but she couldn't stop picturing him roaming the hills and fields of her beloved Willow Spring Farm. Her heart ached with renewed loss. Though her mind asserted that Ray could not be compared to his despicable cousin, her tender feelings rebelled, tying him to Walter Lewis with the unbreakable bonds of family. When Mary Ellen tried to advocate for Dr. Gallagher, Leslie cut her off sharply.

Deep old wounds had been reopened, and the pain welled up again, almost overwhelming her. Leslie relived every dreadful encounter she'd had with Walter Lewis. His loose-jowled, bulldog face, with its superior smirk, floated constantly in her mind's eye.

The only high point of the week had been her triumphant return to work on Monday morning. Reactions to her makeover left her blushing and speechless. Cook's jaw dropped open so wide that Leslie teasingly suggested that he was trying to catch flies in his gaping maw.

Carl whistled appreciatively and exclaimed, "Ooooh Weeee, what in heaven's name have you done to yourself, gal? You look plum wonderful! Talk about attractin' flies. The fellers are gonna swarm around you like bees to the honey. I just hope you won't be tempted to run off with one o' them, and leave me without my best waitress."

"Your only waitress!" Leslie corrected.

Carl's apprehension about his waitress deserting him for a new suitor quickly dissipated, as business and tips picked up. Word travels fast in a small town. It seemed that everyone had heard about the surprising transformation of poor old Les Willow, and wanted to drop by to see for themselves.

Uncomfortable with the unaccustomed attention, Leslie nervously waited on the curious gossips, answering their prying questions quietly. Most meant well and were honestly pleased to see such a pleasant change in the sweet, young woman. But there were also plenty of snide comments from those who sought to put her back in her place, as the easy target of their crude jokes. Few could see that the efficient waitress seemed sadder and more reserved than ever.

Saturday night finally arrived and found Leslie watching the clock, anxiously waiting for quitting time. She had just breathed a prayer of thanks that Ray had thoughtfully kept his distance from her and from the diner, when the bell over the door tinkled ominously. Turning reluctantly, and with a disappointed sigh, she came face to face with Walter and Sharon Lewis. Behind them stood Mindy Tucker, Sharon's best friend since junior high school. Rounding out the foursome was Ray Gallagher.

"Hey there, Les," Walter said cheerfully, nodding in her direction. "Guess it's okay to sit anywhere, since you don't seem too busy."

"Take your pick," she answered, choking back tears.

Walter moved past her toward a large table at the front window. Sharon shot her a smug smile before following her husband. When Ray hesitated and began apologetically, "Leslie, I…" Mindy put her hand on his elbow possessively, to propel him along.

"Come on, sugar. I'm hungry," she whined, leaning against him suggestively. Shrugging helplessly, he complied.

Leslie gave them a few moments to get settled and review the menu before grabbing her pad and pencil and moving to stand at Walter's elbow. "What'll it be?" she asked, keeping her eyes carefully focused on the grungy floor tiles.

Ignoring her, Sharon complained about the plain fare and meager selection the diner offered. "I told you we should drive over to Westlake. There's nothing here worth eating."

"Now, sweety cakes," Walter placated. "You know it's too late to go anyplace else. If we'd been able to pry Ray away from that dilapidated old farm, we could've arranged a nice meal at a fancy restaurant, but with him draggin' his feet till almost dark, this is the best we could do. I'm sure you can find something you like." He turned his attention from his pouting wife, who sniffed snobbishly as she studied the plastic-covered menu, to examine Leslie.

The tall woman shivered involuntarily as his lecherous gaze slid over the length of her. After a second or two, he sucked air through his teeth and sneered. "Well, well, well. Look at you. Now didn't I tell you that you'd clean up nice, if you'd just put out the effort? The job offer I made you last winter still stands, you know. Come by my office when you wise up."

When his prodding failed to elicit a response, he added, "Oh, Les, I think you've met my cousin, Ray." Noting her silent nod, he continued, his tiny pig-eyes sparking with mischief, "I'm so grateful he was stupid enough to take that useless place of yours off my hands."

"Yes, Walter," she snapped, her patience stretched to the breaking point. "I thought you folks were hungry. Do you want something to eat or not?"

"My, my, my, aren't we touchy?" Mindy whined again, pressing her full, lace-covered bosom into her companion's arm. "You'd better be careful how you talk to us, girl. Carl won't take kindly to the help being rude to his customers."

Neither woman noticed how Ray's brows drew together as he listened to the exchange, and both were surprised when he came to the waitress's defense. "It's late and Leslie has had a long day. Let's just place our order."

He deliberately removed Mindy's hand from his sleeve and shifted his body away from hers. "You know what I want," he told Leslie with an apologetic grin, his enchanted-forest eyes boring straight into her heart.

Hands shaking, she marked hamburger, Dr. Pepper, and lemon chess pie on her pad. "How about the rest of you?"

Shocked into subdued obedience by Ray's demand, his companions made their choices. Leslie slipped the sheet to Cook, filled their beverage requests, and hid out behind the counter until the order was up.

She delivered the steaming plates to the table and retreated, only to be called back repeatedly, to bring this or that. Walter enjoyed his position of power, keeping her at his beck and call. Finally, after second helpings, dessert, and three coffee refills, the banker reared back in his seat, making room for his generous belly, and tossed his balled-up napkin on his plate.

Leslie breathed a sigh of relief, praying they were leaving, but to her utter frustration, Walter waved at her once more. Dragging her feet, she made her way back to their table at the front of the diner. "Is there something else?" she asked as softly and politely as she could manage through clenched teeth.

"Oh, no," he chucked, patting his paunch, "The food was passable, and I couldn't eat another bite, but a funny thought just crossed my mind that I have to share with you." His beady eyes shone with malice, twisting her stomach with ice-cold dread.

"Ray, you remember that summer you spent with me and my folks?"

"Sure, Walter," he replied hesitantly, clearly fearful that this was yet another ploy to humiliate Leslie.

"Well, do you remember going with me and my buddies to a dance at the school?"

"That was a long time ago, Walter, and I don't think anyone's interested in hearing about the misadventures of a couple of stupid teenagers. Can we drop it please?" Ray pleaded, obviously not liking where this discussion was headed.

Ignoring his cousin's protestation, the determined bully directed his attention to Mindy, so anxious to sink the knife into his intended victim that he wrung his pudgy hands in glee. "But this is classic. The girls will love it. I'm sure they remember that dance. Don't you, girls?

Both Sharon and Mindy nodded encouragingly. "What happened?" Mindy asked, leaning toward Walter.

"Well, we dared Ray to dance with the ugliest girl in the school, and not being one to wimp out, he accepted the challenge! Could hardly believe my eyes when he went right up to her, standing against the wall in that god-awful, shiny green dress, and stuck out his hand. She was too stupid to know it was just a joke, of course.

"I was sure he'd bolt when she accepted, but no. Old Ray, always a gentleman, danced with the cow for an entire song, and earned himself his reputation for the summer. All the guys were convinced he had balls of pure steel!"

"Walter, that's enough!" Ray barked. "We're leaving, now!"

"Wait, wait, I haven't gotten to the best part yet," Walter

sneered, grabbing Les's arm and pulling her closer. She tried to resist but her limbs were leaden. "Here she is, Ray. Not quite so ugly anymore, but still too tall and stringy for my taste. Why not re-live the old days?

"Sharon, put a quarter in the jukebox," he urged his wife, who joyfully complied, thoroughly enjoying the fun at Leslie's expense.

Ray jumped out of the booth and grabbed for his cousin's shirt front. But before he could get a grip on Walter, the banker pulled Leslie between them. "Go on. Show us you've still got those big marbles!" The trio broke out in shrieks of derisive laughter.

As the first strains of a soft country ballad began, Leslie knew Ray could feel her body, forced against his, trembling in anger and humiliation. She tried to back away, but he raised his arm and encircled her, pinning her against his chest.

Lifting her chin with one long finger, he looked straight into her stormy eyes, brimming with unshed tears. "Our public is calling, my dear," he whispered. "Let's not disappoint them."

Suddenly the dingy walls of the diner faded, the taunting faces disappeared, the noisy laughter evaporated. The only things Leslie Willow could see were the slightly crooked smile and adoring eyes of Ray Gallagher. The only things she could hear were the sweet music and the ragged sound of his breathing. The only things she could feel were his strong arms around her and his heart pounding against her breast. As he swept her around the room, dodging tables, time stopped, and everything changed.

When the song ended, Ray pulled his gaze from hers and searched the room for his cousin. The incredulous look on Walter's face was easy to read. His scheme had backfired, and he knew it. "You and Sharon will have to see Mindy home. I'm staying with Leslie, if she'll have me."

Oblivious to everything but one another, their eyes remained locked, their arms encircling. For the second time in her life, Leslie felt at peace, folded in Ray's embrace, safe, complete. While Carl and Cook stared in stunned silence, and Walter and his retinue shuffled out the door in obvious defeat, Leslie basked in the green-gold glow of Ray's eyes. Long moments passed before she pulled away with a deep sigh.

"I need to get home," she breathed, unsure. "It's late and my cat needs to be fed."

Not waiting for an invitation, the tall man plucked her sweater from its hook, placed it over her shoulders, and pulled open the door.

"Cats like me, you know," he declared, his jaunty grin wide. "I'm great with a can opener."

Watching them disappear around the corner, arm-in-arm, Carl flipped the switch on the neon *OPEN* sign and snickered, "Well, I'll be. That's the first time I seen the tables turned on old Walter Lewis. Must say it's about time."

They walked the short block to her tiny bungalow in silence. Leslie welcomed him in and put on water for tea, while Ray proved his skill by deftly separating the lid from a can of cat food, and dumping it out into the bowl emblazoned with *Marmalade* in bright orange letters. As he waited, the big tabby wound around the man's legs expectantly, purring loudly. "See," he beamed. "I told you cats like me."

"Marme likes anyone who fills his food dish," she teased lightly. "Don't make too much of his praise. He's pretty fickle."

"You're not going to make this easy, are you?" Ray asked ruefully.

"Not if I can help it," she replied, offering a tentative smile. "If you're determined to stick around, make yourself comfortable while I freshen up. The swing on the porch is pretty nice. I'll change and bring out the tea."

"Since I sent my ride off without me, I'll have to take you up on your generous offer. It's a long walk home," he remarked playfully.

"No one twisted your arm, Ray. You can leave anytime you want," Leslie prompted him uncertainly. "You could give Mindy a call. She'd be happy to drive over and pick you up. Her second husband left her a big, expensive Buick that she's anxious to show off. If you're lucky, she'll invite you to try out the back seat."

The bright tears sparkling against her dark lashes told Ray that her sarcasm stemmed from fear and insecurity. She tried to turn away, but he caught her hands and held them tightly, forcing her to look at him.

"Leslie, I'm sorry for what Walter tried to do to you tonight, and for all the pain that insensitive jerk has caused you. I'm not Walter. I'm not like Walter. He can't see what a special person you are. I can. I do. I always have. I saw it twenty years ago, and I see it now. Please don't compare me to him."

Embarrassed by the depth of emotion in his plea, she pulled her fingers out of his grasp and smiled into his eyes. The unexpressed longing took her completely by surprise. "I…I'm sorry, too," she stuttered. "I know you aren't like Walter. Please, please, stay. I want you to. Wait for me. I won't be a minute."

Before he could agree, she whirled around and headed for the bathroom, where she quickly washed up, changed out of her grimy uniform, fluffed up her hair, and applied some lotion to her chapped hands. Finally, she dabbed some light, floral cologne behind her ears and slicked on lip gloss.

Ray heard the screen door squeak and turned to see Leslie pushing her way outside, carrying a huge tray. The light from the hallway poured out into the semi-darkness, enveloping her, and setting her auburn locks aflame. He watched her in awe before unwinding his long legs and moving to help her with the tea and cookies.

She poured a cup for him and a second for herself. Timidly, she slipped into the swing beside him. For a while they nibbled on the shortbread and sipped the steaming liquid in silence, enjoying the lilac-scented evening breeze.

"You don't have any idea how beautiful you are, do you?" he asked her sincerely.

Choking on the tea, she sputtered, "I know I look better than I used to, but I'm not beautiful, Ray."

"You can protest all you want, Leslie, but I love the way you look," he declared, leaning closer and inhaling deeply. "And the way you smell."

"That's just moisturizer. Working with all the disinfectant and hot water takes a toll on my hands," she explained.

"You need to learn how to take a compliment. You're much too modest. Just say 'Thank you, Ray'." he instructed.

"Thank you, Ray."

"That's better," he said, putting his arm around her and pulling her close.

"I think you're pretty handsome yourself," she added bravely.

"No, not handsome," he corrected, "but good-looking enough, in a rugged sort of way, or so I've been told,"

"Now who's being modest? You are the most attractive man I've ever met," she countered, surprising them both with her forthright admission. When he failed to respond after a pause, she prompted,

"Say 'Thank you, Leslie'."

"Thank you, Leslie." He chuckled, deep in his chest, and her body reverberated with the sound of it.

He set his teacup aside and reached for hers. Placing it carefully on the tray, he turned his face toward her and tightened his embrace. "Do you know what I've seen in my dreams every night for the last twenty-odd years?"

She shook her head.

"Your eyes," he whispered, "your stormy, sea-blue eyes. Until tonight I couldn't put them into a face, but I've dreamed about those eyes, your eyes. Sometimes I'd wake up and they'd still be there, haunting me. I'd look over, expecting to find the woman with the stormy eyes lying there beside me; but instead, I'd find my wife. And then I'd feel guilty because I'd dreamt of another woman's eyes."

Deeply moved, heart threatening to explode, she whispered, "Did you love your wife?"

"Not enough, I guess," he admitted.

"What do you mean?" she probed.

"It's hard to explain." He paused and cleared his throat. "For years I searched for the woman of my dreams, the woman with your eyes. I'd given up looking when Wanda came into my life. I was very vulnerable, very needy. It was my last year of college and I was living on a shoestring. My father had just passed away. Wanda took me under her wing, got me through the funeral, and helped me and my Mom put his things in order.

"Dad's death was a killing blow to my future. He left my mother with nothing but a pile of bills she couldn't pay. In addition to his debts, I had thousands in student loans. There was no way I could afford to finish medical school or set up a practice, so I'd decided to quit college, give up my dream, and get a job to pay off bills and support my mom.

"That's when Wanda stepped in. Her family was very well off. She convinced her father to invest in me, pay off what we owed, and give me the tuition for med school. After graduation, he helped me rent and equip a small office in a good part of town. Before I knew what had happened, Wanda and I were married, and Richard was on the way. I don't even remember asking her to marry me; it just seemed the next logical step, so I took it without thinking.

"I'm ashamed to admit it, but I never loved Wanda the way a husband should love a wife. I've carried a bushel-basket of guilt about that, too, and for the other ways I used her to make my life easier. To assuage the guilt and pay her back for what she'd given me, I threw myself into my work, spending all of my days and most of my evenings in the clinic. I guess I thought making a lot of money was the way to absolve myself of my debt to her, but in the end, I found out different.

"I still believe that if I'd been there for her, if I'd been a loving and devoted husband, she wouldn't have died." His eyes grew vacant and his thoughts seemed far away.

"Ray, you can't blame yourself for your wife's illness. You had nothing to do with her cancer. I know you did everything possible to help her, to save her. I can't imagine you doing anything else. You're too kind, too caring," she urged, trying to understand and console him.

"I could have loved her more," he said with a shake of his tawny locks. "I'll always wonder what difference it would've made if I'd been the husband she deserved. She built a life for us, sacrificed everything, including her career, and I couldn't even love her with all my heart."

"Oh, Ray, I never met your wife, and I haven't known you for very long really, but I think you've shown me your heart." She waited until he was focusing on her and her words. "It sounds like Wanda entered into your marriage with her eyes wide open. I can't believe you promised her something you couldn't deliver. She knew you didn't love her with all of your heart, but she was willing to accept the part of your heart you were able to give.

"You say she sacrificed for you, for your future, but didn't she plan that future? Think about it, Ray. You were her career. Didn't she get just what she wanted out of your marriage – a successful husband, a fine son, an attractive house in the best neighborhood?"

Leslie gave him time to recognize the possible truth of her conjecture. "Did your wife ever complain about wanting more from you?"

He answered thoughtfully, "There was one time when she was set on joining a country club, which I opposed strongly, and another when she wanted a bundle of cash for new clothes she didn't need for a trip somewhere, and one when she read me the riot act because I refused to cater to one of her society friends."

"But what about time together, Ray, did Wanda ever complain that you didn't give her enough of yourself?" When no response came, Leslie added, "I didn't think so. You gave her what she needed – your name, your success, your position in the community. She didn't really want more of you – even if you'd been able to give her more. You need to stop blaming yourself."

"What makes you so smart?" he asked, the wisdom of her words seeming to salve the raw wound he'd kept open for so long.

"When you spend your life as an outsider, like me, without many special relationships of your own, you tend to spend a lot of time observing the relationships of others. Over and over, I've seen women like your wife, women who go after men for their potential, or their name, or their position. Once they have the man they want, they put all of their energy into molding that man into the husband they want him to be, and into building the home and family of their dreams. Their marriage is only a means to an end – to build a life that others will admire and envy.

"If Wanda had truly loved you, unselfishly, she would have helped you build the life you wanted. Instead she used you to build the life she wanted."

Her sincerity and insight beginning to erode his mountain of accumulated guilt, Ray noted, "Only an observer of the relationships of others, huh? I can't believe you haven't ever been in love."

She smiled into his eyes, "I have been in love, Ray. Since I was 14 years old and a tall, gangly boy braved the taunts of his friends and dared to dance with me."

Shaking his head incredulously, Ray concluded, "I can't believe I've found you again, after all these years."

"I loved you without ever knowing your name," she whispered as he pulled her close, wrapped his strong arms around her, and lowered his face to hers. The kiss was caressing and soft at first, but soon became more intense and demanding. Years of waiting, of hoping, of longing, were brought to fulfillment in that moment. The exchange was utterly delightful, and totally insufficient, to ease the deep need they felt, so it was several minutes before Ray drew away, reluctantly, stroking her cheek with his knuckles.

"You're the woman of my dreams, Leslie Grace Willow," Ray admitted, his hazel eyes sparkling with golden lights, even in the semi-darkness. "I don't know how it's possible, but I've loved you for a long, long time. I believe we were always meant to be together. I should never have let Walter and his friends drag me away from you."

"No regrets," she declared. "We're together now. We have to trust that our lives took the paths they did for important reasons – reasons we don't understand, but important ones, nonetheless. I'm just thankful we made a connection on that special night years ago, a connection that endured and somehow brought us back together."

Words seemed to fail him, so Ray kissed her again, tenderly. This time it was Leslie who pulled away, many moments later, smiling broadly, and brushing a stray lock of tawny hair from his forehead.

"What happens, now?" she asked uncertainly. He looked puzzled, his brow furrowed in confusion, so she added, "I'm a relationship novice, remember? I don't have a clue what comes next. Where do we go from here?"

"Oh, come on, I can't believe you've never had a boyfriend," he told her with obvious surprise.

"No, really, you're the first," she affirmed.

"Well then…" he said, hesitating, "that does put the pressure on, doesn't it? Since it's been a while for me, too, let's just take things as they come. So far, it's been perfect, don't you think?"

"Yes, perfect!" she agreed, smiling up at him, her sea-blue eyes sparkling.

"Oh, woman, you make me want to shout with joy!" he declared, launching himself from the swing and pulling her along. "I want to tell the whole world!"

"Shh…Ray, please," she begged. "It's late. You'll wake the neighbors."

"You're right, my love. It is late, and you need to get some rest. I know you've had a very long day," he insisted.

Shivering at his endearment, she nodded regretfully, "I was tired, before, well…before you held me, before you told me you loved me. But I won't sleep a wink tonight. I'm too happy."

Hesitantly she added, "I want you to stay, Ray, but I'm not ready for that, yet."

He kissed her again quickly. "It's too soon – for both of us. I'd better go," he said, moving toward the steps. "The long walk will do me good. I can spend it thinking of you and trying to cool down!"

Leslie's amused chuckle echoed deeply and seductively. "You don't have to walk. I have a car you can use. It's not much to look at, but it's dependable. Wait a second, I'll get the keys."

Ray barely had time to draw a couple of calming breaths before she was back, keys in hand. "It's parked around back, in the alley. There's plenty of gas in it, despite what the gauge says."

"I'll take it on one condition," he told her, "that you come out to the ranch with me after church tomorrow and fetch it. I'll fix lunch for you, and show you what I'm doing with the place. I think you'll be pleased."

"Oh, I don't know," she said, her body tensing. "You don't need to cook for me; and besides, I don't need the car. I walk almost everywhere I go. You can bring it back anytime."

"Did I say you had a choice here?" he teased, determined to press his point. "I will walk home unless you promise to spend Sunday afternoon with me. Or maybe I should go call Mindy. Do you know her number?"

"Okay, okay, you win," she sighed with a smirk, throwing up her hands in defeat. "I'll be happy to have lunch with you after church tomorrow, Mr. Gallagher."

"Great. I'll pick you up at 10:30 sharp. Bring some old clothes with you and comfortable shoes." He kissed her soundly one last time, before bounding down the porch stairs and around the house.

Leslie watched as he backed the tiny, blue VW Beetle out of the alley and into the street. She waved a tearful farewell when he tooted the horn and buzzed off down the block.

Despite her prediction to the contrary, Leslie quickly fell into a deep and peaceful sleep, her heart full to overflowing. She was ready and waiting, outfitted in a sea-green suit she'd bought on a whim and had never had the courage to wear, when Ray rounded the corner in his big SUV. He jumped out of the vehicle, almost before it had stopped moving, and grabbed her up, gleefully swinging her around.

After kissing her softly, he announced, "I thought the morning would never get here. I could hardly wait to see you again." She smiled into his eyes, not trusting her voice. He put her down, grabbed her hand, and led her to the car. A few minutes later they were standing at the front door of the church, where Mary Ellen and her girls waited to greet them.

"Hey, Les. Hey, Mr. Ray," the twins chimed simultaneously. Leslie bent down and kissed them both. "Oh, wow, Auntie Les, you look bee-u-ti-ful!" Mary Grace beamed.

"I agree," Ray added, his arm circling Leslie's waist possessively.

"It's good to see you two together," the preacher's wife noted.

"It's good to be together," Leslie admitted softly, reassured by the gentle squeeze Ray gave her. They followed the flow of fellow worshipers and moved inside. Ray urged her to the pew near the front, where they'd sat the previous Sunday, and waited while she slid across the polished boards. Once he was nestled close beside her, he entwined his fingers with hers.

The service passed almost without notice, as Leslie's thoughts were totally absorbed by Ray's masculine presence, the warmth of his thigh pressed against hers, and the clean, fresh scent of his soap and after shave filling her head.

Before she knew it, the organ postlude swelled, and the recessional began. Well-wishers and the merely curious surrounded them as soon as the final note sounded, full of questions for Ray.

"Hello, there." Henry Simpson's booming voice rose above the din. "It's good to have you back with us again." He stuck out his hand and smiled a warm welcome to the newcomer.

Then he looked searchingly at Leslie, clearly amazed by the change in her. Always the efficient businessman, Henry put in a plug for his pharmacy. "Being that you're in the medical field, Dr. Gallagher, we're colleagues of a sort," he suggested. "If there's ever anything you need personally, or for your practice, just holler."

"Thanks, Henry," Ray said politely. "I order most of my supplies and drugs directly from the distributor, but you'll be the first one I call if an emergency comes up."

When the pharmacist moved on, they tried to make their way out, only to have the aisle blocked by Mindy Tucker. "Good morning, Ray," she purred. "I see you're still slummin' it this morning."

She swept Leslie, head to toe, with a look of total loathing before pressing close to Ray. "I'm not accustomed to being cast off like an old shoe, my dear man, but seeing as how you're so handsome, and such a good catch, I'll forgive you this one time."

"That's considerate of you, Mindy," he countered sarcastically, trying unsuccessfully to push past her, "but this isn't the time or place to discuss it."

"Of course, you're right," she agreed, leaning in to whisper. "But be warned. You haven't seen the last of me." Then she pointed an accusing finger at Leslie. "And neither have you." Then she whirled around and pranced up the aisle, her red curls bouncing furiously.

Leslie was thankful they were able to escape the church with no more unwanted encounters. She breathed a relieved sigh when they reached Ray's truck. He deftly steered the big vehicle onto the highway, and headed out of town. The conversation lulled as they neared Willow Spring Farm, and Ray slowed to pull into the long, graveled drive.

Leslie silently surveyed the familiar fields and rolling pastureland, pleased to see them relatively unchanged. She turned to look questioningly at her escort, when he braked to a grinding halt, pebbles crunching under the tires. He said nothing, but pointed to an object standing on the left side of the lane.

Her eyes followed his long finger and came to rest on a newly painted, wooden sign. *Willow Spring Farm* was printed in bright green letters under a raised carving of a droopy willow in full leaf. Beneath the large sign, a smaller one was hung on swivel screws. It read *Gallagher Veterinary Clinic.*

Leslie threw open the door and bounded around the car to examine the attractive sign more closely. Ray followed, smiling as she ran her hand over the letters, almost lovingly. "It's wonderful," she breathed, tears threatening. "Thank you for remembering my family this way. My grandparents would be pleased and honored."

"Well, it is the perfect name for this place. As soon as I heard it, I knew I'd never be able to come up with anything better," he admitted, a bit embarrassed by her show of gratitude. "Don't you think that tree looks like the one that stands over the spring?"

"Yes, yes, it does," she agreed. "When did you have this done?"

"Last week," he said, nervously shifting his feet. "After Glenwood told me about the history of this place, I went over to the woodworking shop in Westlake. It's amazing what they can do from a snapshot."

Still admiring the sign, she commented softly, "You're a veterinarian."

"Of course," he told her, puzzled. "What did you think?"

"A people-doctor of some sort, I guess. You said you went to medical school and had a practice in the city. Henry Simpson said you were in the medical field, so I assumed… It just never occurred to me that you were an animal doctor."

"Well, that's what I am, and your family farm is the perfect place for me to set up my practice." Noting the tears springing to her eyes, he added, "I'm not going to ruin it, Leslie. I'm just fixing it up some. Come on," he urged. "If you like this, I can't wait to show you the rest."

Minutes later, they pulled up in front of the old farmhouse. Leslie could see that he was making good progress with much needed repairs. The siding had been scraped and primed, awaiting fresh paint. A pile of broken shingles was piled in one corner of the yard, giving evidence that the roof had been recently replaced. Looking up, she saw that a sparking gray metal roof now topped off the graceful structure.

He parked the Land Cruiser alongside her ancient Volkswagen, opened his door and came around to open hers. Holding her elbow, he led her up the stairs and onto the wide porch, where a white wicker rocker and settee peeked out from under canvas drop cloths. Les was a bit disappointed to note that the antique cedar swing, where she had loved to sit, reading and dreaming, had been removed.

"Excuse the mess," he apologized. "The exterior isn't finished. The painters are supposed to be back next week. Let's go in. Things are pretty much done inside."

As soon as Ray opened the front door, they were greeted by a wiggling, twisting blur of golden fur. "Hold on there, big fellow," the man scolded gently. "Slow down and show some manners." The soothing tone of his master's voice calmed the excited dog. He stopped his prancing to regard the woman with gentle brown eyes, his generously plumed tail fairly flying from side to side.

"Leslie, this is Max. Max, meet Leslie."

Leslie reached out her hand so the big retriever could get her scent, then she stroked his silky head lightly. "Hi, Max."

"Go on, boy." Ray held the screen and gave him permission to exit. "Have fun, but don't you go running my cows, now, you hear?"

Once the dog was out of sight, Ray told her, regretfully shaking his tawny head, "Max is usually better behaved, but it's just been the two of us for so long, he's overjoyed to have some company. He really misses Richard."

Dismissing his apology, she asked, "When will your son be here?"

"Next weekend, I hope," Ray answered. "I'm planning on leaving for Greenville Friday. I'll spend a couple of nights with Wanda's folks, and bring him back with me on Sunday. Can't wait for you to meet him."

Suddenly nervous and uncomfortable with the uncertainty presented by that inevitability, she changed the subject abruptly. "You've got me here, now, so show me around. I'm anxious to see what you've done with the place."

"You know your way around as well as I do," he concluded. "Why don't you give yourself a tour while I put lunch on the table? You'll find me in the kitchen when you're done."

Nodding agreement, Leslie watched his long strides take him

down the hall toward the back of the house. She pulled her gaze from his retreating back to examine her surroundings. She knew immediately that she liked the changes and improvements Ray had made.

His taste in color, furnishings, and appointments seemed to parallel her own. The walls had been painted a cool, winter white, with baseboards, doors, and hardwood floors polished to a high gloss. The stairs and banister leading upstairs had been carefully refinished, so the wood glowed with a hand-rubbed sheen.

Sturdy and unpretentious, the sofa, chairs, and side tables in the living room had obviously been chosen with care. The neutral colors and durable fabrics, with touches of blue, green, and brown, were homey and welcoming. Photographs of all sorts were the primary accessories. They hung over the fireplace, between the windows, and up the staircase, framed in a variety of rich woods.

She wandered through the dining room, running her fingers over an exquisite Chippendale table of warm cherry. A matching sideboard stood against one wall, and a breakfront, filled with glistening china and crystal, covered half of another. An elaborately carved, silver tea service, adorning the center of the large table, seemed out of place in the otherwise simple elegance of these rooms.

Upstairs she found the same general theme, off-white walls, warm burnished wood, and cool colors. The bedroom, that was tucked under the eaves in the front of the house, had obviously been prepared for Richard. Noting the bright red comforter, gold pillows, and school pennant prominently placed over the headboard of the bed, she cheered, "Rah-rah, Red Valley High!"

Next, she checked the middle bedroom, the one belonging to her grandparents, expecting to find Ray's belongings filling the tiny closet. To her surprise, it appeared to be the guestroom. An ivy-sprigged bedspread and matching curtains complemented the white iron-frame bed, and an old-fashioned, brass alarm clock stood guard on the oak nightstand, under a green-shaded lamp. The only decoration in the room was a porcelain bowl and pitcher placed atop the dresser, in front of a large mirror. A hand towel and wash cloth, in a deep spruce green, hung over the lip of the bowl.

On hesitant feet, Leslie made her way to the back bedroom, the warm, sunny one over the kitchen, the room with the huge dormer window sheltered by the thick, overhanging branches of an enormous hickory tree – her room. She took in her surroundings slowly, feeling Ray's touch permeating the atmosphere.

It clearly wasn't her sanctuary anymore. This room was definitely his now. A clean, masculine scent of soap and pine needles filled the air. Despite the nostalgia she felt for this place that had been her refuge, her haven from the cruelty of others, the sadness she had expected did not overtake her.

"This is nice," she admitted. "Cozy. I like it." From the cherry sleigh bed with its colorful patchwork quilt, to the length of muslin wound around a rod above the window and left to flow freely down each side, to the huge trunk with shining hinges placed against the foot of the bed, this room spoke to her. It welcomed her, invited her to stay. The closets of the old house were very small, she remembered, so to compensate, he'd placed a large, knotty pine armoire on the wall adjacent to the window.

But the very best addition to the room was a wide window-seat, filling the dormer. Growing up, Leslie had spent many hours uncomfortably curled up on the narrow sill, peering out at a fiery sunrise or starlit sky. She couldn't resist the temptation to try it out now. The leather-covered cushion was buttery soft, and before she knew it, she had relaxed completely, lost in memories of the past.

When his, "Lunch's ready," call failed to bring results, Ray went in search of his guest. He found her in his bedroom, perched on the window seat, long legs folded under her, staring off into the distance. She turned toward him just as he crossed the threshold.

At the sight of her, framed by the afternoon sunlight pouring in around her, he sighed, "That spot was made for you." Pausing a beat, he ordered, "Don't move," then crossed to the trunk, opened it and shuffled through its contents. "I want to remember you just this way," he added, pulling out an old thirty-five-millimeter Nikon and pointing it in her direction.

Always uncomfortable with having her picture taken, Leslie fidgeted nervously, until he insisted firmly, "Sit still, please. I promise it won't hurt a bit!"

Ignoring her protests, he snapped several shots before dropping the camera on the bed. "Okay, now you can move." He crossed the short distance between them in a flash and pulled her into his arms. "I can't think of anything nicer than finding you in my bedroom."

Flushing hotly, she smiled into his green-gold eyes, basking in the warmth of his adoration. He kissed her, softly at first, then with more demand. Several moments passed before he pulled away, whispering, "What did I do to deserve you?"

Then he added with some hesitance, "I'd like to keep you here indefinitely, but I promised you food. Let's go eat."

Over delicious chicken salad, rich croissants, and iced tea, they discussed the house, the farm, and Ray's plans for the future. Leslie gave him her stamp of approval on the improvements he'd made so far. She was particularly impressed by the kitchen, where he'd turned the old, well-used space into a modern country-kitchen. The back wall had been pushed out and a bank of windows added, opening up the space and bringing in acres of light. The addition of a sturdy table, large enough to seat six comfortably, and an adjoining family room/library/media center made the space inviting and functional – the hub of family life.

"I was lucky to find a great local contractor right after I bought the place," Ray explained. "I handed him the key and let him go to it, because I was too busy closing up my practice in the city to do any of the work myself. He sent me pictures of the daily progress, so I could put in my two cents, but mostly it's his design and craftsmanship."

When she praised his choice in furniture, he beamed proudly before telling her, "Except for the dining room suite and Richard's bedroom furniture, everything's new, or at least new to me. I did a lot of shopping at second-hand stores. Guess I went overboard on the getting-a-new-start idea, but I couldn't bring myself to move the Victorian and Louis XIV stuff Wanda preferred into this rustic farmhouse. It just didn't fit."

"Like the silver tea service on the dining room table."

"Yes, exactly!" he exclaimed. "I'm so glad you understand. I had to keep that hideous monstrosity, because it's an heirloom handed down to Wanda from her blue-blooded great-grandmother. One day it will belong to Richard. Then he can do with it as he pleases."

"It must be very valuable," Leslie commented, between forkfuls of the savory salad.

"I suppose," he agreed, nodding. "Wanda's family never settled for anything but the best. After I decided to sell the Greenville house and come here, I asked my father-in-law to put her things up for auction in their estate furniture department. The proceeds were placed in a college account for Richard. So far, he has a nest egg large enough for tuition at the school of his choosing, provided he can meet the eligibility requirements. And several of the most expensive pieces are still in storage."

"My goodness, I can't even imagine having that kind of wealth," Leslie said softly.

"Well, it doesn't make you any happier, that's for sure," Ray explained, his brows furrowing. "Before I met Wanda, I had no idea what it was like to have money, shameful, almost embarrassing piles of money. The summer I spent with the Lewis family gave me a hint at the petty, self-centeredness of the well-to-do, but Walter's folks are paupers compared to my in-laws.

"The more time I spent with the privileged rich of Greenville, the more I disliked them. I'm glad to be out of it. If I learned anything from my sixteen years of marriage, it's that true wealth comes from having something more than money, and in accomplishing something more than making bigger stacks of it."

"You're a wise man," Leslie agreed.

"Richard wouldn't agree," Ray noted with disappointment. "He's not happy about moving to the country, to this little 'hick town,' as he calls it.

"His grandparents have spoiled him unmercifully. They've insisted that he live with them, until I get this 'silly notion of a large animal practice' out of my system. Their words, not mine. It took me weeks to convince them that I would not allow Richard to stay in Greenville indefinitely. He's pushing back at me too, but I won't give in. I want him here in time for the beginning of the fall school term.

"I'm really dreading the visit with them this weekend. The pressure will be applied with a heavy hand. And I'm sure they'll play the – 'you're-an-ungrateful-lout' card. They always do. But I won't let them guilt me into giving in this time."

"Oh, Ray, I'm so sorry," Leslie breathed, squeezing his hand. "I wish I could help."

"You have helped, Leslie, more than you know." He smiled into her eyes and her heart somersaulted. "Just finding you, the girl of my dreams, gives me hope.

"I'm doing this for Richard, as much as for myself, and having you here makes it all feel right. You've only been in my life for a week, but I'm more certain of you, and of us, than I ever was of Wanda."

A flood of emotion washed over Leslie, leaving her uncertain and confused. She didn't know what to say, so she said nothing. Sensing her discomfort, Ray adroitly shifted the conversation back to his fledgling attempts at home decorating. "So, what do you think of my photographs?"

"They're yours? I mean, you took all these pictures?" she asked, her eyes sweeping the room.

"Yep, they're mine. Every single one," he declared with a mischievous grin. "Why do you sound so amazed?"

"It's not… I mean, I'm not…amazed, that you took them. It's just that…Well, they're so wonderful! I thought you were a veterinarian, not a photographer."

His lopsided smirk widened. "It's just a hobby, but I'm glad you like them. Wanda wouldn't display photographs in the house unless they were professional studio portraits. She preferred 'real art' to my amateur snapshots. So, I had the best ones framed and hung in my office. The four-legged set didn't object."

"You are a man of many talents," she teased. "What other surprises do you have up your sleeve?"

"Good question," he said with a wink. "Let's go see the barns, outbuildings, and livestock.

"Leave this," he told her when she began clearing the table. "We'll come back later for coffee and dessert. Go change into something more suitable for climbing fences. Your bag is in the hall bath."

When she emerged from the powder room, dressed in rugged denim and beat-up riding boots, she found Ray waiting patiently. He, too, had shed his Sunday finery, looking more appealing than ever in his faded jeans and chambray shirt, sleeves rolled up to the elbows. Leslie swallowed hard.

"Ready?" he asked. She nodded, accepting his proffered hand.

For several hours, they wandered the rolling hills of Willow Spring Farm. Ray showed off his state-of-the-art veterinary clinic, built inside the gutted block walls of the milking shed.

Leslie was impressed by the thoroughness of his design and with the quality of the contractor's work. It was bright and spacious, yet efficient. In addition to a large surgical area and treatment rooms, there was a small office and reception area, complete with modern desks and new personal computers. Ray's diplomas and license hung on the walls of the office, while the other space was ready and waiting for his yet-to-be-hired assistant.

She was pleased with the repairs and expansion he'd made to the stable, barns, and fences. Though she said very little as they walked and surveyed, the knot of pain and loss she'd had twisting her belly gradually relaxed. Ray had done right by Willow Spring Farm. She lifted the large, calloused hand, still gripping hers, and kissed the knuckles, her stormy eyes brimming with tears.

The tour ended at the springhouse, where the huge willow waved lacy fronds above a small stone structure that covered and protected the bubbling headwater. Ray stretched his long legs out on the grass, propped his back against the rough trunk of the tree, and pulled Leslie down beside him. He circled her shoulders with his arm and drew her in, until the back of her bright head rested on his chest. She let herself relax against him, listening to the soothing, tinkling sound of the spring, as it spouted out and tumbled down over the rocky creek.

Long moments passed before she could put words to the gratitude overflowing her heart. Finally, she offered, "Thank you, Ray, for preserving Willow Spring Farm and bringing out its full potential. I wish my grandparents could see it."

Ray smiled enigmatically. "Maybe they can. I believe our loved ones look down on us from heaven, watch over us, and keep us safe. I think they do see this place, through you."

She whispered. "I hope you're right."

"Of course, I am."

They sat in contented silence, watching the sun moving lower in the sky and the shadows lengthening. Leslie could feel Ray's breath caressing the top of her head. The deep gentle rhythm of it told her he'd drifted into sleep. She sat as still as she could for a long time, trying not to wake him, until her aching limbs screamed in protest.

Despite her effort to slip gently out of his embrace, his lids popped open at her first wiggle. "Just where do you think you're going?" he asked her, his eyes twinkling.

"It's getting late. I need to get home. I have to work tomorrow, you know," she said, with chagrin.

"I wish I could keep you here with me forever," he declared, pulling her back against his chest and kissing her deeply and repeatedly. All desire to leave him evaporated, and she melted into his arms.

A while later, he signed in resignation and whispered, "If we don't stop that, this very second, I'll be forced to carry you off to my bedroom and have my way with you. And neither of us is ready for that yet." Gritting his teeth, he pushed up to standing and offered Leslie his hand. "But you can't leave without dessert. Let's go."

The fudge brownies, topped with vanilla ice cream and chocolate syrup, were rich, gooey, and delicious. The exercise and fresh air had whetted their appetites, so they consumed the treat with relish. Leslie helped Ray with the dishes, collected her bag from the half-bath in the hall, and headed for her car. He gave her a gentle goodbye kiss and promised, "I'll see you next week."

And see her he did, every evening. Just before closing, Leslie would hear the bell above the door tinkle and turn to see him coming in, his smile wide. He'd walk her home, join her in a light supper, and sit with her on the porch until time to say goodnight.

One afternoon, the tall, fair-haired man surprised her. He slipped in quietly and took an empty stool at the counter, between Sam, the truck driver, and the pharmacist. Leslie was busy slicing freshly baked pies and failed to notice his arrival, until she heard his voice.

"Hello there, gentlemen." Ray nodded a greeting to his fellow diners.

"Hey there, Dr. Gallagher," Henry Simpson responded. "I'd like you to meet Sam Harris." He indicated the man to Ray's left. "Sam, this here's our new vet."

"Glad to meet you," Ray said, offering his hand. "Call me Ray."

Before Sam could respond, Leslie placed a large glass of Dr. Pepper in front of Ray. He smiled at her warmly, conveying his devotion in an instant.

"It's a pleasure, Ray," the truck driver said, retrieving his meaty palm. "Hey, what did you do to deserve such service? Les is a good waitress, the best there is in fact, but I've never known her to bring me food before I ordered it." Sam sounded just a bit jealous.

Leslie went back to her task, but listened attentively to the conversation as Henry explained things to Sam. "I don't know for sure, but based on the rumors floatin' round, our Les is quite taken with the good doctor here. Just look at the change in her." The pharmacist punctuated his assessment by nudging Ray's ribs with his elbow.

"I see. I see," the truck driver agreed, nodding. "Hey, Les!" he called, his gravelly voice teasing. "Is that right, are you carrying a torch for this tall, stringy fellow? Why I thought you were savin' yourself for me."

Blushing brightly, the waitress wiped her hands on her apron and turned back to the men. "Now, Sam," she began. "You know your wife is as jealous as they come. I'd be a fool to think I had a chance with you." She patted his hand before turning to his neighbor. "So, I guess I'll have to settle for this fellow, since I kinda like the look of him."

Ray responded with a grin. "Sorry, guys, you heard the lady. She's taken." He squeezed her fingers and asked, "Can you get away for a bit? Could we take a little walk?"

"I guess so. We're not busy, and I'm due for a break." Leaning through the window she called for Carl. "I'm taking my break now. Be back in half an hour."

They crossed the street, hand-in-hand, and headed for the tiny town square, where they sat on a wooden bench situated under a large oak. Ray draped his arm possessively across Leslie's shoulders.

For a few moments they sat in silence, enjoying the warmth of the sun on their faces, then she asked him, "What's up? What brings you to town so early in the day?"

"I had several errands to do. I picked up the front porch swing from the cabinet shop where I had it refinished." She rewarded him with a warm smile, pleased to hear he had not discarded the cherished old swing.

"Then I went over to the newspaper office and put in an ad for an office manager slash veterinary assistant for my practice. I talked with Stuart Martin, the editor, and he promised me he'd print it in Monday's edition. I'd like to find someone soon, because I'm starting to get a few patients."

"What type of person are you looking for? I mean, what sort of qualifications do you need?" she asked, her curiosity piqued.

He scratched his head, leaving his tan locks in disarray. "Well, basically, I want someone to answer the phone, make appointments, greet patients, keep the books and charts, do the billing, things like that. You know, manage the office."

"That doesn't sound too hard," she commented, thoughtfully. "You should be able to find someone pretty quickly."

"Problem is, I need someone who would also be willing to help me out with my patients occasionally, assist with treatments, minor surgery, and such. I'm afraid anyone with the skills to do the office work might not want to get their hands dirty with the direct care, but I can't afford to hire two people right now." He paused and leaned closer. "That's why I wanted to talk to you."

She looked puzzled but interested. Her stormy blue-gray eyes held him transfixed.

"I've heard that you do some bookkeeping for Carl and Mary Ellen. You were raised on a farm, so you must have practical experience with animals. So, I was wondering if you'd consider working with me at the clinic. What do you say, Leslie? Are you ready to give up the wonderful world of food service? Just say 'Yes,' and I'll run right back over to the <u>Red Valley Messenger</u> and tell Stuart to nix that ad."

"I don't know, Ray," she answered uncertainly.

"Why not?" he asked, clearly shocked by her hesitance. "You

can't be making much at the diner, not anywhere near what you're worth. I'd pay you well and your hours would be better. And, we'd be together."

"That would be wonderful," she admitted, "but are you sure I'm the best person for the job? You haven't even interviewed anyone else yet. What if you hire me and then find someone else who's a better fit?"

"Won't happen." Ray sounded confident. "You're perfect. You have more than basic office skills, don't you?"

She nodded.

"You have experience with animals, right?"

"Sure," she agreed. "I've helped my grandpa de-horn cows, band baby bulls, give vaccinations, and even more, but that's not the point."

"And what is the point?" he asked, annoyance flickering.

"I don't have any experience working in an office. What if I'm no good at it? I'd hate to sabotage your business before it gets off the ground. You need someone who knows what they are doing, who has done it before. Besides, what would Carl do for a waitress if I quit?"

"I'm sure he can find someone to replace you, but look," he said, sighing, "I want you to have the job, Leslie, but you need to be sure that it's what **you** want. So, this is what I'll do. I'll leave the ad in the paper, and do some interviewing next week, if I have any applicants.

"In the meantime, you think it over. I won't pressure you, but if you decide you want to give it a try, the job's yours. If I hire anyone, it'll be with the understanding that the job is temporary, week-to week. You just let me know when you make up your mind. How's that?"

"Oh, Ray, you're too generous," she breathed in his ear, hugging him tightly.

"Not hardly," he argued, running his fingers along the silky strands of her hair as they caressed his cheek. "I'm selfish. Hiring you would be the perfect way to get my practice up and running, and keep you close at the same time."

Noticing that she was choking back tears, he added, "Okay, I won't mention it again, but I'll be waiting impatiently for your decision." That said, he drew back and regarded her closely. "Now I need to ask you a favor."

"Name it," she said, her smile wide.

He took her hand, opened her fingers, and laid an old brass key across her palm. "I'm leaving for Greenville first thing in the morning, to pick up Richard. My in-laws hate Max, so I have to leave him here. Will you go out to the farm and check on him for me? The large animals will be fine. There's plenty of grazing and the tanks will hold enough water for a week, but poor old Max will be really lonely all by himself."

"Of course, I will," Leslie agreed gladly, fingering the key. "It would be a pleasure."

"Thanks." Ray placed a soft, tentative kiss on her cheek. "You're a real gem, my darling girl." Ignoring the stares of curious passersby, Ray kissed her again, his mouth teasing her full, trembling lips.

Pulling away in embarrassment, she scolded him, "Ray! People are watching."

"Let them," he declared. "I want the world to know how much I want you, Leslie."

Her cheeks flamed and she lowered her head, confused by the passion in his words. Sensing her reticence, he returned to safer ground. "We'll be back by mid-afternoon on Sunday. I'll call you when we get in."

"Okay."

"I don't know when I'll get to see you again," he told her, shrugging. "Maybe not be for a week or so. It'll take a while to get Richard settled in and registered for school. I want him to meet you, but I need to get re-connected with him first, get him accustomed to living in the country, help him make some new friends."

"I understand completely," she agreed. "You two need time together, to catch up. With luck, he'll feel right at home here before long. If there's anything I can do to help, just call. But please, take all the time you need. I'll miss you, but I understand."

"And I'll miss you, too," Ray declared. "I'll call you every day."

He took her hands in his as they rose from the bench. Squeezing them tightly, he looked into her eyes, his green-gold gaze boring into her heart. "I love you, Leslie Grace Willow."

"I love you, too," she whispered, accepting another kiss. With that he was off, long legs quickly covering the short distance to his vehicle.

After work on Friday, and again on Saturday, Leslie drove out to the farm to spend some time with the Gallagher's big retriever. He greeted her warmly, tail thumping furiously, while she refilled his food bowl and freshened his water. She threw a stick for him to fetch and sat on the porch with him for a while.

Suddenly, a thought struck her. "I just had an idea, Max," she told him. "You'll have to let me know what you think of it." His joyful doggy grin seemed to say that he would be okay with anything she suggested.

"I have a ham in the fridge at home. If I skip church and come out early tomorrow, I can bake that ham, along with some beans, make some potato salad and biscuits, and have dinner ready for Ray and Richard when they get here. What do you think of that plan, boy?" Max's eager regard and anxious wiggling was all the encouragement she needed. She put him back inside, locked up, and headed for her old VW with a promise to return, first thing in the morning.

About two o'clock the following afternoon, while Leslie was finishing the final clean-up, Max's ears perked up. He crawled out from under the table and ran to the front door. A few seconds later, she heard tires crunching gravel as the Land Cruiser rolled down the lane.

Extracting a platter, casserole dish, and heaping plate of hot bread from the oven, she placed them on the table. Next, she set out a large bowl of creamy potato salad, a stick of butter, and a new jar of homemade blackberry jelly. She was pouring tea into tall glasses full of ice when the golden dog bounded back into the kitchen, followed closely by Ray and his son.

"Leslie, what a nice surprise, finding you in my kitchen!" the tall man exclaimed, grabbing her, swinging her around, and kissing her soundly.

Setting her back on wobbly feet, he turned to Richard. "Come here, son. I want you to meet Leslie Grace Willow. Her family used to own this farm. Leslie, this is Richard." The boy was a couple of inches shorter than his father, and a bit stockier. His hair and eyes were a deep, warm brown.

Ignoring the welcoming hand she had extended to him, the sullen teen grunted, his dark gaze full of unspoken challenge, "That's my mother's apron. Who said you could wear it? What are you doing anyway? You don't live here anymore, you know."

"Richard! Apologize to Leslie immediately," Ray demanded. "There's no excuse for such rudeness."

"It's all right," Leslie intervened, touching Ray's arm. "Richard's right. I don't live here anymore, and I shouldn't have intruded on your reunion. I'm sorry. It was wrong of me to butt in.

"I just thought you'd be hungry after your long drive, so I put together a little something for you to eat. I hadn't planned to stay, anyway, so I'll be on my way." She removed the frilly, pink apron from around her narrow waist, folding it neatly, and returning it to the drawer where she'd found it.

"I think you have everything you need. I hope you enjoy the meal." Grabbing her purse, she headed for the door, trying to stem the flood of tears stinging her eyes.

Ray followed her to the car, stopping her before she could climb into the beat-up Beetle. "Leslie, I'm so sorry about the way Richard talked to you. Please don't think too badly of him. He's not angry at you; he's furious with me. He blames me for…for a lot of things."

"It's okay, Ray, really. I overstepped. Go to him. He needs you," she urged.

"Thank you for being so thoughtful and understanding." His parting kiss held just a hint of desperation. He hugged her a second too long, as if he feared letting her go. "I'll call you tomorrow."

Ray stood on the porch, watching the dust swirl behind the retreating VW, before heading back inside. "Come on, Richard," he urged. "It smells wonderful. Let's eat." Pulling out a chair, Ray folded his long legs under him and waited for his son, noticing for the first time that the table was set for three. "Not planning to stay, huh?" he mumbled to himself.

Part III

Leslie spent a restless night, tossing and turning, and fretting about Richard's outspoken animosity. He'd made it abundantly clear that he thought she was trying to take his mother's place, and that worried her greatly. She asked herself a million questions, rolling each one over and over in her mind. How should she approach him next time? What could she say that might help soften his attitude toward her? Would he stop being angry long enough to give her a chance?

Finding no answers and finally admitting defeat, she got out of bed, fixed herself a cup of tea, and sat on the front porch swing, with Marmalade, trying to talk it all out. "Why was I so stupid, so presumptuous?" she asked her furry friend, who listened patiently.

"Of course, the kid hates me. He walked into his new home for the first time and found a strange woman standing there, bold as brass, kissing his father while wearing his mother's apron. Could I have possibly been more insensitive?" The big, orange tabby purred and rubbed his face against her hand.

"Ray told me he wanted a few days alone with Richard, to help the boy get settled in. Why didn't I respect his wishes? Given time, Ray would have discussed our relationship with Richard, prepared him for meeting me. Maybe he would have been more open to the idea of his dad moving on and dating. Maybe he would have been more ready to give me a chance – if – if I'd been patient.

"Oh, Marme, I wish I hadn't acted on impulse. I wish I'd thought it through. I wish I hadn't been so anxious to impress Richard, and Ray. I should've left the food I'd prepared for them and given them the space they needed." With a deep sigh, she added, "I've really messed things up."

Despite releasing her worries to the feline's attentive, non-judgmental ear, Leslie slept very little that night, and left for work feeling dreadfully low. She knew she had to be patient, to give Ray and Richard time to work things out, and to wait to see what would happen next, but she found the uncertainty unnerving and unsettling.

Leslie preferred her life to be simple and predictable, but this situation was neither. Her thoughts and emotions rolled in turmoil.

Ray called every evening and they chatted about inconsequential things, which did little to calm her fears. Leslie struggled to be patient and keep focused on her work, but by Thursday afternoon, she was desperate to get out of the diner.

When the lunch rush was over, she told Carl that she needed to get a few staples to hold them over until the next delivery, and walked down the street to the Stop N' Shop. The store wasn't crowded, so she quickly made the rounds of the shelves, dropping several items into her basket.

At the checkout, she fell into line behind Ruth Barnes and her two active boys, who proudly grasped shiny, toy cars in their pudgy fists. The cashier totaled her purchases, while Ruth counted the bills she had folded in her hand. Leslie watched the woman squint at the cash register total and then at the small wad of cash, her cheeks flaming.

The young mother leaned in close to her sons and whispered, "I'm sorry, boys, but we'll have to put the toys back. We can get them another time."

That set up a chorus of wails from the rambunctious youngsters, who stubbornly refused to relinquish their treasures. As the frustrated woman wrestled with her sons, Leslie was shocked to see how old Ruth looked. Though the woman was at least five years her junior, the coarse lines and dark circles under her eyes, and the defeated sag of her shoulders, made Ruth seem much older. Her mousy brown hair was cropped short in an unbecoming style, probably by her own hand, and the old blue jeans and T-shirt she wore were faded and stained.

"How much do you need?" the kind waitress asked.

When Ruth turned toward her, Leslie could see that the woman's dark, chinquapin-brown eyes were sparkling with tears. "I'm two dollars short."

"Here," Leslie offered.

"It's very kind of you, but I can't take your money," Ruth proudly refused. "The boys don't need these cars. We can put them back."

"Please, accept it," Leslie urged, holding out two crisp ones. "I've been in your shoes, leaving home without enough cash in my purse. Happens to everyone sooner or later. You can return it anytime. I know you're good for it."

"Thank you," Ruth said, hesitantly taking the bills, her grateful look silently expressing her appreciation for Leslie's kindness, and her face-saving choice words. "I'll pay you back.

"Say thanks to Miss Willow, boys."

"Thank ya, ma'am," they chimed obediently. Her self-esteem reclaimed, Ruth straightened her chin, turned to the cashier, and handed over the money.

The little family was waiting for Leslie when she left the store, the woman balancing the grocery bag on a generous hip, while her boys raced their cars on the sidewalk. "I was just wondering," she began, hesitantly, "if Carl ever needs anyone to help out over at the diner.

"Since Josh got laid off from the mill, things've been pretty tight, you know, money-wise. He does odd jobs and such, but we've got nothin' regular comin' in. My sister's willing to stay with the boys when they aren't in school, if I can get a job. I'd really appreciate it if you'd let me know if you hear of anything."

It struck Leslie as providential that this needy young woman had come to her, looking for a job as a waitress, just when she was considering Ray's offer. Deciding it must be meant to be, she sent up a silent prayer of thanksgiving.

"As a matter of fact," she began, her words sparking a gleam of hope in Ruth's brown eyes, "I'm thinking of giving up waiting tables, so there might be a place for you. Problem is, I haven't told Carl about it yet. Could you come to the diner tomorrow morning, say around ten? We can talk to him together; and if he agrees, I'll train you immediately. If it works out you could start Saturday."

"That would be wonderful. I'll be there!" Ruth said beaming. She reached out to hug Leslie with her free arm.

"I need to warn you, though, the hours are long and the work is tiring. Do you really want to be away from your boys six days a week, from early morning 'til after dinner?" Leslie asked her.

"Gosh, I hadn't thought about that," the young mother admitted, thoughtfully. After a minute's hesitation she asked, "Do you think we could work out some way for my sister, Sarah, and me to split the job? She could use the money too. If you think it would be all right, she could fill in for me in the evenings, and we could take turns on Saturdays."

"Well, that seems like it could be a workable plan," Les said, nodding, her excitement building. "I can't see why Carl would mind. He'd be getting two waitresses for thc price of one. If he objects, we'll just have to convince him. So, I'll see you tomorrow?"

"Yes, ma'am," Ruth declared. "If Josh is home to stay with the boys, I'll bring Sarah with me, too, so's you can train us both."

"Sounds good," Leslie told her. "Got to get back now. Bye."

"Bye, Leslie, and thanks again."

Charged with optimistic anticipation, Leslie's afternoon flew by. In addition to her usual duties, she prepared the diner for the upcoming training session, making sure everything was spick and span, and that all the supplies were well-stocked and put away properly. She did her best to simplify and streamline processes and tasks for Ruth to take over, and to anticipate any objections Carl might have to the transition.

It was after eight before she dragged herself up the porch steps and into her bungalow. The phone was ringing. As promised, it was Ray. His melodic baritone held a hopeful note that lifted her sagging spirits. Ray said he and Richard were making good progress getting settled in and reconnecting.

He was very excited about a new veterinary client. Martin Bowman, a neighboring dairy farmer, who had called early in the week to ask Ray to check out his herd of Holsteins. Martin had been paying travel expenses for a veterinarian to come out from Westlake, so he was happy to have medical care for his herd closer by, and Ray was delighted to get the work.

The conversation was animated, on Ray's part, as he described his first visit to the Bowman farm, which had taken him the better part of the day, and left him tired, but satisfied that this work was what he wanted to do.

Leslie ended the call with, "I miss you, Ray" and was disappointed when he didn't respond in kind. Nor did he mention the job offer he'd made her. She reminded herself that he'd said he wouldn't pressure her, but she'd hoped he'd bring it up so she could tell him about the possibility of Ruth and Sarah taking over for her at the diner.

After she hung up, she told herself, "It's probably for the best. I'll wait to see if it's going to work out. Then I'll surprise him."

Despite her efforts to put the conversation out of her mind, nagging doubts haunted her. Ray seemed distant and distracted. A couple of days ago he'd told her he loved her, but now he had little to say to her beyond small talk.

She worried that he'd failed to mention the job, because he'd found someone better suited for it. She feared that he no longer wanted her, but didn't know how to tell her. She feared that Richard hadn't mellowed toward her, and Ray was beginning to view their relationship through his eyes.

Trying desperately to shake off those negative feelings, she rationalized, deciding that having Richard within earshot of the phone call had interfered with Ray's ability to speak openly about his feelings for her. He'd kept the conversation light deliberately. Ray was a man of his word, she knew. He promised her he'd wait for her decision about the job, so he would. How could she fault him for being preoccupied with his business and his son?

The long day on her feet kept the tumultuous thoughts from occupying her mind for too long. Following a hot bath and a cup of warm cocoa, Leslie fell into a deep sleep, waking refreshed and alert. As she readied herself for work, she took her extra uniforms out of the closet and stuffed them in a plastic bag. With a little alteration, including several inches of additional hem, they'd be perfectly serviceable for Ruth.

Her breakfast customers were treated to her usual efficiency, along with a brilliant smile, radiating joy and anticipation. She couldn't stop hoping that this might be the last day she'd spend in this dingy diner. Just as she was steeling her nerve to tell Carl about her decision to quit, Ruth Barnes came through the door. Sarah, taller and several years younger than her sister, followed closely behind.

Gathering strength from each other, the three women approached the diner owner, who was known for his gruff demeanor, with their proposal. To their amazement, he nodded with a smile, clearly agreeable, and perhaps even a little relieved. He admitted he'd been expecting Leslie's resignation for some time, and declared that he'd be happy to give Mrs. Barnes and her sister a try.

"You deserve more than a lifetime of toting dirty dishes," he told Leslie, his eyes misting. "I've always known you'd leave me once you wised-up." He took a big white handkerchief out of his back pocket and blew his bulbous nose with a honk. "But I'm still counting on you to do the books."

"It's a deal," she agreed, shaking his calloused hand.

Carl and Cook willingly joined in the training session. With the entire team pitching in, it didn't take long to familiarize the new waitresses with the layout and procedures of the small diner. The young women were quick studies, memorizing the short list of menu items in no time.

By the middle of the afternoon, Leslie felt comfortable leaving them alone for a couple of hours. She promised she'd be back in time to take over before the dinner crowd started rolling in.

In ten minutes, flat, she'd rushed home, changed out of her uniform, and hopped into her blue VW. In twenty-five, she was puttering down the gravel lane of Willow Spring Farm, her nerves stretched taut in anticipation.

She couldn't wait to see Ray and tell him her exciting news. Reaching the house, she pulled into her customary parking space and swung the car door open. Before she could step out, Richard, with Max at his heels, slouched across the porch and down the stairs. The retriever greeted her warmly, his tongue lolling out in a friendly grin, but the youth stood blocking her path, arms folded aggressively across his chest.

"Why are you here again?" he asked belligerently.

"I came by to see your father," she answered softly.

"He's not here," was the abrupt response.

"Do you know if he'll be back anytime soon?" she asked, ignoring his tone and keeping her voice light and friendly.

"Probably not. He's gone over to the Bowman place again." His dark eyes flashed dangerously.

Richard was making it clear that she was not welcome. Leslie didn't want to push, but neither did she want to let the boy get away with intimidating her, so she stood her ground, too anxious to tell Ray that she wanted the job to let this surly teen send her scurrying home like a scared rabbit.

She swallowed hard and told him, "I'm going down to the office to work for a while. Your dad asked me to help him get things organized."

The boy shrugged his shoulders. "Suit yourself, but you're a little late."

"What do you mean?'"

Nodding his head in the general direction of the clinic, Richard grinned. "He's already hired a lady to work for him. She started yesterday afternoon."

Feeling like she'd been gut-punched, Leslie turned toward the renovated milking shed. Parked by the office door was a silver Buick Roadmaster. She didn't have to be close enough to read the "ALIMONY" vanity plate to know the car belonged to Mindy.

Refusing to give in to her first inclination, which was to run for home as fast as her little bug would carry her, Leslie strode purposefully toward the clinic building. She swung open the screen door of the office and stepped inside.

The fiery redhead greeted her with a forced smile. As usual, Mindy had adorned herself in a manner that overstated her overt boldness and blatant sexuality. Her generous curves were accentuated by a tacky, slim-fitting suit in shiny gold. Her make-up had been applied thickly, in a vain to attempt hide the tiny wrinkles around her eyes, and a recent touch-up on her hair color had left it a bit too orange and brassy.

"Why, if it isn't Les Willow," she purred. "What brings you back to the old home place? What's the matter? Can't you give it up gracefully?"

Mindy propped a palm on each side of her trim waist and splayed her diamond-encrusted fingers over prominent hips. Standing nose to nose, she was inches shorter than Leslie, and it was obvious she hated looking up at a woman she considered her inferior.

"Did Ray say when he'd be back?" Les asked, ignoring the look of disdain the smaller woman shot her.

"I'm sure he'll check in soon. Ray likes to stay in close contact with me," Mindy asserted, playing her advantage to the hilt. She crossed the room to reclaim her seat behind the desk. "Would you like to make an appointment with the doctor? Do you have a pet you want him to see?"

"No," Leslie said, shaking her head and gathering her courage. "When he returns, please tell him I've decided to take the job he offered me, as office manager."

"You're too late, Les." Mindy's bright green eyes snapped with glee as she shuffled papers dismissively. "Ray said that if you called or stopped by, I was to tell you that he's changed his mind. After seeing my qualifications and background, it didn't make good business sense for him to hire an unproven applicant when he could have the best.

"Your only real job experience has been waiting tables, right?" Mindy accused. Leslie nodded mutely, shocked speechless and disheartened beyond belief.

"I'm sorry I had to be the one to disappoint you," Mindy offered insincerely. "You can discuss it with Ray, if you like, but I'm sure he'll confirm his decision. He's a bit embarrassed, really. Since he and I've finally had some private time together, we've become very close, and he realizes that his feelings for you were nothing more than pity. I convinced him that he couldn't allow his business to suffer, just because he feels sorry for a homely old maid."

She smiled a smug smile that displayed a row of tiny, shark-like teeth and prodded, "So what do you think of the improvements he's made in your old, run-down house? It's a little too understated and countrified for my tastes, but his bedroom is definitely comfy."

When Leslie failed to rise to the bait, Mindy sniffed and added, "It's almost four; Ray should be back any time. You can wait over there." She indicated a straight-backed chair against the wall.

"That won't be necessary," Leslie murmured. "Please don't tell him I was here."

Almost choking on a lump of bitter bile, she ran for her car, Mindy's pleased, "You can bet on that," and emphatic, "And don't come back!" ringing in her ears.

Richard was nowhere in sight when she climbed into her bug and wheeled it around. Driving back to town through a veil of tears, Leslie felt her heart explode into a thousand tiny shards. She wondered how could she feel such pain and still live.

Pausing for a moment in the alley behind her little house, she vowed to put all thoughts of Ray, and his betrayal of her, out of her mind. In the bathroom, she splashed cold water on her splotched face, slipped back into her uniform, steeled her spine, and went to relieve Ruth and Sarah for the evening shift.

The sisters left smiling. Ruth promised to arrive early the next morning, kissed Leslie's cheek, and thanked her again, enthusiastically, for the job and for the sack of uniforms she had tucked under her arm.

The caring, young mother noted the red rims around her friend's eyes, but Leslie waved away her concern with, "Oh, it's just allergies."

With sheer determination, Leslie held back the flood of tears until she'd finished the dinner shift and regained the privacy of her bedroom. Then, she flung herself across her comforter and let the anguish overtake her. Her body trembled uncontrollably as she cried herself out.

Unanswerable questions plagued her, leading to logical conclusions. Now she understood the cool, impersonal tone Ray had taken during their last phone call. He'd already begun a relationship with Mindy, but hadn't gotten up the courage to break things off with her completely. He'd finally realized that she had nothing to offer him, unlike Mindy, whose position in local society would help his business enormously. But still, he pitied her and wanted to let her down easy.

Her telephone bell jingled, but she ignored it. Minutes later it rang again. This time she struggled to rise and stumbled into the hallway, where she jerked the cord from its wall connection. Two minutes later, her cell phone dinged, so she turned it off. She didn't want to talk to anyone. She refused to open herself up again, to give anyone the opportunity to hurt her. Faint pink rays were painting the sky before she fell into a restless sleep.

Another whirl of questions woke her, swirling around and around in her exhausted brain. Pushing them aside, she set her first priority – figuring out what to do now. With no job and no prospects, she had to come up with some way to make a living.

A shower, fresh clothes, and a forced-down muffin helped her form a plan of action. Folding her last remaining uniform neatly, and placing it in her oversized handbag, along with her savings account statement, she headed to the diner. She found Ruth serving the first customers. Between taking and delivering orders, the thankful woman handed Leslie two one-dollar bills.

"Here," she said, beaming proudly. "It's the money I owe you. I earned it in tips."

"Thanks," Leslie graciously accepted the cash and tucked it into her handbag, glad to see the glow of hope on Ruth's round face. That look cemented her decision to move forward with her plan. Waving a forced goodbye to Cook and throwing a kiss in Carl's general direction, she left.

She turned right and strolled down the block to the First United bank, praying she wouldn't run into Walter Lewis. The president usually left the bank's efficient operation to one or two of the junior employees on Saturday, so she hoped she'd be lucky enough to avoid him.

Handing her savings account number to the teller, she told him she wanted to withdraw her money. Though the amount was a pittance, really, he insisted on giving her a cashier's check rather than cash. Tucking the envelope into her bag without looking at it, she crossed the marble lobby and reached for the door. Just as her hand touched the handle, the huge portal was pushed toward her. She stepped back to allow a portly man to stride through and her mind let out a silent scream. "Not Walter, not now!"

Her attempt to hide behind the door failed. Her nemesis turned and regarded her squarely, grinning slyly, "Hey there, Les." Taking her elbow, he prevented her escape, and drew her with him to his big office at the rear of the building. "I was just over at the diner looking for you. Carl told me you'd quit your job. Come on. We have something important to discuss."

Seeing no way to refuse him, she obeyed meekly. When they entered his private office, he closed the door behind them. Leslie panicked, then realized they were not alone, and relaxed a bit. Her apprehension rose again when her gaze fell on the figure standing by the window. Richard. His dark eyes burned with fury; and as usual, his arms were folded belligerently across his chest.

"Sit down," Walter ordered her.

"I'd rather stand," she refused.

"Suit yourself," the arrogant man responded, flopping into the huge leather chair behind his desk. In what appeared to be a deliberate attempt to extend Leslie's discomfort, he took his time situating his bulk. Finally, he began, "You know my cousin Richard?"

"We've met," she told him. Turning to the teen she added, keeping her voice emotionless, "Hello, Richard. It's nice to see you again." She was not surprised when the lad failed to acknowledge her greeting.

"Let's dispense with the pleasantries, shall we?" Walter's pudgy face was flushed with eager anticipation. "Richard came to me because he wants you out of his father's life – for good. Since I agree with him completely, where you're concerned, I've decided to help him." Leslie said nothing, waiting for Walter to elaborate.

"I'm sure you remember the proposition I made to you a while back." When she nodded, he continued, "Well, I've arranged things to look like you took me up on my generous offer after all."

"What do you mean?" she choked out, her heart pounding. "What do you want from me, Walter?"

"I've placed fifty thousand dollars in your saving account. If you force my hand, Les, I'll make sure this whole town finds out that the money was paid to you for after-hour services you rendered to my business associates."

He paused a beat, leering at her, to let the threat sink in before adding, "I want you to stay away from Ray Gallagher. You will not accept a job at his clinic. You will not see him socially. If he approaches you, you will avoid him, refuse his advances completely.

"If you fail to do as I say, if you have any contact with him whatsoever, I will make sure he knows that you're nothing more than a high-priced whore. Am I making myself clear?" Beads of sweat dappled his upper lip, and his cheeks had taken on a frightening purplish hue.

Pulling the folded envelope out of her purse, Leslie opened it and examined the contents, suddenly calm and clear-headed. Instead of the two thousand dollars and change she expected to see imprinted on the check, it was written for over fifty-two thousand.

Turning the document around so Walter could see it, she commented calmly, "I guess that explains why your teller refused to give me cash when I closed out my account."

Jerking his bulk out of his chair and reaching out a sweaty palm, Walter bellowed, "Give me that!"

"No," she said firmly, returning the check to her purse. Though she didn't understand why the banker was going to such lengths to manipulate her, when Ray had already set her aside, she accepted the unexpected windfall. "You owe me this, Walter, and much more. I'm going to keep your money, and you can tell Ray anything you like.

"Besmirching my reputation will do little good, but I imagine your investors would be more than a tad upset to find out that you've been pimping for your cronies. Such bad press might have a negative impact on your profit margin, and your job. You should've thought out this blackmail scheme a bit more carefully, I'm afraid. Too bad you acted so rashly. I've always suspected that you aren't too smart, and now you've proven it."

"But…but…you can't!" he blubbered.

"Watch me," she declared, turning her steady gaze from the fat man to the tall teen. "Richard, I'm sorry we started off on the wrong foot. If we could've gotten to know one another under different circumstances, we might have been friends.

"Your father loves you deeply. There's no reason to be afraid of me, because he would never allow anyone, or anything, to come between you. Please be patient. Let him show you how much he cares. If you keep an open mind, I know you'll be happy here in Red Valley. With the exception of a few mean-spirited, spiteful souls, folks here are pretty nice."

Her stormy eyes bored holes into Walter. "All in all, it's a wonderful place to live." Head high and shoulders back, she marched out.

As soon as Leslie was out of earshot, the older man challenged the younger one. "This is your fault, you worthless little snot. I had that woman exactly where I wanted her before you came crying to me about her. I put the squeeze on her for your sake, and now she's twisted things around to her advantage. I'll have to do some real juggling to set it all straight."

Leaning in to threaten the boy with his bulk, he snarled, "If you know what's good for you, you'll keep this to yourself. You will not mention it to your father. As hard as it is being the new kid in school, I can make things even worse for you than you can imagine. Remember that."

Then he added one last promise. "Les Willow will get what she deserves, I'll see to it. And you won't mess things up this time. You hear?"

Shocked by the way his cousin had turned on him, and by the venom in the angry man's tone, Richard backed away, his head bobbing. "Sure, Walter, anything you say."

Despite the brave challenge Leslie had thrown down, the last thing she wanted was for Ray Gallagher to hear such a vicious lie about her. She couldn't bear for him to think that she'd had a business arrangement with his despicable cousin, one that was little more than glorified prostitution. Spurred by fear, her tentative plans congealed.

An hour later, she'd packed a small bag of clothing and necessities, and stowed it in the front compartment of her VW. She collected Marmalade, his bowls, and a large sack of dry cat food. With his crate secured in the seat next to her, the cat loudly meowed his objections, as she drove to the parsonage to find her dearest friend.

Mary Ellen didn't open her shop until noon on Saturday, taking the morning for girl-time with her twins. As soon as Leslie pulled in the drive, the girls ran out to meet her.

"Hey, Auntie Les, whatcha doin' here?" Mary Grace inquired, sticking her bright head into the driver's window.

"Oh, boy, you brought Marme!" Martha Joy exclaimed from the other side, reaching in to stroke the feline's silky, orange fur through the window in his carrier.

"I'm hoping you'll cat sit for me for a while. What do you think?" she asked them.

"Yes, oh yes!" they chimed simultaneously. Mary Grace ran

around the car to help her sister open the door and drag out the crate, complete with large yellow tabby.

"Mommy, Mommy, look, Auntie Les brought Marmalade for a visit," they yelled, struggling to carry the animal between them. Leslie followed the excited twins into the house, toting his other things.

Summoned by the ruckus, Mary Ellen held the door open and ushered them inside. "I see. I see. Take Marme to your room, girls, while I talk to Les." She unloaded the bowls and food from her friend's arms and stored them in a large pantry off the kitchen, before pouring two cups of tea.

"Here," the petite blond said, shoving a china mug across the counter top. "You look like you could use this."

"Thanks," Leslie responded, climbing on a barstool. "I sure can."

"What is it? What's going on?" Her friend's bright blue eyes were wide with concern.

After a couple of sips of the restorative brew, Leslie told Mary Ellen about her budding relationship with Ray, the job he had offered her, and the terrible first encounter with Richard. She went on to explain how she'd arranged for Ruth and Sarah to take over for her at the diner, and then she related the details of her short trip to the farm, and the ensuing confrontations with the younger Gallagher, and with Mindy Tucker.

She even told her oldest friend about how distant Ray had seemed, during their last phone conversation, but the incident in Walter Lewis's office went unmentioned. In conclusion, she informed Mary Ellen that she was leaving town to look for work.

"I'd like the girls to have Marmalade, if you don't mind." Leslie's blue-gray eyes filled with tears. "I have no idea where I'll be living, so I can't take him with me."

"Of course we'll keep him. The twins will be thrilled, but Les, I wish you'd reconsider. You know that brazen hussy, Mindy Tucker, will say anything to get herself another husband, particularly a man like Ray. Talk to him first. Make sure where you stand," Mary Ellen urged.

"I can't," the tall woman admitted with an agonized sigh. "Leaving is better. It'll spare me the pain of hearing him say he doesn't love me, and it'll spare him the pain of having to say it."

"Just doesn't make sense." The preacher's wife shook her head in denial. "Ray doesn't seem the type to profess his love to you one day, and then dump you for a gold-digger like Mindy the next. I really thought he felt something special for you. Are you sure you don't want to give him another chance?"

Lowering her face, Leslie responded sadly, "I'm not sure, but I don't have a choice."

"No choice? What aren't you telling me?" her friend asked, intuitively.

Unwilling to reveal anything more, even to Mary Ellen, Leslie offered her a lame excuse. "Richard will never accept me, and I won't drive a wedge between him and his dad. I won't be the cause of any family disharmony."

"Hmm, give it some time. The kid'll come around eventually," Mary Ellen observed thoughtfully. "Sounds like that boy could use a little mothering, and you might just be the person for the job. I'll bet Glenwood could convince him to give you a second chance."

"Mary Ellen, I don't want him to have to be convinced to accept me. Even if Mindy misled me about…uh, things, the fact is, she has the job Ray promised me, and I'm unemployed. There are no options for work around here. What else can I do?"

"Where will you go? Where will you stay?" Mary Ellen asked her, seeing the determined set of her friend's full mouth, and realizing further argument would be senseless.

"I'm headed to Westlake tonight. I'll find a cheap hotel and spend the day tomorrow searching the want ads." Sliding off the tall stool, Leslie hugged her dear friend tightly. I'll be back before long, don't worry. I only brought a few things with me, so I'll come home in a week or so to pick up more stuff. Then once I've found a job and a permanent residence, I'll be back to get my house ready to sell."

"Sounds like you have it all planned out. Call me and let me know where you're staying," the tiny woman choked out, her throat tight with emotion.

"I will," came the tearful response.

Surprised by the calm serenity that had settled over her once she'd made up her mind to leave Red Valley, Leslie guided her tiny car toward the highway. Since the Gallagher farm was on the way, she stopped briefly to place a sealed envelope in the mailbox.

A little over an hour later, she pulled into a small, rent-by-the-week motel. The manager allowed her to inspect a room, and finding it cramped but clean, she paid the deposit, bought a newspaper from the rack in the office, and settled in. Tomorrow she would check out the local library to search online job ads, but tonight, exhaustion overtook her, and she fell asleep reading the help-wanted page.

For the second night in a row, Ray paced the floor in frustration. He'd been trying for over an hour to reach Leslie, by land line and cell phone, and his lack of success was wearing on him. "Where could she be?" he wondered, cursing the circumstances that had kept him so busy all week. "Why won't she answer?"

Then an idea struck him and he rang the Cooper house. Again, no answer. "Oh, shoot, I forgot, it's Saturday," he moaned, running his hands through his tawny mop of hair, "Mary Ellen will be at the shop until late, and Glenwood is probably at the church office, working on his sermon."

In desperation, he tried the diner. Carl picked up with a curt, "Hello," quickly informing him that Leslie had quit her job. Hearing that, Ray's heart did a flip. He tried Leslie's home phone once more, but gave up after numerous rings failed to bring an answer.

Very early the next morning, following a light breakfast, and yet another failed attempt to contact Leslie by phone, he cursed her lack of smart phone and personal computer. She didn't text or use email. Claiming she couldn't afford the expense, she'd purchased the least expensive flip-phone available, and kept it for emergencies only. Initially he'd thought it was old-fashioned and charming. Now he thought it was a darned nuisance.

Grumbling to himself, Ray hustled his sleepy, resistant son into the Land Cruiser and sped off down the lane. Stopping only to pick up the mail, he covered the miles to Red Valley in minutes. The first place he stopped was Leslie's tiny bungalow. Leaving his son in the car, he pounded on the door. When he got no response, he peered in through the porch window, and tried the door. The house was dark and shut up tight.

Sliding back into his vehicle, he drove to the parsonage. "Come on, Richard," he urged, throwing open his door as soon as the wheels had stopped rolling. "I want you to meet Glenwood and Mary Ellen Cooper. Glen is the minister of the Fellowship Church. He's a nice guy; you'll like him. It's early still, but I want to catch them before they have to head over to the church."

With his usual sullen slowness, the tall teen slid out, slamming the door behind him with more force than was necessary. Ignoring the minor display of temper, Ray led the way up the steps and across the porch, pausing to rap lightly on the screen door. The visitors could hear giggles and squeals coming from inside when the preacher's wife pushed it open.

"Ray, it's good to see you. Please come in. I've got to warn you, though, the girls are wild this morning," the petite blonde's smile was wide, making it obvious that she enjoyed the carefree jubilance of her family. "Glen's been roughhousing with them and they're awfully wound up."

"Sorry to bother you so early, Mary Ellen," Ray said.

"No bother. We never get to sleep in with these little…uh…angels around. We're enjoying some family time before we have to leave for the church." Turning her bright blue regard to the younger male, she added, "This must be Richard."

"Yes," the veterinarian confirmed, accepting her invitation to step inside. "I'd like you to meet my son. Richard, this is Mary Ellen Cooper."

"It's a real pleasure." Mary Ellen smiled at the surly teen. "Your father's told me so much about you." Leaning closer to the tall lad, she added softly, "He's very proud of you, you know."

Slowly dusting off his manners, Richard replied, "Thanks. It's nice to meet you too." He offered the friendly woman a small but sincere smile.

"We're having a second cup of coffee. Would you join us?" she asked them.

"That would be nice," Ray said. "It smells wonderful."

At the first sight of Ray, the twins peeled themselves off their father's legs and ran full-tilt toward him, still giggling shrilly.

The amused man knelt down to head off the assault. "Whoa there," he teased, grabbing them both and giving them a little squeeze.

"Hey, Mr. Ray," the more outgoing of the two said, beaming. "Who's that you got with ya?"

"This is my son, Richard." He looked back over his shoulder at the teen. "These lovely ladies are Mary Grace and Martha Joy."

Immediately assuming the younger fellow was a possible playmate, albeit a large one, the girls each grabbed one of Richard's hands, urging him, "Let's go outside and swing." Before he could protest, they pulled him toward the back door. Shrugging his broad shoulders and smiling in mock defeat, he went along.

"I'll be out in a few minutes to rescue you," Glenwood offered.

"There you go." Mary Ellen handed Ray a mug of steaming coffee. "Let's sit in the den. You look like you have something on your mind."

"Am I that transparent?" he asked, taking the chair she indicated.

Nodding silently, she waited for him to begin, noting the strained look about his hazel eyes. He took a deep draught from the cup, cleared his throat, and admitted, "I'm really getting worried about Leslie. I've been calling her for the last two days and getting no answer. Carl tells me she's quit her job, and her house seems totally deserted. What's going on? Where is she?"

Watching the tortured expression on his ruggedly handsome face, the preacher's wife was convinced that the man still had deep feelings for her friend. She wished she could give him more hopeful news. Sighing sadly, she said, "I'm afraid she's gone, Ray. She left town yesterday, headed for Westlake, I think."

"She's gone? Why? Did she say why?" he asked, almost frantic. Before Mary Ellen could respond, he conjectured, "It's Richard, isn't it? She's left because of the way Richard treated her."

"Only partly," the petite woman told him. "Leslie doesn't want to come between you and your son. At least that's the excuse she used. But if my intuition is correct, and it usually is, that's not the whole story. Maybe whatever **it** is involves Richard, and maybe not. She wouldn't tell me everything."

"I wish she'd given me some time. He'll come around eventually. It's really me he's angry at, not Leslie. He blames me for his mother's death, and he can't bear to see me happy." Ray lowered his face to hide the tears that were threatening. "Why did she run off without talking to me, without telling me where she was going? It doesn't seem like her."

"It's not," the woman agreed. "But since she gave up her job at the diner before she found out you'd hired Mindy Tucker for the position at your clinic, she was left with no means of support. She had to go look for a job. Then, after Mindy told her you two were involved, Les was devastated.

"She's endured many disappointments in her life, but being rejected by the man she loves, was more than she could handle. I tried to get her to talk to you first, but she refused. She said she couldn't bear to hear you admit you don't love her."

"Mindy! That lying witch!" the tall newcomer exclaimed, his face contorting in fury. "I'll wring her scrawny neck."

"I smell a rat." Glenwood said.

"A fat, red-haired one!" Mary Ellen confirmed.

"I didn't hire Mindy to help out in the office," Ray announced. "I made it perfectly clear to her that the job was Leslie's, as soon as she was ready.

"That conniving shrew played the part of the generous neighbor to perfection, offering to fill in, temporarily. I should have known she was up to something. She's too close to Sharon Lewis not to be cut from the same cloth. How could I be so stupid?" He dropped his head into his hands.

Clapping Ray on the back, the pastor consoled him, "Don't be too hard on yourself, man You don't seem to have much experience with calculating women. Les isn't gone for good. She promised to contact us and let us know where she's staying. You'll just have to be patient."

"Thanks, Glen." Ray sniffed and looked up.

"Hey, I still have a few minutes before I have to head over to the church. Would you like for me to have a little talk with Richard?" he offered.

"That'd be great," the veterinarian replied gratefully.

"Have another cup of coffee. I'll go fetch him and show him my boat. Maybe we can bond over fish stories. It's worth a try."

The big man grabbed a cap off a peg on the wall and slipped it on. "Ray, don't worry about Les. We'll let you know as soon as we hear from her. We've tried to call her but her cell is off, as usual. She'll check in when she's ready."

With those comforting words, Glen marched outside, calling for his children. They burst through the door just as Ray was suggesting, "I'll drive over to Westlake to look for her. That little beetle of hers would be easy to spot."

Pulling coloring books and crayons out of the magazine rack, Mary Ellen spread them out on the floor to occupy the twins, telling him, "Westlake's not all that big as cities go, but it's huge compared to Red Valley. Besides, Les needs time to sort out her feelings, and you have responsibilities here.

"How would Richard react if you left him to look for the woman he believes is trying to take his mother's place? Would that make him feel any more charitable toward her? You owe it to Les to help Richard understand and accept your relationship with her."

"You're right. You're right." Looking completely crestfallen, he nodded.

"Sure, I am," she said with conviction, refilling his cup.

While Ray and Mary Ellen helped Mary and Martha with their artistic renderings, Glenwood enticed Richard into his garage. "Hey, thanks for being a sport and keeping my little rascals occupied for a while. I hope they weren't too tough on you."

"No," the teen chuckled. "They're fun. I like kids."

"Good to hear. Maybe you'd sit with them some evening for Mary Ellen and me. We're due for a date night soon," the pastor suggested.

"Sure. I'd like that," the boy agreed.

"Well then, we'll plan on it." Pulling the cover off the sleek power boat, he added, beaming proudly, "The girls and I take her down to Sugar Mountain Lake most every Monday, our day off. Isn't she a beauty?"

Admiring the sparkling blue paint and shiny chrome fittings, the lad agreed, "Yeah, it's great."

"Do you fish or water ski?" the pastor probed.

"My grandpa's taken me out deep-sea fishing a couple of times. I've never tried water skiing, but it looks like fun."

"You and your dad are welcome to join us anytime. My girls love the lake, and Mary Ellen's a terrific water skier. She'd be glad to teach you." His warm smile was wide with pride.

"Dad won't have time to go, but I'd like it. There's nothing much else to do in this hick town." Resentment bubbled in the boy's tone.

"Now hold on a minute. I like this hick town, and in my opinion, there's plenty to do here. Maybe not what you're accustomed to, but fun stuff, nonetheless. There's fishing, and all kinds of water sports, picnics, game night and socials at the church, dances and bingo at the VFW. Once school starts, there'll be football games every Friday night. Have you ever played on a school team?"

"No, I went to a small, private academy. We didn't have organized sports. I played rec league soccer one year, but Mom hated it. She complained about the dirt, and the bruises, and having to pick me up from practice. Dad was always working, so he couldn't come to my games anyway." The teen's lips were drawn in a thin, hard line.

"I can see why you'd be angry with your father, but isn't that why he sold his clinic in the city and moved here, so he'd have more time for you?" Glen asked sympathetically.

"That's what he said," Richard snapped, "but I know the real reason – that woman."

"You mean Leslie," Glen surmised.

"Yeah, her. He was seeing her before my mom died."

"You think so?" Glen asked, beginning to understand the depth of the boy's rage and hatred.

"Why else would he buy her farm?"

The young man's erroneous suspicions were clearly undermining Ray's efforts to reestablish a relationship with him, so Glenwood decided to set the record straight. "You know I'm a preacher, right?"

Richard nodded.

"Do you think you can trust a man of God, generally, that is?"

"I guess so," the tall boy said.

"In that case, believe me when I tell you that your father met Leslie at Carl's Diner, about three weeks ago," the minister assured him, keeping his voice low and convincing.

"That's not what cousin Walter told me," Richard contradicted, jutting his chin out in defiance. "He said they'd known each other since they were kids."

"Humph," Glen huffed. "I know he's your kin, but you'll find out soon enough that you can't trust Walter Lewis as far as you can throw him. In this case, however, we're both right. Ray met Leslie once, when she was about thirteen or fourteen and he was, oh I don't know, fifteen maybe. They danced one dance at a school social and never saw one another again, until he walked into the diner a few Saturdays back. Up until then, they didn't even know each other's names."

"If they just met, how come they acted like they did," he asked, unwilling to concede the point, "hugging and kissing and stuff? You should have seen Dad's face when we walked into that old farmhouse and he saw her standing in the kitchen. He never looked at my mom like that – never!"

Pausing to search for the right words to explain, to this inexperienced young man, how love can take on a limitless variety of forms, Glenwood inhaled deeply. "I can only tell you what I've learned about love… Love is different each time you experience it. All of us love in many ways, some much stronger than others.

"What you witnessed between Ray and Leslie is a special, once in a lifetime kind of love. Hopeless romantics like me call it love at first sight. A love like theirs is based on complete understanding and acceptance.

It's an unexplainable connection that few people ever experience."

Seeing the question written all over the boy's face, he added, "Just because your dad has fallen in love with Leslie, it doesn't mean he didn't love your mother, Richard. As a matter of fact, I think he did, very much, but in a different way. He showed your mom that he cared for her by being the successful provider she wanted him to be, and by making it possible for her, and for you, to live the life she wanted. Not as romantic as what you witnessed between your dad and Leslie maybe, but love nonetheless."

The boy shrugged but offered no argument. Glen could see he was still unconvinced.

"As I see it, your father made his decision to buy Willow Spring Farm and set up a practice here for two reasons. The first was to reach for his lifelong dream – of having a large animal practice – a dream he'd given up to please your mother. The second, more important reason, was you. I believe he wants to give you what he couldn't give you in the city, a wholesome environment to grow up in, and more of his time.

"Did Dad really give up his dreams for my mom?" Richard asked softly, somewhat incredulous.

"Yes, he did," Glen told him firmly. "Had your mother lived, your father would have continued with his practice in Greenville, because he loved her and wanted her to be happy. He would have kept on working long hours to pay for the lifestyle you were leading."

"How do **you** know?" the teen challenged, a bit defensively.

"Your dad told me a little about it, and I've pieced together the rest. I've been a pastor for a good number of years, and in that time, I've learned a lot about life and about human nature. My guess is that you and your mother were pretty used to having the very best of everything. I'm sure your dad had to work real hard to make enough money to pay for her expensive tastes, and to keep you in that private school of yours."

"I guess I never thought of it like that." The youth's dark eyes softened, as he began to recognize the truth in the preacher's words. "I just figured he stayed at the office so much because he loved his work more than he loved us."

Sensing a chink in the boy's well-polished armor, Glen widened it a bit. "You're a smart young man, Richard. Think about what I've said. Give your old dad time to show you how he feels, and give him a chance to be happy again. Everyone deserves happiness, right?"

"Yeah, I guess so," he admitted, staring down at his feet.

"And do me a favor. Give Leslie a chance, too, huh?" The minister's bright eyes twinkled merrily. "She's a wonderful, caring woman and Mary Ellen's best friend. My dear wife will never forgive me if I don't do what I can to get her to come back to town."

"Back to town?" Richard asked, obviously puzzled. "Has she

gone somewhere?"

"She left for Westlake yesterday. She told us she didn't want to come between you and your dad," Glen revealed.

"Was that really why she left?" The teen asked hesitantly, suddenly agitated.

"Well, she's unemployed, since the job working for your dad fell through, and there's no other option for her here," The big man studied the boy's reaction curiously.

He nodded, "Oh."

"If there is any other reason, she didn't mention it," the pastor assured him. "Is there something else, something you know about?"

The lad shook his dark head slowly, shrugging his broad shoulders, still looking at his shoes.

"Well, if you think of anything that might be important, I'm sure you'll tell your dad. He's worried sick about Leslie." Glen couldn't help noticing how the young man turned his face away shamefully.

"Better get in. We'll be late for Sunday School if I don't hop to it. The girls still have to be wiped off and dressed up."

When they reached the back door, Ray was standing on the bottom step asking, "Will you text me when she calls?"

"Of course, I will. You have my word," Mary Ellen promised.

"Here," he said, pulling a blue-gray envelope and pen out of his shirt pocket. "I'll write my cell number down for you. We didn't get a land line in the house, but I always carry my mobile, even when I'm working."

Flipping the letter over to see his name written on the front, he examined it carefully. "Hang on a second. This was in the mailbox this morning. Let me see what this is." Inside the envelope was a blank sheet of the same hue, folded around a key.

"What is it?" the pastor's wife asked. "That looks like Leslie's stationery. Is it from her?"

Ray nodded almost imperceptibly, holding the brass key between his thumb and forefinger. "I gave this to her so she could look after Max for me last weekend, when I went to fetch Richard."

"Do you mind?" Mary Ellen reached out her palm. "Can I see it?" The tall newcomer laid the old-fashioned brass key across her fingers.

After a long look, she sighed and told him, "It must have broken her heart to give this up again." Answering the unspoken question in Ray's hazel eyes, she explained, "This was Les's own house key. See the spots of pink nail polish on it?" She held it up for the others to see. "It's almost worn off now, but that used to be a flower.

"On the days when they went to the farmer's market to sell vegetables, her grandparents made her wear this old key tied around her neck with a piece of hay twine. Les had to come home to an empty house after school, and they were afraid she'd lose her key and be locked out. The term 'latchkey kids' hadn't been coined in those days.

"The rest of us had a mother at home to greet us. The mean girls in our class teased Les about the key being ugly, so I painted a pink flower on it and tied it on a silk cord, sort of like a necklace. I guess it was silly, but it made her feel better." Fingering the brass lovingly, she added, "She kept it on that pink string until she had to turn it over to Walter." Tears sparkled in her eyes as she handed the key back to its rightful owner.

"It will be hers again," Ray promised, "if I have anything to do with it. You just let me know when you hear from her."

"Will do," Glen confirmed.

With that, the Gallagher men took their leave of the Cooper home, waving to the tow-headed twins, who stood on tiptoe, peering over the porch railing. As they pulled away, Richard took his father by surprise by asking, "Do you think it's too late to try out for the football team? The first game's scheduled for the week after school starts."

"Well, I don't know, but we'll find out," Ray assured him.

After church services concluded, Ray cornered Coach Cox, the burly, former all-state tackle as he was leaving the sanctuary. He said he'd be happy to give the "strapping lad" a look, even though Richard admitted he'd never played the sport before. They made arrangements to meet on the high school field during the next morning's practice session.

The try-out went well. Richard was unexpectedly quick and powerful, and smart, too, remembering assignments and instructions without repetition. Coach Cox was impressed. When practice was over, the tired boy joined his dad, who was waiting in the car, because Richard didn't want him to watch, anxious to know the outcome. Richard's broad smile told Ray that things were looking up for his son.

After offering his congratulations, Ray started the big SUV, turned back toward Main Street, and pulled up to the curb in front of an ancient brick building. The red and white sign that hung over the door read, *Something Old and Something New,* in huge elaborate letters. Below that in a smaller script, *antiques and framing,* was printed. The veterinarian went inside. Moments later he reappeared carrying an unwieldy package.

"Hey Richard," he called. "Help me with this will you? Open the rear hatch." When the boy complied, he prompted, "Let's unwrap it and take a look. I want to make sure it's right before we haul it all the way home."

Slipping off the string and unfolding the brown paper covering, Ray revealed a huge photograph of a woman and a baby, matted and framed in warm mahogany. "Well, what do you think? I brought it in when I had my other snapshots mounted, but I wanted this one enlarged, so it took a while longer. I thought it would look nice hanging in the foyer above the staircase."

"It's great," the boy whispered, overcome with emotion.

"You really like it?" the father asked, sincerely concerned. When Richard nodded in the affirmative, Ray sighed with relief. "I like it too. Your mother preferred studio portraits, but this was always my favorite picture of her. I took it the day we brought you home from the hospital. Look at the way the mat and frame bring out the highlights in her eyes. When I look at this photograph, I can see how proud she was of you, and how much she loved you."

"Why'd you do this?" Richard asked, perplexed. "I thought the whole idea of moving here, of starting over, was to forget her. Why would you want a picture of Mom hanging on the wall of the house where you want to live with another woman?"

"Hold on a minute." Ray shut the hatch and took his son by the arm. "We need to get some things straight." He led the way to the bench where he'd sat with Leslie a few days before. After a pause he began softly, "Richard, I know you blame me for your mother's death."

"Not exactly, I just..." the boy tried to clarify, but his father interrupted.

"It's okay, I understand…because for a long time, I blamed myself, too. I blamed myself for not being enough, for not loving her enough, for not doing enough to save her. But I met someone recently who helped me see things, and myself, more clearly. I finally realized that I didn't fail Wanda by not loving her enough; I failed her by not loving myself enough.

"I guess that sounds pretty weird, but the truth is, I never felt like I was good enough for your mother. Deep down I didn't believe I would ever be worthy of her. Richard, your mom was the well-bred daughter of a wealthy family. I'm the son of an uneducated factory-worker. Her dad spent his days in an executive office, overseeing a huge company. My dad spent his days on the assembly line, in the finishing department of one of her father's many furniture plants.

"The reason I worked so hard, spent so much time away from you, was because I wanted to be the successful, socially-acceptable husband your mother deserved. But instead of proving myself worthy, I failed her miserably. No matter how hard I tried, I could not be the person she wanted me to be. Money and affluence couldn't change where I came from. No matter how hard I tried to fit into her world, inside I was still the poor kid from the wrong side of town.

"So, after your mom died, I decided to move here, to start over on my own terms, to work for my own goals. I have to stop living in the past, Richard. I hope you can understand that. It's taken time, but I'm learning to forgive myself, and I hope one day you'll be able to forgive me, too."

"She should have had a check-up sooner," Richard snapped. "You know that, you're a doctor, sort of. Why didn't you make her get an exam?" The teen's dark eyes brimmed with desperate tears.

"I tried, many times, but she refused. She had this strange attitude of complete invulnerability, like she was certain that nothing bad could ever happen to her, as long as she avoided exams and tests and screenings that might shake that certainty. I had to drag her to the obstetrician, kicking and screaming, when she was pregnant with you.

"She would spend hours at the gym, the hair dresser, and nail salon, working hard to make her body and face beautiful and fit, but she was terrified of medical tests and hated doctors. There was nothing I didn't try – demanding, begging, promises, bribes – nothing worked. Even after the cancer was diagnosed, she never once admitted that she should have had it checked earlier."

The tall man paused, remembering. "I was always so proud of Wanda's strength, her determination, her drive, but the more she pushed me, the angrier I became. I felt obligated to her, and her family, for giving me a leg up with my practice, so I kept giving in to her demands, even when I knew I should be standing up – for myself, and for you.

"Richard, I want to remember your mother for the special person she was, and for the wonderful gifts she gave us, but I'm not going to sacrifice who I am or what I want to please her memory. I did that when she was alive, but now it's time to start making my own decisions, that is…our own decisions, living the life we want, and not the life your mother wanted for us. So, I brought you here, away from your grandparents' influence, where you'll see another way of life, and have the chance to choose what you really want for your future. What **you** want – not what your mom wanted for you."

"I'm going to work with Grandfather in his business. That's already decided." His prominent jaw was set firmly.

"That's fine, if it's what you really want to do," his father agreed.

"But if you decide you'd rather study forestry and preserve trees, instead of making furniture out of them, that would be okay, too."

Pausing to think, the son asked, "What if I wanted to be a PE teacher and coach? What about that?"

"It'd be great, as long as it's your decision. From now on, we're not going to live our lives trying to please anyone else. We're going to be our own men, make our own decisions, and live with the consequences. What do you think about that?"

Ray's green-gold eyes sparkled with joy when he looked at his son's open face, and saw the beginning of a familiar, mischievous grin, and knew that the thick curtain Richard had pulled down between them was beginning to be drawn apart.

"That friend was Miss Willow, wasn't it?" the younger man deduced.

"What do you mean?" Ray asked, confused.

"She was the person who helped you stop blaming yourself for Mother's death." Richard's head bobbed knowingly.

"Yes, it was."

"You love her a lot, don't you?" the lad added.

"Yes, I do. I love her so much my heart aches. Please understand; my feelings for Leslie don't diminish what I felt for your mother, or for you. Give me a chance to be the father you need me to be. I won't let you down, Richard. And give Leslie a chance too. I think you'll like her."

Ray circled his son's wide shoulders with his arm. The boy tolerated the embrace and even smiled a hesitant smile. "I don't mean to be critical of your mother, but Leslie loves me for who I am, and not for what I do or for what I can give her. She's caring and sensitive, unassuming and sweet. Give her the benefit of the doubt and you'll see."

"I get it, Dad. I get it," Richard teased, his tone taking on a carefree lightness.

"Do you?" Ray asked, sensing a brightening in the atmosphere between them.

"Sure. You know what's funny?" the boy prompted. The father shook his head. "Reverend Cooper said kinda the same thing."

"Well, Glen's a smart man," the veterinarian declared.

"Yep, I think he is, too," the son agreed.

"Come on," Ray urged. "We'll go home, grab a bite of lunch, and get you cleaned up, then we'll ride over to the Westlake Mall and pick up football cleats and whatever else you need."

The trip back out to the farm was made in comfortable silence, as the uneasy tension between the father and the son had all but disappeared. Ray hung the photograph of Wanda and baby Richard with an appropriate amount of pomp and ceremony. That accomplished, he urged his son, "Go get showered while I fix us a couple of sandwiches."

"I'd like ham, if there's any left, and some lemonade." The tall boy ordered before sprinting up the stairs, two at a time.

Later, his stomach comfortably full, Richard pushed his chair back from the table, burped loudly, and said, "Dad, there's something I have to tell you."

"Shoot!" his father replied, putting down the last little bite of his sandwich and giving his son his full attention. "What's on your mind?"

"I think I need to explain why I've been so hateful to Miss Willow." His wide forehead was furrowed with concern. "I feel bad, because I know I'm the reason she left town." Ray regarded him quizzically, and waited for him to continue.

"A couple of days before you came to pick me up, Cousin Walter called me. He said he wanted me to be prepared for what I would find when I got here. He told me you were dating someone, an 'old flame' he said. I'm not sure what he meant by that, but it sounded like you'd been seeing her for a long time, even before Mother died. So, when we got here, and Miss Willow was wearing Mom's pink apron and acting like she was at home in our kitchen, and then with the way you greeted her, I figured Walter was right."

Scrubbing his knuckles over his chin, Ray took a deep breath to push down the fury that was bubbling. "I can see why you'd come to that conclusion. I bet I didn't help my case any by announcing that this used to be Leslie's house."

"Nope, it just confirmed what I already thought about you, and her," the teen admitted.

"And now, what do you think?" his father asked him.

"Reverend Cooper told me you met Miss Willow once, a long time ago, but you didn't get to know her until you moved here. When I thought more about it, I figured that you buying her farm was just a coincidence." Dark brown eyes met green-gold ones in a sincere regard.

"Son, I wish you'd come to me with your fears and your doubts, but I understand why you felt you couldn't talk to me. I haven't been the father I should have been, the father I want to be. It's you and me now, kiddo. We have to trust each other, and take care of each other."

He reached across the table and touched his son's hand. "Don't worry about Leslie. We'll make things right with her."

"You haven't heard the worst part." Swallowing hard, Richard went on, "Remember the other day when I spent the morning with Walter, at the bank?"

Ray nodded, his brows drawing together with suspicion.

"While I was there, he brought Miss Willow into his office and threatened her. Dad, it was awful. He lied to her, tried to blackmail her, and when she didn't react the way he expected, he turned it around on me." The boy's broad shoulders shook with unexpressed emotion. "He said he'd make things go really hard for me here if I told you."

"It's okay, son" Ray calmed him. "Walter's a big bully, full of bluster. Ignore his threats. We can handle him. Tell me what he said, all of it, every miserable, deceitful word."

It took a few minutes for the repentant teen to relate the incident he'd witnessed in the bank president's office. When he was finished, he sighed deeply, tears streaming down his cheeks. "She was so kind to me, so apologetic, even when she thought I was behind it all. Oh, Dad, I'm so sorry. Do you think she'll ever forgive me?"

"I bet she already has, Richard. Leslie's like that. She knows our cousin, Walter, too well to believe anything he says. I'm just happy you got a chance to see how special she is. Maybe now you understand why I care for her so much." Ray's eyes were lit with a warm glow. "She took his money and walked out? I'd love to have seen that."

"Walter was so mad his face was purple. I thought he was going to give himself a heart attack. If I hadn't been so scared when he started screaming at me, I would've laughed.

"Why'd he do that? Why'd he say that, Dad? Why'd he claim it was my fault that things didn't turn out like he planned? It wasn't my idea. I went along with it, but only because I thought he was telling me the truth about Miss Willow. I had no idea what he was going to do until he did it."

"Our poor cousin is a very small man, despite his size," Ray concluded. "When things go right, he's the first to stand up and take credit, but when things go wrong, he's never to blame. Don't let his narcissistic behavior bother you. Only a tormented mind like Walter's could come up with such a hateful, twisted scheme. I'm thrilled Leslie turned the tables on him."

"But she still left town. So, in a way, he won." Richard frowned. Rubbing his forehead thoughtfully, Ray conjectured, "His victory will be short-lived. Leslie will come back, and when she does, I'll be there to greet her. I won't let her slip away from me again."

Max growled. A beat later, they heard the crunch of tires coming up the gravel lane. "That'll be Mindy." Ray slid back his chair. "Can you clean up this mess and put the things back in the refrigerator? I've got a few things to straighten out with that woman."

"No problem," the lad agreed. "If she gives you any trouble, let me know. I was standing outside the office and heard every word she said to Miss Willow. Don't let her lie to you, too."

The father opened the screen door and paused to ask, "And when were you planning to tell me about that?"

Richard shrugged. "I kept it to myself at first, because I wanted Miss Willow out of our lives, and Ms. Tucker was helping my cause. With all the stuff with Walter, I started to tell you, but then I figured that this was your mess to straighten out, not mine. You're the one who promised Miss Willow a job and gave it to someone else."

"Thank goodness Mary Ellen was more helpful than you," Ray teased. "Until this morning, I had no idea Mindy was claiming me, along with the office manager job. I thought I'd made it clear to her that she was only here temporarily."

"Come on, Dad. I know you haven't been around much, but I can't believe you're that gullible. I'm only a kid and I can see that Ms. Tucker has her hooks out for you. I guess she'll do anything to get you."

"That doesn't worry you?"

"Naw, 'cause she's not your type. You'd never fall for a cheap-looking, conniving female like her." Richard grinned.

Ray howled with laughter at his son's insightful assessment.

"This won't take long. We'll head into town as soon as I send our unwanted visitor on her way."

As predicted, the confrontation with Mindy was short, and very one-sided. Ray caught her just as she was unlocking the office. He took her by the elbow, removed the key from her hand, and propelled her back to her long, silver automobile, ignoring her surprised, but cheerful greeting.

Politely taking the handle and swinging the car door wide, he gently ushered her inside. "Good-bye," was the only word he spoke.

Sensing defeat, the pert redhead shrugged, "Well, I knew my chances with you were slim, but I had to give it a shot. Then she jerked the heavy door out of his hand and slammed it shut, rattling the windows. A cloud of dust billowed out behind the big Buick as it roared down the lane.

Part IV

Leslie spent Monday and Tuesday scooting around Westlake, tracking down job leads and dropping off applications. By the end of the second day, she'd set up three interviews for early the following week. Wednesday, she scoured the city for available apartments, and by that evening, she had two promising possibilities to consider.

That accomplished, she was reluctant to endure another restless night on the lumpy motel mattress, so she checked out, deciding to make a quick trip home to collect essential items for her interviews.

Once she was on the highway, the former waitress let her mind wander. "I'll pick up my good suit, my dress pumps and handbag, and a couple of blouses, but I'll wait to buy more clothes after I have a job. I'm going to make Walter's money last a very long time."

That decided, she yawned, "And I'll sleep in tomorrow morning, in my own bed! Then I'll spend a couple of days cleaning up the house and getting it ready to sell. I can stay until Sunday, so I'll be well rested and ready for my first interview on Monday morning.

"What am I going to do about Mary Ellen?" she wondered. "She'll be mad that I've ignored her calls and voice mails. I'll have to go by the shop, I guess, show her I'm okay, and leave her the name of the motel where I'm staying." Her upturned nose crinkled in distaste. "I'll have to go back there for a while. I can't put a deposit on an apartment until I'm definitely employed and know what I can afford."

About forty minutes later, Leslie stopped her tiny bug in front of the Clip N' Curl. She almost collided with Glenwood as he burst out of the shop. "Hey, gal, it's good to see you. Love to talk, but gotta run!" he blurted, practically sprinting down the street.

Shaking her auburn curls in amusement, Leslie entered and scanned the busy room for her friend. "Where's Mary Ellen?" she asked Carol Simpson, the pharmacist's wife, who was seated under the first dryer, her hair coiled on large pink rollers. The prim lady gestured toward the back of the building.

Crossing to the storeroom door, Leslie drew aside the curtain and called out, "Mary Ellen, are you back there?"

"Is that you, Les? I'm behind the shelves. Can you give me a hand, please? The petite hairdresser's voice was muffled by the clutter of boxes stacked everywhere.

Leslie circled through the maze until she located her friend, who fidgeted in frustration. "I can't seem to find any warm reddish-brown hair dye. There's got to be some here somewhere. I know I ordered it last week. Do you see it? Maybe it's on that top shelf. I'm too short. Will you look?"

Obliging her, Leslie stretched on tiptoe to carefully check each hair color kit. "Nope, there're all shades of brown, but not one warm reddish-brown. Sorry, kid."

"Help me look on these lower shelves, then," Mary Ellen demanded. "It's here. I just know it is. It has to be." When they'd searched the entire storeroom and come up empty, she insisted they start over. Leslie complained good-naturedly, and checked each rack again.

"There's no reddish-brown here, my girl., warm or otherwise. You'll just have to accept that fact," Leslie teased.

Looking quite sheepish, the tiny woman chuckled, "Did I say reddish-brown? Silly me. That's the old name for it. Now it's called 'brownberry.' How could I forget? And here it is. Thanks, Les." She grabbed the box and moved to a big sink and worktable. Leslie followed smirking.

"What's with you and your silly husband today? He almost knocked me over, the big oaf, then he took off down the sidewalk like his pants were on fire, and I find you here, totally lost in your own little world of hair color. You two are truly weird."

When Mary Ellen failed to comment on Leslie's wry observation, she added, "Anyway, I just stopped by to leave you the address of the motel in Westlake where I'll be staying temporarily." She took a piece of folded paper out of her pocket and handed it over.

"About time you checked in," Mary Ellen scolded, hugging Leslie hard. "I called you a dozen times, but you were being too stubborn to answer. Why didn't you respond to my voice mails? I was worried about you!"

"I know," Leslie replied softly. "And I'm sorry. I just needed some time to get things straight in my head, and to figure out what to do next."

"Well…you've had your time, and from now on you need to keep in touch. You have to let me know how you are, and where you're going to be," her dear friend insisted.

"Okay, okay," Leslie agreed, "I'll be home until Sunday. Then I have to go back for an interview first thing on Monday morning."

"Wow, an interview already. That's great…I guess." The hairdresser's enthusiasm was underwhelming. Noticing the forlorn expression on her friend's lovely face, she set aside the plastic container she was using to mix tint, and reached out to embrace her again. Mary Ellen could feel Leslie's body trembling, fighting back tears, and she asked her, "Are you all right?"

"Yeah, yeah," Les sighed, pulling away and sniffing. "Full of hope for the future!" Squaring her chin, she put on a brave smile. "Um, I hate to ask, but I need another favor."

"Don't be silly. You can count on me for anything, Les. You know I'd help you hide the body if it came to that!" Mary Ellen told her with a wink. "What can I do?" Her pale blue eyes sparkled with sincerity.

Leslie ignored her friend's attempt at dark humor. "It'll be hard to make arrangements to show my house from out of town. Could I list your phone number on the 'For Sale' sign, and in the ad I'm putting together for those real estate websites?" The tall woman stuffed her fists deep into her pockets to stop them from shaking.

"Sure, I already have a key. Between Glen and me, it shouldn't be a problem to go over whenever we need to." She shook her fair head sadly. "Are you sure you want to sell your cute little bungalow? I hate to see you take such a big step so fast."

"Hey, Mary Ellen! What's taking you so long?" a customer summoned from the front.

"Be with you in a minute!" the hairdresser called back. "Ignore them, Les," she urged her friend. "They can wait."

"I figure it'll take a long time to sell in this market, so I'd better put it out there as soon as possible. If I get one of the jobs I'm interviewing for next week, I'll move into a small apartment. When I sell the house here, I may be able to buy something in Westlake."

Shrugging her elegant shoulders, she added, "What choice do I have?"

"You could talk to Ray," Mary Ellen told her bluntly. "Give him a chance to..."

Leslie interrupted. "Give him a chance to confirm my worst fears, tell me he made a foolish mistake, and he really doesn't want to see me anymore? No thank-you, I couldn't bear it."

"Why are you so convinced he'll reject you?" her tiny friend objected. "He stopped by the house, desperate to find you. When I told him you'd gone, he was positively frantic. It was all I could do to keep him from tearing off to Westlake to look for you."

"But he's with Mindy now. That doesn't make any sense," Leslie argued.

"He's not with Mindy, you idiot. She lied to you. Ray was furious when he found out about what she said to you, that scheming witch. You're the woman he loves, my dear." Curling her heart-shaped mouth into a knowing smile, she said with confidence, "He'll be thrilled to see you."

"But what about Richard? He hates me! And if Ray hears..." her voice trailed off.

"Hears what?" Mary Ellen asked, her intuition screaming.

"Nothing. Never mind," Leslie brushed off her question. "It doesn't matter." She turned to leave, putting on a forced smile.

"Look, you've got customers, and I have to go. The house needs some deep cleaning before it'll be ready to sell." Pausing, she winked at her friend. "Thanks, Mary Ellen, for everything. I'll stop by to see the girls and check on Marmalade before I leave."

Minutes later, Leslie slipped her little car into the alley behind her house. Slinging her overnight bag over her shoulder, she grabbed a large yellow and black "For Sale" sign out of the back seat. Lost in thought, she circled to the front and started up the stairs. Her foot was on the top step before she realized that the big porch swing was occupied. As soon as her eyes touched him, Ray was on his feet.

"Hello, Leslie," he breathed, his deep voice sending shivers down her spine. "I'm happy to see you. There's so much I need to say to you, I don't know where to begin."

Leslie couldn't move, couldn't speak. She waited silently for him to continue.

"I guess I should start by saying I'm sorry for being such an insensitive fool, for hurting you. Can you forgive me? I love you so much. I can't bear to lose you."

He reached out one long finger and brushed a stray, dark curl away from her eyes. That simple gesture shattered the barriers she'd carefully constructed around her wounded heart. She dropped the things she carried and fell into his waiting arms.

He kissed her long, tenderly, and deeply. When he raised his head, his green-gold eyes were filled with tears. "Promise me you'll never, ever, run away from me again."

"I didn't run away," she objected. "I just left. I wish I could promise you I won't leave again, but..." Her voice was hesitant as she turned away from him.

"There are no buts," he argued firmly. "I need you here, with me,"

"I have job interviews next week. And I **need** a job," she asserted.

"You already have a job. I need your help, Leslie. I'm beginning to get some patients." He smiled smugly.

"What about Mindy?" She eyed him sheepishly.

"Don't mention that insufferable woman to me." Almost growling in frustration, he told her, "I fired the lying Ms. Tucker. That's not exactly correct. I couldn't fire her because I never hired her. Oh shoot, I'm making a mess of this. Leslie, she's gone – for good."

"You shouldn't have been so hasty." Picking up the bag and sign, she crossed to the door and pulled her key out of her pocket.

"What do you mean?" Ray followed her, obviously puzzled, but still determined.

The lock clicked and the door swung open. "Go talk to Walter. When you hear what he has to say about me, you'll likely want the lovely widow Tucker back in your life, and me out of it, for good."

Brushing off his efforts to assist her with her bag, she stepped inside. Ray grabbed her arm and forced her to face him. "Leslie, I love you. Nothing Walter can say will change that. If you're referring to that conniving snake's attempt to blackmail you, I already know about it."

"You do? How?" she stuttered, incredulously.

"Richard," Ray answered, grinning proudly. "Richard told me everything. He feels terrible and wants you to know that he had no part in it, despite what my cousin implied. The whole scheme was Walter's."

"I don't understand."

"You impressed my boy when you stood up to that hateful bully and called his bluff. After you left the office, Walter turned on Richard, blaming him for the failure of his plan, and terrifying the kid. I'm sure it was an awful experience, but it opened his naïve eyes."

"I never thought Richard was responsible. Please tell him I don't blame him for anything."

"I'll do that," he agreed, "but you have to answer one question first. Why did you tell Walter you didn't care what he said about you, then prove exactly the opposite by leaving town, running away?"

Taking his hand, she led him to the kitchen. "Come on. I'll make some tea while we talk this out." He watched her move around the cheerful room, gracefully and efficiently, while he waited. She set the kettle on the eye and leaned against the counter.

"I was bluffing. I couldn't let Walter win, so I said I didn't care what he told you. The truth is – I was terrified you'd believe the lies he was threatening to spread. Add that to Richard's animosity toward me, and Mindy's declaration that she had my job and my place in your heart, and retreat seemed my best option. I'm not much of a fighter."

Pulling her to him and hugging her tightly, he chuckled. "I understand, but I don't agree. I think you're a pretty tough opponent. You got fifty thousand dollars out of tight-fisted Walter Lewis."

"I did, didn't I?" Smiling widely, she slipped a folded paper out of the back pocket of her jeans and smoothed it out. "What I should do with it?"

"You haven't deposited it yet?" he asked incredulously. "What're you doing for money?"

"Oh, I had a little cash tucked away. With that and my one little credit card, I've been able to get by so far." She lifted her chin proudly. "I wish I could figure a way to get a couple thousand out of this check, without taking the rest."

"You should keep it all. He owes you that, and a lot more, considering the way he cheated you on the farm. It'd serve him right."

"I suppose it would at that. Maybe I will." When the pot whistled, she poured two mugs full and dropped in tea bags. Placing the steaming cups on the table, she pulled out her chair and gestured for Ray to join her.

"I'll go down to the bank with you on Monday. And hope I get the chance to confront my dear cousin." His eyes flashed dangerously.

"You wouldn't hurt him, would you?" Leslie asked, blowing on her tea to cool it.

"I wouldn't lay a finger on him."

"So, what are you thinking of doing, then?" she asked curiously.

Grinning widely, his lopsided smile brilliant and beautiful, Ray said, "I'll tell him we're going to use his money to pay for our wedding."

"Our wedding?" the surprised woman almost choked.

At that, Ray slid out of his seat and crouched down on one knee. Reaching into his pocket, he retrieved a blue velvet box and opened it. Holding it up where she could see the contents clearly, he slipped his free hand into hers.

The sparkling oval solitaire was set in a gleaming, exquisite, platinum setting.

She gasped, "It's lovely."

"Leslie Grace Willow, will you marry me?" he asked her. He removed the ring from its case and held it over the third finger of her left hand.

"Ray, Ray, you can't…I mean… How can you? I mean… You've only known me for a few weeks. How can you be sure you want me to be your wife?" Her cheeks were flushed, and her blue-gray eyes sparkled with excitement, despite her protests.

"I'm surer of you, of us, than of anything else in my life. You're the woman of my dreams. Remember?" His melodic baritone echoed blissfully in her ears.

"And you are the man of mine," she whispered, pressing her lips to his softly.

"Is that a yes?" he teased, sliding the silver circlet onto her finger.

"Yes, yes!" she shouted, throwing her arms around his neck.

Her joy was short lived, as a disturbing thought intruded into her happiness. "What about Richard? He won't be happy about this."

"Don't be too sure," Ray countered. "He's coming around. He helped me pick out your engagement ring."

Noting the look of amazement on her beautiful face, he expounded, "Walter poisoned him against you before he ever met you, by implying that we'd been involved with one another for a long time, even before Wanda died."

"Oh, no…that's horrible! No wonder he hates me," she concluded sadly.

"He doesn't hate you. Glenwood had a long talk with him, and so did I. Richard knows the truth of our relationship now, and seems honestly willing to give you a chance."

"Poor kid. With you and Glen ganging up on him, he probably just gave in to get you to leave him alone." Her tone was as light as her heart.

"You'll find out for yourself soon enough. Come out to the farm with me so we can tell him you accepted my proposal."

"Don't you think it's too soon? Maybe you should break it to him slowly, then bring me into the picture a little later on," she suggested.

"Coward," he teased. "Can't face down a measly teenager, huh?"

"Okay, okay. Give me a minute to freshen up." She put the mugs in the sink and started down the hall. Then she turned back and asked, "Hey, how'd you know I was in town?"

"Glen called me," he admitted, "right after you pulled up in front of the beauty shop." Leslie doubled over laughing.

"What's so funny?"

"Mary Ellen and her silly husband. He practically ran me over, trying to get out to call you, and she kept me busy on a wild hair-color chase until you could get here from the farm."

"I guess I owe them a big thank-you then," he replied. "Listen, since you've already got your overnight bag packed, throw in another change of clothes and stay with me for a couple of days."

Peeking around the doorframe so she could see his face, she asked, "Do you think that's a good idea, with your son in the house?"

"I wasn't implying that you'd share my bed, though it's nice to know you're willing." His hazel eyes twinkled merrily. "We have a guest room, you know."

"Oh, you!" she groaned, shoving a clean pair of blue jeans, a couple of shirts, and a pair of hiking boots at him. "Here, put these in my bag. It's there next to the front door where I dropped it. I'm almost ready."

When he looked up again, she was standing beside him, auburn locks brushed to a lustrous shine. The blue-gray sweater she wore making her large eyes seem almost luminous.

"Come here, my love," he whispered, gathering her in. He trailed soft kisses from her left ear lobe, down her neck, to her shoulder. Leslie trembled under his touch.

"Wow," he breathed, releasing his iron-like grasp. "I want you, Leslie. Waiting until we're married is going to be torture." She smiled her agreement into his eyes.

"So, let's set a date," he prompted. "The sooner the better."

"If Richard's okay with it, maybe we could be married after Labor Day," Leslie suggested timidly.

"Perfect." Throwing her carryall over his shoulder, he asked, "You ready?"

She nodded, picking up the yellow sign. "What should I do with this?"

"Bring it along. I'll put your phone number on it and attach a stake. You won't need this place after you move into Willow Spring Farm with me."

While she locked up, he retrieved his car from its hiding place around the corner, and loaded her things into the back. "I was afraid you'd see my Land Cruiser sitting in front of your house and bolt," he told her, grinning mischievously.

She waited patiently for him to open the door for her, and offered him a quick kiss before climbing in. When they were settled inside, she squeezed his arm gently and said, "Thank you, Ray."

"For what, my love?" he responded softly.

"For everything," she replied. "Less than an hour ago I was miserable because I'd lost you. I was dreading the tasks facing me – getting my home ready to sell, finding a job, and a new place to live.

"Now, I have a fiancé, and a job. I'm actually happy about selling my house, and looking forward to moving back to the farm…with you. Do you realize what a huge difference you've made in my life?"

Winking at her, he grinned again. "Happy to oblige, my lovely lady. You were ready for a few changes, weren't you?"

"More than ready," she admitted, "but I never dreamed such a wonderful future was possible."

Her admission touched him. Clearing his throat, he told her, "My life before I moved to Red Valley, and met you, was dreary. I had great plans for my business, of course, but never expected to find love, because I was carrying too much baggage.

"So, Leslie, I'm thanking you for helping me crawl out of the deep pit of guilt, where I was wallowing. And for giving me hope, and joy, and the promise of a bright future."

When he glanced away from the road, turning his forest green gaze on her, Leslie's heart lurched. Ray slipped his arm around her shoulders, pulling her against him. They rolled to a stop in front of the farmhouse where Richard and Max came bounding down off the porch toward the SUV.

"Dad," the tall boy called out. "You found her!"

"I did," Ray said, beaming joyfully. "And I convinced her to stay with us for a couple of days."

Opening the car door and helping Leslie out, Richard swallowed hard, then said, "Miss Willow. I hope Dad told you how sorry I am about everything."

"Yes, he did." She regarded the young man warmly. "Don't worry, Richard. I never believed Walter's lies, or blamed you for what happened. Thank you for giving me a chance, and please, call me Leslie."

"Okay, Leslie," he said, returning her grin. It was the first time she'd seen him smile. The lopsided smirk bore such a resemblance to his father's that she was shocked.

"Take Leslie's bag up to the guest room, please, son," Ray prompted, handing him the small knapsack. "I'll go put on the pasta."

"The sauce is simmering on the back of the stove, and the salad is in the fridge," the boy informed him. "I made iced tea and set the table."

While Ray dropped the noodles into boiling water, Leslie buttered thick slices of bread and set them under the broiler. When dinner was ready, Richard joined them, proudly showing off his new football gear. Over the delicious meal, they discussed the boy's successful bid to become a member of the Red Valley High School varsity football team. Ray's pride in his son's achievement was obvious.

Basking in the glow if his father's approval, the young man seemed to be maturing right before Leslie's eyes. Richard was animated. He described, in detail, the trip to the sporting goods shop and jewelry store, and was sincerely pleased to see her wearing the ring he'd helped select.

They spent a delightful evening discussing their future as a family. Richard agreed that the Saturday after Labor Day would be the perfect day for the wedding. The weather should be ideal, still warm, but with a hint of the fall to come.

"We'll ask Glen to conduct the ceremony, of course" the anxious groom concluded. "But will September give you enough time to do everything you have to do?" Ray's brow furrowed with concern, unsure of the details surrounding the event.

Leslie reassured him with a smile, "There's not much to do. I can send out a few invitations the first of the week. The women's fellowship group will be happy to help with food for the reception. Should we plan on using the church social hall?"

"No, let's have the reception here, out back, make it a real party. We can set up tables under the trees. I've got some old plywood sheets we can put down to make a dance floor. Richard can play disc jockey. What do you say, Rich?"

The boy bobbed his head agreeably. "That would be fun!"

Though the possibility excited her, the bride-to-be was hesitant.

"What if it rains?"

"It wouldn't dare!" Ray moaned, grinning. "Seriously. In case of inclement weather, we can move everything into the barn. It's practically empty right now. Everybody around here enjoys a good barbecue, and most appreciate a lively barn dance. We can have both. What do you think of that plan?"

"I love it, and I love you!" she proclaimed, kissing him soundly. Remembering Richard, she flushed hotly and pulled away. Sheepishly, she cut her eyes in the teen's direction and was pleased to see that his face held an approving smile.

When the three entered the church Sunday morning, Leslie on Ray's arm and Richard following closely behind, all heads turned. To the shy woman's chagrin, Dr. Gallagher marched them down the aisle to an empty place beside Mary Ellen. The entire congregation heard the squeal of delight from the pastor's wife, when she saw the sparkling solitaire on her friend's hand.

After the service concluded, inquisitive faces, anxious to get the news, swamped them. Most offered their sincere congratulations and best wishes. But Leslie noted a small group, led by Mindy Tucker, lagging at the back of the sanctuary, eyeing her maliciously.

Glenwood was thrilled to hear of their engagement, and delightedly agreed to perform the marriage ceremony. Ruth Barnes offered to coordinate the reception, with help from Carl's Diner and the women of the Red Valley Fellowship Church. Leslie's former employer begged to stand in as father of the bride, saying he'd always loved her like a daughter. Stuart Martin, who ran the local copy shop and printed the weekly newspaper, promised to have invitations ready for her to send out on the following Tuesday.

With the willing help of the church and community, Leslie had most of the wedding details worked out by mid-week. On Wednesday morning, Ray drove her to the bank, where she opened a checking account with Walter's cashier's check. Unfortunately, the president's office was noticeably vacant, so Ray didn't get the satisfaction of seeing the angry, defeated look on his cousin's pudgy face.

Mary Ellen took Thursday off to go into Westlake with the

bride-to-be, to look for wedding gowns. At Leslie's insistence, they started their search in a small, vintage clothing boutique.

"This dress was made for you," the shop owner told Leslie, as she pulled it off the rack and removed the protective bag. "Few women have the height or build to handle a gown like this. That's why no one has snatched it up. It's never even been worn. The woman who brought it in changed her mind, deciding she wanted something frillier and more modern. Such a shame. The dress is simple and gorgeous. And originally quite expensive."

The rich, ivory satin drew her touch. Leslie stroked it reverently, noting the elegant cut and wide, flowing skirt. The heart-shaped neckline was adorned with seed pearls, and set atop a tightly fitted bodice. She couldn't imagine herself in this beautiful gown. "Oh, Les," Mary Ellen crooned, "You have to try it on."

Mrs. Ellis, the storekeeper, helped them maneuver the voluminous bundle into the dressing room. While the bride slipped out of her jeans, Mary Ellen undid the long row of pearl buttons running down the back of the gown. Leslie stepped inside the opening and pulled her arms through the straight sleeves. She liked the way the cuffs came to points over her hands, reaching almost to the fingers. She turned toward the three-way mirror.

Mary Ellen fluffed the billowing skirt out around her, as Mrs. Ellis retrieved the headpiece from its bag and placed it lightly on her auburn curls. Held in place by a rope of matching pearls, the filmy veil floated around Leslie's shoulders like a sheer cloud.

"What did I tell you? Perfection," the storeowner declared firmly. "Not one woman in twenty could pull off this dress, but on you, it's perfection."

"She's right, Les," her friend agreed. "You look like an angel."

Swallowing hard, Leslie stared at the unfamiliar figure facing her in the mirror, blue-gray eyes wide with wonder. She couldn't believe the reflection was her own. Fearing the answer, she stuttered, "How...how much is it?"

Rubbing her chin thoughtfully, the plump, silver-haired woman sighed. "Most of the time, folks bring in a valuable designer gown like this for me to sell on consignment. They get their asking price, plus a little commission for me. But the young woman just wanted to be rid of the dress.

"The girl had more money than sense, so I bought it outright, for a fraction of what it's worth. When I was putting it away, I found the original receipt in the bottom of the bag. You'll never guess how much she paid for this gown."

Leslie shook her head, her stomach knotting with dread.

"Twenty thousand dollars! This dress and veil cost twenty thousand dollars."

Her face downcast, the bride-to-be sadly removed the headpiece, "Well, that's settled. I can't afford it."

"No, wait, dear," Mrs. Ellis chirped. "This gown was meant for you; I couldn't bear to see it on anyone else. If you want it, you can have it for what I have in it – five hundred dollars."

Unable to believe her ears, the tall young woman repeated, "Five hundred, are you sure?"

"Quite, quite." The matronly shopkeeper smiled.

A few minutes later, the dress and veil were zipped into the protective bag and hung in the back of the Cooper family van. The excited women sped toward the mall, in search of shoes to compliment the gown. That task was accomplished in short order, and the delighted twosome headed for home.

"It's a shame you won't have time for a real honeymoon," Mary Ellen complained. "I'd love to help you shop for a complete trousseau."

"You'll have that pleasure soon enough," Leslie assured her. "Ray says we'll take a cruise over the Christmas holiday, all three of us."

"I'm so happy for you, Les. It looks like you're going to get some of the happiness you deserve."

"Thanks." The new bride sniffed back tears of joy. "I'm happy for me, too."

The next two weeks flew by. Richard started high school and began making friends. To his delight, the football team won its opener against a big county rival. The athletic teen played most of the fourth quarter, carrying the ball several times, and catching the eye of a pretty little cheerleader.

With Leslie efficiently manning the phones and handling the books, Ray's practice blossomed. He spent mornings making visits to area farms, and afternoons in the clinic seeing small animals. Their partnership proved to be a lucrative and compatible one. Thanks to her training and experience on the farm, Leslie was just as comfortable and capable in the operating room, assisting in minor surgery, as she was behind the computer, running account statements.

Late Friday afternoon, on the day before the wedding, Leslie was wrapping up to leave, so she could get ready for the rehearsal, when the clinic door swung open. In sauntered Walter Lewis. "Where's Ray?" he demanded sharply. "I have to talk to him, alone."

"He's in the back," she informed the banker calmly. "He'll be out any minute." Picking up her purse, she added, "You can wait here."

"You don't have to leave on my account," he sneered.

Before Leslie could respond, the handsome veterinarian stepped through the archway at the back of the office, slipping his arms out of a soiled lab coat. Ignoring his cousin, he dropped the coat on the back of a chair and approached his fiancée. "So, you're off?"

She nodded. "I'll pick you up about six thirty, okay?" She nodded again, not trusting her voice. He kissed her cheek lightly.

When Leslie was gone, Ray turned to the red-faced man, his contempt barely concealed. "What do you want, Walter?"

"I came here to talk you out of making this…this…terrible mistake." His voice dripped false sincerity. "I'm family, Ray, and I'm worried about you, and about Richard. Even if you don't care about yourself, you should care about him. Your son is used to the finer things in life. He won't ever be happy living here on this crap-hole farm with that…that **slut** trying to replace his beloved mother.

"You can't believe you'll be happy, yoked, for the rest of your life, to that homely piece of poor white trash. Wake up, man, she's not good enough for you. And this life isn't good enough for your son."

Bitter bile rose in his throat. The poisonous words his cousin spoke repulsed him. Choking back the indignant reply that sprung to his lips, Ray waited for the pompous banker to finish his tirade, sensing where the dialogue was headed.

"I hate to tell you this, but your fiancée is nothing more than a common whore. She's been in my employ for several years, as a paid escort for my business associates. Come by the bank tomorrow and I'll show you the proof." He puffed up his chest and stuck his receding jaw out as far as it would go.

"If that's true, then that makes you nothing more than a despicable pimp." Ray's eyes flashed dangerously, but Walter was so caught up in his practiced lies that he failed to notice.

"Well, I…I mean…That's different. A good businessman does what he must to make deals and bring in profits. It's just how things are done."

Brushing off the insult, Walter redoubled his attack on Leslie's character. "Your fish-faced slut has fifty thousand dollars of my money deposited in a checking account at the bank, and do you know how she got it? On her back, spreading her skinny legs for every man I chose. I want you to know the truth, so you won't be so anxious to crawl between those thighs, where so many have gone before you."

"The truth! That's hilarious, Walter. You wouldn't know the truth if it jumped up and bit you on your fat behind. You're wasting your breath. I know where Leslie got the money, because Richard told me the whole sordid story.

"I urged her to open the account. She wanted to return every penny you put into her account, but I encouraged her to keep it. It won't please you to know that we're using that money, your blackmail money, to pay for our wedding.

"By the way, I hope you and Sharon are coming to the ceremony and reception. It's going to be a great party." At the sight of his cousin, face scarlet, jowls flapping in frustration as his mouth worked mutely, the fury drained out of Ray, leaving him sadly amused.

"You're a small, pitiful man, Walter. You put on a good show for your fans, but Leslie sees through you and knows you for who you really are, she always has. I pray that one day you'll see yourself through her eyes."

He turned to walk out, then hesitated. "Wait, that's it, isn't it? That's why you hate her so much, and why you've bullied and tormented her – you do see yourself as Leslie sees you. You always have."

Wasting no more time on his cousin, Ray left with an order to, "Close the door behind you. I have to get ready for our rehearsal. And Walter, you **will** be on your best behavior tomorrow, and you'll keep Sharon, and that predatory cat, Mindy Tucker, on short leashes, too. I know I can count on you." The groom wasn't surprised when his pleased grin wasn't reciprocated.

The wedding rehearsal went off without a hitch, and afterward, the party adjourned to Carl's Diner for a small celebration. Despite the fact that everyone was having a wonderful time, the group agreed to cut the festivities short, so they'd be well rested for the big day.

The next morning, just as Ray guaranteed, the sun smiled down on them from the heavens. He gave his tie one final tug to straighten it, and went to help Richard. With the usual portion of moaning and groaning, about the constraints of his suit, the teen finally managed to dress.

Understanding his son's aversion to the formalwear, Ray was grateful that Wanda has insisted on purchasing tuxedos for them. As bad as tuxedos were, ill-fitting rentals were worse. As they stood admiring one another in the freestanding mirror, the Gallagher men agreed that they looked pretty darned good.

At the church, Mary Ellen buttoned Leslie into her gown, pinned on her headpiece, and touched-up her hair and make-up. The bride admired her friend's delicate, hand-made frock, amazed that the busy mother of two had designed and constructed the striking dress in less than two weeks, while caring for her family and operating her shop. But miraculously, she had. The cut accentuated her petite figure, and the delicious shade of fresh peach complimented her creamy complexion.

A soft tap sounded on the door. Their simultaneous cries of, "Come in!" were quickly answered. Carl stepped into the parlor, his bald pate shining, bereft of the grimy baseball cap he usually wore.

"My, oh my, you're so beautiful, like a fairy princess," he beamed at the bride. "And you look darned good too, for an old married woman," he teased Mary Ellen, kissing them both on the cheek.

Leslie had never seen her former boss dressed up before, and was pleasantly surprised at his polished appearance. She let out a whistle. "You clean up pretty good yourself, old man," she teased. "Is that a new suit?"

Carl shrugged and looked embarrassed. My wife said it was about time I got one. I'll probably never wear it again, except for a funeral maybe."

"Well, I'm honored that you bought a suit, just for my wedding," the bride whispered, hugging him tightly.

Clearing his throat uncomfortably, the man grouched, "Your groom and his best man are here. If you're going to back out, now's the time. If not, we'd better get out there."

Leslie smiled at his discomfort, and she reassured him, "I'm ready." The Matron-of-Honor took two bouquets out of their vases, keeping the nosegay of tiger lilies for herself, and handing the bridal bunch to Leslie. The movement sent the intoxicating scent of gardenias wafting throughout the room.

"Thank your wife, again, for the lovely flowers," she told Carl, lifting the white blossoms to her nose. "They're so lovely. She must really have a green thumb."

"She loves fooling with her garden, and she's happy to know you're pleased." The diner operator took a deep breath then asked curiously, "I thought you said this was gonna be a small shindig. The church is full. Who all'd you invite?"

"I sent out a few invitations and gave an open invite to the church congregation," the bride admitted.

"Well, they must all be here," he concluded. "Now, let's go gal. It's time I got you married and outta my hair, what little I have left."

Chuckling at his own cleverness, the thoughtful man held the door for the women to precede him.

The 'Wedding March' began, signaling Mary Ellen to begin her slow walk down the aisle. She gave Ray an encouraging wink when she reached the front, and took her place to her husband's right. The organist redoubled the volume to signal the impending arrival of the bride.

Patting the hand Leslie had placed in the crook of his arm, Carl propelled her forward. All heads turned. Completely oblivious to the, "Oohs," and, "Aahs," and comments of, "Isn't she lovely?" and, "I never would have believed it," the groom's attention was riveted on the vision in ivory approaching him. Richard, proudly serving as the best man, regarded his future stepmother with admiration.

As she passed the row where the pharmacist was seated, Henry Simpson whispered to his wife, "I always thought she was pretty. Not many folks could see it, but I did."

Carl completed his father-of -the-bride duty by placing Leslie's hand in Glenwood's, then he retraced his steps and took a seat on the pew beside his wife. Leaning toward her ear, he told her, "It was love that did it, you know."

"Did what?" she asked softly, puzzled.

"Love brought the shine she had on the inside out where everyone can see it." Tears of joy stung his eyes.

The music ebbed. Glenwood Cooper, minister of the Red Valley Fellowship Church, placed the bride's hand in the groom's and led them through the meaningful, life-changing words of the ceremony. When the vows had been spoken, and rings exchanged, he gave permission for the kiss.

Before he lowered his lips to hers, Ray looked deeply into Leslie's stormy sea-blue eyes and promised, "I will love you forever." And he did.

ABOUT THE AUTHOR

Donna Minnix Proctor began writing romantic fiction in the 80's, on a dare. Since then, she's penned historic, contemporary, and sci-fi/fantasy romances. In collaboration with her husband, Cary, she's co-authored, directed, and performed in dozens of religious plays and skits. The Proctors are from Vinton, Virginia. They currently reside on Briarwood Farm in Franklin County.

SDC Publishing, LLC was established to promote and encourage aspiring writers and artists. It is a family oriented vehicle through which they can publish their work.

Contact SDC Publishing, LLC at allenfmahon@gmail.com

Or on the web at SDCPublishingLLC.com